THE MANSTEIN ALTERNATIVE

PART 1: THE GREAT WAR
PART 2: PRELUDE - THE SPANISH CIVIL WAR

BY JOE AVINGER

DORRANCE
PUBLISHING CO
EST. 1920
PITTSBURGH, PENNSYLVANIA 15238

Dorrance Publishing Co
585 Alpha Drive
Suite 103
Pittsburgh, PA 15238
Visit our website at www.dorrancebookstore.com

ISBN: 978-1-6366-1470-0
eISBN: 978-1-6366-1726-8

THE MANSTEIN ALTE

———⟫◆⟪———

Erich von Manstein had always felt he was dest
on the battlefield. A Russian's bullets had othe
Great War was passing him by. While rehabilitat
a chance encounter with Erich Ludendorff, se
Germany's armies, set him on a political care
military one. Manstein's efforts cause World W
tiated peace. Alliances in this new postwar wor
ent from ours as Charles de Gaulle and Benito
push the world towards a second world war.

I

THE GREAT WAR

January 9, 1917
    – Schloss Pless, Germany

I knew why my boss brought me to the meeting but it was still unnerving to have those three sets of eyes staring at me. Chancellor Bethmann-Hollweg was the first to break the silence caused by my simple question. "Why? We need to unleash the U-boats to have a chance to win the war. Are you deaf as well as blind?" Kaiser Wilhelm II added, "And don't forget we'll be giving them a taste of their own medicine. Let's see how they like it when food riots start in England." Paul von Hindenburg, Field Marshall, Chief of the General Staff and virtual dictator of Germany, simply continued to stare at me. I came to attention and returned his stare, knowing that he was the key.

The Chancellor and the Kaiser both turned to Hindenburg, wondering why he was quiet. Hindenburg ran his fingers down his mustache and turned to my boss, Erich Ludendorff, First General Quartermaster. "So, Erich. I presume this is the young man you've been hiding."

Ludendorff smiled and said, "Hauptmann Erich von Manstein." I wondered how Hindenburg would handle this as the Chancellor and Kaiser tried to figure out what was going on between the leaders of Germany's war effort. Hindenburg looked me up and down before saying, "At ease, Hauptmann. I presume Erich brought you here for discussion not inspection. Kaiser, Chancellor, meet Hauptmann von Manstein. I believe he's the young man who helped Erich come up with his 'elastic defense'. The basis for the Hindenburg Line." I saluted and relaxed a little. As I had expected, uncle Paul was going to keep this on a professional level.

Ludendorff nodded, adding to the Kaiser and Chancellor, "He has an interesting way of looking at things and questioning basic assumptions. I met him when he was convalescing after being wounded in Poland. I was visiting the wounded and trying to raise morale when von Manstein made it clear that he didn't agree with everything I said. When events proved him right, I decided to put him on my staff and talk to him when there's a question with a lot of perspectives."

My nervousness reminded me of the night before any offensive. I knew my arguments since I'd been through them with General Ludendorff. Then again, that had simply been a discussion when he'd asked my opinion on returning to unrestricted submarine warfare. I knew he'd been for it but I also knew he'd listen to my arguments even if they didn't eventually sway him. I was under no such illusions here, wondering if Hindenburg would be more or less inclined to listen because of our relationship.

"I presume you had a reason for your question..." prodded the great Field Marshall. It reminded me of the first time I met my boss, Erich Ludendorff, First General Quartermaster of the German Army...

It was March 12, 1915, and I was at the Army hospital in Wiesbaden for another check on my recovery. It had been almost four months since I was wounded on the Eastern Front. One bullet hit me in my left shoulder and another got me in the left knee. I counted myself lucky that everything still mostly worked. The docs said I needed another couple of months of therapy and I'd be able to get back to where I belong. I always felt I would do well in the army. I have the confidence, training, knowledge, and courage to lead men and had been doing a good job of it right up until the moment I got shot. I guess I should have spent more time on learning to duck.

Doctor Becker had just spent ten minutes squeezing and twisting my knee while I gritted my teeth through the pain. He'd shaken his head ruefully when I assured him that nothing hurt. He'd also scheduled another appointment for me in two weeks for more of the same. I'd just thanked him and stood to leave when there was a commotion in the waiting room. Some General was there to boost morale and tell us how everything was going according to plan. The same plan that said the war should have been over by the end of 1914.

I exited the doctor's office and came to attention just as the visiting high and mighty was telling us how our U-boats would starve the British into submission. If I had realized the Feldwebel with his arm in a sling was part of the General's staff, there's no way he'd have seen me roll my eyes. It was a mistake I didn't find out about until several minutes later after the General had droned to a conclusion.

My knee throbbed from standing at attention after the doctor's ministrations but since he'd followed me out his door, I had to do my best to keep up appearances. The "At Ease" order came as an immense relief and I shifted most of my weight to my good leg. I even managed a smile as I turned to Doctor Becker and told him I'd see him in two weeks. That was when I saw his eyes get very big. That and a minor stampede of clicking boot heels told me I should turn back around. Back to attention and a smart about-face. At least that was the intent. My abused knee gave way about halfway through the turn and I grabbed Doctor Becker and the person on my right as my eyes registered the horrified look on the face of the Feldwebel with the sling. I finished my turn and came back to attention with a helping hand from the person I'd grabbed. And then the blood drained from my face. There in front of me sporting a now crinkled uniform was Generalleutnant Erich Ludendorff. He was the Chief of Staff to my Uncle Paul von Hindenburg, the Commander-in-Chief of our armies on the Eastern Front. That was definitely not how I'd envisioned meeting him.

"Would you like to take a seat, Leutnant?" Ludendorff's gravelly voice had belied the twinkle in his eyes.

I had started to automatically reject the offer when Doctor Becker answered for me, "Don't ask, General, or he'll stay standing here until he falls over again."

After I was sheepishly led over to a chair, General Ludendorff had sat next to me and continued, "Feldwebel Wagner tells me you didn't appreciate part of my speech. Normally when an officer rolls his eyes there's a morale or discipline problem but based on what just happened, I doubt that's the problem here. So why don't you tell me why you were rolling your eyes, Leutnant."

I'd almost panicked as I realized I had to say something and the only thing I could think of was the truth. "General Ludendorff, Sir, it was the part about our U-boats starving the British. It won't work, Sir."

An amused smile played across Ludendorff's lips and then quickly disappeared. "Be careful when talking to Generals, Leutnant. Not many of them like being told they're wrong. But you've got my ear now so tell me why it won't work."

"Well, Sir, if we can sink enough ships to starve the British, why don't we simply sink their troop transports and keep them off the continent? The French would fold without the British army to support them."

Ludendorff looked disappointed. "We don't because they move their troops in heavily escorted convoys. It would be suicide for our submarines to attack them."

He shook his head and started to stand. I knew I had to act quickly. "Exactly, Sir."

That stopped him.

"If we sink enough merchant ships to cause them supply problems, won't they start organizing convoys for the merchants? They have more than enough escorts to handle the job."

Ludendorff sat back down and stared at me for a moment. "Running convoys for their merchants would generate its own supply problems."

"Yes, Sir, it would. The question is whether or not it would cause them enough problems to knock them out of the war. The figures I've generated seem to show that the British would have to ration things but would be no worse off than we currently are."

Ludendorff had gotten a kind of far-off look in his eyes as his math and logistics background came into play.

Time to play my last card. "My gut says that this is all a trap. The unescorted merchants are the bait and the ambush party is the neutral countries, especially the United States, that will be pushed into the Entente's camp as we sink their merchants. The convoy system won't even cause many supply issues if we add their navy and merchant fleet to the equation."

Ludendorff looked at me for a moment before answering. "We're committed to this course so we'll have to see how this plays out. I hope you're wrong but if you are right, what would you have us do instead?"

"I don't know, Sir. I hadn't really thought about it."

General Ludendorff smiled and stood up. He took a couple of steps before stopping and turning back to me. "A word of advice, young Leutnant, Generals may not like it when you tell them they're wrong but they really don't like it if you don't have an alternative for them."

Two months later we sank the Lusitania and two months after that the Americans had issued an ultimatum. The British had expected the Americans to join the war and they almost did. Germany was vilified as a pirate nation and U-boat operations were curtailed....

I swallowed and took a deep breath before charging the enemy guns. At least this time I had an alternative. I fired my opening shot with "As with any battle plan, we have to examine the current situation, overall objective, the forces available for both sides, their logistics, possible responses by the enemy, the probability of success and the price of failure."

Hindenburg's eyebrows went up on that last point and I felt there was a chance of surviving this battle.

"Here's how I see the current state of the war," I continued. "Serbia, Montenegro, Albania, Poland, Lithuania and most of Rumania have been occupied. The Russian government is teetering while its armies are losing ground steadily. The French and Belgians have taken heavy losses and their land has been chewed up by the fighting. The Turks and Austro-Hungarians are unsteady but stable for now. The British and Italians have taken heavy losses in men but their home fronts are generally prospering. We have proposed peace negotiations that were rejected by the Entente. We are withdrawing to a shorter, stronger defense line in France and Belgium. We too have taken heavy losses in men but our biggest problem is feeding our people and supplying our troops."

I paused to gauge their reactions. The Chancellor and Kaiser appeared to be indulgently bored. Hindenburg's face had taken on the bland but attentive features of most commanders at a staff briefing. My hopes rose and I pressed on.

"We have given up on winning the ground war on the Western Front and wish to reach an advantageous negotiated peace. The primary impediment to this is Great Britain. The current plan is to resume unrestricted submarine warfare in an attempt to starve the British into coming to the negotiation table. We will have between

100 and 120 U-boats available through this year with 80 to 100 at sea at any given time. The enemy already knows how to counter the threat so there is no chance of success. Failure...." I stopped since both the Chancellor and Kaiser were now on their feet calling me a lying, defeatist communist among other things.

After a minute or two of their venting, Hindenburg cut through the noise with "GENTLEMEN... I would like to hear why the young Hauptmann has put his career, and possibly life, on the line by making such a claim."

After a few more grumbles they both sat back down and petulantly looked at me.

I explained, "The Entente already uses the convoy system when moving troops to minimize losses. The only reason it isn't used by their merchant fleet is it introduces inefficiency in the delivery of goods. That inefficiency is currently higher than the losses caused by our U-boats. That equation will change if we press the U-boat war. The U-boats have been ineffective when attempting attacks against convoys. Therefore, while we will hurt their war effort, we will not be able to starve Britain to the negotiating table."

I came to parade rest and joined the other three looking at Hindenburg for his reaction. He ran his fingers down his mustache again and I knew I would survive.

"And your 'price of failure'?" he asked.

"It will be a propaganda coup for the Entente," I replied. "Neutrals will shift even further in favor of them. The US may join the war against us further diminishing the effect of the U-boats. The biggest price will be at the negotiation table. We will be branded as the barbarian pirates who have no respect for international law. The eventual peace treaty will be very harsh with little chance of maintaining any of our overseas colonies or Eastern Front gains. I do not believe the Entente would allow this government to stay in power."

I was surprised to see that Chancellor von Bethmann-Hollweg seemed pleased by my comments. General Ludendorff had said that one of the three had been against resuming unrestricted operations but based on their reactions I had assumed it was Hindenburg. My already high respect for the great man rose. The Kaiser looked despondent. Hindenburg was back to thoughtfully stroking his mustache while splitting his attention between Ludendorff and me.

I was confused for a moment as the great general looked at me while addressing my boss. "So, Erich, since you are still smiling and von Manstein is still standing as if he has more to say, I presume he has a proposal that has some chance of bringing this war to a successful conclusion."

Ludendorff nodded and said, "He has come up with a series of steps that I believe have at least a reasonable chance of success. Hauptmann...."

I smiled for the first time during this meeting since I enjoyed the irony of what I proposed. "Regardless of the position and actions of the US government, there appears to be a significant group of its citizens that are sympathetic with us. Their Secretary of State, William Jennings Bryan, resigned when Wilson rejected our arguments against the British blockade in 1915. The sailors on the merchant submarine *Deutschland* have been treated as heroes by the Americans. They have no historical reason for siding with the British. Their motives appear to be primarily profit based. Let's offer them a higher profit and get them working for us.

"First, stop all sabotage efforts in the US. Second, we begin negotiations with the US for peace on the Western Front. We can even present the withdrawal to the Hindenburg Line as a display of our sincerity. Third, we push the Russians as hard as possible with the intent of forcing them out of the war before any peace agreement is reached with Britain, France and Italy. And finally, we use the convoy system against the British. We take over the *Deutschland* and send it to the US with bullion and enter their financial markets like the British have. We then use the money to guarantee payment for goods that would not normally be considered war material and their shipment. We schedule these shipments to meet at a point in the Atlantic outside the blockade zone where they are met by fifteen to twenty U-boats. The U-boats will act as escorts, torpedoing any British that make contact with the convoy. If needed, the convoy can use the neutral waters of Norway, Sweden and Denmark for the final leg of the journey while the High Seas Fleet sorties towards London to pin down the fleet at Scapa Flow. The merchants are paid here and loaded with any exports we can ship. The merchants will not be escorted back to the US since they won't be violating the blockade. If the British harass them on their return leg, it will be an even bigger propaganda win for us.

"There is a higher risk to our U-boats but it will be easier to keep them supplied since their patrols will be shorter. With the U-boats acting as escorts, the British will be forced to either let the merchants go or fire on them from range. We win either way. They may expand the blockade zone or intercept the merchant ships outside of the blockade zone. Both would pin down far more British ships and I doubt either would be popular with the neutrals. They could sink the merchants and blame it on us. But as soon as they're caught, the backlash would probably shift all the neutrals into our camp. They might be able to convince the American government to outlaw the shipping but we should be able to convince either Sweden or Denmark to receive the shipments and then send them on to us.

"I think this will give us a good chance of either loosening the blockade enough to continue the war or forcing an advantageous peace treaty at a fairly low cost in war material. We should know within a month or two whether we can get American merchants to attempt the shipments. If they won't, we can turn the U-boats loose.

Since our people won't be starved out in the next twelve to eighteen months, we can try this strategy for six months. If it doesn't work, we can still attempt unrestricted submarine warfare." I stopped and waited for some reaction.

Von Bethmann-Hollweg was the first to comment with "I like it. We should be able to get some needed supplies while keeping the Americans out of the war."

Kaiser Wilhelm scoffed, "Bah! The Americans won't be able to influence the war until at least 1919. And even if they could, why would they turn their backs on the British?" The Kaiser stopped as he realized Hindenburg was slowly shaking his head back and forth while scrutinizing him.

With a sigh Hindenburg said, "I thought your tutors had taught you better. You should know the Americans have few ties to the Brits and that the blockade is hurting American shipping. The British blockade violates several of the rules of war by starving our civilians. Add that the Brits are impressing Norwegians and virtually stealing their merchant fleet, something the Americans went to war about around a hundred years ago, and it shouldn't take much to get them to at least try shipping us 'non-war' material."

Ludendorff finally joined the conversation. "While discussing this with Manstein, I came to the conclusion that we also weren't doing a good job of presenting our case that this war is Russia's fault. Ambassador Bernstorff needs to ask the Americans how they'd react if a Mexican with military training used Mexican Army equipment to kill Vice President Marshall. What would they do if they found evidence that the assassination was carried out with the knowledge and consent of the Mexican government? And if the British mobilized to 'protect' Mexico? Would they back down or would they attack Canada to prevent the British from using it as a base?"

Hindenburg actually smiled. He leaned back and said, "It may work. We'll need to approach the Norwegians and Swedes about shipping through them and keep the orders to our subs as secret as possible at least for the first shipment. The cost is minimal and the potential reward is very high. Congratulations Major von Manstein. Not many have changed my mind after I've made a decision."

"Thank you, Sir!" I replied.

As the discussion continued to plan details and additional options, I happily realized I'd not only survived the battle without a wound, I'd actually gotten a promotion.

The planning continued into the night. Both the Chancellor and Kaiser eventually said their goodbyes. I expressed my honor at getting to meet them. Hindenburg laughed quietly when the Kaiser claimed he was glad to meet me, too.

Once they'd been gone for a few minutes, Hindenburg laughed openly. "Glad to meet you? I bet he'd have rather met a cobra."

Ludendorff laughed too. "I don't know about a cobra but definitely one of those disappointed but overly patient tutors from his past. Anyway, would you mind telling me why you wouldn't let me leave earlier?"

I had noticed that General Ludendorff had made several comments and moves that I had come to understand meant he was through with a meeting. I thought that Hindenburg had simply ignored them or didn't know them. Apparently, he had ignored them for a reason.

"I wanted you to meet my nephew," he replied.

General Ludendorff was surprised to hear of my relationship to Hindenburg, but he understood why it had been kept quiet. I knew Uncle Paul had a twisted sense of humor, but I didn't realize how twisted until he announced I would oversee my plan and named me a military attaché to Ambassador Bernstorff. I pointed out that I didn't even know if I got seasick and that I knew very little English.

Hindenburg simply smiled and said that we could work on the English and the seasickness would resolve itself. I smiled weakly as Ludendorff suggested it might be useful to advertise my relationship to Hindenburg to give me more authority.

The next week would be consumed by selecting personnel for my staff, learning what the strategic plan was for the next six months and how I could use it to our advantage in negotiations, and intensive training on the people I'd be dealing with in the United States. All of this is sensitive information so there's no way I can take it on the submarine with me. Improving my English would have to wait for my ride across the Atlantic.

February 3, 1917
Baltimore, Maryland
Fresh air, open space, and ground that doesn't move! After seventeen days on that infernal submarine where diesel fumes permeated everything, even the food, I simply stood on the dock and breathed deeply for a few moments. My brief stints topside had done little other than convince me I wanted out of the submarine. It seems I'm a little claustrophobic.

Kapitän König stopped a dozen feet ahead of me, turned and said, "Major, I believe the rest of the crew would also like to enjoy the fresh air."

Abashed, I turned and smiled apologetically at the line of men patiently waiting for me to get out of the way.

I continued down the dock and Kapitän König smiled, saying, "Don't feel bad. I did the same thing on the first voyage. The only problem was there wasn't anyone willing to urge me to move. They say I stood on the dock for almost thirty seconds before I got moving again."

So here I was in the USA with twenty handpicked leutnants as my assistants. It was hard to tell with the afternoon sun behind them, but unless I was mistaken, there at the end of the pier were my greeting parties: one German from the embassy and one American to keep me out of trouble. I also noticed several people watching us that weren't part of the official welcome. They didn't look like security and they were too eager to avoid eye contact to be casual observers or the press. It appeared the Entente knew of our arrival, too.

I was a little surprised to see that Bernstorff himself led the embassy group. I was very surprised to recognize the leader of the American group. Secretary of State Robert Lansing was a distinguished man in his early fifties. His trim white hair and salt-and-pepper mustache made me think of every bank manager I'd ever encountered. Either that or my information about the man was affecting my observations. He would be the second hurdle I would have to jump. While he was against the British blockade because it hurt American trade, he wasn't thrilled with the expansionist tendencies of Germany either.

I greeted my first hurdle, Ambassador Bernstorff, and let him make the introductions. "Secretary of State Lansing, I believe you've met Kapitän König of the *Deutschland*, and may I present Major Erich von Manstein."

At least I was fairly sure that's what he said. My English was still a little rusty despite the drilling by my assistants, all of whom spoke it fluently.

I bowed and shook Lansing's hand, saying, "I didn't expect the honor of being met by you. I'm happy to meet you."

"I'm happy to meet you, too, Major. And welcome back, Kapitän König," he replied. "We were expecting a return to unrestricted submarine warfare by your government, but it hasn't happened. And then we're informed that Hindenburg's nephew is about to arrive with special instructions for Ambassador Bernstorff. Add in that the British have already started trying to discredit you. Strangely, the American government wants to know what you're doing here."

I smiled at what I took to be sarcasm and then had to fend off one of Bernstorff's assistants as he tried to relieve me of my attaché case. Lansing raised an eyebrow in question and I informed him, "If we can meet soon, I will present these documents to you. I would like to discuss them with the ambassador first."

Lansing nodded his head, replying, "I expected as much. I've cleared my schedule on Monday and the meetings for the rest of the week have been informed they may be moved. Will the rest of today and tomorrow give you enough time?"

I agreed and our delegations headed off for our trip to Washington. My leutnants stayed with the ship to keep an eye on our cargo.

Bernstorff was barely cordial on the trip to Washington. I tried to find out where things stood from his viewpoint but was rebuffed with a terse "We will discuss things at the embassy. Tomorrow." While my relationship to Hindenburg may have caused interest in the US State Department, it appeared to cause little other than contempt from my country's own ambassador. Either that or he thought I was here to replace him.

It was late when we arrived at the embassy, one of the ambassador's assistants informed me that my leutnants would be staying at a nearby hotel since there wasn't enough room at the embassy itself. I noticed Bernstorff had stopped at the door to the embassy and was watching me for my reaction to this pronouncement. He appeared surprised when I readily agreed to the arrangement. I turned to the assistant and asked about entertainment and food for the leutnants since their services wouldn't be needed in the immediate future. He assured me their needs would be taken care of by the staff and that they would be met at the train station and led to the hotel. I turned back to find that the ambassador had disappeared into the building. I sighed. At least I could look forward to a hot bath and a bed that didn't sway.

February 4, 1917
German Embassy, Washington, D.C.

It was still dark when I awoke. I tried to just lay there and wallow in the bed but my mind wouldn't let me. It kept going over the ideas and info I needed for the coming days. I found that I looked forward to the end of the war, not just for the end of the death and destruction, but for being able to wake up at my own pace with only mundane worries on my mind. I sighed and got up. At least I would have a steady floor when I shaved.

Bernstorff was already eating when I arrived at the dining room. A member of the staff asked what I wanted for breakfast and directed me to the chair opposite the ambassador. I took my seat and discussed my options while the ambassador ignored me and continued eating. My guess was he intended to slight me. Personally, I was glad for his silence. Either the embassy cook was very good or the diesel fumes had cleared from my nose enough to let it recognize the smell of food. My stomach growled loud enough to earn a look of disdain from Bernstorff. He finished his breakfast while I was still waiting for mine and I expected him to say something. Instead, he picked up the morning paper and began to read.

I waited patiently until my breakfast arrived. Orange juice, milk, pancakes, sausage and an omelet arrived together. I inhaled deeply. My nose was in heaven. My stomach was impatient. The growl it let out made the server smile. The third bite was on its way to my mouth when Bernstorff put down his paper and cleared his throat. It was going to be one of those kinds of discussions. Another growl, this time in protest, escaped my stomach as I sighed and put down my fork.

"Good morning, Ambassador."

He simply stared at me for a moment before responding. "I trust the accommodations were acceptable?"

"Everything has been fine and the food smells delicious." I picked my fork back up hopefully but the hint was ignored.

He glanced down at my hand and then back to my face and waited until he heard the clink of my fork being set back down. "You will tell me why you are here and if there is anything illegal in it, I will throw you out of the embassy regardless of who your uncle is. I will not have another von Papen here."

I smiled as I finally understood why I was persona non grata. Franz von Papen had been the last military attaché. He'd set up a spy ring and group of saboteurs here in America. Bernstorff's honor had been compromised when von Papen's activities were discovered.

"I give you my word of honor that I and my men are not here to conduct any espionage. I will happily explain why I'm here but ask your indulgence. I've been stuck on a submarine for almost three weeks where everything, even the food, smelled like diesel oil. Food from a mess at the front would taste wonderful to me right now. What's on my plate is torture in that I am not eating it."

The ambassador stared at me for a few moments trying to decide if I was telling the truth. He finally nodded and said, "I'll meet you in the study when you are ready to discuss why you are here."

I nodded my thanks and found my fork was loaded with omelet and already nearing my mouth. He got up and left the room as I enjoyed a meal more than I ever had in my life.

When I finally finished, I thanked the server and sent my compliments to the cook. I went back to my room to wash up and get my papers for the meeting with Bernstorff. When I entered the room, I found a member of the staff cleaning it. I also found that my attaché case was missing. When I asked, the maid informed me that the ambassador had come by and picked it up about fifteen minutes earlier. It appeared Bernstorff didn't really trust me. I had been planning to tell him the whole plan anyway but was disappointed in how things were going. Sighing, I shook my head and went to the bathroom to clean up.

There was a crisp and competent-looking young man waiting for me when I emerged. He escorted me to the study and closed the doors behind me. I found Bernstorff had my papers scattered across several tables in the study. He was currently reading the main outline of the plan. I waited for him to finish but, after a minute or so, I realized he wasn't moving.

"Ambassador?"

He seemed to come back to the room and responded, "Is this real?"

"Yes, Sir."

"I thought the Kaiser and the military were all for this war."

"They were, Sir. But they expected a short war. I think everyone did. The only countries benefiting right now are England and possibly Italy, at least as far as their economy goes. Even they have lost a lot of men. I've been given the opportunity to see if we can force them to the negotiating table with the help of the U.S. If I fail, we will return to unrestricted submarine warfare as an attempt to win the war. I think all we'll accomplish is our own destruction if we do that. And in case you're wondering, Ludendorff didn't know I was Hindenburg's nephew until after I had changed his mind and he'd agreed to this plan."

"Then it will have all been for nothing?"

"Hopefully not, Sir. We hope to have a peace treaty with the Russians in place before negotiations progress too far with the Americans. Of course, that's not something we wish to advertise."

"I understand. What can I do to help?"

"Trust me and keep reading. I planned to share all of this with you." I picked up a still carefully wrapped package that had been at the back of my papers. "Except for this. This you will see at the appropriate time."

The ambassador looked at me for a moment, then with a nod he went back to reading.

He stopped several more times over the next half-hour but never asked me any questions. His eyes simply glazed over for a few moments and then he'd shake his head a little and go back to reading. I took the time to study him and where he paused in reading the documents. I started trying to guess when he would pause based on what he was reading. I was wrong only once.

When he finally stopped, I asked, "What about us investing more heavily in the American markets made you pause?"

"The idea is fine. I was simply putting together puzzle pieces. I was informed that not all of your men made the trip to Washington. I was concerned that they might be up to mischief. When I read about the investment strategy, I came to the conclusion that a security detail had been left behind with the cargo of the *Deutschland*."

"That would be correct. Kapitän König was in charge of finding them places to stay that were convenient to his warehouse. It's also one of the reasons his ship wasn't taken over by the Fleet. We believed that Kapitän König had the contacts required to safely store our shipment and that his merchant vessel would receive a friendlier reception than would a ship run by our navy."

"Should I arrange for more security?"

"The ten leutnants that stayed behind should be enough. If they aren't, I doubt a hundred extra men would be."

"So be it." Bernstorff sighed and shuffled back to the main outline. "If it is okay with you, I will pass along the recall of Boy-Ed's 'friends' immediately. That will please me and the Americans, too."

I agreed and he called for Franz, one of the staff members.

After a few moments, Franz entered the room with a disgusted look in my direction. A smile soon crept over his features as he listened to his instructions. He bowed to the ambassador and then to me before he left to carry out the recall. Apparently the activities of the saboteur groups Boy-Ed had set up with von Papen were still causing problems.

I noticed that the crisp young man was still outside the door. As I turned back to the ambassador, I noticed he had followed my gaze and was also turning back to me.

"Security?"

"He cuts down on eavesdroppers. There are several others stationed around the grounds. Anyway, it is a grandiose plan but I don't see how it can work. If you can get the American government to agree to the shipments, how can you get them past the blockade? I assume there are details not recorded here."

"Indeed there are, Mr. Ambassador...."

He raised his hand to stop me. "You may call me Johann. And what should I call you?"

I realized he had yet to use any name when talking to me. He had used my full name and rank when he introduced me to the Secretary of State but he had addressed me as little more than an unwelcome servant since then. I guess I was too used to how some generals acted to notice the slight. "You may call me Erich or Manstein as you wish." I seemed to have cleared the first hurdle.

"Very well, Erich. You were about to mention these other arrangements...."

We talked for about a half an hour with Johann chuckling at the idea of the U-boat escorts. He offered several suggestions on how to approach the Americans and was pleased to learn that I wanted him as the lead negotiator. When our discussions wound down, he turned to look at the still unopened package I'd retrieved earlier.

"And that?"

"You will get to see it tomorrow since you will be the one translating it for Lansing. I want him to see your honest reaction to it."

"Normally I don't like entering a meeting without all the information available. Considering what I've seen so far, though, I'm looking forward to finding out this new piece of the puzzle. Shall we adjourn?"

"That's fine with me. I'd like to check on my staff and see how they're doing. I'd also like a chance to just walk around. The bed last night was very comfortable but I still have more than a few kinks that need to be worked out. I am definitely not someone who wants to spend a lot of time cooped up on a submarine."

Johann smiled and raised his voice "Otto!"

The security guard opened the door and looked expectantly at the ambassador.

Johann turned to me. "This is Otto, my head of security."

"Nice to meet you, Otto."

He responded with a simple "Sir."

After the introductions were concluded, Johann turned back to the guard. "Major von Manstein may be going for a walk later today. Please see to his needs personally."

Otto nodded and held the door open since it appeared our meeting was breaking up.

I smiled at Otto as I gathered up my papers and nodded.

The ambassador's chuckle made me turn toward him as he said, "Don't think ill of him, Erich. It's how he approaches his job. He only wants you to know one name so if you need him you know exactly who to yell for. He speaks as little as possible because if he's engaging you in conversation, he's not focusing on his job. He has a wealth of knowledge of Washington and pays attention to everything so you can ask him questions. Just don't expect him to look at you or give you long answers when he responds. You can trust him with your life and your honor."

I turned back to Otto to find him scanning the foyer and hallways outside the study.

"Would you like to put your papers in our safe? I give you my word of honor that your mysterious package will not be disturbed."

"I would appreciate that very much, Sir," I responded and Otto led us away.

When we got to the safe, Otto shielded my view of the ambassador as he opened the safe and placed my documents inside. The safe door clicked, I heard its dial spin, and the ambassador came back into view.

"Well, Erich, is there anything else you want to discuss? Sunday is normally my day off and you've given me a lot to think about."

"That's it for the moment, Mr... Johann. Your suggestions have given me things to think about, too."

"Then I'll expect you for dinner at six. If you want to bring any of your leutnants along, please let Otto know and he'll get word to us here. If there's nothing else...."

"Actually, there is. Would it be possible to get a car sent to the hotel a couple times a day to ferry some of my men here and back?"

"I guess you don't trust the phones?"

"Security on some of the information is very important."

"Very well. A car will be put at your disposal."

I thanked him and headed back to my room to prepare for my venture into the streets of Washington.

Otto was waiting for me when I exited my room and the assistant from the previous night was waiting in the lobby. She already had a couple layers of clothes on as well as some sturdy-looking boots. A heavy coat was draped over her arm. She smiled and introduced herself.

"Good morning, Major. I'm Brenda. I understand you want to see the rest of your group?"

"Good morning, Brenda. It's nice to see you again and yes, I'd like to see my leutnants."

"It's about a half-mile to their hotel. Are you sure you want to walk?"

"I'm sorry but yes. Between the submarine, the train and the cars, it feels like I haven't been able to stretch my legs for far too long."

I put on my coat as Brenda put on hers. I turned to find that Otto's coat had magically appeared on him and he was headed to the door.

As Brenda buttoned up her coat she smiled and said, "I can understand that. I get fidgety by the end of my shift. I just asked because a lot of the people I've dealt with are trying to prove something."

We headed out the door and as she pointed the way, I noticed that we weren't alone. I stopped and turned to Otto as he was closing the door.

Before he even turned around, he said, "Security, Sir."

I noticed he was locking the front door and he turned around to face the street. He simply stood there scanning the street over my shoulder.

"C'mon, Major. Otto's just locking up because half the security detail is out here. It's standard procedure."

I turned back to Brenda and heard a quiet "Americans and British, too." I simply nodded, trusting that Otto would notice my acknowledgment of his warning.

"I'm beginning to feel a little guilty about the number of people I'm making take a walk in the cold."

"Don't worry about it, Major. We don't do this all the time but we do it often enough that it isn't a problem. I'll admit we don't usually have quite this much of an audience, but your arrival seems to have caused a bit of a stir."

"Good. Maybe the Americans will listen to what I have to say. That's half the fight."

"What are you planning on telling them?"

"Things the American government may not want to hear. Things the Entente governments don't want the Americans to hear. What the Alliance governments hope the future will be. The truth as I see it."

"That could be dangerous on many different fronts."

"You've got that right. Sometimes I think Hindenburg and Ludendorff sent me on this mission because they consider me expendable."

"Either that or they think you're the only one who can successfully complete it."

"Ah, the hopeful outlook of one who has not spent time at the front. Please keep your optimism, I may have need of it."

Brenda laughed and continued to ask questions as we walked to the hotel. Yes, she was collecting information for Bernstorff but I didn't mind. She was good company and my body was finally starting to unwind from my trip.

It was hard to keep from laughing as we entered the hotel. There were seven people scattered around the lobby. All of them seemed to be trying to watch each other without being obvious about it. One of them was one of my leutnants, the senior member of the group here. He stood and headed in our direction.

"The others?" I asked.

Brenda looked at me questioningly as behind us, Otto responded, "Two each of ours, the Americans and the Brits."

Brenda's head snapped back around to look at the other people in the lobby.

"And here I thought she was one of yours."

"No, Sir. Just friendly, chatty, and nosy."

"A useful combination." I returned the salute I was receiving. "Ah, Leutnant Weber. It's good to see you again."

"You too, Sir. I don't think it's safe to talk here. We're on the second floor if you'd like to come up."

"I think I'll have to agree with you on that point." I turned to Brenda. "Brenda, I thank you for your pleasant company but I'll probably be here for some time."

She smiled warmly and said, "No problem, Sir. I enjoy getting outside. Even on brisk days. I'm happy to wait."

Weber sighed and mutter something about rank having its privileges as Brenda took a seat in the lobby.

I turned the other way. "And you, Otto?"

As expected, his "We stay" was terse and brooked no argument. I nodded and then had a mischievous thought. I suggested that he bring the other members of the security detail inside and then headed to the front desk. Weber trailed me on my left while Otto followed on my right. I didn't see what Otto did but one of the men in the lobby headed outside.

The young man looked a little worried but still smiled as we approached. "Can I help you?"

"Yes, please," I replied. "Would it be possible to provide some lunch for the gentlemen in the lobby and those who will be coming in soon?"

"Certainly, Sir. I can have one of the waiters go around and get their orders."

"Excellent. Please do and put it on the bill for...."

"The second floor," Leutnant Weber supplied with a smirk. "Are we going to stay and watch?" he asked me.

I shook my head and replied, "I'm sure Otto's people will let us know how it goes."

We headed up the stairs to where the rest of the group was. Two of my leutnants were seated in the hallway and snapped to attention as we arrived. Apparently the entire second floor had been booked and, since only half of my assistants had made the trip, there were several empty rooms. Weber directed us to one of them that had been turned into a meeting room.

I sent him in first with a reminder that we weren't in uniform or on duty so there was no need for jumping up or snapping to attention. The two in the hallway relaxed a bit and went back to their seats and their turn at watch. Otto and I entered the room to find two tables pushed together and a poker game in progress and Weber holding a broom pointed at the ceiling. I got a few nods of greeting from those not in the current hand and decided to wait until it was over. Hoffman won the hand and was obviously winning overall. As I started to speak, Weber began tapping the ceiling and several of the leutnants started tapping their feet.

"I was going to see how you were doing but it seems that at least one of you is doing quite well. Should I ask where you got the cards?"

Weber smiled and said, "Hoffman supplied the original deck but after a few hands, we got a couple of new decks from the hotel. And no, that hasn't slowed him down."

"Have you received any word from Kapitän König?"

"Not today. Last night he said it would take him a couple of days to get things organized with up to a week to get things ready to ship."

"That's faster than what he told me on the sub."

"He contacted several shippers while we were unloading. He said they were more than happy to try to run the blockade with the stipulations he gave them. He also said they were willing to try it regardless of how your meeting goes tomorrow."

"The idea is to get rid of the friction between us and the Americans so I would prefer we get the blessing of the US government. There's already some friction between them and the Brits and we want to foster it if possible. I expect the Americans would be more upset if the Brits interfere with officially sanctioned shipments. Until we know more, a car will come by to pick up someone around noon and five for updates."

"Yes, Sir. I guess that and Otto mean that things have been ironed out with the ambassador. Yesterday, it seemed like he didn't want us here."

"He thought we were replacements for von Papen. He seems to be much happier with what our mission actually is. Is there anything else you need?"

"Unless you can get rid of nosy neighbors, we're fine."

"Who?"

"It looks like the Americans are upstairs and the Brits are downstairs."

"Not surprising. We'll head off and let you rest your arms. Good luck."

The incessant tapping stopped as Weber bid us a good afternoon. I smiled when we got to the first floor. I took a seat near Brenda while she and the other members of the security detail ate the food that had just arrived. I asked for some sandwiches for Otto and me, savoring the roast beef when it arrived. Meanwhile, the British and American watchers were still fending off the helpful hotel staff that was trying to feed them. Their antics while trying to remain unnoticed amused me for a while. Then I wondered if anyone in Germany would so readily refuse food and the crushing weight of their hunger brought me back to the seriousness of my mission. I was quiet on the walk back to the embassy despite Brenda's best efforts at conversation.

February 5, 1917
Department of State, Washington, D.C.
The trip to the Department of State was uneventful. I was surprised that we had to wait once we got there but the secretary informed us that Secretary of State Lansing was in a meeting. Ambassador Bernstorff and I took seats to wait while Otto found a corner where he could watch both doors into the room. Bernstorff's face mirrored my own with a combination of concern and puzzlement.

It seemed longer but it was actually only a few minutes before the door to Lansing's office opened. We stood, expecting to see Lansing inviting us into his office. Instead, two young men with the same look about them as Otto came out and looked us over. One of them took a position near and was obviously watching Otto. The other kept an eye on me and informed the door to Lansing's office that it was clear.

I was getting more concerned. If Lansing thought we were such a potential danger, there was little chance of success for my mission. I looked to Bernstorff in hopes he had some insight and found him smiling and straightening his suit. He continued to smile as two more of Otto's cousins entered the room and exited into the foyer. Another announcement that things were clear and the door to Lansing's office opened all the way. A gentleman I didn't recognize was shaking Lansing's hand. He turned and entered our room followed by two more security types.

I turned to Bernstorff for some guidance as he extended his hand with a "Good morning, Vice President Marshall."

Marshall stopped and looked at me. "I guess I have you to thank for helping create more jobs for Americans."

Neither he nor his security seemed very happy. Me? I had no idea what was going on.

"Mr. Vice President, Major von Manstein has given me his word that he isn't here to carry on von Papen's work."

Aha! Now I remembered. Marshall had been the object of a bomb plot that some thought was the work of von Papen. No wonder he wasn't happy to see another German military attaché here.

"Mr. Vice President, I assure you I am here to try to bring an end to this war and the animosity between our governments." I extended my hand and found it nearly touching the stomach of one of the security people.

Marshall placed a hand on the shoulder of the guard and said, "Easy."

The guard relaxed a little but didn't move.

"We'll see, Major." He turned to Bernstorff and with an "Ambassador" extended his hand.

After a brief shake and nod of greeting, Marshall left the room trailed by his security. Bernstorff sighed and shrugged at me.

"Well, that was awkward. C'mon in."

Lansing was standing in his doorway with a smirk on his face. It was a lot more encouraging than the virtual scowl that had been on the Vice President's face. We entered the office and took the seats indicated by Lansing. I planned to let Bernstorff do most of the talking and Lansing seemed to expect it.

"As you might guess, the good news is that President Wilson is interested in what you have to say. The bad news is he sent Marshall to notify me of his interests. I think Wilson is trying to use Marshall's sense of humor against him. The security detachment was an added dig."

Bernstorff smiled. "That's right. Marshall refused security even after the bombing, didn't he?"

I thought I now understood the job comment. It was apparently meant as a joke.

"Yes, he did. And it didn't make everyone happy. Anyway, can I get you anything before we get started?"

Bernstorff looked at me and I shook my head.

"Not at the moment, Robert."

"Fine. Will you or Manstein be doing most of the talking?"

"I will. There's something that he will bring out at some point but he's briefed me on everything else."

"That works for me, Johann. So what's going on and why is Manstein here?"

"What's going on is a major shift in how my government wants to end this war. Manstein is here because he's the reason for the change."

Lansing looked at me again then turned back to Ambassador Bernstorff. "Really? That sounds like an interesting tale."

"It's less interesting than you might think. He caught Ludendorff's attention when he was convalescing in east Germany. Apparently, Ludendorff likes to discuss ideas with him because he looks at things a little differently. They discussed the return to unrestricted submarine warfare. Manstein pointed out some issues that Ludendorff eventually agreed with. After some more discussion, they came up with a different path to peace. Ludendorff had Manstein pitch it at Schloss Pless, not realizing that Manstein is Hindenburg's nephew. It was agreed to give the new plan a try and after a lot more discussion, Manstein was sent here. As you might surmise, America plays a pivotal role in this new plan. Before you ask, no, it does not involve America going to war with anyone."

"And just what does it involve?"

"You know our position on this war being Russia's fault. We—"

"Stop, Johann. We aren't going to change our position on that."

"Mr. Lansing, if I may?" I asked.

He flicked his hand, sat back and looked at me with a sigh.

"I believe you currently have a military force in Mexico pursuing Pancho Villa?"

He nodded.

"What if, rather than raiding the town in New Mexico, Pancho Villa had assassinated the man who just left, Vice President Marshall?"

Lansing's eyes looked at me sharply.

"Further, what if the Mexican government was shown to be behind the assassination?"

He sat forward. "Pershing would have a few more troops with him and Mexico would be getting a new government."

"Even if another country, say the United Kingdom, had guaranteed Mexico's sovereignty? Making them feel protected against retaliation."

"We'd tell the Brits to stay out of it."

I nodded and smiled. "Much like we told the Russians to stay out of the issue between Austria-Hungary and Serbia?"

That question earned me a dirty look from Lansing.

"And what would your country do if, like Russia, the British chose to mobilize to protect Mexico?"

He sat back again and stared into the distance for a moment. "We'd probably begin general mobilization and enact war plan Red—the invasion of Canada." He looked back at me with concern on his face.

"Much like we moved against France since they would be involved in the war and they were the immediate threat."

I stopped to let Lansing think things through. Bernstorff was looking at me with a bewildered smile on his face. He seemed to think I had finally made our case for who was ultimately responsible for the war.

"There are a few more pieces to our puzzle, Mr. Lansing." He turned back to me with a shake of his head.

"In our case, the Black Hand of Serbia assassinated their own king in 1903 to put someone else in power. Someone more in line with their thinking. They have made no secret of wanting to take large chunks of Austro-Hungarian territory. Would your government be more or less lenient with a Mexico that was clamoring for a return of the territory it lost in the 1840s and saw political assassination as a valid method for achieving its aims?"

Silence reigned in the room for several minutes. Lansing mulled things over while Bernstorff urged me to keep my peace. I pulled the sealed package out of my case and waited.

Lansing turned to the door to his outer office and said, "Did you get that, John?"

A barely muffled reply of "Yes, Sir," answered. I'd thought that we would be monitored in some way. The confirmation was pleasing.

"Your arguments will be taken to the President."

"Thank you, Sir, but there is something else that should also be taken to him. If I may?"

"By all means...."

I unsealed my package and pulled out a map. Lansing moved a few things and I spread it out on Lansing's desk. He looked at it in confusion as Bernstorff moved around so he could read it.

With a small gasp, Bernstorff looked at me and asked, "Is this real?"

"There are numerous examples of the Archduke's signature. The notes and signature on the bottom right looked genuine to me and Uncle Paul assured me they were."

Lansing kept looking at the map but said, "John. Could you come in here for a minute?"

The door opened and a young man came in, nodding to us. He closed the door and walked across the room.

"What can I do for you, boss?" he asked.

Lansing indicated the map. "Could you tell me what this says?"

As John came around the desk, I moved away. It was getting a little crowded on that side and I had already seen the map.

John looked it over and then looked up at me. "Really?" he asked.

"As far as I know. Kaiser Wilhelm wasn't overly fond of it."

John went back to looking at the map.

After a moment, Lansing's patience gave out. "Well? I can see it's a map of Austria-Hungary but what does the writing and all this strange shading mean?"

John pointed to the large bold lettering across the bottom of the map. "That says: 'The United States of Greater Austria.' The shaded regions are the planned state boundaries. The written comments order that a constitution be drawn up based on ours and the Brits'. It requires that the constitution be ready before Emperor Franz Josef's death. It says the writer will bring their country into the modern world. It was signed by Archduke Franz Ferdinand on June 15th, 1914. Less than two weeks before he was assassinated."

Lansing sat down and looked up at me. "This will have to be authenticated."

"I understand. The German and Austro-Hungarian governments simply request that you be very careful with it. If the plan it contains ever bears fruit, it will be a national treasure for the Austro-Hungarians."

He nodded and John carefully folded the map back up and I helped him put it back in the packing in which I'd carried it. He looked to Lansing when we had it repacked.

"Take it and go. Tell Bill he has the duty."

John opened the door to leave. There was another man there who nodded, stepped out of the way, and closed the door behind John. It appeared that Bill had heard.

Lansing gestured for us to return to our seats. "If I remember correctly, we had just started our discussion."

Bernstorff thought for a moment. "Ah, yes. Since we don't blame France or England for starting the war, we do not want anything from them. The territory of Belgium and Luxembourg has been occupied and disrupted and we feel there should be some form of reparations for them. We are prepared to withdraw to the prewar boundaries on the western front and cease hostilities.

"The Balkan areas occupied by our allies should stay under their control. Considering they were the center for wars in 1912 and 1913, we feel the Serbians will continue to be a threat to the stability of the region if they are an independent country. The hope is that they could be incorporated into the US of GA.

"The Russian empire appears to be breaking up. We believe that to be good. We would like to reestablish the Polish-Lithuanian Commonwealth as well as a free Ukraine. Rumania would lose some of its western territory and add Bessarabia to the northeast.

"The Ottoman empire would lose those areas currently occupied by the Entente. Its border with Russia would be based on wherever the front was at the time of a peace accord.

"Our Pacific colonies would go to their current occupiers. Our African colonies would revert to our control." Bernstorff stopped for a reaction.

"That's an interesting list. It's not exactly how President Wilson wants things to end but it has some merit." Lansing paused for a moment, then continued. "I notice that you still haven't gotten to what you want us to do for you."

"That is simplicity itself. We would like you to ship us fertilizer, food and other non-war materials. The very materials that you protested to the United Kingdom about being included in the embargo. The British are waging war on our civilians by starving them. If they were rounding them up and shooting them, your government would be protesting in the strongest terms. As it is, they kill thousands and no one cares."

"Please, Johann. I've read the Bryce Report. I know what your people have been doing to the civilians in Belgium."

Bernstorff turned to me with a wave of his hand.

I turned to Lansing. "Have you read the White Book? It details some of what the Belgian civilians have been doing to German soldiers. There is a small-scale guerrilla war going on in Belgium. I know there have been some issues. There are in every war. No army works well if such things are allowed and we have been meting out discipline to those we catch. I am certain that what was reported is a colorful version of what the reality is.

"Anyway, consider the source. You may find Bryce to be honest but that says nothing about his sources of information. Even some members of the committee have expressed reservations about their findings. Finally, consider what kind of responses we would get if we sent someone to northern Mexico and asked them what your troops have been doing? Do you think we might get a less than sterling version of their actions?"

"You just love that we have troops in Mexico, don't you?"

"It does provide a useful context for our reasoning."

Lansing sighed and sat back. He looked back to Bernstorff. "I believe I understand what you meant when you said he has a different way of looking at things. Besides shipping you non-war material, what else do you want us to do?"

"We would like you to help negotiate an end to the war. We have approached the Entente and been summarily rejected by the British. I believe they have responded to President Wilson's peace initiative with the Central Powers paying for everything, losing lots of territory and the dissolution of both Austria-Hungary and the Ottoman empire."

"Allowing different ethnic groups to determine their own futures is something that we support."

"Really? Very admirable. When can we expect to hear of free elections in the territories you control?"

Lansing's face took on a rather unpleasant frown.

"And when will we have the honor of recognizing the Confederate States of America?"

"Ambassador," I interjected.

"I'm sorry, Manstein, but we have to bring this up at some point. They need to consider whether they are following the same rules they want to impose on us. They want to prevent or limit future wars and they think they can do this by creating large numbers of small countries. If they haven't learned anything from the constant wars in the Balkans then we might as well leave."

"If I may?"

Bernstorff looked at me for a moment before disgustedly waving his hand for me to proceed. "Fine, go ahead. I seem to have stepped on Mr. Lansing's sense of propriety."

"Mr. Lansing, we understand your desire to let people determine their own government. It is one of the reasons that Germany itself is looking into transitioning to a constitutional monarchy and that we have hope for Archduke Ferdinand's dream for Austria-Hungary. We do not believe that the proliferation of smaller nations is a good idea.

"The Balkan Wars of 1912 and 1913 demonstrate to us that these countries will squabble over their borders, often as a method for keeping their people in line by introducing an outside enemy. These small countries will gravitate to different great powers for protection and then use this protection as a license for their own ambitions.

"This is exactly what Serbia did with Russia. Italy did the same thing with the Entente for a promise of part of Austria-Hungary. So did Romania. I believe even the Belgians have stated a desire to annex some of our land. With the guarantees of the great powers, these countries are far more willing to go to war to further their ambitions. If a small country doesn't have a great power as its protector, one of them will take the role regardless of the small country's desires. Greece was neutral, the British didn't like it and so they've been pushing a civil war to replace the Greek government with one they can use.

"When the ambitions of these small countries are found to be useful by a great power, a general war erupts over small issues. This is basically how the current war began. Russia wanted to reassert its prestige after its losses to the Japanese. France was eager for war so they could regain Alsace-Lorraine. By the way, a territory where a large majority of the people are Germanic, and only around ten percent are French. We believe that same line of thinking is why England entered the war. They wanted to divert attention from the Home Rule issues in Ireland and saw it as an opportunity to take land from the Ottomans as well as our colonies. Do you truly believe the Japanese have entered the war to protect Serbia?

"If you really desire to prevent or limit future wars, then a proliferation of small countries and the inevitable proliferation of defense treaties is exactly the wrong way to approach it. Especially when these small countries have a long history of mutual animosity."

Lansing took a deep breath. "Interesting arguments. I notice you're happy to point out the territorial ambitions of the Entente and yet you don't mention your own."

"That's because we don't really have any. The Kaiser has agreed that the cost of Pacific colonies has been much higher than their benefit. The escalating naval expenditures required have done little other than possibly help destabilize the peace. The African colonies are a more reasonable investment. There will probably be some adjustment of our eastern frontier as the Polish-Lithuanian Commonwealth is created but both they and the Ukraine should be large enough countries to keep them from being viewed as easy targets for expansion.

"The territorial changes for Rumania would mostly be territory it recently acquired from Bulgaria. Serbia would bear the brunt of territorial changes since it would be dissolved. Then again, they are the ones who instigated three wars in three years."

"Yes, and I remember the rest of your proposal. I will pass it along to the President but I doubt he'll believe you are very sincere. And I have no idea whether or not he'll agree with your line of reasoning."

"If you doubt our sincerity, I am prepared to send a message that will activate a plan to demonstrate it."

"And that would be?"

"We are prepared to evacuate some of the territory we occupy. I will not tell you where but I will say it would take a couple months to enact."

Bernstorff looked at me like I'd lost my head.

"I don't know if it would work but it would be a good start. If you want it to demonstrate your sincerity, I suggest you simply do it rather than trying to use it as a bargaining chip. Is there anything else?"

"That's it. We would like to put a few men on the boats to help them navigate the route to Germany. We do not want them to run if they are challenged by British warships. We would put payments for shipments in escrow here with the funds released if the ships successfully return with other payment. If their cargo is seized, the payments would go to the shippers and the British would get the cargo for free."

"Really?"

"Yes, really. The only ways to end this war are by being starved out by the British, by starving out the British, or by loosening the blockade enough that the British agree to a negotiated peace. Every other country is suffering to some extent. They've lost some men but they're using the war to expand their empire and fleet. Ask the Norwegians where their merchant fleet has gone."

"Yes, we know the Brits have been effectively stealing it and some of the Norwegian merchantmen too."

"Didn't you fight a war with them over this same activity?"

Lansing smiled ruefully and nodded.

"Until the Brits have some reason to come to the negotiating table, they will continue to grab as much land as they can. And if you're not happy with Serbia's policy of coup by assassination, how do you feel about the British policy of coup by starting a civil war?"

"We aren't happy with it either. But I'm fairly certain that what you hope to do is engineer some incidents between us and the British."

"We wish to reestablish the freedom of the oceans for trade. Something the British have unilaterally decided to end. We do not want to put your merchants in harm's way and we want to see trade resume between our countries. We offer to guarantee the profits for your merchants. Is there the possibility of an incident? Yes. But such an incident would require the British to fire on your unarmed merchants when they are following the orders of the British. Not something that is likely to occur."

"Fine, Major von Manstein. Your message will be taken to the President." Lansing stood "It appears that despite your earlier assertion, you have done most of the talking."

Bernstorff was still looking at me quizzically as we stood.

I extended my hand. "I'm sorry about that, Sir. I've been told I have a tendency to jump into conversations."

Lansing smiled and shook my hand. "That's a bit of an understatement. Manstein, Ambassador Bernstorff." Lansing turned and shook his hand as the door opened.

We were directed out of the room and to a waiting car. The trip back to the embassy was a quiet one.

The quiet lasted until we were in the embassy. We had barely removed our coats when Bernstorff rounded on me.

"Alright, Erich. Just where did this idea of a withdrawal come from?"

"Hindenburg and Ludendorff. We are already preparing a secondary defensive line on the Western Front. The plan is to begin the withdrawal to it in the next few weeks. The intent is to free up a number of divisions to act as reserves or be used in offensives on other fronts."

"Not something the Americans need to know. And here I was worried about your ability to play the diplomat. I get upset while you try to wring advantage out of an already planned action. Well done."

"Thank you, Johann. It comes from dealing with generals who don't like being told they're wrong."

"Any other little surprises I should know about?"

"Not that I can think of at the moment."

Bernstorff simply snorted and shook his head.

February 7, 1917
Department of State, Washington, D.C.
The message from Lansing had arrived late yesterday afternoon. It requested our presence here today but gave no indication of what had been decided. Bernstorff had expected a response to take several days. He said that such a quick response usually indicated either a

flat refusal or a full acceptance. As you might expect, both Bernstorff and I were more than a little nervous as we waited in the front office.

We had spent the last day and a half going over possible reactions and arguments against them. We just needed to find out which way the Americans would jump, if they jumped at all. The door to Lansing's office was opened by John. I nodded a greeting as he invited us in. Lansing was sitting behind his desk and another gentleman was seated on his right. He was wearing a cowboy hat and simply smiled as John directed us to our seats.

"Good morning. I'd like to introduce you to Colonel House. Colonel House, this is Ambassador Bernstorff and this is Major von Manstein."

Colonel House tipped his hat and simply said, "Mornin'." Then he started chuckling.

I glanced at Bernstorff trying to figure out what was going on and who this new person was. Bernstorff face showed a pleased respect for House.

"I think you should know that the VP didn't like you using him as an assassination example. Nope, not at all."

I'm sure Bernstorff's face looked as shocked as mine did. This was definitely something we hadn't anticipated.

"He was stomping around claiming you were baiting him. Wanted to throw you out of the country, preferably into the ocean without a boat."

House started chuckling again and I relaxed a little as I realized he was chuckling at Marshall and not at our stupidity.

"Hell, I didn't even have to say anything. Woodrow pointed out that it was just an equivalent position to the one ol' Ferdinand held. Said you were just trying to get us to understand how serious the assassination had been for Austro-Hungarians. Marshall eventually calmed down but I bet he provided a good fifteen minutes of entertainment, struttin' around like a rooster tryin' to keep his hens. Anyway, thanks for twistin' his tail, whether or not it was intentional."

Bernstorff replied with a simple "You're welcome?" which made House go back to chuckling.

Lansing rolled his eyes and shook his head. If nothing else, we seemed to be on good terms with this person who called the American President by his first name.

Colonel House stood up and began pacing around the office. "Down to business. We're glad to hear you're stopping the sabotage and you're not going back to sinking everything with your subs. What we want to know is just what you plan to accomplish with our merchantmen."

Bernstorff turned to me. "Do you want to take this or should I?"

House stopped next to Lansing. "Before you decide that. I know what you said your intention was but I also know you have to have some ace up your sleeve or you wouldn't be trying this. I want to know your real plan. We ain't real happy with either the Brits or you. Tell us plain and we're more likely to believe you."

Bernstorff looked at me and said, "Colonel House is Wilson's most trusted adviser."

I looked at the floor and sighed. I'd come across a few ranking officers who were like this. The full truth was the only thing that ever worked.

"We plan on using the convoy system against the Brits."

"And just how will you do that? The convoy system only works if there are escorts...." He paused for a second. "Submarines?"

"Yes, Sir. The merchants will rendezvous with submarines at one of several points we've designated."

House held up a hand and smiled. "Let me guess. The convoy starts its run and your High Seas Fleet sorties away from the convoy. The Grand Fleet has to respond and is pulled out of position. Anything that intercepts the merchants has to move nice and slow to escort them to port, making them big fat targets for your subs. Our guys are used as bait with a minimum of risk to them."

I nodded. "If the Brits intercept your ships outside the blockade zone, they're effectively committing piracy. They don't have the ships to cover an expanded blockade zone. And the only other way to stop your ships would be to fire on them."

"Which wouldn't go over very well. It sounds like you're trying to get us into the war on your side."

"I think the only way that would happen is if the Brits started shooting at your ships. There is the possibility that they'll do just that and then claim it was our ships. I've spoken with Hindenburg and the Kaiser. We will not be shooting at your ships. We need the supplies those ships will be carrying.

"I'll give you one more reason to agree to this, the people of Europe. We've overrun large areas of the Balkans, Belgium, and eastern Europe. As our food supplies dwindle, who do you think will get what food is available? The people of the occupied territories? It is not something we want to do but if the blockade continues, we will be forced to starve them to feed our own people."

"That's something that Woodrow is worried about, though the Brits dismiss the idea every time we bring it up. I'll let him know your plans but I don't know which way he'll decide. And yes, we'll keep this quiet. Advertising it seems like a way to increase the risk for our boys. Anything else y'all have to say?"

I shook my head as did Bernstorff.

"We'll be in touch."

We shook hands with the Americans and left. I think we were both surprised by the brevity of the meeting. It seemed things were moving much faster than we'd expected.

When we got back to the embassy, Bernstorff asked, "Do you really think it's a good idea to reveal so much?"

"I was told this is my project and the decisions were mine. I was given six months to try this and some people respond to the bald truth."

"From what I've heard of him, Colonel House is one of those. The real question is whether or not Wilson is, too."

February 9, 1917
Department of State, Washington, D.C.

This trip to Secretary of State Lansing's office was a little different than the previous ones. We had two cars of security men as escorts. Bernstorff heard that Lansing had met with British Ambassador Spring-Rice after he met with us on the 7th. Unfortunately, he hadn't gotten any details on what was discussed. Then again, that might bode well for the confidentiality of our meetings.

Lansing was standing in his doorway as we arrived and waved us into his office. He looked more than a little annoyed and Bernstorff and I shot worried looks at each other. He directed us to our usual seats and closed the door behind us. He sat down and glared at us while shaking his head back and forth.

"Do you know how big of a mess you two have caused?"

I started to answer but he held up his hand.

"That was rhetorical. You probably know I had a meeting with the British ambassador. We started out discussing their peace demands, which happened to be very close to what you thought they'd be. Anyway, we never got to how countries who joined the war for territorial gain could demand reparations because they were losing. No, Spring-Rice didn't like it when I asked how he could ask for self-determination for the Balkan peoples while requiring Alsace-Lorraine go back to the French. When I asked him when the Brits would allow their colonies that same self-determination, he got rather annoyed and told me that was to be determined by the British government and no one else. When I told him that was fine and pushed on to ask about the Middle East, he just stared at me for a while then got up and left."

"We got a message from him yesterday saying the British would, quote, 'work with the various groups to help bring them into the modern world and establish stable governments. This will, of course, take time,' end quote. The President didn't like that response one bit."

Lansing stopped and contemplated us to gauge our reactions. I had no idea what Bernstorff's reaction was. I'm sure I looked somewhere between smug, thankful and hopeful.

"Thank you for asking him," I said.

"Don't doubt that there's going to be a reevaluation of our relationships, but don't be so quick to thank me. Our people picked up some chatter that more than a few Brits would be happy if you had a fatal accident."

Bernstorff exclaimed, "What? They're contemplating assassinating a diplomat? What kind of precedent would that set? It'd throw international relations back thousands of years."

"Von Manstein isn't a diplomat. He's a military attaché. I'm sure that if anything happens to him, there will be plenty of evidence found with him to make him look like von Papen."

I swallowed as I came to understand the reason for the extra security on the trip over here. "At least you know the truth. If I'm to die serving my country, so be it."

"There's just one problem with that. The papers would report the story the Brits want. The only way we could prove them wrong would compromise your plans as well as reveal that we spy on our 'friends.' Neither of us would benefit from that. So how about we work on keeping you alive for your country?"

I nodded. "That sounds good to me but I'm afraid that there will be a few more issues if you go ahead with shipping food. The Brits will quickly figure out that my leutnants know the sea rendezvous options. They'll probably figure it out after the first convoy. My leutnants will be targets too, once that occurs."

Lansing smiled. "So the President was right."

When I appeared puzzled, he continued.

"There was a discussion over how you'd keep your rendezvous location secret. Colonel House thought you'd use a special code just for it. Wilson said there weren't that many different paths you could use and all you'd have to do is name each one."

"The simple solutions tend to be best."

I decided not to point out that Colonel House was right, too. The entire German navy was going to switch to our new codes when the first convoy sailed.

"We've already got extra men watching your leutnants and the crew of the *Deutschland*. If the shipment is allowed, we'll put a few more people on it. For now, it would be a good idea if you give us a call any time you feel the need to leave the embassy. I'll let you know when I get instructions. Until then, remember to duck."

The ride back to the embassy was uneventful, though Bernstorff did keep looking at me like I was crazy. I guess he didn't like my smile.

When we were safely back and he asked why I was smiling, I simply said, "If your enemies want to kill you, you're doing something right."

He walked away shaking his head and muttered something that sounded like "Crazy soldiers...."

February 14, 1917

Department of State, Washington, D.C.

Bernstorff had been surprised by the request for a meeting on Valentine's Day. I was just glad to have something to do. Reports of the British peace demands and the meeting with the British ambassador were in the local paper. Some of the stories even questioned why countries that had been bribed with promises of territory to go to war should be due reparations. I had the feeling that Lansing had pushed that angle. There was also a story that the Germans had begun a general withdrawal on the Western Front. The timing couldn't have been better. I had high hopes for this meeting.

Lansing was not alone when we entered his office. "Good morning, Johann, Erich. This is Josephus Daniels, our Secretary of the Navy."

He rose and shook our hands. "Just call me Joe."

We greeted him and took our seats. I'm sure I had a smile on my face. Lansing hadn't used my first name in any of our previous meetings.

Joe remained standing and started things off. "Ease up on the glee there, Erich. We will stand by international law that several items on Britain's list are not actually contraband. Yes, we're going to allow the shipments but we have some requirements." He paused to make sure we understood.

Bernstorff answered with a smooth "And they are?"

"First, all shipments will be inspected before leaving port. They will only carry items that Britain cannot legally embargo.

"Second, you'll pay fifty percent above the shippers' standard rates to cover hazardous duty pay and days when the ships sit idle waiting for the convoy to form up.

"Third, you'll pay the insurance for the shipment. We won't have our boys losing money if things don't work out. If you want to keep those costs down, make your system work.

"Fourth, if there is no return cargo, the shippers will receive fifty percent of their standard rates to cover their operating expenses. This would include if the ship is detained by the British and offloaded there.

"Fifth, we will send observers with the convoy. We do not want to see any of your U-boats. We will follow standard shipping protocols. Our ships will not stop for your ships or the Entente's. They will expect to be met by pilots when they approach your ports."

Bernstorff turned to me. "I believe the first four terms are within the limits you set. I don't know how the fifth condition would work."

"It's fine if they want to treat it like standard shipping. The problem will be with the British. I'm sure they'll try to stop the American ships due to 'safety concerns' or something similar." I turned to the Secretary of the Navy. "Would you have an issue if we patrolled along your intended path looking for potential trouble?"

Joe thought for a moment before answering. "I think that would be okay. If you spot something, notify us. We will not let you make it look like we're running with you as escorts."

"That would work for me. Our main goal is the resumption of legal trade. Are there any other stipulations?"

"Just that all the merchantmen be volunteers. But that's something for us to worry about. I believe Kapitän König has been arranging your first convoy."

I nodded and he continued.

"I'll need a list of his contacts and you can proceed once I've talked to them."

"I noticed you didn't say anything about us prepaying for the actual goods."

"That's because we're going to treat this just like normal shipping. If it's legal for us to ship it to Germany then there shouldn't be anything special about how you pay for the cargo."

"Thank you. That's more than I hoped for."

"There are more than a few people getting tired of Britain flouting the law whenever she wants to. That goes for Germany, too. International law says some of what both of you have been doing is illegal. We got you to stop the unrestricted sub warfare. We'll see what we can do about Britain's abuse of the 'contraband of war' lists. We believe that the laws apply to everyone."

With that, the meeting was concluded. Our car was sent for and security arranged for our trip back.

Once we were back at the embassy, Bernstorff pointed out, "It appears your leutnants won't have anything to do."

"For the moment. Things have taken a different path than I thought they would. This may be better. The big question is what the Brits will do. How far will they push the Americans and what will they do to change this policy shift back to what it was?"

February 17, 1917

German Embassy, Washington, D.C.

The newspaper and Bernstorff's watchers had become our main sources of information. Lansing responded politely to our messages requesting information without actually providing any.

Thursday's paper reported the shift in policy along with outraged reactions by the British government. The policy was presented as the Americans upholding international law and the British reaction came across as a bully throwing a tantrum. The impressment of Norwegian sailors and the forced sale of their merchant fleet were compared to what the British had done in the past. The argument that many of the civilians saved from starvation would be those of Britain's allies was dismissed as an outright lie by the Brits. The British claimed that the Americans were violating their policy of neutrality and siding with the Germans. I crossed my fingers for a good outcome.

The leutnant who came for dinner that night was excited. Kapitän König had been contacted and the shipment he'd been working on was given official sanction. He would be responsible for ordering and payment. It appeared that the Americans wanted to keep things away from any connections with the German government. Kapitän König would need access to the funds we'd brought across with us. It looked like my leutnants and I might not have much to do for the foreseeable future.

Friday's paper contained several stories refuting the British arguments, as well as several that blamed the Germans for everything. The most important story was the one from the State Department. The official position was that a neutral should treat and trade fairly with both sides of the conflict. No war materials would be shipped to either side. Shipment of non-war material would be made to both sides. All shipments would be inspected in America and no interference with American ships would be tolerated. I nearly whooped for joy. I was so pleased I almost missed the short story that the American congress had approved accelerated war preparedness measures.

Today's paper continued the back-and-forth arguments on the policy shift. It also announced that the first shipment to Germany had sailed in the pre-dawn hours. No mention was made of escorting ships so I wondered if the Americans were naively taking a moral stand or if they were exercising good operational security. Time would tell. There was also a story about shipments to Britain that were being canceled. The American government was purchasing the shipments for use in its shipbuilding program.

This afternoon, Bernstorff received a cable from Hindenburg. He is pleased with the progress we're making even if it isn't along the path we expected. Apparently, several other neutral countries are expected to follow the American example on shipping. He also said that Norway, Sweden and Denmark have approached the United States about a closer relationship. Karl I of Austria-Hungary also appears to be supportive of the current initiative, and of a future change in government style for his country. Almost as an afterthought, Hindenburg informed us that the shift to the new naval codes would be implemented at midnight Berlin time. The next few days promised to be very interesting indeed.

February 20, 1917

German Embassy, Washington, D.C.

Today's newspaper reported the first incident for the convoy. I smiled as I read the story. Apparently two Canadian destroyers sailed right through the convoy in the early morning hours of the 19th. Several merchant ships had to take evasive maneuvers to avoid collisions. The destroyers sent a message warning of a submarine sighting as they came upon the well-lit convoy. The destroyers made another pass through the convoy "chasing the submarine" and dropped a number of depth charges perilously close to several merchant ships. They had turned back for a third pass through the convoy when American escorts that had been shadowing the convoy arrived on the scene.

The Americans informed the Canadians there was no submarine sighting and ordered them away from the convoy. The Canadians sent their submarine sighting warning again and headed back toward the convoy. The Americans put several shots between the Canadians and the convoy with a warning that further reckless endangerment of American ships would be considered an act of war. The Canadian destroyers broke off and said that they would file an official complaint over the action of the Americans. The Americans responded with a similar message.

The American complaint got an interesting response from the British. They claimed the submarine sighting message was probably a ploy by the Germans to cause friction between the two countries. In a statement by Josephus Daniels, it was pointed out that the American navy had pickets out in multiple directions from the convoy and none of them had picked up the sighting message. He didn't say that the

British were lying but it was the conclusion the reporters came to. Apparently, the Americans weren't as naive as I thought.

February 28, 1917

German Embassy, Washington, D.C.

Today's newspaper reported the second incident for the convoy, though it wasn't reported as such. The American navy released a report that one of the destroyers escorting the convoy had been damaged during rescue operations. A British ship approximately fifty miles east of the convoy broadcast a message that they were being attacked by a German submarine. A few minutes later, the German submarine broadcast the location of the now sinking ship. They also sent the ship's name and that she was a minelayer. Two American destroyers sped to the scene and rescued a number of the British sailors. One of the American destroyers was damaged when it hit a free-floating mine.

The location was interesting because the convoy has been broadcasting its position every night and it was in the direct path of the convoy. There was no comment from the British other than thanking the Americans for their assistance. The rescued sailors were transferred to British ships that showed up about an hour after the Americans arrived at the scene.

March 2, 1917

Department of State, Washington, D.C.

Yesterday, Secretary of State Lansing asked for a meeting this morning. Bernstorff's sources said the next convoy should be ready to sail in the next day or two so we arrived wondering what we would hear. We had to wait in the front office for a few minutes and the secretary seemed nervous which made us even more curious.

Lansing finally opened his door and invited us into his office. He closed the door and directed us to our seats. We both became more intent when Lansing didn't sit in his chair but stood behind it holding onto its back.

"The convoy arrived in Kiel this morning. That's the good news. The bad news is the Brits haven't been happy with the change of policy. We expected their government's reaction. We didn't anticipate the reaction against our merchantmen in their ports. There have been several violent incidents that were ignored by their local police."

"What incidents for the convoy have come to your attention?"

Bernstorff answered for us. "We read about the Canadian destroyers and the minelayer off the coast of Norway. That's all we've heard about."

"There were two other incidents. A British cruiser coming out of Bergen ran right through the convoy. The escorts hadn't anticipated any issues from that direction and at least it didn't turn around for another pass. Two of the merchants bumped into each other but there was no serious damage. The cruiser ignored all hails and acted as if the convoy and its escorts didn't exist.

"The second happened off the northwest Danish coast. Two torpedoes were fired at one of the escorts while it was in Danish waters. The destroyer dodged them and its Captain rightly decided to stay on station rather than pursue the submarine that appeared to be firing from long range. Unfortunately, that means we can't positively identify whose sub it was.

"The British have apologized for the first incident, claiming it was an unfortunately literal interpretation of a harsh Captain's orders by an inexperienced subordinate. We haven't mentioned the second incident since we don't have any proof.

"What this means for you is that there is a growing faction in our government that's against the recent shift in policy. On the other hand, the Scandinavian countries and Brazil are looking to us for leadership and protection. Hell, Norway asked if we'd like to station a battle squadron in Bergen to provide convoy protection. It's probably to help protect the Norwegians too. A lot will depend on what happens with the second convoy."

When Lansing paused for a moment, I asked, "Is there anything we can do to help?"

Lansing stared at us for a few moments before answering. "In many ways, President Wilson is happy with the developments. He believes it's the first real step towards creating a group of neutral nations that can help prevent or shorten future wars. His concern is for the immediate future. The Brits will have more time to figure out how they want to deal with the second convoy. It will have a heavier escort and the Entente will be warned that close approaches will be viewed as hostile.

"Regardless, our boys will be a long way from home and any help our navy can provide. We don't expect the Brits to do anything too overt but if they do, we'd like to know what kind of support our sailors might get from you."

He looked at Bernstorff for a few moments before turning to me with an expectant look. It took me a moment before I realized that Bernstorff was looking at me, too.

"I presume you wouldn't want us shooting at Entente ships without your permission."

"That would be correct. We'd prefer that no one even know you're there."

It seemed like some of my ideas might actually get tested. "If your convoy is willing to take a few of my leutnants with you and follow the course they give, I think something can be arranged."

"That's what we were hoping to hear. The next convoy will be ready to sail from New York in a few days. When can your men be ready?"

"They've been ready since we got here. All they need is to get to your ships."

"That's what I expected. We'll send someone tonight to collect them. Do you remember John? The young man who came in to look at your map of Austria-Hungary?"

"I think so...."

"That's fine. I'll get him over here before you leave and he'll go with you. If you can drop him off with your men, he'll be able to verify their contact tonight."

"That sounds good to me." I strained to see if I could hear someone outside leaving to get John. I did hear the outer office door close and counted a small victory. I smiled until I realized that Lansing was looking at me with a patient expression on his face.

"Yes, we're still being listened to and yes, someone has left to collect John. Back to business?"

Bernstorff smirked a little and said, "Ah, finally, a crack in the armor. Good diplomats are supposed to pretend they don't notice such things."

I felt like I was five and had been caught with my hand in the cookie jar.

Lansing stifled a small laugh before saying, "Don't worry about it. You're doing just fine."

"Anyway, if things go really bad, we may need your fleet sortie idea to draw the British away from the convoy. Is that still an option?"

"The order for the submarines is also an order for the fleet. We'll need to get one of the submarine Captains to forward the change in orders but that shouldn't be a problem."

"I wondered if you knew the new codes your navy was using. We didn't know that we were sending the first convoy through just as you were changing them. It definitely added to the British confusion." Lansing smiled. "Another one of your ideas?"

"Yes, thank you. And no, we don't have the codes. Security in case anything goes wrong."

Lansing nodded just as there was a knock on the door. Lansing said, "Come in, John," but was surprised when his secretary entered.

"Sir, Ambassador Jusserand has requested a meeting and is on his way over. He should be here in fifteen minutes."

Lansing nodded and she closed the door. "I've been wondering when he'd show up. I think it'd be best..."

Another knock at the door interrupted Lansing's comment, though I was fairly certain it was a dismissal. This time it was John and we left for the hotel and my bored leutnants.

March 5, 1917
German Embassy, Washington, D.C.
Leutnant Weber led the group of five that headed to New York. Since the other four members of the team were picked by a game of chance, Hoffman was among them. I figured it wouldn't hurt to have someone lucky with them.

As expected, the French lodged a protest concerning the change in American policy. President Wilson responded by reiterating his policies of strict neutrality, freedom of the seas and what materials could be embargoed. Official notice was taken that the US was sending war material to France and these shipments were stopped. Other members of the Entente have apparently decided to take the hint and haven't made any complaints.

We were informed last night that the convoy would sail today and when we got confirmation this morning, Bernstorff sent the initial convoy message to Berlin. I wondered what all the different snoops would think since it was in our standard diplomatic code, something I was fairly certain had been broken by a number of countries. All it said was "Convoy New York, path one, 5 March 7 A.M."

This had been a minor sticking point back in Germany. The Kaiser was convinced we should do something more elaborate. Ludendorff had finally convinced him that the convoy would be shadowed so any extra security or misdirection efforts would be meaningless. It also meant that we didn't need to know the new naval codes so there was less chance of any accidents.

For me, all this meant was another couple of weeks of worrying. I was developing a greater understanding of how the people running both sides of the war could react calmly even in the face of disaster. Usually, if something went wrong there was nothing they could do to salvage the immediate situation. You simply made the best plans you could and trusted the commander on the scene to be able to adapt to any changes. If things went bad, you tried to determine why and how to avoid it in the future. Either that or a lot of men died for no reason. At least the men in Europe had people to talk with and places they could go to blow off steam. I was still effectively under house arrest and Bernstorff wasn't very useful at talking tactics. I found I had to limit myself to two drinks a day.

March 13, 1917
German Embassy, Washington, D.C.
Today's paper contained the first news on the convoy. It reached its first way point on path one last night, about six hundred miles south of Iceland. Two Canadian destroyers had been shadowing the convoy and reporting its position every two hours. A distress signal was received on the afternoon of the 12th that indicated two British destroyers about ten miles east of the convoy were under attack by multiple submarines. Two American destroyers

were dispatched and picked up a number of survivors before returning to the convoy.

Bernstorff seemed quite pleased with this until I reminded him that the Americans didn't want us shooting unless they requested it. I did admit I was pleased that the group submarine attack had worked which placated Bernstorff to some extent. My real concern was whether or not the submarines had been contacted and given the order change. If they had, the rescued British sailors would almost certainly have seen it. If they hadn't, would there be more incidents for the Americans to complain about before they were contacted.

March 16, 1917
German Embassy, Washington, D.C.

And the answer is—there was contact. The rescued British sailors were released on the 15th at the Faeroe Islands, not far from the second way point on path one. They immediately began reporting that the Americans were colluding with the Germans and using the convoy as bait. The Americans also dropped off a spokesman to present their side of the story.

The British issued a complaint about the American use of their neutrality to lure British warships into hazardous positions. They also reiterated their stance that the Americans were dangerously close to causing an incident that would irreparably harm Anglo-American relations.

The American spokesman admitted there had been contact with a German submarine but it was well after the combat was over. Apparently, the American admiral in charge of the convoy didn't like his convoy being used as bait either. The German Kapitän had apparently replied that he had been heading out to find the stupid Canadian destroyer Captain who had been broadcasting his position every two hours for the last several days. He just happened to be in the path of two British destroyers that were going to meet them.

The British claimed this was an outright lie since the Germans hadn't broken the British naval codes. The American said he'd asked the Germans about that very point. They said maybe they had, maybe they hadn't. If they hadn't, they might have simply used the data of when the Canadians had come into range of different wireless stations and done some fancy math.

Neither side appeared to be overly happy with the incident but the most interesting thing mentioned was about Sir David Beatty, Commander in Chief of the British Grand Fleet. He apparently made an official comment that these kinds of incidents would not be tolerated. It will be interesting to see what the Americans do.

There was one other interesting item in the paper. The Russian Czar abdicated yesterday. I expect their new government to push for an offensive to improve morale and show that they are more effective than the czar was. With any luck, we'll be able to use the extra troops sent to that front to take advantage of their efforts.

March 17, 1917
Department of State, Washington, D.C.
It was just after 10 A.M. when the car arrived at the embassy to collect us. We'd gotten the phone call from Lansing's office just a few minutes earlier. Since the chauffeur drove as sedately as ever on the trip to the State Department, my guess was that he'd already been on his way when we were called and not that he'd driven like a maniac.

Lansing was standing in his doorway when we arrived and waved us into his office. He looked a more than a little worried, so our guess that something was up with the convoy seemed likely to be correct. He waved us to our seats and flopped into his chair.

"We've received a message that the convoy encountered elements of the British fleet west of Bergen at 3:30 P.M. local time. The commander of the escort sent a message in the clear that...." Lansing picked up a piece of paper and read from it. "'We have encountered a force of three British battlecruisers, eight cruisers and at least thirty destroyers conducting anti-submarine operations. The convoy has been ordered to stay at least five miles from the British squadron. Efforts to detour around the British squadron failed. The British ships keep moving their area of operations to interpose themselves between the convoy and any progress east or south. Please lodge an official complaint regarding this blocking of sea lanes. Also, please inform the Germans of the location of this force.'"

Lansing looked up. "My question to you, von Manstein, is what you think Hindenburg will do?"

I thought for a moment before answering. "The High Seas Fleet should be ready to sail and should do so soon. The timing will depend on how many submarines are in the vicinity of the convoy and how soon they can organize an attack. There's been enough time to get pickets out to report on the movements of the Grand Fleet so that shouldn't be an issue. I believe Hindenburg will take this message as a request to engage but there's a small chance he may wait in an attempt to force a more overt call from your ships."

"Trying to force us to drop our neutrality and commit to your side. You know that's not going to happen."

"Yes, Sir, but Hindenburg may not believe it. There's also Scheer and Holtzendorff to consider. Scheer has been reluctant to engage the British since Jutland. Holtzendorff has been against this idea from the beginning. Either one could slow down a response. But I'd assume Hindenburg would be keeping a close eye on them."

"In other words, you think your strategy will be implemented but you aren't sure." Lansing let out a heavy sigh and said, "Great."

"There are other factors that make me fairly confident that action will be taken."

"And those are?"

"First, the British squadron is conducting anti-submarine operations. They might be doing this if there's been an increase in submarine sightings near their warships. And second, from what I've seen in your newspaper, there has been a significant drop in British merchant ship losses in the last week."

"Like they were pulling back for some other purpose?"

"This would be expected if they were adhering to the original convoy plans. The encounter on the 12th may have sent the submarines back to their patrol zones but I think Hindenburg would keep things in place, hoping for this kind of opportunity."

Lansing leaned back and closed his eyes. "At least there's hope."

"Surely the convoy's position isn't that precarious."

Lansing's eyes popped open and he sat forward with a confused look on his face. "Precarious? Ah, I see. My hope is that the German forces are NOT in position to do anything. The convoy commander was under orders to only call for help if his ships were fired upon. He's currently in the brig on what was his flagship. An apology has—"

The knock on the door interrupted Lansing and the door was opened without any leave from him. A gentleman I'd seen around the premises entered with several messages in his hand.

"Sorry for the interruption, Sir, but I thought you should see these immediately."

Lansing's annoyed look made me think he was going to have a "discussion" with the newcomer once we were gone. I'd seen the same look on more than a few officers who'd been interrupted by subordinates at inopportune times. I didn't envy what the messenger would have to endure. He gave the messages to Lansing and beat a hasty retreat. The pensive look on his face indicated he knew what might be coming. The messages must be important. We waited while Lansing read through them to see how important.

Lansing sat back with what appeared to be relief. "It seems that the British squadron has been recalled. The convoy reports that the commander of the British squadron sent them an apology for the delays and began steaming southwest. We also received a formal apology from the Brits about the incident. It appears we aren't the only country with people exceeding their orders and a squadron commander in the brig. Now if we can get out of this without an encounter between the Brits and your people, we may get to keep this from causing too much trouble."

While I understood Lansing's sentiments, I hoped our Navy would do something to show we would be there if needed. That and I'd like to see if our plan worked. At the very least, I might be able to deflect any blame for future incidents.

"When did this occur?"

"About two hours ago, a little after 4 P.M. local. Why?"

"Was a message broadcast in the clear about the changing situation?"

Lansing didn't answer for a moment. "The German Navy doesn't know that things have changed." He sat staring into the distance for a few seconds before picking up the phone.

"Get me the President."

Bernstorff and I exchanged glances. Lansing didn't seem to care if we heard this. After a minute or so, Lansing started to run through the situation and pointed out the problem with communicating with the German fleet. He listened for a while before slumping a little and closing his eyes.

"Yes, Sir, I'll be there soon." He took a few deep breaths before opening his eyes and looking up at us. "I should be getting another message shortly, assuming I'm still here. It appears the British squadron ran into several German submarines about an hour ago. We don't know the results of that encounter. We do know that the convoy was attacked by a submarine about fifteen minutes later. One merchant ship and two destroyers were sunk. They sank the submarine. It had German markings and the wreckage from the sub was consistent with it being German. And just to keep things exciting, your High Seas Fleet has been sighted leaving port.

"Either the Brits are getting very sneaky or everyone is having trouble keeping their navy in line. Unfortunately, it appears your people are trying to keep up their end of the bargain to render assistance. I'm not sure how this will affect the current arrangement, but I'm sure it will. If you'll excuse me, I have things to attend to. Good afternoon."

We used the time while waiting for our car to observe the staff of the State Department. My impression was that of an anthill that had just been kicked. Lansing and several other people came out of the building as our car was pulling away. Bernstorff stared out the window for the whole trip back to the embassy. I spent the time damning a certain sub Kapitän to every hell I could imagine.

March 18, 1917
German Embassy, Washington, D.C.
The headlines were all about the betrayals. Both the British and Germans were blasted for interference with the convoy though we got the worst of it. The official apologies from both governments were generally treated with scorn and one story even wondered if the two "rogue Captains" hadn't been working together to get the US involved in the European war. President Wilson was expected to appear before the American Congress to discuss any policy changes. I wasn't sure if my head was pounding from the desire to throttle the already dead German Kapitän or as an aftereffect of the large amount of schnapps I'd had last night. Sleep had not come willingly.

Having hopefully gotten through the bad news, I looked for any news of what was happening with the rest of the fleet. Each paper had a story about what I presumed was the action with the interfering British squadron. One battlecruiser, three cruisers and four destroyers were reported sunk. Both of the other battlecruisers, two cruisers and five more destroyers had been damaged. The squadron encountered five of our subs. The subs had apparently fired torpedoes from close range and then charged to get off a second salvo. All of the subs were sunk, two of them by ramming.

I stopped to wonder if the Kapitän who attacked the Americans had been assigned to the group that had attacked the British squadron. The tactics employed by our subs only made sense if we were making an all-out attack on the British fleet. Regardless, the sub commanders had to know it was a suicide mission and that the American convoy was ultimately the reason they were being sent to die. It was not a path I would have chosen, nor was it the honorable one, but I could at least understand how someone might opt to attack the cause of his death.

There were also stories about the High Seas and Grand Fleets sailing. Everyone expected a naval engagement today. The relative strengths between the two sides were compared and the changes since the Battle of Jutland were discussed. One writer seemed more perceptive than the others. He noted the drop in British merchant ship losses and the results of the squadron that had encountered five submarines. He wondered where the German submarines were and whether they would have a major impact on the coming battle.

March 19, 1917
German Embassy, Washington, D.C.
Special editions were printed yesterday afternoon reporting the big naval battle. There was little information other than reports that many ships on both sides had sunk. Today's papers had more details. Details that were both grim and satisfying.

The High Seas Fleet commanded by Admiral Hipper shelled Great Yarmouth in eastern England. He was apparently attempting to force an engagement with the Grand Fleet commanded by Admiral Beatty. Beatty obliged and the two fleets met about forty miles off the British coast. The High Seas fleet was withdrawing to the east with the Grand Fleet in pursuit when they abruptly turned back toward the British. The British ships turned to form a line of battle just as ten of our submarines surfaced less than a thousand yards in front of them. The submarines scored numerous torpedo hits and threw the British formation into chaos.

The careful Jellicoe and Scheer had led these same fleets against each other last year at Jutland and there had been few losses. Both Hipper and Beatty are known for their aggressiveness and my guess is that Hipper was under orders to take the fight to the British. This time the losses were huge. The British lost twenty battleships or battlecruisers, eight cruisers, fourteen destroyers, and nearly thirty thousand men. We lost twelve battleships or battlecruis...

Knock, knock, knock....

October 4, 1936
Manstein residence, Berlin, Germany
I lowered my hand from my son's door and waited.

"Come in."

I prepared to enter the maelstrom and opened the door. How one teenager could create, let alone live in, such a mess was beyond me. If only Brenda had made it through the Spanish flu. Otto was a great bodyguard and worked well with Brent, but his concerns were primarily our security. Past attempts to get that discipline to carry over into other aspects of Brent's life had met with massive resistance from both Brent and Otto.

The door seemed to have its usual problems opening. Yes, another shirt that had been draped on the knob was now on the floor and partially under the door. Dad's fault, of course. Clothes were strewn everywhere except the bed and his desk. At least there didn't appear to be any multi-day-old half-eaten food lying about. Several books were open on his desk, but his history book was on top and there was a stack of paper next to it. Brent was sitting on his bed with my journal from the Great War in his lap. My eyes finally got to his face and found his blue eyes surrounded by a face of bored annoyance.

"Are you finished with the inspection?"

"I just wanted to let you know that dinner will be ready in fifteen minutes."

"Already? Okay, I'll be down in a few minutes."

"If you didn't bury your clock under a pile of clothes...."

"Dad...."

The annoyance on his face had gone from bored to active. "I'll expect you down soon then."

Another look around the room made me shake my head and Brent sigh in exasperation. I closed the door and headed back to the kitchen, this time shaking my head at myself. The powerful Chancellor of Germany was in control of so many things, just not his sixteen-year-old son.

March 19, 1917

German Embassy, Washington, D.C.

Special editions...

The High Seas Fleet commanded...

The careful Jellicoe and Scheer.... We lost twelve battleships or battlecruisers, four cruisers, twelve destroyers, all ten of the submarines that made the critical attack, and nearly twenty thousand men. About half of all the capital ships involved were sunk and all were damaged to some extent. The Dutch reported that four of our surviving battleships were heavily damaged and struggling to remain afloat as they made their way back to Germany.

Both sides claimed victory, though the real test will be whether Beatty and Hipper keep their jobs. Regardless, there's been a significant change in the balance of naval power. The Grand Fleet is down to a little over twenty capital ships while the High Seas Fleet is down to ten to fifteen. Neither fleet is in shape for another major engagement. The Americans have a dozen modern battleships in their navy. What will they do?

March 21, 1917
German Embassy, Washington, D.C.
My request for more information about the Battle of Great Yarmouth, or the Sunday Slaughter as one of the newspapers called it, apparently crossed paths with Hindenburg's request for information on the American reaction to it. One good thing the battle did was to push the follow-up stories about the German attack on the convoy to the back pages. Our requests to meet with Lansing have been put off so far, probably because Wilson and the American Congress are still meeting behind closed doors. We do know that the British ambassador hasn't met with Lansing either.

The response to my query was that the reported losses were accurate. Two of the badly damaged ships that limped back to port have been scuttled. They were older battleships and repairing them would have cost more than they were worth. The other two will take at least six months to repair.

Hipper is a little depressed despite being hailed as a hero. The entire battlecruiser squadron, his former command, went down with few survivors. On the other hand, the morale of the sailors is surprisingly high.

Apparently, they were frustrated by not being able to do "their part" in the war. One of the biggest differences is the attitude of the surface fleet sailors to the submarine sailors. No longer are they viewed as glory hounds that try to avoid real fights. The respect being given to them has become a grim source of pride. The general population and the army seem to have had a similar change in attitude about the navy.

The only information I had for Uncle Paul was based on rumor and speculation. The rumors indicated that Beatty was out as commander of the Grand Fleet and Jellicoe was back at the helm. That, and the British shipyards were now working around the clock. Neither was very surprising. The speculation was that the Americans were going to do something dramatic. Their leaders were still meeting but all of their new battleships have put to sea over the last two days. The question is, where are they going? Operating near England from bases here in the United States would put a strain on their logistics. Iceland and Norway were my best guesses with an expectation of Norway. The presence of an American fleet might keep the British from taking more Norwegian freighters for their own use.

March 23, 1917
Department of State, Washington, D.C.

Friday morning dawned crisp and clear. Our morning breakfast was interrupted by the arrival of a driver from the US State Department. Lansing wanted to see us as soon as it was convenient for us. We hurriedly finished our breakfast, dressed and headed to our meeting. We needn't have rushed.

We waited in Lansing's outer office for about twenty minutes before his door finally opened. British Ambassador Spring-Rice came out in a huff. I don't think our presence improved his mood. He simply glared at us for a few moments and then stomped out of the office. When I turned to Bernstorff, I was met by one of his rare smiles. I smiled, too.

The look on Lansing's face when he invited us in was definitely not a smile. He looked at me then at Bernstorff, rolled his shoulders and with a sigh said, "Do you want all the flowery language or do you want the basics of our policy decision?"

Bernstorff replied without even looking my way. "The basics, please. Some of us are more adept at interpreting nuance than others."

Lansing smiled and snorted, "I think everyone here does just fine with interpretation. I also think you know I'd rather speak plainly so I'll just thank you and get on with it.

"The naval losses suffered on Sunday make it far more reasonable for us to station a fleet in Norway. This fleet will be there to protect future neutral convoys and the Norwegians from the types of abuses that have been occurring. It will also be used as an incentive to both sides to reach a negotiated peace. More instances of indiscretion like those our last convoy encountered will not be tolerated. The addition of a dozen battleships to either side would radically shift the balance of power.

"President Wilson is forming something he calls the League of Nations. This alliance of neutral countries will work to stop this and future wars. Acts that are outside of international law such as unrestricted submarine warfare, the embargo of food, and seizure of neutral shipping will not be tolerated. Restriction of trade and possible military intervention will be used to encourage the resolution of conflicts. Arbitration of disputes will be available upon request. Countries that limit expansion of their military will receive favorable trade agreements.

"A dozen countries have agreed to follow our initiative in this. More have been invited. There will be peace. We would prefer it sooner rather than later."

I thought for a moment before responding. "Not a change of the alliance system, but an addition to it. An alliance headed by the US that will economically favor either side if they demilitarize. An alliance that would keep enough forces to provide a decisive power shift if a military conflict occurs, thus allowing both it and the faction it favors to spend less on their military while maintaining security. Interesting. What would this League of Nations have done about Serbia?"

"That exact question came up during Wilson's conversations with Congress. League personnel would have been sent to determine the involvement of the Serbian government. Guilt would have been assumed if the Serbians refused to cooperate. Once their government was implicated, a total economic embargo would have been put in place. This would include countries trading with them. Everyone found to be involved would have been turned over to Austria-Hungary for justice."

"And if the Serbs had ignored the embargo and continued trying to overthrow the Austro-Hungarian government?"

"Military action would have been authorized. Even if Russia guaranteed their security. Do you think the war might have been over by now if we and the other League countries had been on your side at the outset?"

"And what happens when you have a new president?"

"The same thing that happens to any country when their government changes. Any desired changes are brought up and negotiated. The alliance continues."

Lansing pulled a set of documents out of a desk drawer and offered them to Bernstorff. He took the proffered documents and had just started to look through them when Lansing spoke up.

"The flowery language version. Please send it on for any response from your government. They'll have already received the basics in a cable we sent earlier today."

I thought for a moment. "The British ambassador didn't seem to like this at all."

"True. I still have his copy of the League's statement in my desk. What was it he said? Something to the effect of 'So you think you can economically strong-arm us? We'll see about that.'"

"I presume he's being watched to see what he does."

"That would be a prudent precaution."

"And I presume we will be watched and monitored, too."

Lansing smiled. "Now why would you think that? We're all such good friends here."

I turned to Bernstorff. "Mr. Ambassador, I believe I detect some of that nuance you mentioned earlier."

"Really, Major? Perhaps we should explore that nuance and realize that Secretary Lansing is implying they have a method of monitoring our actions as well as those of the British."

I turned back to Lansing, who simply smiled at me.

The trip back to the embassy was a quiet one as I thought back through the things I'd discussed with Bernstorff in what I thought was privacy. How many of those conversations had the Americans heard? If they had heard them, what did it mean for the current situation?

As we entered the embassy, Bernstorff turned to me with a smile. "I see there are still some things about diplomatic nuance that you need to learn. The easiest way to throw a mission into chaos is to convince them their security's been compromised. They may watch us from outside. They may have broken our codes and be able to read what we send by cable or wireless. They can only guess at what we say or do inside these walls."

I nodded in understanding. But now that the idea was planted, it didn't want to go away.

October 4, 1936
Manstein residence, Berlin, Germany
I wait patiently for Brent's arrival. He'd inherited his mother's knack for arriving at an appointment precisely on time. I wish some of my advisers had it. They never seemed to be on time or ready to do anything. Ah, footsteps in the hall. Wait for it... and he steps into the dining room just as the hall clock starts chiming six o'clock.

"Hey, Dad. Hi, Otto."

"Hi, Brent," we both respond.

He also inherited her height and blonde hair. She had only been ten centimeters shorter than my own one hundred and eighty. Brent tops me by five centimeters, though he's still five short of Otto. He is thin like her, too, and that thinness is even more accentuated when he's near Otto's muscular frame. Unfortunately, that thinness also means the Proud Prussian nose he got from me looks even bigger. Still, he lights up the room like she did when he smiles.

He takes his seat as Otto and I take ours. Beatrice comes in from the kitchen with a tray of soup that smells delicious. She's the same smiling, slightly plump woman I hired eleven years ago. I smile at her and nod. She nods back. Talking to her while she's cooking or serving is a no-no, but nodding is fine. With the way she cooks, I'm fine with following her rules. Why we aren't all more than a little plump is something beyond my understanding. Things are getting back to normal. Life is good. I turn back to Brent.

"How are things going?" Even as I ask it, I know it sounds formulaic.

Unlike other teenagers, Brent usually answers honestly. I guess it's difficult to be too intrusive when you only get to see him for a few hours a week.

"Mostly okay. Mr. Fisher wants us to write a paper on how we view the Great War and its aftermath."

"Is that why you're reading my old journal?"

"Yeah. I remember most of what you told me over the years but I figured it wouldn't hurt to actually read what you'd written. Mr. Fisher said he's 'expecting some interesting papers' from some of us."

The way he rolled his eyes meant that yet another teacher was out to "correct his misconceptions" about our history. Luckily, even if Brent did find these revisionist teachers annoying, he'd decided to deal with them by presenting well-researched papers that were hard to attack. I'm fairly certain that Otto taught him this method of dealing with difficult superiors.

"It's not due tomorrow, is it?"

"No. It's due a week from tomorrow but I figured I better start on it today so I can ask you about any questions I have."

A deep sadness grips me. I hate that my son feels he has to schedule time to talk with me. At least it's better than if I were still in the army. That and being Chancellor does have some perks. Brent and his best friend Peter Hipper had enjoyed the Olympics. He'd even brought a girl out of hiding for two of the events.

"Dad."

I came back to the dinner table and smiled. "Sorry. Just wool gathering."

"It's okay. I know you'd like to be around more and I know why you can't be. Just remember that I'd rather have you as Chancellor than any of the other nutcases out there."

"Other nutcases?"

"You know what I mean."

I scowled and said, "Yes. I guess I do." Unfortunately, I couldn't hold the scowl very long before laughing. "So, what questions do you have?"

"From what I've heard, Mr. Fisher thinks we could have won the war if we wanted to. You've told me differently and some of your reasons for feeling that way. Why do you think the Americans would have joined the Entente if we had pushed into France in 1918?"

"What is the purpose of the League of Nations?"

Brent rolls his eyes again, just like he always does when I answer one of his questions with one of my own. "To prevent or end wars by economic sanctions or military intervention."

"And how did we get the Americans to push their agenda?"

"We quit violating international law with our subs and you finally got them to understand that Russia started the war."

I smirk a little. "I got them to believe that Russia was to blame for the war."

My son looks at me quizzically. "Isn't that the same thing?"

"I thought it was. At least until several years later. Hindenburg had moved me up in his staff and showed me some of the correspondence between us and the Austro-Hungarians from just before the war. The documents are in the library but have been mostly ignored. Russia was modernizing and the Kaiser and Hindenburg wanted a war with them before they got too far. We supported the Austro-Hungarians in taking a hard stance with Serbia with the hope of going to war with Russia."

"So you lied to the Americans?"

"Not knowingly. It was one of the reasons they didn't tell me the truth. They figured I'd be more convincing if I believed what I was saying."

Brent shakes his head for a moment before Otto makes one of his infrequent dinner comments.

"You know your dad isn't a very good liar. He used to be even worse."

Brent's nod and chuckle means there are probably a lot more people out there with lower opinions of my efforts at tact and subterfuge than I thought. If my son can readily tell when I stretch the truth, I'm sure that a lot of political and business people I'd dealt with hadn't always been fooled. Before this gets any worse, I clear my throat.

"Back to the question, please. If the Americans believed we were fighting the war because the Russians started it, what would they have done if we'd gone back on the attack in France?"

"They'd have at least embargoed us like they did in 1917, when we went back on the offensive in Russia." He stops and thinks for a moment. "If I remember correctly, they had four or five of their over-sized divisions deployed in Norway and Spain by early 1918." He understands my nod of agreement but continued silence to mean he should keep going. "So if we had attacked France in early 1918, the U.S. would have probably felt like they'd been used and jumped into the fray with both feet."

I smile again. "Well reasoned and exactly what the American ambassador warned us would happen. Copies of those letters are in the library, too. Wilhelm II was surprised at how quickly the Americans had gotten troops into Europe. It's possible we could have taken Paris but it wouldn't have ended the war. All it would have done is prolonged it and destroyed the credit we'd carefully built up with the Americans. A gain in the field would have been a loss at the negotiation table."

Brent nods his head thoughtfully. "So we attacked on the peripheries rather than the main front to keep from annoying the Americans too much. They built up their army in areas that could help or hurt the Entente so they could apply pressure to both sides though it seems to me they were in a position to hurt the Entente more." He looks at me thoughtfully for a moment. "Okay. What am I missing?"

"What happened in America during the summer of 1917?"

Brent stops with a fork full of roast beef halfway to his mouth and stares into the distance. He's been a student of history almost since he could read. I can almost see the wheels turning in his mind. "Their stock market crash?"

I smile as I see him realize what had happened.

"The Brits caused their stock market crash? That's what their ambassador was warning about in your journal?"

It still amazes me how he can put puzzle pieces together that many adults miss. "They'd been investing in the U.S. markets to finance the war. They quadrupled wheat and corn prices in one week and bought and sold stocks to devalue companies that were dealing with us. The Americans weren't happy with being forced to implement controls on their free-market system. On the other hand, those same controls probably kept the recession of '29 from getting too bad."

"It was still bad enough that we ended up changing to a constitutional monarchy and France went fascist. Do you really—"

His question was interrupted by Oberst Ernst Weber entering the room and coming to stiff attention. Ernst has put on a few pounds since our time together during the Great War, though his black hair has yet to show any gray. He's also added a small mustache like so many have. I think it looks silly on him.

"Yes, Ernst?"

He passes me a piece of paper and makes his report. "The item you were worried about when the Pope excommunicated President Azaña of Spain. We have..."

"...confirmation that the French are in Spain?" Brent's comment is more of a statement than a question.

Oberst Weber's frown at being interrupted doesn't reach his eyes. There the expression is one of surprised admiration. "Yes. The French are in Spain with at least six divisions and the Italian navy is off their coast."

"I guess the Non-Intervention Agreement they signed a couple months ago didn't mean much to them." Brent seems to be getting good at connecting the dots in international politics too.

I look at Brent as I wonder if I'll be sending him off to war. "I was afraid it might be a ruse to keep us and the Brits out of the Spanish Civil War. Chamberlain was too busy crowing about how he was keeping Europe from another great war to pay any attention to my concerns. With the excommunication, de Gaulle and Mussolini can claim they're acting on behalf of the Spanish people."

"And it'll probably hurt the morale of the Republican troops," Brent mutters while shaking his head.

"Don't forget the support of the civilians. Many will be torn between their faith and their support for their government. If the people don't support their troops, the fight won't last very long.

"Isn't it convenient for de Gaulle that the Third Serbian Insurrection started just two weeks ago? That ties down the Austro-Hungarian troops that would have been the backbone of any League military response."

Brent frowns for a moment before responding. "I guess that means it's up to us and the British to do something."

"It looks that way. Unfortunately, since our surface navy is tiny, about the only thing we can do is put more men on the border. But if we do something that aggressive, Hoover will use it as a reason to do nothing and the Brits will think we're making a land grab. Now the question is whether the French and Italians can make a decisive difference before we can get the League to organize a response."

Oberst Weber leaves as Brent and Otto return to eating the soup. Brent pauses on his second spoonful as he realizes I haven't gone back to eating. He puts the full spoon back in his bowl as his brows furrows and he stares at me intently.

"Okay, Dad. What am I missing?"

Otto stops eating at Brent's comment and looks at me for a moment before his puzzled look changes to one of comprehension.

Is it good to know that my mind still sees things that theirs don't or is it a sign of too many political games? I nod to Otto to see if his reading is the same as mine.

He turns to Brent. "What if it wasn't a ruse?"

Brent starts to protest before he stops and looks thoughtful. I wait patiently for the twenty seconds it takes his mind to catch up to the conclusion that Otto and I have reached.

Brent looks at me, still unsure of his theory.

"Bargaining leverage?"

Nodding, I say, "It's possible."

Encouraged, Brent continues. "Franco has been trying to get French assistance since his initial push failed. The French hadn't intervened so either they wanted to stay out of it or they wanted something from Franco that he wasn't willing to give them. The French have intervened so it isn't that they wanted to stay out of the fight. So the French make the non-intervention deal as a way to turn up the pressure on Franco to give in on their price for intervening?"

I smile ruefully. "Welcome to the wonderful world of political intrigue. The question is, what Franco has decided to do for the French?"

Brent smiles at me before he shakes his head. "I don't know what the Spanish have promised the French but this isn't the world of political intrigue. It's how power works."

Now it's my turn to look puzzled.

Brent's smile grows bigger. "You've been on the power wielding side too long. You, my teachers, heck, even my friends wield power over me in some way. If you want something, you offer me something. If I don't agree, you either up the offer or you issue a threat. If that doesn't work, you enact the threat with a promise of relief if I do what you wanted me to do."

I simply offer a grunt of agreement as I realize that Brent has just summed up international politics as schoolyard peer pressure. I think I better pay closer attention to my future efforts to get him to do things.

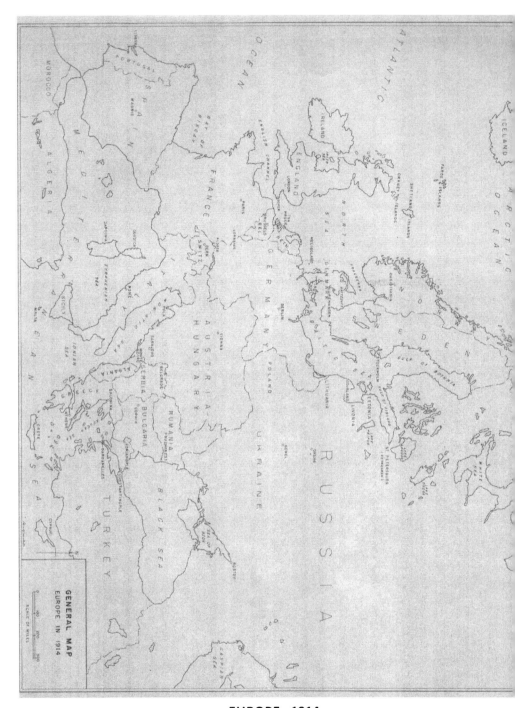

EUROPE - 1914

REFERENCE: PART I

THE GREAT WAR

HISTORICAL FIGURES

GERMANY

Erich von Manstein –   One of the best strategists and field commanders during WWII. Nephew of Paul von Hindenburg. Wounded on the Eastern Front during WWI.

Paul von Hindenburg –   Chief of the General Staff from 1916. Leader of Germany in all but name.

Erich Ludendorff –   Quartermaster General of the German Army. Formed the Third Supreme Command with Hindenburg. Actually ran most of the German war effort.

Theobald von Bethmann-Hollweg – Chancellor until 1917. Favored moderate policies.

Kaiser Wilhelm II – Militaristic, pro-navy Emperor. Impetuous and prone to outbursts which cost him most of his power.

Johann Heinrich von Bernstorff – Ambassador to the United States and Mexico.

Paul König – Kapitän of the merchant submarine *Deutschland*.

Franz von Papen – Military attaché to Bernstorff. Expelled from the United States for espionage activities.

Karl Boy-Ed – Naval attaché to Bernstorff. Expelled from the United States for espionage activities.

Franz von Hipper – Aggressive admiral given command of the German High Seas Fleet. Replaced Reinhard Scheer, who resigned when unrestricted submarine warfare was not renewed.

UNITED STATES

Robert Lansing – Secretary of State. Vigorous advocate for the principles of freedom of the seas.

Thomas R. Marshall –   Vice President. Target of an assassination attempt by a German professor.

Edward House –   Texan known as "Colonel House." President Wilson's chief adviser on European politics and diplomacy. Advocate of peace through diplomacy.

Josephus Daniels –   Secretary of the Navy. Proponent of innovation.

AUSTRIA-HUNGARY

Archduke Franz Ferdinand –   Heir presumptive to the Austro-Hungarian throne. His assassination started WWI. Advocated forming the United States of Greater Austria.

Emperor Karl I –   Succeeded to the throne in November 1916. Sought peace and a change to the Austro-Hungarian government.

UNITED KINGDOM

Sir Cecil Spring-Rice –   British ambassador to the United States. Not trusted by the Wilson administration.

David Beatty –   Succeeded Sir John Jellicoe as Commander-in-Chief of the Grand Fleet. Known for his dashing and aggressive style.

TIMELINE:

Jan.1917 Germany adopts the Manstein Alternative.
Unrestricted submarine warfare is not resumed.

Feb.1917 Germany begins withdrawal to the Hindenburg Line.
The USA reasserts international law and resumes shipment of non-war material to Germany.

Mar.1917 Nicholas I abdicates due to Bolshevik revolution.
Multiple incidents between US and British ships.
Riots in British ports kill 87 US sailors in three days.
Naval battle of Great Yarmouth between Germany and
Britain results in massive ship losses.

Apr.1917 Allied attacks in France repulsed with heavy casualties.
Central Powers push Russians back in Galicia.
The League of Nations is formed by the USA.

May1917 French troops mutiny. First Russian armistice ends after
two weeks.

Jun.1917 Russia signs Treaty of Brest-Litovsk to end fighting.
American stock market crashed by British and French.
The USA reluctantly institutes tighter economic controls.

Jul.1917 Provisional government for the Kingdom of Lithuania
and Poland created by Germans.
German troops in Belarus and the Baltic States begin
looting food.

Aug. 1917   Provisional government for the Ukraine created by Germans.
Starvation rampant in eastern Europe.

Oct.1917   Battle of Caporetto begins. Italians routed with heavy losses.
USA increases food shipments to Central Powers in an
effort to reduce civilian casualties.
Multiple US-British naval incidents.

Nov.1917   Central Powers overrun northern Greece. Battle of Cambrai.
Battle of Caporetto ends.

Dec.1917   The Entente begins peace negotiations.

Mar.1918   The Treaty of Washington ends the Great War.
Many territories change hands.

Austria-Hungary - Adds northern Serbia.
Adds Albania, part of Romania.
USA advisers sent to help create constitution.

Belgium - Receives reparations from Germany.
Adds part of German East Africa.

Britain - Adds Palestine, Jordan, Saudi Arabia.
Adds Iraq, part of German East Africa.
Adds part of Togoland.
Adds German South-West Africa.

Bulgaria - Adds Macedonia, Southern Dobruja.

France - Adds part of Togoland, Cameroon.
Adds Syria, Lebanon.

Germany - Loses its Pacific possessions.
Loses African possessions.
Adds territory on its eastern front.
Reparations to Belgium.
Reparations to Luxembourg.
Ukraine recognized.
Kingdom of Lithuania and Poland recognized.

Japan - Adds the Marianas, Carolines, Marshall Islands.

Romania - Loses Southern Dobruja, counties west of Ilfov
and Prahova.
Adds Bessarabia.

Russia - Loses Georgia, Armenia, Nakhchivan.
Loses Finland, the Baltic States.
Loses Ukraine, Poland, Belarus.

Turkey - Loses Palestine, Jordan, Saudi Arabia.
Loses Syria, Lebanon.
Adds Georgia, Armenia, Nakhchivan.

June 1918	Spanish Influenza epidemic begins. Fifty million will die.
Oct. 1918	Russian civil war ends with Bolshevik victory. Russian Soviet Federative Socialist Republic (RSFSR) formed.

May 1920   RSFSR invades Estonia and Finland. Estonia falls in a
            week. Finland holds on until July of 1921.

July 1920   The United States of Greater Austria is formed. It joins
            the League of Nations in September.

Apr. 1921   RSFSR invades The Kingdom of Lithuania and Poland.

June 1921   Thirty thousand German advisers arrive to aid the King-
            dom of Lithuania and Poland.
            The war ends in July with no change in territory.

May 1922   RSFSR changes its name to the Union of Soviet Socialist
            Republics and celebrates by invading the Ukraine.

June 1922   The Kingdom of Lithuania and Poland changes its name
            to Lithuania-Poland and celebrates by sending ten divi-
            sions to help the Ukrainians.

Aug. 1922   Thirty thousand German advisers arrive to aid the Ukraine.

Oct. 1922   The USSR officially recognizes Ukraine.
            Mussolini stages a coup and takes over in Italy.

Feb. 1923   First Serbian Insurrection begins and quickly spreads to
            Albania and Macedonia.

Apr. 1923   Revolt in Macedonia ends after Bulgarians kill
            thousands.

Aug. 1923   First Serbian Insurrection ends with Serbia and Albania receiving full rights as states in the United States of Greater Austria (USGA).

May 1925   The USSR attacks the Ukraine. Lithuania-Poland joins the Ukraine in June.
The war ends in August with no changes.

May 1927   The USSR attacks Turkey.
Lithuania-Poland and the Ukraine mobilize.
Germany deploys five divisions to the Ukraine as part of a joint military exercise.
The USSR pulls its troops back.

Oct. 1929   Financial crisis rocks the world.
Controls enacted during the Great War ease effects in USA.
Charles de Gaulle becomes French President.
In Germany, Kaiser Wilhelm II abdicates in favor of Wilhelm III.
Germany adopts constitutional monarchy.
Manstein becomes Chief of Staff of German Army.

Nov. 1929   Second Serbian Insurrection begins. Economic disparities cited as reason.

Mar. 1930   de Gaulle pushes modernization of French Forces.
French nationalism surges.
Religious rhetoric also rises as Protestants are blamed for failures in the Great War and for the financial crisis.

Apr. 1930   Second Serbian Insurrection ends with spending amendment to USGA constitution.

Sept. 1931   Japan invades Manchuria.

Jan. 1932   League of Nations warns Japan against further expansion.

June 1932   New Entente formed between France and Italy.
Pope Pius XI denounces Fascism.

Oct. 1932   Japan and Britain formalize alliance.
Spheres of influence are laid out.
Pope Pius XI dies under questionable circumstances.

Nov. 1932   A hardline French cardinal is elected as the new Pope.
He takes the name Pius XII.
Hoover wins second term as US President.

Dec. 1932   Pope Pius XII declares de Gaulle and Mussolini to be defenders of the faith.
Non-Catholics begin leaving France and Italy.
Numerous spies are included in their numbers.
Many are turned away by England and Germany and settle in the USA and the USGA.

Jan. 1933   France and Italy announce exit taxes for non-Catholics.

Mar. 1933   Numerous non-Catholics caught attempting to leave France and Italy with "religious" property.
Anger at the theft of national treasures promoted.

Apr. 1933   Manstein becomes Chancellor of Germany.
Catholicism made the official religion of France and Italy.
The New Entente is renamed The Catholic Entente.

Non-Catholic religious sites looted.

May 1933	Thousands arrested for heresy in France and Italy. Influx of confiscated money and available jobs spurs economic growth. Those who can pay exit taxes are sent to other countries. Those who can't are sent to work at government-run munitions factories near Orléans and Milan to earn their exit fees.
June 1933	Unrest in French and Italian colonies quelled when Pope Pius XII announces tolerance of other religions. Papal primacy is renounced and tensions between Eastern Orthodox and Roman Catholic Churches ease. Protestantism is named as a heresy, not a separate religion.
July 1933	Central Coalition formed by Germany, Ukraine, and Turkey. Lithuania-Poland joins as conditional member. Defensive pact only applies to the USSR. Slave labor conditions at Orléans and Milan are denounced by the League of Nations. France and Italy denounce exploitation and treatment of religious refugees by other countries.
Apr. 1934	Bulgaria and Romania join Central Coalition. The Dust Bowl begins in North America.
Oct. 1935	Italy invades Ethiopia. Conquers it in May 1936.

July 1936   Spanish Civil War begins.
Republicans supported by USSR and Mexico.
Nationalists supported by Portugal, Italy and France.

Aug. 1936   Non-Intervention Agreement signed to prevent foreign involvement in the Spanish Civil War.
Most signatories almost immediately start violating the agreement.

Sept. 1936   Third Serbian Insurrection begins and quickly spreads to Albania and Macedonia.
Lack of state participation in federal government cited as primary issue.

Oct. 1936   France and Italy intervene in the Spanish Civil War.
The League of Nations vacillates on what action should be taken.
Tensions mount between the Catholic Entente and the United Kingdom.

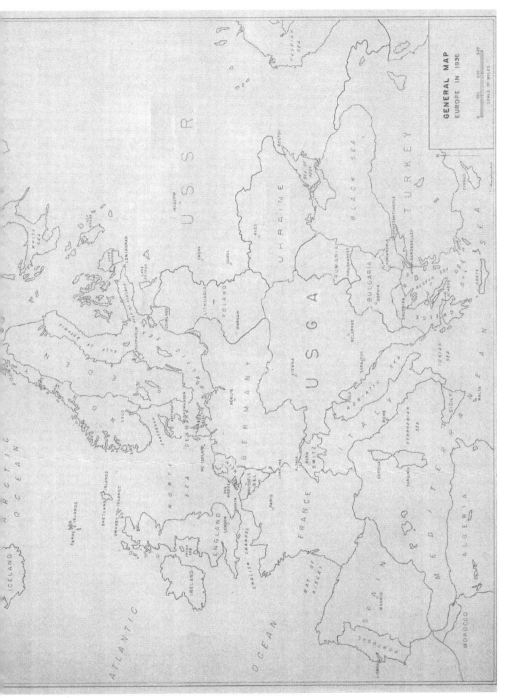

NEW EUROPE - 1936

NE SPAIN

II

Prelude – The Spanish Civil War

October 5, 1936

Northeast Spain

Lieutenant-colonel Roger Noiret was bored and the constant hum of the tank tracks wasn't helping. He had recently been put in command of the elite 1st Battalion of the 507th Armored Regiment. Since they were the only battalion with the new Char G1 tanks and General Charles Delestraint wanted a field test, Roger had expected to see some action when they'd been ordered into Spain. Unfortunately, General Maurice Gamelin was in charge of this operation and he had other ideas. The other two battalions in the 507th had Char B1bis heavy tanks so obviously they should lead the attack towards Barcelona. Who cares that the G1's armor was as thick or thicker than the B1bis'? The label said medium tank so here he puttered along with one of his companies and a company of armored cavalry protecting another column of trucks. It probably didn't help that Roger's dark hair, thin mustache, and boyish face made him look younger than his forty-one years of age. That youthful appearance seemed to make subordinates more willing to bring up new ideas but it made some of the older generals think of him as a brash youngster.

Roger sighed. If nothing else, the lack of action gave him time to think. He reviewed the tactics he'd agreed on when he'd talked with Commandant Philippe de Hauteclocque, the head of the armored cavalry battalion that was temporarily under Roger's command. Aristocratically snooty or not, the major seemed to have an idea of what to do with his men and the desire to use them. Capitaine Michel Thomas was in charge of the fifteen SOMUA S36s of the armored cavalry platoon that were accompanying Roger's platoon. At one hundred and seventy-five centimeters, he was slightly shorter than Roger but had the same trim, athletic build of most military men who didn't sit behind a desk all day. He knew what was expected of him and seemed eager for action. Roger couldn't come up with anything else to do there.

He stood up in the tank's cupola to look around. Northeastern Spain was beautiful. The mountains at the border had been majestic and the view down into Spain had made him feel like a conquering hero. The woods and farmland north of Figueres reminded him of the land around Toulouse. Roger sat back down as he finally realized what had been bothering him. This was his third escort mission in the four days since President Charles de Gaulle had sent French troops to help the Nationalists in Spain and Roger had seen few signs of fighting. There were some shell craters around the border and a few buildings in Figueres were a little worse off than they'd been a few days ago but nothing to indicate a major engagement.

His first escort mission had been peaceful and boring. He and his command had spent the time looking for places where guerrillas might set up ambushes. The second escort mission had been livelier. There had been several squadrons of French fighters patrolling just north of the border and two ambushes. Both had been carried out by lone Republican soldiers that had apparently been missed in the sweep south. One had badly injured a convoy truck driver, but neither had done any real damage.

The fighters had been overhead at the border again but the first good ambush spot had been empty. So where were the Republican forces? And why had Gamelin taken the better part of four days to advance less than fifty kilometers against virtually no opposition?

The second question was easy enough to answer. General Gamelin was still fighting the Great War. That's why Roger was escorting yet another supply convoy to the forward supply dump. The next time he got to the front, Roger halfway expected to see trenches at the positions north of Girona. If General Gamelin took long enough he might eventually find someone to fight. That brought Roger back to the first question. Where were the Republican forces?

For that matter, what had changed that made de Gaulle willing to send troops to Spain? Lieutenant-colonel Noiret didn't think it was because of the excommunication of the Spanish president. He was pretty sure that the Pope's action was at de Gaulle's request, not the other way around. Franco and the Nationalists had been requesting help since early August, and France had sent weapons and supplies just like everyone else was doing. But if it'd accomplished nothing else, the Non-Intervention Agreement had at least kept other countries' troops out of Spain.

Roger stood up and took another look around the road his column trundled down before he went back to musing. He didn't think de Gaulle cared what the League of Nations would do. The League had abandoned its original lofty goal of preventing war and slowly redefined that to keeping the great powers of Europe from fighting each other. The League justified non-intervention when the Soviet Union invaded Estonia and Finland by saying it was all part of their protracted civil war. The League hadn't done anything when the

Soviets invaded the Ukraine though they did start making noises when first Lithuania-Poland and then Germany had sent men to help the Ukrainians. The German intervention ended things before the League decided what to do.

If the Japanese takeover of Manchuria hadn't shown the League was worthless then the Italian invasion of Ethiopia certainly had. The USA's President Hoover had even justified the invasion by saying the Italians were going to help modernize Ethiopia. Considering that Ethiopia was a member of the League of Nations, the other smaller members of the League were predictably nervous. No, Roger doubted the League had any influence on his President's decision.

Roger thought for a few more minutes but kept coming up with the same answer. The Nationalists had promised something to France. The remaining question was what. Was it as simple as trade concessions or did it go all the way to Spain joining the Catholic Entente with Italy and France? Roger didn't think it was simply to test the new equipment but even that was a possibility.

"Colonel, we're coming up on ambush site two."

Sergeant Pierre Murat's warning broke Roger's train of thought. Just past a bend in the road a copse of trees came within fifty meters of its east side while a ravine came within twenty meters on the west. There were three places like this on the road to Figueres that were good spots for the Spanish to set up ambushes. Nothing had happened at any of them so far but the practice helped break up the routine boredom. He ordered his radio operator, Caporal André Rinck, to signal the rest of his command.

"Rinck, tell the rest of the escort to keep their eyes open, standard formation, and pick up the pace."

He turned to make sure everyone had gotten the message. The trucks began to drop back from his platoon of tanks as the trailing armored cavalry vehicles took to the sides of the road. The tank commanders normally watched in shifts, but soon all of them were standing in their cupolas to get the best view they could. These spots always made Roger's heart beat a little faster. His concern was primarily for the vital supply trucks he was escorting and only distantly for his own safety.

It wasn't long before the platoon had taken up a V formation with the point tank driving down the center of the road and a sizable gap had opened up between them and the supply column. Roger's tank was about ten meters back with its left track on the road and its right running on the shoulder. Lieutenant-colonel Noiret started to order Caporal Guy Morin to load a high explosive round but stopped when he saw that his redheaded gunner was already loading one. When they rounded the bend, they were still a couple hundred meters from where the clearance was narrowest. Roger had Morin turn the main gun in its direction.

The ambushers must have worried that they'd been spotted since they fired almost immediately. Roger's duck was as instinctive as it was useless. It wouldn't have helped if the enemy's shot had his name on it. God would call him when He wanted. Roger's ears rang as the Spanish anti-tank round ricocheted off the hull of his tank. Morin adjusted the turret and fired back. The report from the seventy-five-millimeter main gun was loud even through the headphones Roger was wearing. A section of the dirt embankment exploded sending stone and dirt near the gun spraying into the air.

Two Spanish machine guns opened up on the tanks and Roger shouted for another HE round even as Caporal Morin was shoving it home. Sergent Murat pushed the tank for all it was worth for about five seconds before slamming the brakes. His crew was performing just as they'd practiced so many times. Roger sprayed bullets from his cupola machine gun while the tanks on either side of him, commanded by Lieutenants Francois Martin and Jacques Jeannin, added to the cacophony as they fired their main guns. Not wanting to be left out, Caporal André Rinck fired the hull-mounted machine gun in bursts at anything that might have been movement.

The surge forward gave Lieutenant-colonel Noiret a better view down the ravine. He spotted more men trying to set the anti-tank gun back up for another shot at his tank while Roger lined up his machine gun. He shouted "Two o'clock!" to Morin even as he felt the turret begin turning. He squeezed the triggers even as he tried to compensate for the turning turret and was rewarded when his spray of bullets caught the crew of the anti-tank gun. Roger watched them dive or fall to the ground as Caporal Morin fired the main gun again. The flash from the shot blinded his view for a brief moment, not long enough to avoid the sight of body parts flying through the air. The sound from the tank's gun was loud enough that his stunned ears couldn't make out what Rinck was reporting. Roger swallowed as the sight brought back memories of far worse horrors from the Great War.

"Say again."

"Radio reports of mortar fire on the road," came the response.

"Tell everyone to get their asses in gear. Keep up suppressive fire."

His command surged forward as more shells landed near and on the road in the vicinity of the supply trucks. Roger noted that smoke was rising from part of the woods on the east side of the road. There must have been an ambush group over there too. He scanned the ravine for any signs of movement while firing bursts in its direction. He didn't see any more targets. Unfortunately, that included the Spanish mortar teams. And while he didn't know where they were, he was sure they knew what the ranges were for the road. That left running the gauntlet as the best option. He didn't like it but he ordered Murat to take them to the top of a small rise fifty meters off the road.

Roger called to Caporal Rinck, "Tell Martin to check the far side and the rest of the platoon to roll. We'll catch up in a few."

It was a few moments before Rinck joined him in spraying machine gun fire at everything bigger than a bush on this side of the road. A quick glance to the other side of the road showed that the trees there were starting to burn as Lieutenant Martin took his tank off the road. Looking back, Roger saw two columns of smoke that were too big for mortar shells. A couple more shots landed near the road as the Spanish tried to adjust their aim for the now fast-moving convoy but no more damage was done.

Rinck reported that airplanes had been sighted and Roger added the sky to all the things he was trying to watch. Moments later they were identified as French, partially by their colors, partially by them strafing an area just over the rise where the Spanish mortar crews might have been. When his tank crested the rise a few moments later, Roger Noiret saw the fighters' target. There had been two mortars set up for the ambush. The survivors of their crews were working to get one of them set back up for firing. Caporal Rinck sprayed bullets in their direction but the terrain provided them with some cover. Caporal Morin aimed the main gun once again. For the second time in a few minutes, Roger saw men turned into flying body parts. The old memories of his time in the trenches during the Great War fluttered once more through his mind before they were ruthlessly suppressed. Better them than us.

They spent a few more minutes checking the area for other ambushers. Then they spent another minute with Rinck and Morin leaned over the side of the tank spewing their breakfast across the Spanish countryside. It had been the first taste of combat for both of the Caporals and they'd gotten clear views of the effects of their guns on the people they'd shot. Roger knew he'd have to chat with them that evening. Wine. He'd need some extra wine for that conversation. He remembered it helping him in those trenches so long ago. They sped south to rejoin the convoy.

Roger got the damage report for the convoy when they returned to its head. He ordered Caporal Rinck to radio the garrison at Figueres to let them know about the guerrillas and report his losses. All things considered, losing a fuel truck and a food truck wasn't too bad. Maybe the blessing they'd received this morning had done some good. The fighters patrolling at the border had helped limit the damage. Four men dead and three with minor wounds wasn't nearly as bad as it could have been.

Maybe General Gamelin wasn't as clueless as Roger had thought. The armored cavalry would have had a tougher time of it if the tanks hadn't been here. Two of his tanks now had scars from anti-tank rounds that probably would have destroyed the SOMUA S36s the cavalry drove. Then again, if the Italian alpine troops at Figueres had been doing their job, there wouldn't have been an ambush. That was one more thing to report. The convoy rolled south.

October 5, 1936
La Linea, Spain
Carmen Esperanza groaned as the jangle of the alarm clock woke her from her pleasant dream. In it, Luis was here and they'd just finished their glasses of sangria with a promise of some time alone. She turned off the alarm with a sigh since reality was nowhere near as nice.

La Linea was now in rebel hands and Luis was somewhere northeast of here near Malaga. Of course, that was assuming her prayers at mass yesterday had been heard and he was still alive. The troops loyal to the Republic had been barely holding their ground. They hadn't been at their best around here. How were things going to go now that the French and Italians had piled on? Would the British in Gibraltar do anything? Would God listen to her prayers when the head of the government Luis fought for had been excommunicated?

Carmen shook her head and got out of bed. After using the bathroom, she splashed cool water on her face to help push the cobwebs away. That seemed to be part of her new morning routine. She used to wake up refreshed and ready to meet the day. Not anymore. At least, not since the civil war had made worry her favorite pastime at night. She said yet another silent prayer for her husband and then one for herself and Carlos. She was sure God understood the position in which Luis found himself. Many of their countrymen now found themselves fighting for a government whose leader had been labeled as ungodly. The government itself was still just and righteous.

Carmen kept trying to convince herself that her thoughts were true as she finished washing up and removed her nightshirt. She stared in the mirror for a moment. Her long black hair hung almost to her waist. Her face still retained its youthful look except for the dark circles under her eyes. There weren't any wrinkles yet but her nose was too big. She cupped her breasts. They were still firm with only a little sag and the rest of her body only had enough fat on it to keep her shape appealing. She sighed and put on the same dress she'd worn yesterday. It was shapeless, plain and a bit dirty but these days that was an advantage. An appealing shape wasn't. She pulled her hair back into a ponytail to try to accentuate her nose then made her way to the kitchen for the rest of her morning ritual.

She got the fire going in the stove before heading to Carlos' room to wake him up. Once she was sure he was getting up, she headed back to the kitchen. A look in the pantry confirmed what she already knew. They were running low on everything but eggs and orange juice. It looked like potluck omelets for breakfast again. She'd have to stop by the market on the way home this afternoon. Hopefully there would be something worth buying. Normally they'd be enjoying what they'd grown in their garden. Not now. Someone had told the rebels that her Luis was a Sargento Primero in the Republic's army. The rebels had stripped her garden bare and after looking her up and down told her that she was lucky that was all they took. She hadn't worn make-up or anything but her drab-best clothes since then.

Carlos eventually stumbled into the kitchen still rubbing sleep from his left eye. His right one was still swollen shut and the bruising around it was a vivid purple. Carmen was thankful that the rebel soldiers hadn't taken her twelve year old son's bravado seriously. Carlos had kept them from raiding their garden for about thirty seconds. That was how long it took the squad leader to stop laughing. The backhand that had so bruised Carlos' face had also knocked him senseless for several minutes. She'd talked to her son that night and hopefully convinced him to keep his head down.

Carlos mumbled something that sounded like "Good morning" before plopping down at the table. His first coherent words were "Do I have to go to school?"

Carmen frowned with concern. Carlos normally loved school. "Does your head hurt or did something happen yesterday?"

Carlos stared at the table for a moment. "The guys at school are giving me a hard time because of Dad. Even Pedro and Jose are joining in and their dads are in the army just like Dad is."

That didn't sound too bad. "They're probably just trying to keep the other kids from picking on them. Have you gotten in any fights? Doctor Garcia told you to be careful."

"I know and no, I haven't gotten in any fights."

Carmen figured that was the main part of the problem. Carlos wasn't shy about brawling. It was the only thing the teachers complained about. "Do the teachers know about it?"

"Uh-huh. Some of them are even encouraging the other kids."

Great. It was probably the same teachers who complained about him getting into fights. They probably thought they were teaching him a lesson when all they were really doing was setting things up for more fights in a week or two.

"You know I've got to go to work today. Can you stay out of trouble and clean up your room?"

Carlos smiled as he looked up. "Yes, ma'am. I'll even see what I can do to get the garden straightened up."

"Okay. Pour us some juice, breakfast is almost ready."

Carlos got the pitcher that contained the leftover juice from last night and split it between two glasses. He brought them back to the table just as Carmen was bringing the omelets. For once she was glad Carlos kept quiet during breakfast. It gave her a chance to think about what she could do about the school problem. She discarded every idea she came up with as more likely to make things worse.

Carmen rose from the table still trying to come up with a useful idea. "If you're staying home, you can wash the dishes."

The eagerness with which Carlos agreed to the task, something he normally hated doing, proved to Carmen just how serious this problem was. She decided that if she hadn't thought of anything by lunchtime, she'd ask Major Hawkins. She kissed Carlos on the forehead, put on her coat, and headed off to work.

It was still dark out as she headed south on Calle Gibraltar. This was the easy part of the day. The streets would be crowded when she came home this afternoon. More people meant more rebel soldiers. More of the rebels meant more chance of being bothered. With a husband still fighting for the Republic and a job working for the British, the rebel soldiers had more than enough reason to bother her. She desperately didn't want to give them any more.

Carmen smiled for the first time of the day as she neared the British guard post for entering Gibraltar. The British territory was the only place she actually felt safe these days. The guards knew her and greeted her with welcoming smiles.

Sergeant Terry Sanders nodded as she approached. The blonde Brit with a thick mustache was well tanned from years in the field. His one-hundred-and-eighty-five-centimeter frame tended towards pudgy which seemed to fit his gregarious nature. He greeted her with his usual "Good morning, Mrs. Esperanza," but his smile vanished as he took in her rumpled appearance. "How are you and Carlos doing today? Any better than yesterday?"

Carmen gave him a wan smile. "Good morning, Terry." She was NOT allowed to call him Sergeant Sanders. "Things are about the same as they have been. At least Carlos is doing better."

Sergeant Sanders smiled again. "Glad to hear it, ma'am. Make sure you leave through this gate this afternoon. Me and the boys have something for you."

"I'll make sure to stop by. And thanks for asking about Carlos."

Carmen wondered at how strange her life had become as she continued south toward Major Hawkins' quarters. Her Spanish neighbors in La Linea treated her like an outcast because her husband kept his honor and fought for the rightful government. The British here in Gibraltar treated her well for the same reason. Either way, she felt safer when she passed soldiers here. Even before civil war wracked Spain, there had been leers and the occasional crude comments from Spanish soldiers when she passed them. The British soldiers here in Gibraltar had never done more than follow her with their eyes. She didn't know if that was better discipline in their army or the fact that she worked for several officers. It was probably a little of both. Add in the food the border guards had been giving her, without expecting any kind of "payment," and it was easy to understand how she felt more comfortable here in a fortress of Spain's traditional enemy than she did at home. It still made her shake her head as she continued her daily journey.

Lights were on in the Major's quarters and she tried to straighten up some as she came to the door. Major Thomas Hawkins was dressed from the waist down but only wore an undershirt on the top when he opened the door. He was shorter than most men, just five centimeters more than Carmen's one hundred and sixty centimeters. He was thin and swarthy. He could have passed for a local Spaniard if not for his blond hair. His smile stayed in place as he greeted her but Carmen could tell by the way his eyebrows pinched that he was concerned by her appearance.

Major Hawkins held the door open for her. "Good morning, Mrs. Esperanza. Please come in. I'll be back out in a few minutes." He closed the door behind her and headed back to his bedroom.

Carmen hung up her coat and headed to the kitchen. There, next to the sink, sat a bundle of butcher's paper. A quick look confirmed that Major Hawkins still enjoyed the way she made liver and onions. She smiled as she realized that the thought of making this standard breakfast for the Major had a very calming effect on her. When the world was crazy, the routine things became precious. She sighed as she retrieved one of the Major's frying pans and started her work.

October 5, 1936
Genoa, Italy

Capitano Guido Nobili walked toward the barracks where the men of his squadron were housed. His breakfast with group commander Maggiore Tarcisio Fagnani had been informative and sad. Guido had been Fagnani's executive officer for almost two years. They had been through the Ethiopia campaign together and still shared a bond of brotherhood earned in battle even though they were so different. They were both one hundred and seventy-five centimeters tall but Tarcisio's brown hair was showing gray at the temples while Guido's hair was still jet black. While Guido's skin was almost pale from his time spent reading and playing poker, Tarcisio's was deeply tanned from outdoor activities like his favorite, soccer.

They were the only two who had actually engaged an enemy in the air though Fagnani had gotten both kills. But barely a month ago, Fagnani had been promoted to group commander and Guido had taken his place as squadron commander. Now the squadron would be going back into combat and Maggiore Fagnani wouldn't be accompanying them. Capitano Nobili could see the pain and longing in his mentor's eyes as he gave Guido his orders. Both would find out if Guido had learned Tarcisio's lessons and could handle the still new responsibility of running their squadron and safeguarding the tight knit family.

The squadron was going to Spain, specifically an airfield near the town of Figueres. There they would pair up with a squadron of French pilots and be under the command of a French group commander. The rebase was a stretch for their CR.32s, so there would be a stop in Toulon along the way. Now it was time to see how ready his men were.

As Capitano Nobili climbed the stairs to the barracks door, his expectations were low. He'd told his men yesterday that they would probably be going to Spain but would any of them have made any preparations? Probably not. He doubted if even his executive officer, Capitano Francesco Rossi, had prepared. Guido sighed more at himself than his men. Fighter pilots flew on the edge or they weren't any good. That tended to make them less worried about tomorrow and more concerned with the here and now. Forcing them to plan ahead on things other than flying was a way to dull their edge, something Guido hoped hadn't happened to him during his month as squadron commander.

Capitano Nobili cleared his throat as he walked into the room, more to let his men know he was there than to get them to come to attention. When your life would almost certainly end up in the hands of your men, being too much of a stickler for protocol was not the best way to live a long and healthy one. His men did stand and come to an approximation of attention. While Guido might think it was best not to push protocol too hard, his men knew not to take too much advantage of the leisurely attitude. It was a comfortable balance they all enjoyed.

Once they were all looking in his direction, Nobili addressed his men. "It's official, we head out this afternoon at two. Maybe now you'll get things packed."

Rossi replied for the group, "In a bit, Sir. There was talk of a poker game at breakfast. Do you want to join in?"

Guido inhaled deeply and started to object. Then his eyes registered the changes that had occurred since yesterday. All the loose items that were usually strewn about the barracks were missing. Neither clean nor dirty clothes were draped anywhere. Pictures and mementos that usually sat on tables or dressers were gone. For once, they had listened and actually prepared to move. Guido didn't have any children but was pretty sure that this was how parents felt when their kids surprised them in a good way.

The pleased surprise must have made its way to Nobili's face for when he looked back at his men they were grinning ear to ear. He came to attention and snapped a crisp salute at them and said, "Poker it is!"

They played. They joked. They drank. They told dirty jokes and laughed. They reaffirmed the bonds of brotherhood they'd formed. Even as they bragged about their sexual exploits, Guido's private thoughts kept returning to the fact that they were going to battle. Yes, there were thoughts of glory but there were also thoughts of dread. Would he survive? Would his men? Would they be able to squeeze their triggers when they knew there was another person in the airplane they were trying to destroy? How would they react when the bullets were flying at them? Hesitation could mean death.

Capitano Nobili shook his head to chase away the evil thoughts. It turned out to be a lucky move for him. His wingman and the replacement for Maggiore Fagnani, Sottotenente Corrado Ricci, thought it meant he was bluffing and so he called Guido's last bet. Poor Corrado proudly displayed his two pair and winced when Guido showed his flush.

"Unfair! How am I supposed to read you when you're not thinking about the game?" he protested.

Guido smiled to cover his real thoughts. "Sorry, I was thinking about the ladies in town that I'm going to miss."

"Ah, but think of the Spanish ladies we'll get to meet."

"True, but some of us will be working to get everything set up and straightened out so we won't have time to interview the local talent."

Capitano Rossi groaned and shook his head. "Thanks for the bleak prospects, boss."

This brought a smile back to Sottotenente Ricci's face. He raised his glass. "To the Capitanos! They work so we can hunt!"

Nobili and Rossi shook their heads ruefully as the rest of the men cheered. At least their men were in good spirits.

October 5, 1936
30 miles east of Barcelona, Spain
Vice Admiral Sir Geoffrey Blake happily scanned the latest report from his scout planes. His task force was headed to the Spanish coast near Palamós. Despite the growing tensions with France and Italy he felt confident in his men's ability to handle whatever might happen and the clear autumn evening had a relaxing effect on him. It didn't hurt that he had a new flagship. The *Marlborough* wasn't the newest ship in the fleet but it was powerful and fast. She was the second of the *Iron Duke*-class battlecruisers that sported nine sixteen-inch guns

and could hit thirty-two knots. The *Marlborough* and her sister ship, the *Benbow.* had arrived two weeks ago. They'd replaced the *Hood* and her sister ship, the *Tiger,* in the First Battlecruiser Squadron. Their sisters, the *Lion* and *Princess Royal*, were still part of his squadron along with the *Renown.* With the *Ark Royal* providing air cover, Admiral Blake wasn't worried about what the Italians might do.

Their older battleships weren't worth worrying about but they had five of their new *Littorio*-class battleships. Those were a match for the *Lion* and *Princess Royal* but not the new ships. It would be a lot more dicey if they teamed up with the French. The French had all four of their *Richelieu*-class battleships based at Marseilles. But that was a potential problem for the future.

Right now he was concerned with the French and Italian intervention in Spain. They'd signed the Non-Intervention Agreement just like Britain had. It hadn't even slowed the flow of weapons and supplies going to Franco's troops. Then again, here he was escorting a similar shipment bound for Republican troops. Whatever influence the agreement had had on keeping the fighting confined had been lost when the Catholic Entente sent troops across the border. Blake doubted that the League of Nations would do anything in the next few months. The United States of Greater Austria was dealing with another Serbian revolt and the United States of America was dealing with its dust bowl and a presidential election. That left the Commonwealth, the Germans, and the Soviets to do something. Unfortunately, they were three countries who didn't have a history of cooperating with each other.

Vice Admiral Blake looked back at the reports. The local fishing ships were headed back to port. It seemed no one wanted to arrive in port at night when they might be mistaken for someone worth shooting at. He couldn't blame them. It seemed like the Spanish were just like people everywhere, relatively indifferent to who ran things. They were far more concerned about where their next meal would come from and who might shoot at them. That's the way it was everywhere once the shooting started. In calmer times, people might speak up and try to make things better. Once there were bullets flying around though, keeping your head down was the best way to survive.

Regardless of why, the actions of the local fishermen meant there would be fewer prying eyes to see what he was doing. The destroyer *Firedrake* was loaded with small arms, four portable anti-tank guns, explosives, and enough ammunition for a short firefight. They were going to deliver the munitions to a point just east of Roses tonight. The idea was that the locals would disrupt the Franco-Italian supply line through Figueres, or at least keep some of the French and Italian troops chasing them around the countryside.

Geoffrey hated how the Great War had ended. He'd been a gunnery officer on the old dreadnaught *Iron Duke* and seen action at Jutland and Great Yarmouth. While Admiral Jellicoe had kept the Grand Fleet in fighting trim after Jutland, Admiral Beatty had walked into a trap at Great Yarmouth. That trap had done enough damage for the Yanks and their League of Nations to keep the Huns from starving and pressure the Entente into a negotiated peace. The stain to British honor was a bad taste in every officer's mouth, but lessons had been learned. Aggression is good, but know what you're getting into. Never trust the Americans. Never depend on the French or Italians. At least the Empire had picked up some overseas territories for the years of bloodshed.

Thinking back on that first lesson, the Vice Admiral ordered the *Ark Royal* to send another group of scout planes out to sweep the surrounding waters. He liked having the brand-new carrier at his disposal and wanted to know what the Italians and French were doing while keeping them in the dark about his actions. It was the last chance to do some reconnaissance before dark and landing planes on a carrier after dark was always a dicey proposition. That also meant that if the scouts didn't find anything, there was little chance his delivery would be noticed by the wrong eyes.

The second lesson still held true, too. The American-led League hadn't done a thing about the French and Italian intervention except tell them to stop. There had been no trade embargo, no mobilization, and definitely no actual intervention. Hell, the Yanks hadn't even rattled a sabre.

And the third lesson? After Great Yarmouth, neither the Italians nor the French were willing to put their navies in harm's way to enforce the blockade. They cowered like sheep and pushed for ending the war, while their armies mutinied. Then, they turned around and blamed Britain for their losses. There wasn't an honorable man in the lot of them.

Well, that had turned his mood dark. That probably wasn't the best frame of mind when one of your ships was going on a dangerous mission soon. As long as the scouting report came back as clear as the skies were, the *Firedrake* wouldn't have any enemy ships to worry about. The mission itself was another matter. She'd be running with no lights and get as close to the shore as she dared. There shouldn't be any problems if it stayed clear there. Then crewmen would take the loaded ship's boats in to shore. The beaches in the area didn't pose any risk of sinking a boat, but the people on the shore might. The boats' crew would have a rough time of it if the guerrillas weren't the ones to meet them. If the drop went well, the crew still had to navigate back to an unlit destroyer in the dark. They'd have to get pretty close to the ship to see her and currents or bad weather could have them lost just like those planes trying to find their carrier at night.

Vice Admiral Blake asked for the latest reports from the British agents ashore and on the weather. He stopped and smiled to himself, confidant that Captain David Eakes on the *Firedrake* was doing the same thing. There wasn't anything to do now except rely on the skill of British sailors, and that was something he was always comfortable doing.

October 5, 1936
Manstein residence, Berlin, Germany

It's nearly eight as Otto and I walk up the steps to the front door. Oberst Weber is off parking the car. I nod to the guard at the front door but barely notice the byplay between him and Otto. It had been a long day and I relied on Otto to keep things secure at home. At least Beatrice would have made sure Brent and the guards had eaten and that there would be something delicious and nourishing for us. I begin to wonder if I could function on my own anymore.

Sighing, I let Otto open the door and enter before me. I quit arguing that point years ago. I remove my hat as I enter, a habit as old as the military tradition that ingrained it in my actions.

A bellow of "Is that you, Otto? How are things?" greets us from Brent's room upstairs.

"A little worse than usual," Otto calls back.

"Glad to hear it. I'll be down in a couple."

Even this now ritualized greeting serves a purpose. Any response that things are fine or good means that we've been taken hostage and Brent should escape to the roof and set off the security distress flare. Brent used to ask me how things were until about two years ago when I got home after a particularly rough day and sarcastically said that things were just great. Boy, was that a mess.

I take off my jacket and put it on a hangar that Otto has retrieved from the foyer closet. Otto takes it from me as I remove my tie and undo my collar button. I close my eyes and inhale the aroma from the kitchen and take an almost involuntary step in that direction before stopping myself. That is Beatrice's domain and I am at best tolerated when I invade her kingdom.

I must be tired. I've forgotten part of the ritual that I insist on. I open my eyes and turn to Otto.

"Thanks, Otto."

"You're welcome, Erich," sighs Otto as he takes my tie. He's given up on protesting when I thank him for him doing what he considers to be just a part of his job. He's probably heard my explanation for it dozens of times. Expected or not, I want him to know that I appreciate what he does for me.

We head down the hallway to the front powder room where we wash our hands and faces. Beatrice would be flabbergasted if we arrived at the table looking less than presentable. Brent would probably just snicker and try to use it as an excuse for him to do the same.

Even here in my home, Otto leads the way into the parlor and then the dining room. At least I've gotten him to quit pulling my chair out for me. Two glasses of iced water wait at our usual table spots.

Over the years, Beatrice has gotten very good at estimating our arrival time from the Chancellery and Edna, my current secretary, would face Beatrice's ire if she didn't notify Beatrice when we left the office. Otto had selected Edna for me and I still wasn't sure if I should thank him or curse him. She is one hundred and seventy centimeters tall with long blonde hair just like Brenda had been. She's shapely like her too, though she is a bit more buxom. Though she is a few years older than Brenda had been when she died, Edna's face says they could have been sisters. She is both a comforting sight and a source of sadness for my missing wife.

Otto and I smile at each other as we tuck in our napkins. Regardless of the stresses of the day, Beatrice's cooking always restores me and provides the calm relaxation of a stomach filled with good food.

No sooner have I sighed in anticipation than she enters with two plates. Steak, potatoes, green beans, and kohlrabi are artfully arranged on my plate. Otto and I smile up at Beatrice and nod. Actually saying thank you to her tended to fluster her, but she accepts our nods and smiles, and returns her own before heading back to the kitchen.

I try to savor tonight's offering but my hunger makes it disappear in bare minutes. I lay down my fork and knife, sitting back to find that Brent has managed to join us without me noticing. He's grinning from ear to ear.

"You can chew, you know."

I chuckle. "Thanks. I needed that."

The clank of Otto's utensils being put down summons Beatrice from the kitchen to clear the table. I notice that Brent seems to be sitting up very straight and smiling at her expectantly.

She stops beside the table and looks at him.

"And just what do you want? You ate earlier." I ask.

Brent pipes up, "I finished my homework and my room's clean."

"And now you expect a reward for doing what you're supposed to do?"

Brent has learned over the years too. "Expect? No. But I hope."

Beatrice sniffs and turns back to the kitchen while we smile at each other. This usually means there is something chocolaty for dessert. She returns in moments with three more glasses and a pitcher of milk which she pours for us, dragging out the anticipation of what is to come. Another trip brings plates and clean forks. We all begin to hope and suspect... yes! She returns with a triple-layer chocolate cake smothered in icing. I look down at my waistline and shrug. Too bad for it.

We all wait patiently for her to cut and serve us each a slice of her specialty dessert. It's fluffy and moist and would all disappear if she left it on the table. She returns our grins with a haughty stare as she doles out the delectable treat. We all sit eagerly awaiting her word as she finishes and picks up the knife and cake tray. She nods once before turning back to the kitchen uttering her magic command, "Enjoy!"

The next few minutes involve much clanking of fork on plate with the occasional slurp as one of us gulps some milk. Starving hounds couldn't do a better job than us. Far too soon the slice is gone and my fork can find no more morsels to scrape from my plate. I look up to see Otto in a similar fashion while Brent's head has disappeared behind his plate. He sets it down after licking it clean and I have to chuckle. I tap the end of my nose just as he notices the icing on the tip of his. No napkin is used here. That would waste part of the treat. After wiping it off with his finger he greedily sucks the icing off, licks his lips, and smiles. Otto and I smile, too.

"If she ever serves that at a state dinner, I'm going to be the laughing-stock of Germany."

Otto jokingly replies, "Unless you let them have some of the cake."

Brent looks alarmed and holds his fork up like a weapon. "Never!"

A stifled snicker from the kitchen means that Beatrice knows her efforts have been thoroughly appreciated. We all sit back in contented bliss for a few minutes before Beatrice returns to clear the table and shoo us out of the dining room.

We head to the parlor where Otto and Brent sit in their usual chairs.

"Schnapps?" I turn to my bar as I ask, knowing that now is one of the few times Otto will drink alcohol or let me serve him.

His mumbled agreement comes as I'm almost through pouring the second glass. I hesitate for a moment before getting a third glass and filling it halfway.

After giving Otto his drink and passing the third glass to my surprised son, I ease into my favorite chair with a sigh. Peppermint Schnapps is the perfect way to complement the cake. I close my eyes and almost drift off to sleep. The only interruptions are my efforts to lift my drink for a sip and the sounds of the other two doing the same. After somewhere between a few seconds and a few hours, Brent puts his glass down on the coffee table with a small clunk. I breathe heavily and open my eyes.

"Sorry, Dad," he says quietly.

I look at Otto. His blond hair is thinning after all these years but his face still shows the strength of character he's always had.

"I'm awake so stop staring at me," he yawns.

"Rough day?" Brent asks.

"Long and tedious," I reply.

"I figured it would be. The French intervention was in the paper this morning and even the teachers were talking about it at school."

"And what did they have to say?"

"Some of them think the French are going in to try to save Spanish lives. Some others think it's a land grab. Some think they plan on putting their own guy in charge of Spain like Napoleon did. Most think they're just doing whatever the Pope tells them to do. My art teacher is the only one who brought up the idea that Franco had offered some kind of concession for the help. Peter asked what he thought the Spanish could offer and Mr. Hitler came up with a few things."

"Such as?"

"A place to get the French army some combat experience on the low end. You know, let them try out their new equipment, get the men blooded, check out how their logistics work. The Spanish might join the Catholic Entente and provide men and resources for fighting. They also still have some influence in Latin America and might be able to sway some of their governments to join the Entente or at least leave the League of Nations."

I look confounded for a moment. Brent's art teacher has seen as far down the road as I have. It's something that could create a whole new set of problems for the English. Brent stops for a moment while he watches me as I revisit that line of reasoning. He continues when he sees my eyes focus again.

"He thinks if the Entente can get enough countries to leave the League then they'll be strong enough to wage a war without fear of the League tipping the balance against them." He looks at me questioningly.

"Someone in France or Italy has probably had similar thoughts," I admit.

"Which means that unless something is done, there's a reasonable chance of a new war in the not-too-distant future." Brent looks down at his empty glass and back at me.

"The only time I get Schnapps is when something bad has happened. My guess is that someone else in Germany has had similar thoughts but hasn't managed to convince anyone else of the probability."

I quietly look down at my own empty glass for a moment, confirming Brent's analysis. For the first time in his life, I wish my son wasn't quite so perceptive. I look back up and raise my glass.

"I think we could use a little more. You pour."

Brent looks at me in consternation for a few moments before rising to get the bottle. That he didn't immediately jump for the chance at extra Schnapps means he can tell just how worried I am. So much for protecting my son.

October 6, 1936
Figueres, Spain
Lieutenant-colonel Roger Noiret had started his day with his usual bathroom regimen followed by prayer at the chapel. Even though there hadn't been a shower, the sponge bath, brushing his teeth and shaving helped him feel renewed for the new day. The prayers to God had helped him center the Lord, his wife, and their two sons in his

heart. And Catherine could definitely use the prayers when dealing with Guy and Junior. They tried to help and did their best to stay out of trouble, but fifteen- and thirteen-year-old boys had a knack for accidental mayhem.

Breakfast had been filling but the tastes had been muted because he knew what today would be like. Now he sat at a desk in the field office doing paperwork. This was not his idea of how to start a workday but he didn't have much choice in the matter. His executive officer, Commandant Robert Olleris, was with the first platoon of B Company on today's escort mission. He could have made the run again but that would have been bad for the morale of his men and it would have messed up the system he and Commandant Philippe de Hauteclocque had created.

Noiret had set up a rotation for the 1st of the 507th after their initial escort mission and de Hauteclocque had done the same for the 4e Cuirassiers. One day for the escort missions, empty trucks north then loaded ones south, the next day for repairs and maintenance, and the third for paperwork. Roger paired himself and A Company with Philippe's C Company, then both B companies with both executive officers, and finally his C Company with Philippe and his A Company. One platoon from each company made the entire escort trip. The others went to the crossroads near Capmany and Pont de Molins to secure the southern section of the run.

Unfortunately, Roger was sure that one day wasn't long enough for the amount of paperwork he had to do. That's why Sergent Murat was in charge of the maintenance on their tank and Roger was here at his field office. This was the downside of running a unit with new equipment. There were the usual reports for the attack on the convoy he'd been guarding and its list of recommendations for his superiors, as well as notes for himself on how his people had performed. There were also the reports on how his tanks had performed. The design bureau wanted details on everything from actual gas consumption to equipment issues to crew comfort and recommendations. When they were going through their initial field trials around Verdun, the design bureau had its people meet with his men every evening for a debrief. He'd thought those sessions were tiring. Now he longed for them.

Roger understood their desire to make the G1 a better tank, he just wished it was someone else typing up the reports. Well, technically it was someone else. Caporal Jean Martin was doing the typing, Roger just had to dictate. If he had been doing the typing, he would have needed at least a week. At least Roger didn't have to write the condolence letters for the truck drivers. That was a job for someone else.

Lieutenant-colonel Noiret stopped in mid-dictation to jot a note to himself. Thinking about the death of the drivers made him think about his family and how much he missed them. Death had a habit of making people think of their loved ones. Even more so when they weren't nearby. A letter to his wife was one more thing to write, though there wouldn't be any dictation for that letter. His sons were back in school and his wife would be using the time to catch up on the chores that he normally did when he wasn't off on deployment. Even though he prayed for them during his morning time at the chapel, he added another mental prayer asking for their health and safety before realizing that Caporal Martin's typewriter was silent as he patiently waited for Roger to quit woolgathering. With a smile, Roger decided that God tested everyone in different ways. Back to work....

Roger spent the rest of the morning dictating as Caporal Martin banged away at the typewriter and patiently waited while Roger decided on how to phrase things. That was another part of being an officer he'd never expected when he started his military career. Poorly phrased criticisms of superiors could hurt his career and make long-term enemies. Critiques of subordinates could be just as bad. Saying something to them in private was far different than putting it in an official report. Not only did Roger have to make sure that the soldier truly deserved the praise or condemnation, he also had to be aware of who the soldier had as patrons or enemies. He'd gone into the military to avoid office politics. He silently laughed at his own naivete.

That was one of the things he liked about the Warriors for Christ. Honesty and bluntness were considered to be virtues not liabilities. Giving and accepting criticism without malice was part of the path to improving oneself. Penance and repentance went hand in hand to make the members better people and better examples for those who had strayed from the path to salvation. Roger knew that the soldiers he fought against in Spain weren't bad people. They had simply been led off the path by the leaders, both political and religious, that they trusted. He hoped they could be brought back into alignment with the Church and God with a minimum of loss. He also knew that he would deal with those who couldn't be redeemed. Their preference to follow a different path was the work of the great deceiver and it was better to remove them than to allow their influence to corrupt other souls.

The lack of real action wasn't helping either. Roger remembered when he'd been through it in the Great War. The youthful exuberance, the pent-up energy, the brief action with death flying through the air. When you followed that up with inaction and boredom, morale and morals both began to slip. If his unit continued on escort duty for supply missions there would be problems in both of those areas.

Lieutenant-colonel Noiret understood the need to tolerate the sins of his men though their transgressions were minor. That didn't mean he didn't try to get them back to the true path. The priests led the men when they were in church, Roger tried to do the same when they were in the field. While he could restrain their baser actions, he couldn't make their private choices for them. All he could do was pray and set an example.

All this musing made Roger sad for where the people of the world were headed. Those who didn't know the joy and serenity of Christ were doomed to damnation. The musing was also making the work of dictating the reports go slower than he had hoped. He'd only just finished with the reports for the engagement and it was already lunchtime. Roger told Caporal Martin to take off for lunch and return in an hour. Roger would get a light lunch before he spent some time in the chapel centering his spirit. If he had any time left before Martin returned, he'd write his personal notes on his men's performance. The letter to Catherine would have to wait until tonight. If he could keep his mind on the tedious task of the detailed report of the Char G1's performance, it might not even be too late when he got to his wife's letter.

Tomorrow would be worse. His men would be filling out their maintenance sheets today and he would have to go over them tomorrow. Caporal Martin would have to fix the inevitable spelling errors while he would have to make notes on what his men's ideas were and crosscheck them with his notes to determine if they left anything out. His men would finish by noon so they could enjoy the rest of the day. He and Caporal Martin would be here until late in the evening again. Martin would finish up any leftover notes and bundle things up while Roger led his next escort mission. Only then would Martin have his half a day off.

Lieutenant-colonel Noiret stopped for a moment as he headed to the mess hall. A thought had struck him. While he was sometimes bored by the tedium of the paperwork he had to do, it also had always given him a sense of calm when it was done. Even the boring paperwork was a part of his service to Christ, the Church, and France. In some ways, it was like prayer. He unburdened his troubles to a higher power. He strode on with renewed resolve to make sure he always did his best to support the great crusade that he was a part of.

October 6, 1936

La Linea, Spain

The day sped by, or so it seemed to Carmen Esperanza. The constant work kept her from fretting too much about how things were going in her little part of the world. Carmen felt the heft of her purse and smiled as she walked the last few blocks to home. Two pounds of salted beef and another of dried fruits made the handbag bulge and feel heavy at the end of a long day. But the food and the money she'd earned would keep her and Carlos well fed, if not necessarily well liked by all of their neighbors. She hadn't come up with a solution to Carlos' school problem but Major Hawkins had said he would think about it.

She was greeted with a wave by old Isabella Sanchez when she made the last turn on her route. Mrs. Sanchez rocked back and forth in her porch chair as she surveyed the area. The great grandmother now lived alone but kept the peace in the neighborhood as if everyone else was one of her children. The rocking stopped and a rare smile came to the matron's weathered face as Carmen detoured across the street to her front porch. As she'd passed the gate from Gibraltar to Spain, Sergeant Sanders had given her several of the candied apricots that Mrs. Sanchez so enjoyed. They were the only form of payment that the watchful woman would accept for keeping an eye on the house and Carlos.

A smile came unbidden to Carmen's face too. Even as the rest of the country tore itself apart, life here in La Linea kept a semblance of normalcy. She walked up the steps of the porch and greeted her friend. The paint on the small yellow house may have been faded, but the porch was clean and the bushes around it neatly trimmed. Mrs. Sanchez wouldn't have it any other way.

"Good evening, Mrs. Sanchez. How are you and Nosey doing today?"

The greeting was required by habit alone. Carmen knew from the wave of greeting that everything was as normal as it could be. Mrs. Sanchez had greeted her with a curt nod and her hand held flat, palm down, the day the Nationalist forces had moved into La Linea. It was the hand signal she used to tell her dogs to stand guard. Nosey, Reina, and Amber had been at the bottom of the stairs looking menacing. Today, Nosey lazed on the porch looking back and forth between his master and Carmen.

"We're doing as well as the world will let us," Mrs. Sanchez replied before turning to her dog.

"Go ahead. I know you want to."

The medium-sized brown hunting dog went from laying on his side to all fours in one fluid movement before ambling the few steps over to Carmen's outstretched hand. A turn of the head indicated that today's itchy spot was behind his left ear. Carmen obliged and continued her ministrations while she turned back to the human she was visiting.

"Nosey seems to think you brought me a present," Mrs. Sanchez said with a smile.

"Maybe he smells the beef in my handbag."

"If he smells that, it must be salted the way those Englishmen keep it. He seems to think you've got something for me, not him."

Carmen frowned down at the dog and gave him a vigorous scratch.

"How am I supposed to surprise her when you keep giving away my secrets?" she complained.

The first time Carmen brought some of the candied apricots for Mrs. Sanchez, she'd gotten to the top of the stairs and found Nosey with his head up and cocked to one side. When Carmen had asked Mrs. Sanchez about it, she'd been informed that Nosey smelled something he couldn't identify and he wanted to know what it was. Now that he knew what the smell was, he knew it was for Mrs. Sanchez and the look back and forth let her know that Carmen had something for her. A thumping tail greeted gifts that his nose said were for him.

Carmen reached into her purse and pulled out the candied apricots. As she handed the treats over, she said, "Candied apricots from your friends on the other side of the street." Even here, she was reluctant to use the word British lest someone overhear and make a wild accusation to the new rebel overlords.

Isabella Sanchez's lips and tongue worked in that peculiar, humorous process that only those with few teeth can manage. The display of greedy anticipation brought a smile to Carmen's heart and a mental note to tell Sergeant Sanders how well his gift was received. She should say something to Major Hawkins, too. After all, he was the one she'd told about Mrs. Sanchez's refusal to take any form of payment for helping Carmen. The donations of sweets had started a few days later. It was their third attempt that had discovered Isabella's soft spot for candied apricots.

Mrs. Sanchez gave a slight nod as she accepted the small bag. Neither she nor Carmen would explicitly acknowledge that Carmen had anything to do with procuring the treats. Then they would have been payment—strictly against Mrs. Sanchez' code.

"Please give those young men my thanks. They could teach some of the people around here these days about manners and respect."

The Nationalist soldiers had been rude towards everyone who had wielded some form of power before their arrival. It was a form of intimidation intended to reinforce the new power structure in La Linea. Those who kowtowed to the new bosses were left alone and put into positions to help solidify the Nationalist control of the town.

"And how are Amber and Reina?" asked Carmen. She was less likely to forget to inquire about the other two dogs than she was to forget the children of her neighbors. After all, the dogs had always been friendly to both Carmen and Carlos. That was something that couldn't be said for all of her neighbors or their children.

"They're fine, out sniffing around the area as usual." That was another euphemism. The dogs, one red with a white blaze on her chest, the other black with a tan blaze, were the only ones in the neighborhood and considered it to all be part of their yard. And while they had learned to accept the comings and goings of other people, they kept an eye on things that didn't belong. They also played with the children in the area and tended to look sad and starving whenever someone came by with anything that smelled interesting.

Carmen smiled. "That's good to hear. I better be off. There's no telling what mischief my son has gotten into and I need to get dinner started. Can I set an extra place for you?"

"Thank you, but no. I've got some left over salmorejo that I need to eat before it goes bad. Maybe tomorrow or Thursday."

"I look forward to it. Have a good evening."

"You, too," Mrs. Sanchez replied.

Carmen saw Mrs. Sanchez reaching into the bag of apricots as she turned and headed for home. Maybe she'd make some churros to say thanks to the gate guards. They had liked the last batch she'd made and had almost fought over the ones she'd sprinkled with cinnamon.

She was still thinking about what had been a good day as she passed two Nationalist soldiers walking the other way down her street. She didn't notice the leers they'd given her as she approached them. She didn't see the glance they exchanged as she passed. Nor did she hear them stop and change the direction of their walk.

She had just gotten to the steps up to her own front porch when something did penetrate her musings. Three short sharp whistles brought her up short. That was Mrs. Sanchez' alarm. Carmen spun to see what was wrong and found herself facing the unknown soldiers, one of whom was drawing a knife, both of whom wore evil smiles that chilled Carmen to her core. Her thoughts almost immediately went to hoping Carlos wouldn't notice and would stay safe.

Two visages would be imprinted on her memory for the rest of her life. The first was the countenance of the men as they saw her fear and grinned even more at their expectations of what was to come. The second was the look of surprise and pain as both men suddenly sprouted dogs attached to their wrists. Only after they had clamped down on the would-be attackers' wrists did Reina and Amber start to growl. The dogs yanked and pulled the Nationalist soldiers off balance then both did quick releases and bit the men a little further up their arms and continued yanking. The soldier with the knife dropped it and began screaming. The other was made of sterner stuff and yelled as much in anger as in pain. He managed to hit Reina in her chest with a thunderous right that hurt the dog but didn't make her lose her grip. He was pulling his arm back for another blow when Nosey arrived, flying through the air to latch on to the man's right arm.

A cry of "Mama!" got Carmen to turn back toward her own door. There stood Carlos with her cast-iron skillet. They met in the middle and Carmen turned back to help her rescuers. Both men were on the ground. Amber was growling next to the one who had drawn the knife. He was whimpering but had stopped fighting and was staring at the dog. The other soldier was half-sitting, half-laying in the yard with both dogs circling as he tried to fend them off and pull his pistol with his damaged right arm. Another sharp singsong whistle and Reina and Nosey closed ranks on the side of the soldier away from Carmen. The soldier thought the dogs had screwed up and growled back "Stupid dogs" as he finally got his pistol out of its holster. Then there was a loud gonging sound that seem to come from far away and the dogs seemed to vanish along with everything else.

Carmen stood over the limp body and shook with rage and adrenaline. It was only another moment before the still spry Mrs. Sanchez arrived carrying her double-barreled shotgun.

Over her shoulder Mrs. Sanchez said, "Carlos, go get Doc Garcia." Then she turned back to the bloody scene in Carmen's front yard. "It's okay, Carmen. You can put it down. It's over."

Carmen stood frozen still trying to process what had happened. Another plaintive call from Carlos seem to get her brain slowly working again.

It got Mrs. Sanchez to raise her voice. "I said move, boy! Do it now!"

Carlos turned and ran up the road as fast as his short legs could carry him. She then pointed her shotgun at the ground away from everyone and pulled one of the triggers.

The blast snapped Carmen out of her mental fugue and made her look at her old neighbor questioningly.

Mrs. Sanchez nodded. "That should bring the police. You go get something to bandage them up with. There'll be more trouble if they die."

Carmen nodded and headed into her house still clinging to her skillet. When she came back out a minute later, she had her bag she used to treat Carlos' scrapes in her left hand. The skillet was still firmly gripped in her right. Mrs. Sanchez figured that she would have to pry it out of Carmen's hand at some point but she wouldn't want to try that for a while. Hopefully Carmen would be willing to let it go by the time the police showed up.

October 6, 1936
Toulon, France
Capitano Guido Nobili and his squadron of Fiat CR.32s had arrived in Toulon. They were supposed to be heading on to Figueres tomor-

row but Capitano Francesco Rossi's plane had been misfiring for the last fifteen minutes of the flight here. Their best ground crew was on a cargo plane that wouldn't arrive for another hour but at least they would have their own men working on the airplane.

Capitano Nobili and his men were greeted by a courteous liaison officer named Lieutenant Michel. Michel tried to load them all on a bus for their guest quarters and became flustered when Guido refused. Lieutenant Michel's Italian was even more limited than Guido's French so the squadron commander patiently explained for the second time that one of their planes needed some work and he wasn't leaving until arrangements were made. At least that's what he thought he said. The French lieutenant had become flustered, told them to "wait here," and left on the bus with a scowl on his face.

The "here" where they'd been told to wait was a hangar that had been totally empty before they'd rolled their CR.32s into it. There were racks and stains on the floor but there wasn't a single tool or piece of equipment in sight. Capitano Nobili thought that the airbase was supposed to have a full wing of fighters with all of its support personnel and had expected to find a ground crew to assist his people when they arrived.

The waiting lasted about thirty seconds before the fighter pilots' desire for action took over and the Italians decided to look around. There were three other large hangars in the area so Capitano Nobili decided they should be investigated. Guido had intended to send one man to each but within moments it was just him, Capitano Francesco Rossi, and Sottotenente Corrado Ricci standing at the entrance of the hangar with their airplanes.

Guido watched his men jogging off towards the other hangars and shook his head. He turned to Francesco.

"I guess I shouldn't be surprised."

The smirk on his executive officer's face showed that he wasn't. "What? That fighter pilots left alone on a foreign airbase, scatter at the first opportunity?"

Capitano Nobili had to laugh at that comment. "Yeah, I guess them standing around is a bit much to ask. Though Ricci is still here."

Sottotenente Ricci answered deadpan. "I'm your wingman, Sir. I'm not supposed to go running off even if it looks fun."

That made Capitano Rossi laugh. "After we spent a couple hours in the cockpit? Yes, Sir, standing around might be a bit of a stretch, even for your wingman."

If Francesco was trying to bait the young lieutenant into anything, he failed. Corrado Ricci ignored the taunt and watched the rest of the pilots scamper down the taxiway. After a moment he did muse, "So what are the odds that they come back with a bottle of wine?"

Sottotenente Ricci didn't get an answer to that question. Three of the men had arrived at the nearest of the other hangars and while two of them now jumped around waving, the third was whistling as loudly as he could. Capitano Nobili waved to acknowledge their find and turned back to his compatriots. He looked back and forth between them for a moment before Capitano Rossi rolled his eyes.

"I know. I'm the XO. I stay with the planes. I wouldn't want to try to separate you from your wingman."

Sottotenente Ricci just stood there smugly. He knew that if anything happened, Capitano Nobili would be in the middle of it. And that meant that he would be too. The kid was bright and eager to learn. That was one of the reasons Guido had selected him as his wingman. When Francesco got his own squadron, Corrado would be bumped up to replace him.

Guido smiled, first at Capitano Rossi and then at Sottotenente Ricci. "I'll send someone back to relieve you." With a shake of his head, he began walking toward his men who had been successful in their search. He didn't need to look around to know that Sottotenente Ricci was a couple of steps to his right and one step behind. He even held station on the ground.

Guido' men had found people they assumed had the equipment to fix Rossi's plane. Guido then spent the next half-hour trying to convince the French mechanics stationed here to let them use the space and tools he knew would be needed for the job. He had expected a full ground crew and maintenance shop but there was only a skeleton crew and two of the M.S. 406s that were now the front-line fighter for the French. The French mechanics had been stubbornly trying to shoo him and his men out of the hangar since their arrival. His men had been doing what Capitano Nobili wanted to do, look over the big French fighter.

The French mechanics were back to trying to chase his pilots away from their single-wing fighters when an official-looking group finally arrived. Capitano Nobili came to attention as he saw the insignia of a full Colonel leading the arriving group which included several MPs. The Colonel may have been five centimeters shorter than Guido but the sour look on his face and no-nonsense purpose in his stride announced him as someone to be taken seriously. Guido's salute was as crisp as his uniform was rumpled from the long flight to Toulon.

The Frenchman stopped in front of Guido and looked him over for a moment before returning the salute.

"Just what are you and your men doing in this hangar and why didn't you board the ground transport I arranged for you?"

The Colonel's Italian was flawless and Capitano Nobili felt a sense of relief that he wouldn't have to try to explain things in French again. Guido stayed at attention as he explained the issue with Rossi's CR.32 and their need for the space and tools his flight crew would need to fix it. The French Colonel seemed to relax as Capitano Nobili's explanation wound down.

"At ease, Capitano Nobili. Sorry for the problems. It seems Lieutenant Michel's Italian is good enough for trying to pick up women but it isn't up to explaining an airplane's mechanical issues."

"My French seems to need some work too, Sir. If we're going to be working together, I think my men and I need to expand our vocabulary a bit."

The tension eased and the Colonel introduced himself.

"I am Colonel Jacques Bernard, the base commander. Most of the base's assets are off on a maneuver and we are a bit shorthanded. We will be happy to provide whatever you need to the best of our abilities. If you have no objections, I suggest you and your men plan on staying until tomorrow afternoon rather than leaving in the morning. That should give your mechanics adequate time to both rest and fix your ailing airplane. Starting a combat tour with rushed fixes and a lack of sleep is never a good idea."

"That sounds great to me, Sir. Some time to relax and maybe get a closer look at your new fighters would be welcome."

Colonel Bernard seemed to consider something for a moment before responding.

"I'll see what I can arrange, Capitano. I may even let a couple of your men take a 406 out for a spin in the morning."

Guido's "Thank you, Sir!" was accompanied by a quick salute and big grin.

October 6, 1936
20 miles east of Roses, Spain

Vice Admiral Sir Geoffrey Blake leaned on the bridge railing of the *Marlborough*. He was always nervous before every real operation and this one had been changed at the last minute. He scanned the area to see what little he could make out by the light of the waning moon before checking his watch. Captain David Eakes and the *Firedrake* were due to leave for their arms delivery to Cadaqués in ten minutes. Scout planes from the *Ark Royal* had landed a half of an hour ago at dusk. There was a French fleet not far from Marseilles, a couple of French scout planes near the Spanish border, and nothing else other than a few fishing boats that were doing their best to stay away from anything with guns.

One of those fishing boats, the *Peces Abundantes*, had been reporting engine problems all day. She and her partner ship were limping back to Roses at a bare three knots. The new plan he'd received was that the engine on the *Peces* would conk out in about ten minutes if they were alone. The *Firedrake* would go to render assistance and in the process of helping the Spaniards fix their engine, four tons of weapons for the locals would make their way aboard the stricken boat and its partner. Normally Sir Geoffrey didn't like last-minute changes but this one would keep his men out of harm's way if it worked. If there were complications, they'd go back to the original plan of delivering the weapons themselves.

Transferring cargo at sea was something that English sailors had been doing for centuries. Captain Eakes' men would generously offer to help the fishermen out by purchasing their catch to ease the strain on *Peces'* engine. Boxes would go over loaded with munitions and come back with fish. It might or might not fool prying eyes, but it was a cover story they could stick to if they got caught. Not that any of the other countries sending weapons to Spain seemed too interested in examining things too closely.

That would probably change soon. The invasion by the Catholic Entente put troops on the ground in this area and Vice Admiral Blake doubted the Entente would appreciate the British Empire giving guns to people who would shoot at those troops. Then again, he didn't care what the Italians and French thought. If he hadn't been under orders to do this quietly, Geoffrey would have sailed his ships into Roses and offloaded at the harbor. He would also happily turn his guns on any of those Entente troops he could find.

Vice Admiral Blake had been at the Battle of Great Yarmouth. He'd witnessed the carnage of that engagement. What he hadn't seen was a single French ship at the battle. His countrymen bled and died for the French on the waters and the fields of northern France while they rioted and refused the call to battle. And while King George V was ready to continue the fight against the Huns and the Yanks if need be, it was the French and Italians who decided to go to their peace talks. How long had it taken after the Treaty of Washington was signed before their former allies had started blaming Britain? It may have weeks but it seemed like days.

It had been less than a year before those same former allies began saying that the Great War had been a Protestant plot to destroy the power of Catholic countries. They didn't care that there were Catholics, Protestants, Hindus, Muslims, and any other religion you could think of fighting for each side. They just wanted someone else to blame and to rile their people up for the next war. Sir Geoffrey found it sadly humorous that the United States led the League of Nations and was a primary target for that hate and blame even though they were the major deterrent to his countrymen stopping the Entente's invasion of Spain.

The Vice Admiral shook his head and looked down at his watch. It was five minutes until the scheduled "breakdown," time to start the next ball rolling. He walked back into the bridge.

"Any news?"

"None, Sir," replied the *Marlborough's* commander, Commodore John Moore.

Sir Geoffrey nodded. That was good news. The *Peces Abundantes* was supposed to broadcast a "thanks for the assistance" message if they weren't alone.

"Begin anti-submarine operations."

"Aye, Sir."

Commodore Moore passed the order on to the rest of the First Battlecruiser Squadron. Soon the destroyers would be running their search grids using active and passive sonar to annoy any submarines in the area and hold their attention. There hadn't been any indications of them in the area but a submarine just sitting on the bottom was hard to find. The hope was that if the Entente had one scouting in the area, it would do its best to stay hidden rather than reveal its presence. And if it was staying hidden, it wouldn't be able to see what the *Firedrake* was up to. Vice Admiral Blake headed back out to the railing and more waiting.

Four hours had passed since the *Firedrake* left to transfer its cargo to the *Peces Abundantes*. Four hours where Vice Admiral Blake stayed at the rail staring at the calm seas of the Mediterranean. Four hours where men under his command were in a position where he could do nothing if they got into trouble. Four hours where Sir Geoffrey had stayed at the rail rather than infect the bridge crew with his nervousness. He would have had fewer qualms sending his men into combat than one of these covert operations. Knowing he wasn't allowed to assist them if anything went wrong was what rankled the most.

The only reprieve from his lonely vigil had been an hour into it when Commodore Moore had come out to join him.

"It's been an hour, Sir," was all he'd said. Continuing the anti-submarine operations for much longer would raise suspicion if there were any eyes watching or ears listening. A simple nod from Sir Geoffrey canceled the operation.

Four hours passed before Captain Eakes reported that the *Firedrake* had successfully repaired the *Peces Abundantes* and Vice Admiral Blake could relax until the next covert mission.

October 9, 1936

Manstein residence, Berlin, Germany

It's finally Friday, but somehow I don't think this will be the end of the work week. Otto is already sitting at the table reading the newspaper when I enter the dining room. I take my usual seat at the other end and close my eyes. The sound of Brent finishing his morning preparations mixes with those of Beatrice bumping around in the kitchen. Both will converge on the room in about thirty seconds, but for now I can just relax and enjoy the aroma of Beatrice's apple strudel wafting through the house. A deep sadness grips me as I realize that while I love my country, I hate my job.

I open my eyes as Brent enters the room. He stops halfway through pulling his chair out.

"Are you okay, Dad?"

"Just wishing I didn't have to go to work today."

The smile on my lips never reaches my eyes and I can see the concern on my son's face as he sits down. He starts to say something but stops when I raise my left hand a bit. I glance at the kitchen and he nods his head. Beatrice won't serve breakfast if we're talking. She wants our attention so we can properly appreciate her offerings. And appreciate them we do, at least according to the growl from my stomach. This time the smile reaches my eyes, and Brent's too. Otto takes it as his cue to put away the paper before looking up expectantly. Beatrice takes the crumpling paper noises as her cue to present our breakfast. Sometimes I feel like my life is a play where everyone is very concerned with hitting their marks.

I smile at Beatrice as she places the strudel in the middle of the table, and distributes our drinks. She breaks from our normal routine as she's dishing up the strudel and stares at me for a moment before placing an extra-large portion on my plate.

"You look like you could use an extra helping today."

"Thank you, Beatrice."

Long ago I learned that she doesn't want me to explain or protest. She knows what goes on in the house so she'd know if the problem was there. Since it isn't, it has to be work. If it's work, I probably can't say anything about it. My thanks are enough. Apparently, I look concerned enough this morning that she pulls out her only other way of helping.

"I'm off to the market. I won't be back until after you're all gone. There's extra coffee and juice in the kitchen if you want it. Have a good day."

"You, too!" we say almost in unison.

Beatrice thinks we'll talk more freely without her around. That might have been true when we first hired her but it isn't the case after eleven years. If we can't trust her, we're doomed. Still, she had learned the habit in her first years of caring for us and change is something she rarely condones. We can hear her bundle up and head out as we finish off our initial servings of strudel. Brent is reaching for more when I finally break my silence.

"How can I get the Brits or the Americans to see the coming storm when I can't even get most of the Reichstag or Bundesrat members to see it let alone prepare for it? I know I sound plaintive but I'm running out of patience and I think we may be running out of time."

"Maybe I can get Mr. Hitler to come talk to them. Art class has been mostly political discussions this week and he seems to be good at getting the class to agree with his points. And if he can get us to agree with him on things most of us don't care about then maybe he can get through to the knuckleheads in parliament."

"He's the one who saw the implications of the Entente intervention in Spain, right?"

"Yep. I don't know if he does it in his other classes but he keeps bringing it up in mine. He hasn't asked me or Peter anything that would be inappropriate, he just discusses events and makes some predictions on where things will go."

"Have there been any interesting predictions?"

"He came up with one yesterday that got the class going. He said that the Entente attack near Girona was a trap."

Brent stops when he sees me glance at Otto before I turn back to him.

"And just how did he reach that conclusion?"

Brent sits back with a stunned look on his face before answering as he realizes that his art teacher's assessment matches my own. I look at him expectantly and he gathers his memory of his teacher's argument.

"Let me see if I can remember his points. The French have pushed into an area that's the base of support for the current government but they stopped as soon as it looked like they'd have to attack a major population. It's like they're looking for a fight while trying to keep from attacking the Spanish civilians in the area. There hasn't been a similar reluctance to engage civilians in the other areas where the Entente has committed ground troops even though the people in those areas are less solidly loyal to the Republicans. There must be something different with the attack in northeastern Spain.

"Apparently all of the newest French fighters and tanks have disappeared. I'm not sure where he gets his information but he said that we, the Belgians, and the Brits had been reporting their new tanks and planes acting aggressively along our borders with France. That stopped two weeks ago. I pointed out that the French had announced they were conducting maneuvers and those were over. Mr. Hitler agreed but asked if it were just the end of the maneuvers, wouldn't some of the new equipment still be seen near the border? There weren't any big reports of problems with the French equipment so if they weren't pulling it out of service to fix issues, wouldn't they have left some of it where they expected to use it? Where did it all go? There are reports of some of it in the Girona drive but the equipment in the other French drives is all older. Why aren't the French battle testing their new equipment?

"Similarly, the number of trains and trucks delivering supplies to the French border armies has dropped well below what it was before the maneuvers. Where are those supplies going now? With the way things are in Spain, everyone would know if the supplies or vehicles were there. What could they reach quickly if they're concentrating in France? His answer was the Girona area.

"Then there's the French fleet. Their Atlantic fleet has been actively assisting the Nationalist and French forces along the coast but their Mediterranean fleet has been sitting at Marseilles. Why? It's like it's waiting for something to happen. Something that isn't too far away from where it's currently waiting. Some place like northeastern Spain.

"He also pointed out that all the reports from Spain seem to indicate that a lot of the Republican forces are pulling back like they're trying to mass a force for a counterattack somewhere. The logical place for that would be either Madrid or the exposed French force near Girona. Mr. Hitler said he doubts they could get more than five or six divisions together and while that would help around Madrid, it wouldn't be decisive. Overwhelming the French near Girona would protect their support base and might win something internationally. It might convince the French to leave them alone or other countries to come to their aid.

"And his last point was the Pope. He canceled a scheduled appearance on Wednesday and hasn't been seen publicly since then. Where is he? If the Entente is hoping for some kind of major victory, who would be better to try to end the fighting and bring peace to Spain?

"I think that was pretty much it."

I was amazed at how my son's art teacher had put together a situation analysis that mirrored my own with far more limited resources. The angle on the Pope was one we hadn't considered.

October 9, 1936

Figueres, Spain

Lieutenant-colonel Roger Noiret was actually looking forward to his paperwork today. The last two days had been uneventful. No ambushes, no breakdowns, no squabbles among the truckers. Things had settled down to a steady hum. Now if he could just keep it that way.

His first stop of the day was the barracks where his enlisted men quartered. His men would be doing the maintenance on their tanks before taking the rest of the day off and unlike his officers, he didn't trust them to not cut corners so they could head into Figueres early. Their reports from three days ago had been pretty thin.

"Attention!" greeted him as he walked into his men's quarters.

The barracks was tidy with just those few things out of place indicating things were being done. Sergent Pierre Murat brought a smile to Roger's face. His tank driver was halfway through shaving and his half-lathered, half-cleanshaven face looked pretty comical. He looked around the room for a moment to make sure he had everyone's attention before starting.

"At ease. I just wanted to remind you that there are people at the design bureau who actually read and pay attention to your reports on our tanks. The last reports were a little short. I want you to put down everything, and I mean everything, that you like and don't like about our tanks in addition to any ideas you have on how to make them better. I don't care if you think you're being repetitive. The people reading your reports may dismiss something if it's only in one report. They'll pay attention if it's in every report.

"Sergent Murat. Didn't I hear you cussing yesterday after you banged your elbow?"

The smiles that spread around the room indicated that most of the men had heard of the incident. Sergent Murat came to attention before answering.

"Yes, Sir! The offending outcropping of metal will be summarily reprimanded in my report, Sir."

The seriousness of his tone combined with wafting bubbles from his shaving cream made everyone chuckle.

"Very good, Sergent. That's the kind of enthusiasm I want from all of you. If we're going to fight in these tanks, we want them working for us rather than against us. Anything that the designers could do to make our tanks better fighting vehicles should be in your reports. And no, Caporal Morin, they will not be installing women in the tanks regardless of how strenuously you request them."

That was greeted by a good laugh from his men. Caporal Guy Morin was the undisputed champion of the battalion when it came to smooth talking the ladies. His 180-centimeter frame had been athletic before he became the loader/gunner for Noiret's tank three months ago. Now he looked like he could give Hercules a run for his money. Add in good looks, a deep voice, and his exotic red hair and women had a tendency to throw themselves at him. There was also a keen mind behind the rugged chin and if he ever got past just chasing women, Roger would be more than happy to push Morin's career onto the commissioned path.

"On a similar note, don't forget that time in town is a privilege. That privilege can be taken away if things get out of hand."

Lieutenant-colonel Noiret looked around the gathered faces to see if anyone looked confused and hadn't heard about the incident from Tuesday. His men usually spent their nights "off" at the local cantinas in Figueres. While the interactions between his men and the local patrons hadn't gotten out of hand, they were definitely cool. The barmaids were a different story. They had to interact with his men and things hadn't gone smoothly last night. After several rounds, one of C Company's men had grabbed the ass of one of those barmaids. The beer mug she'd smacked him in the head with had been empty so the damage wasn't too bad. Just a couple of stitches. Luckily, the rest of C Company's men had laughed at the incident and sided with the barmaid. Things could have gotten ugly if they hadn't. So a reminder to his men that roughhousing would end up with them being confined to base should keep them in line.

Once he'd looked in the eyes of each of his troopers and gotten a nod of recognition, he nodded back before breaking back into a smile.

"Okay, then. Today, note down everything while you're doing maintenance. They want reports on fuel usage, engine wear, tread wear, everything you check. Tomorrow, write your reports like you're explaining things to your six-year-old nephew."

Roger let the round of laughter and comments about the design bureau die down before he gave a nod to Sergent Murat.

"Attention!"

Roger looked around the room with pride.

"This evening, relax and enjoy yourselves. Dismissed."

Roger nodded and headed to the building where they had set up their headquarters. Tomorrow was supposed to be their paperwork day. Assuming there were no incidents tonight, he wouldn't see his enlisted men again until Sunday morning mass. He didn't expected there to be much trouble from his men for now but worried what would happen if they kept having little to do.

At least the road report for yesterday was going to be easy. There hadn't been any incidents either way. While it meant more boredom, it also meant less paperwork and no letters to his fellow Frenchmen about the loss of their sons and loved ones. The Italian alpine division based here in Figueres had sent several columns east. The regiment they'd sent to Roses was catching the brunt of the action. Either the local Spaniards had stockpiled a lot of weapons or the British and Russians were running guns to them. But unless things got significantly hotter, that was their problem, not his.

Lieutenant-colonel Noiret was a few minutes early when he got to his headquarters tent, but wasn't surprised to find Caporal Jean Martin already there banging away at his typewriter. Caporal Martin was the glue that held the battalion together.

"Good morning, Jean."

"Good morning, Sir."

One of the things Roger would have to deal with today was the report from C Company commander, Commandant Henri Dubois, about the cantina incident. Sergent Delort, now sporting stitches above his left eye, had been docked a day's pay and confined to base. Forms would have to be filled out and sent up the chain of command with copies for his file. Delort had been in trouble before and had gotten away with a slap on the wrist each time. Maybe something harsher was needed this time.

"Could you get me Commandant Dubois' report on Tuesday's cantina incident and Sergent Raoul Delort's file?"

"On your desk next to yesterday's road report, Sir."

Roger smiled at Caporal Martin's ability to figure out what he would want. Then again, it was the major news of what was looking like a short day of paperwork. Roger sat down at his desk and picked up Delort's file. Before he opened it, though, he looked back at Caporal Martin.

"Is there any scuttlebutt about why Delort got out of line?"

Like any good military operation, the commander's clerk was the unofficial channel for information from the enlisted men to their officers as well as the official rumor mill.

Caporal Martin stopped typing and turned his chair to face his boss before answering.

"Well, Sir, everyone knows that he's been having trouble at home. His wife, Dawn, isn't happy that he's not home more, though I'm not sure what she was expecting since he was already in the army when they got married. She probably thought they'd move every couple of years but they'd live near his base and he'd be around most of the time.

"They don't have any children and Raoul doesn't want any but his wife does. They had a big fight about it just before we were deployed and apparently Raoul got a letter from her Tuesday afternoon. Charles said that the letter said that she had found a man who would give her the children she wanted if Raoul wouldn't. Charles didn't actually see the letter but said that the other men in his barracks said Raoul muttered something about Dawn cheating on him and wanting a divorce.

"Anyway, Charles said things were fine at the cantina. Raoul was drinking a little more than usual but he wasn't drunk, just a happy in-between. Then their waitress, the same one who usually takes care of them, started trying to cheer him up, flirting with him. You know how they do when they're trying to sell more drinks and get a bigger tip. So anyway, she'd asked if there was anything she could do to get him to smile and he, Raoul, Sir, just shook his head no. Then the waitress turned around to help one of the locals and someone, Charles doesn't know who, whistled and said that, you know, pointing at the waitress' rear end, would bring a smile to the face of any man who wasn't dead. Well, everyone heard the comment and the waitress looked over her shoulder with a stern look on her face until she saw that it had indeed bought a smile to Raoul's face. Since she'd been trying to cheer him up all evening, she smiled at him and gave her hips a little wiggle. Unfortunately, Raoul was tipsy enough to take that as an invitation so he reached out and grabbed a handful. The waitress wasn't mad, she actually does seem to like Raoul, but several of the locals stood up from their tables while grabbing knives, and bottles, and such. Only then did the waitress grab an empty mug off her tray and hit Raoul with it. Then she started laughing at Raoul and making fun of his feeble attempt to get her attention. The locals and the C Company men joined in the laughter and everything settled down. Charles got everyone gathered up and their tab settled and as they were heading out, the waitress came over to check on Raoul and even gave him a kiss on the cheek. Charles thinks that the only reason she hit him was to keep the locals from starting a fight.

"There were a couple of the other C Company guys there and they backed up Charles' story, so that's their official version of what happened, Sir."

Lieutenant-colonel Noiret nodded while he worked out the twists in Caporal Martin's story. Charles would be Caporal Charles Bernard, the clerk for C Company's commander Commandant Henri Dubois. Like Caporal Martin, Charles would be the battalion fountain of information. During the day, they typed up their commanding officers' reports so they heard the official news before the other enlisted men and most of the other officers. They hung out with the other enlisted men at night picking up and spreading gossip. When you added in that they handed out the mail, they were every enlisted man's friend. That also meant they got to see how those men reacted to their mail. The odds were very good that Caporal Bernard had a good grasp of what was going on in Sergent Delort's life.

Roger looked through Sergent Delort's file. The two other times that he'd been in trouble also involved alcohol. They also involved problems from home. Sergent Delort's father had died three years ago and Delort had ended up picking a fight in a bar in Toulon. His sister had been killed in an automobile accident last year. There wasn't any violence that time. Just a drunk and disorderly for throwing up on the shoes of a Parisian constable before he passed out.

It seemed like Delort had an issue dealing with bad news more than anything else.

"Jean, type up a suggestion for Commandant Dubois that he send Sergent Delort to Father Lobau for counseling about his marriage issues. Also, suggest that the Commandant get Charles to keep an eye on Sergent Delort for future signs that things at home might interfere with Delort's performance of his duties."

Caporal Martin had stopped in the middle of his typing and had begun looking through the papers on his "finished" pile. He grabbed two sheets before turning back to Roger.

"Do you want to suggest some kind of public apology from Sergent Delort to the waitress, Sir?"

"That's not a bad idea, Jean. It might help soothe the locals' sense of indignation. Add it in."

Caporal Martin reached into his pile and added the third and fourth sheets of paper to his holdings. Roger simply watched with a slightly amazed smile as his aide straightened the papers before stapling them together. He then turned and handed the pile to Roger before turning back to his "finished" pile and assembling another stack. Roger signed the cover sheet to Commandant Dubois as he heard the stapler being used by Caporal Martin. Roger then handed the signed orders back to Jean in exchange for a duplicate set which he signed and placed in Sergent Delort's file. Meanwhile, Caporal Martin had placed the first copy in his out basket and grabbed a sheaf of papers from the bottom of his finished pile. He handed them to Lieutenant-colonel Noiret.

"Here are Wednesday's reports from the men for the design bureau, Sir."

"Corrected and retyped so they don't look like were done by children?"

"Curse words and coffee stains removed and scribbled additions included, too, Sir."

Caporal Martin turned back to get the next set of papers that required Roger's signature as he began skimming and signing this batch. The tedious but calming routine continued throughout the morning.

October 9, 1936

La Linea, Spain

After the attack on Tuesday, Mrs. Sanchez had left Amber on Carmen Esperanza's front porch that night and she'd been sleeping there since. The dog provided a sense of comfort and protection that Carmen desperately needed. Amber happily accepted the little treats Carmen gave her and nuzzled and woofed at both Carmen and Carlos. On Wednesday morning, Amber had followed Carmen all the way to the Gibraltar gate before heading home.

Carmen had been worried about what would happen to Carlos when he was at school. She had almost kept him home on Wednesday but that would have meant she would have stayed home too. That was something Carmen didn't want to do. They needed the money and Carmen wanted to get away from the site of the attack even if only for a few hours.

Wednesday had been a blur at work. Between the questioning from the police and the jitters from the attack she'd gotten even less sleep Tuesday night than when Carlos was a newborn. Carmen had been emotionally and physically exhausted when she finally left Gibraltar Wednesday afternoon. Amber had been waiting outside the gate guard house and had walked back home with Carmen. Mrs. Sanchez had simply waved a greeting as Carmen went by, but the real surprise was when Carmen got home. Carmen had been worried about Carlos but there he was in the living room playing with three of his classmates. He'd jumped up when she opened the screen door and come flying across the room for a hug. She carefully maneuvered him into the room so she could shut the door.

Carlos finally let go and backpedaled a couple of steps before proudly coming to his best rendition of a soldier at attention.

"Look what I got, Mommy!" he said as he proudly puffed out his chest.

Carmen bent down to examine a ribbon pinned to her son's shirt. She recognized it since Luis had three of them. It was an actual infantry combat ribbon.

"And where did you get that?" she asked.

"A teniente came to school and gave it to me for helping you last night. He said I was a brave little boy and would grow up to be a fine soldier one day."

The smile on Carlos' face and the awed look from his classmates made Carmen heave a sigh of relief. If the military had given Carlos a medal it was a pretty good bet that they weren't going to blame them for what had happened. It probably also meant that Carlos wouldn't get bothered at school for a while. She proudly smiled at her young man.

"I bet you will. I know that you're my guardian angel."

Carlos blushed before grabbing her hand to pull her over to see what he and his friends were working on. They had piles of paper and crayons scattered around the floor.

"We're making medals for Amber and Reina and Nosey and Mrs. Sanchez, too."

"What a nice idea. Does anyone want something to eat or drink?"

Enthusiastic yeses had sent her to the kitchen while the children worked on their medals. They had then used one of Carmen's hairpins to attach a medal to Nosey before heading over to Mrs. Sanchez' to present the rest of them. Carmen had needed to shoo the other children home as dinnertime approached. At least it didn't look like she needed to worry about any reprisals aimed at Carlos.

Carmen managed to get better sleep Wednesday night. There was only one nightmare that she remembered but it still didn't seem like she got nearly enough sleep. Amber happily greeted her as Carmen headed to work and she once again walked with her all the way to the Gibraltar gate before heading home. Work on Thursday was better, but Major Thomas Hawkins and the gate guards had seemed very concerned about her.

Last night's sleep had been blessedly uneventful. No dreams or nightmares, just restful oblivion until the alarm had gone off. Today Amber had joined Carmen on her walk to work but she stopped at Mrs. Sanchez' house. Carmen had taken another half a dozen steps before she realized that Amber had stopped. When she turned back to the dog, Amber had her nose up like she was scenting something and just woofed at her. Carmen guessed it meant it was time for her to brave the trip on her own again and called goodbye and thanks to the dog before they headed their separate ways, Amber to her house and Carmen to work.

When she arrived at the Gibraltar gate, she was greeted by Sergeant Irvin Havens but his usual companion at the gate, Sergeant Terry Sanders, had been absent. Carmen couldn't remember the last time that Sergeant Sanders hadn't been there on a weekday. When Carmen asked about Sergeant Sanders, Sergeant Havens had cheerfully told her not to worry he was off for a personal matter this morning.

Once Carmen arrived at the quarters of Major Hawkins, she felt better than she had the last couple of days. She decided she was getting back to her old pre-attack self. As she looked around the Major's quarters, she noticed that she hadn't been doing a very good job the last couple of days. It was a good thing that she normally only worked a half a day on Fridays. She would need some extra time to fix the poor job she'd done during the last two days. That probably explained the Major's concern. She hoped he wasn't so disappointed with her that he started looking for a new housekeeper.

October 9, 1936

Figueres, Spain

Capitano Guido Nobili and his squadron of Fiat CR.32s had arrived in Figueres on a brisk Wednesday evening. All of the pilots in the Legionary Air Force were volunteers and their morale was high. They had been scheduled for transfer to Cadiz but when the French bogged down north of Girona, they'd been sent to where the action was. At least that's what he'd been told.

Maybe the first mission of today would be more exciting than either of the two he'd flown on Thursday. His planes were nimble and great in a dogfight. Unfortunately, there wasn't anyone to fight. There hadn't been any signs of the Republican Air Force. That left him and his men with little to do other than strafing Republican troops—a job that Guido felt was more dangerous than any other. His plane was designed for maneuverability and a lot of its body was fabric, not a good combination when flying low and straight.

Capitano Nobili looked over his squadron and made sure that everyone had gotten into formation. Then he ordered them to turn south towards Girona. The early-morning sun glinted off Sottotenente Corrado Ricci's engine as his wingman banked his biplane and took the lead. The squadron began its climb to ten thousand feet as it cruised south towards the front.

Nobili's eyes scanned the skies during the couple of minutes it took to get to Girona. It looked like today would be another day spent looking for targets on the ground. The skies were clear except for the dozen French planes that his squadron were relieving. As he reached for the radio, he heard the call from Commandant Thomas Juin, the leader of the French combat air patrol.

"Welcome to the peaceful skies of Girona, Capitano Nobili. Try not to fall asleep."

"Thank you, Commandant Juin. We'll do our best."

"Be careful when—"

"Trucks! Say again, trucks!"

Nobili wasn't sure which of the Frenchmen made the report, but two of the M.S. 406s turned and began dives on the road south of the city. There were about twenty trucks making a dash for the safety of Girona's houses. The French fighters started their strafing runs as half a dozen anti-aircraft guns in Girona began filling the sky above the Spanish trucks with shrapnel.

The French monoplanes could hit over four hundred and fifty kilometers per hour when flying level. They were doing over five hundred as they dove on the trucks. The canvas was thrown off the front two trucks. Each revealed a pair of machine guns pointing up which quickly began hammering away at the strafing planes. Unfortunately for the Spanish, the speed of the French planes didn't give the gunners much time to aim. The French pilots reported a couple of pings as the sped back into the air but no apparent damage. The M.S. 406's metal wings and fuselage had stopped what little lead had found them. Six trucks were left burning on the road while the others disappeared into Girona.

Commandant Juin came back on the radio. "As I started to say a moment ago, be careful when strafing. The Spanish have started mounting machine guns in some of their trucks. They've also figured out that we aren't shooting at the town itself so they're running the gauntlet to deliver supplies."

"Thanks for letting us know, though I'm not sure how you managed to time that demonstration. Go back to base and get some rest."

"We'll see you at the cantina. Juin out."

As Capitano Nobili watched the French squadron head north, he wondered how well his CR.32 would do when it was his turn to deal with a truck convoy. He loved the way his plane floated through the air but the speed and toughness of the French planes looked awfully appealing right now. Both aircraft had two machine guns but the French plane also sported a twenty-millimeter cannon that chewed up ground targets and would probably be deadly in air combat. It would be interesting to see which of the planes fared better if the Republican air force ever showed up.

According to Juin, the Spanish had been running trucks into Girona two or three times a day. They seemed to coordinate with the Girona defenders on the way into town but they didn't on the way out. Anti-aircraft covering fire from the town was fairly heavy when the convoys were inbound, but it was sporadic at best on the way out. Add in that the empty trucks were faster when they left and the standing orders were to just ignore them.

Guido had his squadron take up stations about five kilometers south of Girona. Capitano Francesco Rossi and his wing man, Tenente Guillermo Bianchi, dropped down to four thousand feet while the rest of the squadron circled at ten thousand. Guido had set up a rotating schedule of who would get the chance to shoot up any supply trucks, a privilege that now came with extra risks.

The French forces had closed the roads that headed north from Girona and only the southern ones were open for the Republican forces. According to Commandant Juin, those roads had been crammed with people fleeing the French for the first few days in October. Now there were very few people on the road. The Spanish had quickly figured out that the French weren't strafing the refugees headed south but they were shooting at almost anything headed north. Since roads clogged with slow-moving civilians headed south tended to make anything headed north a slow-moving target, the Spanish had taken to clearing the roads before they ran anything into Girona.

Capitano Nobili enjoyed the view from his cockpit. During each lap of his patrol, he got a fine view of the Pyrenees, the Spanish countryside, and the beautiful Mediterranean. He picked up his microphone.

"Keep your eyes sharp when you're looking through the glare off the sea," he reminded his men.

Their nonchalant acknowledgments echoed Guido's own disappointment with the squadrons' role in the campaign.

October 9, 1936

50 miles southeast of Barcelona, Spain

Vice Admiral Sir Geoffrey Blake stood at the railing of the *Marlborough* and scanned the seas. Here he cruised southeast of Barcelona trying to intimidate and disrupt the Catholic Entente's navies without shooting at them. He hated days like today. There wasn't anything wrong with the weather or the seas, both were clear and calm. It was the waiting with his hands tied.

Regardless of what they said, there was only one real reason for the French to intervene in the Spanish Civil War and its name was Gibraltar. He may not be privy to the Army's plans but all the extra men and supplies had to come through the port. And the harbor was buzzing with the preparations. Vice Admiral Blake would much prefer that his countrymen start fighting the Entente as far from Gibraltar as possible, but that wasn't his call. So he waited and planned.

Things would get dangerous once the French and Italians got moving towards Girona. They had air cover around Girona so he'd been ordered to keep his scouts away from the area. That didn't keep him from checking the seas and the surrounding Spanish countryside. It also didn't keep him from letting the Republicans know what his planes reported.

What those planes were reporting made Vice Admiral Blake smile. The French still hadn't tried to outflank the Spanish at Girona and the Italian fleet was patrolling the coast but not shooting at anything. Far more interesting was what the scouts had noticed as they returned from their missions. The planes that were scouting west of Girona reported large troop movements heading northeast from Barcelona. They also reported a large number of Soviet I-15 fighters. It looked like the Soviets had decided to violate the Non-Intervention Agreement just like everyone else. Maybe the French and Italian troops north of Girona were in for a rude surprise. He'd sent that information back to Gibraltar along with a request.

Vice Admiral Blake's orders had been to observe and report on the Entente ships operating off the Spanish coast. He understood that he wasn't supposed to cause an incident but he had an idea that might help the Republicans without getting directly involved. All he wanted to do was take his ships on a little cruise to the north. He didn't plan on getting closer than ten miles to the French and Italian ships. He'd be visible and well within gun range but wouldn't even train his guns on the Entente ships. Since the British had permission to sail in Spanish waters, there wouldn't be anything wrong with where he was taking his ships.

His hope was that the French and Italian ships would worry about why he was there. All he hoped was to slow down any reinforcements or supplies they were carrying or prevent them from providing gunfire support. It wasn't much but it was the only thing he could come up with that might provide any help to the Republicans without starting a shooting war. He just hoped the Admiralty would respond before it was too late.

The Italians were pushing towards the ports he'd been using to supply the Spanish guerrillas and so the Admiralty might end the gun runs. It meant that Britain's efforts to harass the Entente supply lines had worked and troops had been diverted from the front north of Girona. The question was whether or not the Republicans would get their counterattack underway before the Italians finished mopping up the partisans.

Vice Admiral Blake wanted to get the shooting started sooner rather than later because he didn't know what the Admiralty would do if the Nationalists won and Spain joined the Entente. Gibraltar would probably hold out for months or years if the Entente started shooting. The problem was that if the Entente did start shooting from Spain, Gibraltar wouldn't work as a naval base. Malta wouldn't work for the same reason. Would his ships be sent to Egypt, Bermuda, South Africa, or even back to Britain? None of those would be good for her majesty's ships in the mid-Atlantic.

The materials to feed Britain's people and factories sailed on those ships and they would be hideously vulnerable to raiders based in Spanish ports. Add in that those supplies would have to sail around Africa rather than through the Mediterranean and the Entente raiders wouldn't have to be too successful for the people at home to feel the pinch. Supplies would have to come from the Americas in that case. And that meant being friendly with the damned United States of America. The very people who had kept the Great War from ending in an Allied victory. Wasn't that a bitch.

Well, at least he had his answer for why he wasn't allowed to shoot at anyone. The Entente would be able to buy from Africa and possibly eastern Europe with fairly secure supply lines. The United States of Greater Austria had never had much of a navy. Their army was pretty big but the League favored economic warfare rather than shooting. Add in the USGA's central position surrounded by neutral neighbors and any punitive mission they might launch would be pretty small. The Entente wouldn't be that bothered if the League of Nations quit trading with them, they would just ship things through one of the neutral Balkan countries.

Britain's supplies would have to run along the western side of the Atlantic or come from the League itself. A long-term embargo from them would be disastrous if the Entente could block the western

Mediterranean. If the League joined the Entente in shooting at British ships, things would be bleak.

Logistics. It always came down to logistics and Vice Admiral Blake didn't like where things were headed for his country.

October 11, 1936
The Chancellery, Berlin, Germany

I sat at my desk pondering the latest response from the League of Nations. They couldn't really believe the French story that Spanish Republicans had crossed the border and raided Céret. It didn't make any sense. The League must be looking for a way to delay any response until after the American elections. It looked like Roosevelt would beat Hoover this time and Roosevelt was pushing a far more aggressive foreign policy.

Regardless, it didn't look like there would be any real response until too late. Two French divisions were helping the Nationalists clear the north coast of Spain. Bilbao was expected to fall any day and then those troops would be available for the drive on Madrid. Two more French divisions and a panzer regiment had turned the stalemate around Madrid into a slow advance as the Republicans fought tenaciously for every yard of ground. The only good news was that the two divisions, one French and one Italian, and the panzer regiment that were heading towards Barcelona had stalled north of Girona. Whoever was leading the Republican defense had to have run a hell of a bluff. Our estimates were that he only had around a thousand men available when Gamelin's troops first showed up. He was up to a full division now but with little panzer or air support. It still wasn't a good situation for the Spanish.

Our agents reported almost double the normal number of British merchants in Republican-held ports even though they were publicly sticking to non-intervention. They had even warned other countries that they would search unusual traffic bound for Spain. Fortunately, the Turks and Ukrainians had been doing a fair amount of trade with the Spanish for years. Our first large shipment of weapons would be setting sail from their ports tomorrow. I'd been proud of finding this way around the British search policy until both the Turks and Ukrainians had reported the Soviet Union had been doing this since early September.

A knock at my door interrupted my musings. Oberst Ernst Weber poked his head into my office and came the rest of the way in when I nodded. He resisted the old habit of coming to attention and instead unceremoniously flopped into one of the chairs across from my desk.

Since I was looking at him rather than something on my desk, Weber started his report without any preamble. "The Dutch and Belgians have both responded with a 'Thanks, but no thanks' to our offer to join the Coalition. Both of them also expressed their appreciation of our concerns for their security and said they might be open to joining at a future date if the international situation changes."

"That's more positive than they've been to our previous overtures. Something good may yet come out of the Entente intervention in Spain."

"That's not the interesting news, Sir. We also have reports that the Republicans are preparing a counterattack from Girona."

"Any reports on what they've assembled for the attack?"

"Becker, head of our agents in Barcelona, estimates three divisions are moving to join the one already at Girona. He also figures they have at least a hundred panzers and two hundred aircraft in support."

I thought for a moment. "That's most of the infantry and more of the panzers and planes than we thought the Republicans had in reserve. I know the French had been trading them their older equipment for resources but I didn't think they had traded so many panzers. Maybe the Russians have been sending them more equipment than we thought."

Oberst Weber shrugged. "Becker thinks Gamelin and the French are in for a rude surprise. The French have built some light trench works and don't seem to be interested in pushing the fight."

"Let's hope he's right."

It was Weber's turn to look thoughtful for a moment. "Do you think the French are up to something?"

"Either that or they're really stupid. I know Gamelin has a reputation for being overly cautious, but that's not true of de Gaulle and Delestraint. The French have had the largest panzer force around since the end of the Great War and de Gaulle and Delestraint have been pushing them. They must know that a move towards Barcelona would get a reaction from the Azaña government since the area is a base of their support. So why make a move there with just two infantry divisions and panzer support? Reports are that Gamelin has half of the Italian division north of Girona running security on his supply line but even with them he doesn't have enough boots to hold much of that area of Spain. It just doesn't add up."

"Maybe the French are worried about supplying a larger force?"

Oberst Weber held his hand up at my look of derision almost as soon as I made it.

"I know, Sir. The obvious solution to that is to commit enough force to take Barcelona and use its port. Hmm, if they aren't worried that we or the Brits will start shooting, I'm down to hoping they're stupid."

"Me too, Ernst. Me too."

October 11, 1936
Figueres, Spain

Lieutenant-colonel Roger Noiret rolled out of his bunk and promptly stubbed his toe on his foot locker. He could almost hear his curses over the wailing air raid siren. He was outside in under thirty seconds, though no one would accuse him of being dressed. No bombs were falling outside so he used one hand to carry his boots and socks while the other kept his pants from hitting the ground as he ran towards the headquarters building. He passed half-dressed men from his battalion who were running for their tanks and nodded to them. Talking or saluting was out of the question.

Roger pelted into the building to find half a dozen officers in much the same state of dress as he was. The two exceptions were the duty officer, who was ignoring everyone but the radio operator, and Commandant Philippe de Hauteclocque, who looked like he'd had all the time in the world to get dressed. Roger just shook his head and dropped his boots in front of an empty chair so he could finish dressing. Phillipe came over as Roger plopped into the chair to pull on his socks. Roger couldn't believe it. He had a cup of coffee in his hands.

He cocked his head to one side for a moment and let out a sigh of relief as the siren finally fell silent. "Good morning, Colonel. It looks like things are getting interesting."

"They better be or someone is going to be chopping a lot of onions. What's going on?"

"The Italians were flying the dawn patrol today and they reported about twenty enemy airplanes headed towards our lines north of Girona. The duty officer was trying to decide whether or not to scramble our pilots when the number of enemy planes was pushed to around a hundred and a lot of artillery was seen shelling our lines."

"Damn, we figured that Gamelin's dawdling would cause something like this. It sounds like things are going to get hot down there. When do we move out?"

Commandant Philippe de Hauteclocque smiled at how his counterpart's immediate reaction was to go to the fight. He admired the older man and his thirst for a fight. "We don't." As Lieutenant-colonel Noiret's face took on a look of consternation, Philippe continued,

"We're under direct orders from General Gamelin to ensure that Figueres is held. It was part of the first message we got from headquarters. Gamelin expressed concern over a possible Republican advance from Besalú on our flank."

"And that's why we've got a company of our Italian friends near Besalú. They're supposed to keep an eye on things over there." Roger finished lacing up his right boot before continuing. "They should be enough unless Gamelin has reason to believe the Spanish are coming."

Commandant de Hauteclocque shook his head. "There wasn't anything in the orders, but who knows. This whole foray has been more of a camping trip than an attack. We're all alone out here in an area where virtually everyone supports President Azaña. If the Republicans don't know exactly what we have out here, they're complete idiots."

"True. And if Gamelin doesn't realize that then he's a lot less competent than he's shown in the past. So either Gamelin is losing it or he has reason to believe the Spanish may actually put in an attack from Besalú."

When Philippe simply shrugged, Roger scratched his chin. "I think I'm going to go inspect the position our Italian friends have selected around Besalú. I'll leave C Company here under your command in case there's any excitement and I'll take your C Company with me."

"That sounds good to me, Sir. I love our S36s but your Char G1s make me think about requesting a transfer."

Roger smiled and having finally finished dressing stood to go. "Send your company to the ammo depot for extra ordinance and then over to our parking field. Meet me back here in five minutes and if there's nothing new, I'll move out."

Philippe nodded and replied with a smile "Will do. I'll even get some of my men who aren't going, to run by the mess hall to get a picnic basket or two for your men."

The mention of food made Roger's stomach growl loud enough to be heard over the din. "That sounds like an excellent idea. I'll see you in five."

Caporal Jean Martin arrived as the armored cavalry commander left. Lieutenant-colonel Noiret immediately turned him around and sent him off towards the battalion's makeshift chapel. Capitaine Louis Lobau, the battalion chaplain, would normally be preparing for today's sermon. Father Lobau hadn't been in the army that long and might not know what his duties were when combat was imminent. If Roger's men were going into battle, he wanted them knowing that God was looking out for them.

October 11, 1936
Gibraltar

Carmen Esperanza was doing something she'd sworn she'd never do. She was in Major Thomas Hawkins' kitchen preparing his breakfast but she was straining to hear the conversation in the living room. She had arrived at the Major's door just as a young lieutenant had begun knocking at it. The young officer had waited until she left the room to start talking with Major Hawkins in hushed tones. At least it had started as hushed tones. At the Major's exclamation of "Good for the Republicans!" Carmen had started trying to listen in on the conversation.

Something was going on around Girona. That's where her Luis was. His first letter after the Republicans had pulled back from La Linea was from Malaga but she'd gotten one yesterday from Barcelona. In it Luis said he'd been involved in an ambush on a French convoy. His description of getting strafed by French planes made it sound like he thought it was exciting. It terrified her. The thought of bullets thudding into trees around her husband's head had kept her awake much of the night. The bags under her eyes were bad enough that

Major Hawkins had pressed her when she responded to his morning pleasantries with a vague comment of being fine.

The bang of the front door meant that her musings had prevented her from hearing any more of what was going on up north. She sighed and went back to cooking with a gusto to cover what she'd been doing. When Major Hawkins entered the kitchen and simply watched her for a few moments, she began to worry the he knew she'd been listening. He didn't show it if he did.

"Mrs. Esperanza, I have some good and bad news for you."

Carmen pulled things off the stove and steeled herself before turning towards the British officer she'd come to like over the years. The worry on her face was still plain enough for Major Hawkins to quickly realize the potential misunderstanding and hold his hands up defensively.

"Sorry, ma'am. I don't have any news on your husband." He waited for Carmen to relax a little before he continued. "I've been informed that the Republican forces near Girona have started a counterattack against the French. We've been expecting this for several days but of course, I couldn't tell you. Though now that it's started, everyone will know by the time you head home today."

Major Hawkins watched as Carmen fought through a kaleidoscope of emotions. She was relieved that there wasn't bad news about Luis, proud that the government troops were attacking the cowardly French, and she ended back up at worried. Luis was probably in more danger of being killed now, than at any time since his "adventure" began.

When she seemed to settle on worried, Major Hawkins nodded and began talking again. "We think your husband's unit is west of Girona so hopefully he won't be involved in the worst of the fighting. I'll let you know if we get any information on him."

Carmen stared at the Major for a moment. That last comment implied that he was trying to keep tabs on her husband for her. Was it because he liked her more than might be appropriate or was he just a very decent man? Either way, the tears welled in her eyes as she murmured her thanks for the news.

Major Hawkins appeared more than a little discomfited by Carmen's emotional vulnerability. He smiled slightly and said, "Right, ma'am. I still need to finish dressing before I can enjoy breakfast." He left the room faster than Carmen had ever seen him move which brought a smile to her eyes if not all the way to her lips. Whether or not the Major had personal feelings for her, he was definitely a decent human being.

Carmen turned back to the stove and worked at finishing her cooking. As she did so, she said a short prayer for her family's well-being. For the first time in her life, she included one of her British employers in those prayers.

October 11, 1936
The skies north of Girona
Capitano Guido Nobili was sweating. He'd never done that while flying before today. Then again, he'd never worked this hard in an airplane. His squadron had jumped the first group of Republican planes he'd seen. The Spanish fliers weren't very skilled and his CR.32 was a good match for the Soviet I-15s they were flying. He'd just shot down his second Soviet biplane when Sottotenente Ricci's cry had made him look at more than his quarry. The sky was filling with planes and they weren't friendly. He'd ordered his fellow pilots back toward Figueres until they got some reinforcements.

That had been over an hour ago. The French fliers had arrived about forty-five minutes ago. Unfortunately, far more Spanish planes had arrived than French. At least most of the Spanish were bombing and strafing the French troops on the ground in support of their now advancing countrymen. That left the Entente fliers only outnumbered about three to one on the north end of the battlefield. His men had shot down fourteen of the Spanish pilots. Four of his own had also fallen from the skies. Guido wondered if he would soon be joining them.

Capitano Nobili had managed to shoot down one more enemy plane before he ran out of ammunition. That was almost ten minutes ago and he'd been trying to work his way back towards Figueres since then. Five Spanish planes were now circling around him as he slipped and rolled for his life. They'd sent Sottotenente Ricci on a smoking spiral to the Spanish countryside only moments before and Guido was fairly certain they knew he was out of ammo. His maneuvers only moments before had put one of the Spanish broadside in front of him at only fifty meters. If he hadn't taken that shot, it meant that he couldn't.

The Spanish fliers grew bolder as Guido began working his way north and lower. He knew that making it back to Figueres was out of the question so he was looking for a place to put his plane down or at least a place to crash where he might survive.

He feinted left, rolled right, and made a tight turn to the left which put him behind the pilot who'd been on his tail. Nobili squeezed the trigger on his guns in the vain hope that there might be an answering stutter from his guns. His mouth twitched with a smile as he heard the staccato sound of machine gun fire. That lasted for the briefest of instants before he realized his guns weren't firing and the sound of fabric being punctured made him throw his CR.32 in a tight turn to the right. That got him out of the sights of his quarry's wing man and almost stalled his plane. Guido dove lower for speed and almost hit a tree. He looked around for both a landing spot and his nearest opponent when the most beautiful sight he'd ever seen greeted his eyes. Three of the Spanish planes were smoking and all of them were being pursued by French M.S. 406s. Part of Guido's brain had registered the increased chatter on the radio but he'd been too busy staying alive to contemplate its significance.

Capitano Nobili checked his plane and found only a few more holes in his fuselage and wing before climbing a little as he headed northeast toward his airfield. He saw six other CR.32s headed home and hundreds of French planes battling the Spanish. The French had a definite numerical edge and their planes were faster and better armed. More Spanish biplanes began smoking and losing altitude as Guido turned his attention to getting his wounded plane home.

Despite his best efforts, Nobili couldn't figure out when the desperate voices coming from his radio had turned to gleeful shouts but turn they had. Regardless of his own joy at their rescue, Guido refrained from joining the shouts for vengeance from his countrymen and allies. Almost half of his squadron, men he'd come to know as friends, had fallen from the sky. He hoped some of them had survived their crashes and would be able to rejoin the squadron. It wasn't even noon yet but he was positive the drinking, both in celebration and sorrow, would begin as soon as they got out of their planes.

October 11, 1936
70 miles east of Barcelona, Spain
Vice Admiral Sir Geoffrey Blake was pushing the limits of his orders and he knew it. However, as second in command of the Mediterranean fleet, Sir Geoffrey could exercise a good bit of his own initiative. He was supposed to keep an eye on the Italian ships near northeastern Spain without provoking them. Still, forming his battlecruisers in a line of battle barely ten miles west of the Italians and directly in their path was probably a little too provocative.

The log books showed that both the *Marlborough* and the *Benbow* were having issues with their scout planes. That was absolutely true. What wasn't in the log books, and better not ever show up there, was that a couple of seasoned mechanics were taking their time repairing problems that they had carefully created as part of a "training" exercise. Vice Admiral Blake had been assured that the planes could be up and running in five minutes if he needed them, though the official log showed that there was some trouble in finding certain essential spare parts. Blake could have used planes from the *Ark Royal* but that would have reduced her air arm's effectiveness if it was needed for combat missions. Honest.

Sir Geoffrey knew it wouldn't stand up if there was an inquiry but that would only happen if someone started shooting. Without an inquiry, his motives might be questioned but he and his captains should be fine. No one could say he wasn't following his orders. He was definitely keeping an eye on the Italian ships. They'd slowed to a crawl when they spotted his ships broadside across their path. They'd just turned northwest and picked up their speed. Either they were trying to get around him or they were forming their own line of battle.

"Take us due north at twenty knots. Signal the *Ark Royal* to go to battle stations."

The responses from the bridge crew barely registered on Vice Admiral Blake as he let his binoculars hang loosely around his neck. He wanted to see the Italian fleet as a whole so he could better gauge their actions. The men on his battlecruisers were already at battle stations though everything looked like they were at general quarters. He didn't want an inquiry into his actions but even more, he didn't want to get caught with his pants down.

The Italians appeared to have settled at a leisurely ten knots and if he didn't slow his ships they'd run right past the Italians.

"Drop us back to ten knots. Let's see what they're up to."

Once again he was only peripherally aware of his crew's response. The Captain and crew of the *Marlborough* were the professionals that England had been cultivating for hundreds of years.

Sir Geoffrey went back to watching the Italians. It looked like they were heading for the Spanish coast somewhere east of Girona. He smiled at the irony. His ships had been up at Roses only last night dropping off a load of arms for the local Republican fighters. The Italians wouldn't be doing anything to interfere with the Republican offensive if they maintained that heading.

"Sir."

Vice Admiral Blake took a deep breath of the soothing and stimulating salt air before turning to the *Marlborough's* Captain.

Commodore John Moore had been Captain of the *Marlborough* for almost a year and had been working with the Vice Admiral for eight months. He patiently waited for Blake to turn towards him but knew better than to wait for a prompt from him.

"It looks like they've got the *Littorio* and the *Roma* over there along with the *Andria Doria* and the *Caio Duilio*. We've also spotted four heavy and six light cruisers, about a dozen destroyers, and ... something different."

Sir Geoffrey looked puzzled for a moment. One of the issues with the scout planes "mechanical problems" was a reduced ability to accurately determine the opposing force. But "something different" was not a report he'd ever heard before. After a moment, it looked like Commodore Moore was reluctant to provide more detail.

"Someone reported something, Commodore. Would you care to explain?"

A look of consternation crossed Moore's features before he responded.

"One of the lookouts on the *Benbow* reported what he swore looked like a yacht, Sir. Not only that, but he said it wasn't flying an Italian flag. There's been no confirmation but it looks like the Italians are trying to hide and shield whatever it is."

"Did he say what flag the yacht was flying?"

"He didn't recognize it, Sir. It was gold on the left and white on the right with a design he couldn't make out in the white field. I've sent him to the ship's library to see if he can find anything that matches."

Vice Admiral Blake thought for a moment before a look of stunned concern came over his face.

"Take the squadron southwest at twenty knots. Contact the *Ark Royal* and have them send up a single scout plane, I repeat, just one, to confirm the sighting. Get the planes on the *Marlborough* and the *Benbow* up and running." He then turned back to the sea and raised his binoculars back to his eyes.

"Aye, Sir." Commodore Moore's training took over and he issued the orders even while his brain was trying to catch up. The Vice Admiral never repeated an order, he expected his men to hear and obey promptly. Given the apparent gravity of the situation, Moore stayed with the radioman to ensure the order was conveyed as given. He still had no clue about what had just happened and was getting ready to return to Sir Geoffrey when a message came in from the *Benbow*. Moore still didn't understand Sir Geoffrey's reaction when he heard its contents. He returned to the Vice Admiral's side to report the news.

"Sir."

Vice Admiral Blake continued to scan the Italian fleet and Commodore Moore was about to repeat himself when Sir Geoffrey said "Yes?" without turning.

"The *Benbow* reports that they believe the flag belongs to Vatican City, Sir."

"Damn. Well, at least nothing happened."

"Sir?" Commodore Moore couldn't keep the confusion out of his voice.

Vice Admiral Sir Geoffrey Blake lowered his binoculars and turned to the confused Commodore.

"I thought it sounded like their flag. The only way a yacht would be flying that flag is if the Pope were on board. And here I was playing chicken with them to see if I could cause an incident."

He shook his head and shuddered as Commodore Moore absorbed the information.

"Can you imagine what would happen if the Pope is over there and we had started shooting?"

The *Marlborough's* captain responded, "War."

"War? Try a holy war with every Catholic on the planet wanting our blood. We'd be lucky to keep our heads. Not exactly a good career move."

"No, Sir. I'll get you the report from *Ark Royal* as soon as it comes in."

October 11, 1936
The Chancellery, Berlin, Germany
The door to my office is already open so when I look up at the sound of a knock, Oberst Ernst Weber meets my gaze.

"Chancellor, sorry to interrupt but there's news on Spain."

"Come in, Ernst. Please give me some good news." I held up the paper I'd been reading. "The Austrians are echoing the official League of Nations position that everyone should stick to the Non-Intervention Agreement. They're even threatening sanctions if we take any action that violates the spirit of the agreement."

"Maybe this will help, Sir. The Spanish counterattack at Figueres has begun. It's about what we expected. They've got four infantry divisions and about a hundred and fifty panzers, though most of them are old French models. Our reports confirm they've got about two hundred aircraft supporting them."

"Any reports on how they're doing?"

"Yes, Sir. They're in complete control of the skies and are pushing the French back on the western end of the front. They appear to be trying to flank the French positions and push them east of the main road to Figueres."

"Are there any signs of a surprise by the French?"

"None so far, Sir. We did get a report from a Turkish frigate that's been shadowing the Italian fleet off of Spain. It looks like they've been playing chicken with the British battlecruiser squadron based out of Gibraltar. They were stymied for about ten minutes but then ran for Spanish waters and the Brits broke off."

"Where does it look like the Italians are headed?"

"Somewhere up the coast from Barcelona, Sir. We thought they were planning on shelling some of the Republican staging areas and supply routes. They could have caused some trouble if they'd done that. We have no idea of what they're up to with this new heading."

The sound of booted feet running towards us down the marble hall makes both me and Oberst Weber come to our feet. A breathless Feldwebel skids to attention while holding out a piece of paper. Weber takes the paper and scans it quickly.

"Planes, Sir. Our team in Girona says that a large number of French fighters just showed up in the sky over the battlefield. They outnumber the Spanish fliers at least two to one and are slaughtering them."

I close my eyes for a moment. It looks like my fears were right on target and the trap has sprung. When I open my eyes, I turn to the Feldwebel.

"Send the orders for our men to pull back to Barcelona and be prepared to move on to Tarragona."

Oberst Weber gives me a quizzical look as the Feldwebel leaves with more decorum than he had when he arrived. I sit back down and Weber does the same. I hold up my hand to forestall the question forming on his lips and dig out my map of southern France and north-eastern Spain.

"Think, Ernst. When you set a trap, you need bait and then something to crush whatever shows up."

"But why go to all this trouble? Wouldn't it have been simpler to just roll in with a larger force, Sir?"

"Simpler, yes. But probably less effective. The Entente pushed a force into the heartland of the Republican territory. A force that was big enough to cause problems but small enough to invite attack. The Republicans seem to have scraped up everything they could to drive the French away from Barcelona. If those reports are accurate, they've pulled more than they could afford from other fronts for this counterattack. The troops, panzers, and planes that would have taken the Entente and Nationalists months or years to hunt down are now out in the open as they attack. The fact that a large number of Entente planes arrived not long after the Spanish started their land attack makes me think this was carefully choreographed."

"You think the ground attack was the signal?"

"Stopping a fight once it's been started has always been one of the hardest things to do. We may have better communications than armies of the past but getting the message down the chain of command still takes time. Time the Republicans may not have."

"Don't forget the time it takes the commander to figure out that things are going wrong and decide what to do."

"This seems like something that de Gaulle and Delestraint cooked up. The relief force probably rolled for the border as soon as the Spanish planes showed up. My guess is that the relief force would wait to cross into Spain until after the Republicans committed their troops. Assuming they were based in Perpignan, they'd be able to get to Girona in a couple of hours though they'd seriously clog the roads."

Oberst Weber thought for a moment. "That may be why they've been running so many convoys up and down those roads. More bait to roust out anyone who might impede the relief force."

I sit back for a moment and smile. Weber still has trouble coming up with intricate strategies but once he's started down the path, he can figure out where they lead. "Makes sense to me."

Oberst Weber smiles at my agreement but displays his typical optimism. "Let's hope the Spanish have a surprise or two that can disrupt the French."

"We can hope, Ernst. I just wouldn't put any money on it. We know most of what's happening on both sides in Spain and we haven't been devoting many resources to it. I'd count on the Entente having intelligence that's at least as good about where the Republicans are and what they're doing."

"True, but the Republicans showed up with more men and equipment than we expected. Maybe it'll be enough to throw the Entente off their plan."

"Sorry, Ernst. It may even the odds some but I doubt it will make much of a difference. President Azaña may have gotten more to the fight than we expected but his planes are still heavily outnumbered. I doubt it'll be much different when the ground troops show up."

"Then what can we do, Sir?"

"We can find out what the Italian Navy is doing and use whatever happens to our advantage. If the Entente gets drawn into a long guerrilla war in Spain, we'll have enough time to send the Republicans equipment and supplies. If things end quickly, it should put enough concern into the people that we'll be able to expand the military. A lot will depend on what happens with the League of Nations after the American elections."

"I'll push our assets to find out what they can about the Italians. The League? Sorry, Sir, but I just don't see them doing anything useful."

"I agree if Hoover wins. But Roosevelt has been using the League's inaction as a hammer to pound Hoover's hands-off approach to government. It'll be interesting to see what happens if Roosevelt wins."

October 11, 1936

Just east of Besalú, Spain

Lieutenant-colonel Roger Noiret had his command deployed the way he wanted them. The fifteen Char G1s of his B Company were in a line running north and northwest from the road to Figueres while his A Company was in a line running south and southwest from the road. He was with a small command group on the road barely a hundred meters behind their juncture. All the rest of the support units of the 1st of the 507th were back at their base near Figueres. Everyone had done their best to camouflage their positions. Lieutenant-colonel Noiret didn't think they'd fool anyone for very long but ten seconds might be critical if there was a battle.

The Italian company that was stationed here was on a low rise two hundred meters west of his position. Their commander, Maggiore Verdino, had received the warning about a possible Republican attack. His reaction had apparently been to bluff at the poker game he was playing. He'd been called by one of his officers and lost that hand. Roger hoped the Italian commander fared better with the Republicans. The Italians hadn't moved in days and since they could see into Besalú, the people in the town could see them too. Part of the problem was that the Italians couldn't see the west side of the town so they couldn't tell if the Republicans were moving up. If the Spanish did show up in force, Roger expected the Italians to have a rough time of it.

Right now, most of his men were snacking at their stations. A few were sleeping in the shade of their vehicles. Roger wasn't sure if this reflected the confidence of his men in their ability to handle any attack or their belief that none was coming. The only thing Roger was sure of was his own frustration at not being in the fight.

Radio reports said the Republicans had launched their ground attack at ten o'clock and he'd seen several hundred French fighters headed south about twenty minutes later. A group of around a hundred bombers, Roger thought they were the new MB.174s, had been spotted headed south about twenty minutes after the fighters. The reports since then said that the Republicans were pushing his countrymen back but were taking a terrible pounding. And here he sat with the best tanks in the world hoping for something to do.

It was a couple minutes after eleven when all hell broke loose. The area of the rise around the Italian command post erupted in explosions as Republican forces blew it apart. Lieutenant-colonel Noiret's head swiveled to his radio operator to give the order to report the attack but de Hauteclocque's Sergent was already making the call. All that was left for Roger to prove was he could still run as he bolted for his tank, the nearest one in A Company. Three more spots on the low rise exploded into columns of dirt and smoke as he ran down the road towards his tank. Those would be the gun emplacements the Italians had set up. Roger thought that was a good sign. If the Republicans had enough toys to swamp the command post and hit the guns at the same time, they might have enough to overrun his position. Since they were doing it sequentially, Noiret expected to give them a rude surprise on this side of the crest.

When Lieutenant-colonel Noiret got to his tank he was treated to the curious sight of Sergent Pierre Murat and Caporal André Rinck staring at their wristwatches. Before he could ask, Murat raised both hands with a triumphal yell and grabbed a couple of bills that were sitting between them on the tank.

"What the...."

Caporal Rinck interrupted the question with his own. "Couldn't you have tripped a little on something, Sir?"

Sergent Murat laughed before chiming in with "I told you he'd make it in under thirty seconds. And he hasn't even figured out he should be breathing hard."

Rinck muttered something that Roger didn't quite catch as he climbed aboard. He thought he caught the word adrenaline but he wasn't sure and any thoughts about the comment quickly disappeared from his mind.

It took Lieutenant-colonel Noiret less than a minute from when the first shell landed on the Italians to get himself and his tank ready for the coming battle. His undignified run down the road was wasted since it was close to ten minutes before the enemy first crested the rise. They appeared to be sixty Soviet T-26s with infantry and they were spread along the rise centered on the road. Roger was grateful for those minutes since it gave the routed Italians a chance to clear the slope and reform near the command group behind his line.

Noiret called to Caporal André Rinck, "Send a go for fire plan beta."

When he'd set up his position, Roger had decided on two basic firing plans. If the enemy came down the road in column, his flank G1s had been assigned sections of the road for their initial shot with the tanks near the road shooting at anything that got through the initial salvo. Roger had selected a bush by the side of the road as the signal for when to open fire. Since they were advancing in a spread formation, they would be using the second option. Each G1 had a section of the slope to cover. Roger's tank would initiate the firing in this case. In either case, the tanks machine guns were only to be used after the enemy returned fire.

Roger felt the turret swivel slightly to the left to adjust for the secondary target location. It was about thirty seconds after the first Republican tanks were spotted before he decided it was time. He patted Caporal Guy Morin on one of his broad shoulders and the gunner sent his shot on its way.

The results from their initial shots made Lieutenant-colonel Noiret smile. There were thirty burning tanks on the slope. He had just enough time to enjoy the feeling before another wave of tanks crested the rise. Things were getting serious.

Noiret's smile got even bigger as he realized they had achieved complete surprise. The Republican troops had been scanning the slope for any stray Italians that might have regrouped from the shelling so the location of the French armor was still concealed. The remaining tanks of the first wave had stopped while the second wave continued down the slope.

The semi-automatic loader for the main gun let his men get their second shots off barely five seconds after their first. The results were just as devastating as the first rounds. The infantry accompanying the Republican tanks had sought shelter around and behind the remaining vehicles and were shredded when those tanks blew up. The most astonishing thing from Roger's perspective was what was going on with the second wave of tanks. The commander of one of the tanks near the road was waving a red flag over his head for all he was worth. The advancing tanks of the second wave came to a ragged halt as their infantry began a jogging advance down the slope.

Roger spoke into his radio, "Rinck, machine guns with the next salvo." He then lined up his cupola gun at his selected area and waited for Morin's next shot.

The whole battle was over in less than a minute. The relative quiet was a stark contrast to the frenzied noise of the battle. Morin had fired five times and scored hits with every shot. One hundred and twenty burning hulks and hundreds of men were scattered across the east side of the low rise and nothing else was willing to come over it. The ambush had worked perfectly, now came the tricky part. He radioed his command to advance to the top of the rise and give the burning metal coffins of the enemy a wide clearance. Some of them were still cooking off their ammo.

His companies pivoted to form a skirmish line about two hundred meters long centered on the road. As they were forming up, the infantry of the Italian company joined them forming up about twenty meters to their rear. An Italian Capitano approached Roger and, in fluent French, requested permission to advance to the crest and scout the other side. Maggiore Verdino was nowhere to be found and the remaining Italian troops had not been happy with his retreat order.

The Italians formed a skirmish line and headed up the slope. When the line neared the crest of the rise, the Italians started shooting at something on the other side. Lieutenant-colonel Noiret smiled as he ordered the advance. That's when things went wrong.

The Char G1s were called medium tanks but they still weighed almost thirty tons. There had been some moderate rain over the last several days and while this Sunday was a warm clear day, the ground was still moist and soft in many places. By the time his lead tanks had covered half the distance to the crest, barely a hundred meters, his command was no longer in anything that could be called a formation. Between dodging burning enemy hulks and the muddy patches of ground, some of his tanks were already forty meters behind his lead elements. So much for interlocking fire zones.

His tank and Commandant Robert Olleris', the leftmost one of B Company, were in the lead since they were closest to the road where the ground was firmer. The main gun was loaded with a high explosive round and Roger had both hands on the cupola machine gun. They were still 20 meters from the top of the rise when dirt-covered men started coming over it. Roger realized they were Italians a split second before pressing the trigger. Caporal Rinck appeared to come to the same conclusion since the hull-mounted machine gun also stayed quiet. The same couldn't be said for Olleris' tank. Several of their allies twirled like rag dolls as they were sprayed with machine gun fire.

"Friendlies! Friendlies! Friendlies!" was barely out of Caporal Rinck's mouth and over the radio waves when more men came over the crest.

Moments later, the Italians that Noiret and Rinck had spared started hitting the dirt. Some of them wouldn't be getting back up. The men of the command detachment were supposed to help provide anti-infantry defense with their machine guns and their fire came streaming from behind him. The open turret hatches gave his tank commanders some protection from stray bullets. They didn't help the machine gun crews from misidentifying the muddy Italians at a hundred meters. It couldn't have been more than a second or two before the bullets quit flying but they felt like hours to Roger as he helplessly watched Italians perish in the hail of lead.

The friendly-fire spectacle almost cost Lieutenant-colonel Noiret his life. The limited view from Caporal Rinck's vantage point kept him from getting distracted so when Spanish infantry crested the rise, he was quick on the trigger. Roger yelled "Halt!" as he ducked from the whine and ricochet of bullets. He felt like a turtle with his nose pressed against the top of the turret and his helmet for a carapace. His right arm extended up to his grip on the cupola machine gun. He knew his fire was wild but kept it up anyway, hoping he didn't hit any more Italians.

The exchange was over in moments, far quicker than Roger expected. The tanks that had been slowed by the mud had been presented with clearer targets than those that were closer to the crest. As he uncoiled from his crouch, he found a dozen of the Italian infantry crouched around his tank with guns pointed uphill. He heard Rinck on the radio warning of Spanish infantry across the rise as one of the Italians stood up.

"Hey, Frenchie! I think that's most of them. Let's get the rest of the bastards. You watch the front and we'll clean up the gaps."

Roger nodded and then smiled as he realized he'd just taken "orders" from an Italian Sergent. The battlefield made things a little foggy sometimes. He started to give the orders to roll when a thought penetrated that fog. Why had so few infantry come over the rise? There had been less than a company's worth that had made the last attack. Was it the infantry from another tank group?

Roger ordered the rest of his tanks to form up just short of the crest of the rise. While the tanks struggled up the muddy rise, he turned back to the Italian infantryman.

"Sergent! What's on the other side?"

The Italian recognized the voice of command and realized he'd been a little too familiar with an officer. He snapped to attention before replying, "Truck mounted infantry, Sir."

Lieutenant-colonel Noiret's reply of "This isn't the parade ground" took him by surprise and he smiled as he ducked his head and resumed his previous crouch.

"Any more tanks or artillery?"

"Not that I saw, Sir."

It was close to five minutes before the plan for attack was set and both the French and the Italians knew what was expected of them. Roger looked up and down the line of his formation. Everything looked good except for Lieutenant Jacques Jeannin's tank. It was still halfway down the rise with what looked like a thrown tread. The remaining Italian infantry was clustered around his tanks. No use waiting.

"Let's go have a look, shall we? Sergent, watch the gaps. Rinck, move 'em out easy."

Colonel Noiret found himself crouching down in the cupola again as they crested the rise. There he found a curious sight. There were close to four hundred Spanish infantry with their weapons on the ground and their arms raised. The lone exception was an area near the road where several Spaniards had their guns trained on a dozen officers who were kneeling on the ground. An elderly priest stood in their midst.

Noiret barked "Hold your fire!" unnecessarily as Sergent Murat and the other tank drivers stopped their machines.

One of the Spanish infantrymen tapped the priest on the shoulder and helped him head up the rise to the waiting French tanks. Roger thought for a moment before dismounting his tank and heading towards the approaching men. When he saw Commandant Olleris start to do the same, he motioned him back. No sense in risking them both if things went bad.

The old priest had a livid bruise on his right cheek and was leaning on the Sergent who was helping him up the rise. The soldier bore marks of fighting too, with a black eye and his own limp. Roger wasn't sure who was helping whom on their trek to meet him. As they neared, the pensive look on the priest's face faded. He pointed at the Warriors for Christ tabs on Lieutenant-colonel Noiret's collar and said something to his helper.

Roger nodded his head to the clergyman and smiled. He was still trying to figure out what was going on when the priest began to talk in fluent French.

"Sir, these men wish to surrender themselves and their officers." The disgust in that last word was palpable. "I assume I can have your word that they will be treated well?"

"Lieutenant-colonel Roger Noiret, Father. I will gladly accept their surrender and give my word on their treatment, as long as you tell me why they're surrendering."

The priest nodded gravely and said something to Sergent, it looked like Esperanza. The Spanish soldier turned back towards the group they'd left and waved. A series of signals seem to go back and forth and soon there were several hundred more Spanish troops emerging from the town behind them.

"I'm Father Pedro Garcia. Those officers," again that thick contempt, "arrived with their men yesterday. They have been looting my flock and my church. They forced themselves on several women. I was beaten when I tried to stop them. They urinated on me while chanting that the Church was dead. This man came to my defense and was beaten too. The tank crews turned their guns on the others to keep anyone else from joining his protest. Their crews are Russian and they laughed at our humiliation.

"When the attack was launched, most of the men stayed wary lest the Russian tanks come back and turn on them. They hoped when they heard the explosions and saw the dense smoke from over the ridge. After they saw the infantry from the second wave come back over the crest, they refused the order to follow their fellow soldiers to a useless death. We were released and the officers taken into custody. When the remaining Russian infantry saw what was happening, they headed back over the crest. I guess they preferred to take their chances with you.

"Many of these men had doubted the excommunication of President Azaña by the Pope, but the actions of their officers have made them far less interested in laying down their lives for the Republic."

Roger formally accepted their surrender and had Olleris and B Company take up a position between them and Besalú to screen them. The men from his A Company rounded up and disarmed the Spanish. Roger left Olleris in command and headed back to his command base. His command hadn't suffered any casualties and Jeaninn's tank should be back in action soon. The report to Figueres was going to be interesting. What would happen when it was reported up the chain of command was anyone's guess. He did know that he wanted to personally hear whatever orders came down to deal with this. His orders might be interesting and miscommunications were the bane of all military men.

In the meantime, he needed to find out who was in charge of what was left of the Italian unit and see if he could get them to screen an advance into Besalú. One or two hold out snipers could cause a lot of damage to exposed tank commanders.

October 11, 1936

Gibraltar

It was close to noon when Carmen Esperanza finally headed back up the steps to Major Thomas Hawkins' quarters. After making breakfast for the Major and cleaning up in his kitchen, she'd headed off to morning mass back in La Linea. There had been muffled arguments after the service as rumors of the Republican counterattack clashed with Nationalist counter-rumors. Try as she might, Carmen didn't hear anyone with any real news of what was going on near Girona. A number of people didn't even believe that the Republicans were attacking. Carmen knew better but held her tongue to keep from drawing the crowd's attention.

Carmen had just finished preparing fish and chips, the Major's Sunday standard, when he arrived at the house. She'd set it on the small dining table and turned back toward the kitchen when Major Hawkins cleared his throat in that annoying British way of requesting attention without just saying something. The look on his face when she turned around made Carmen suddenly afraid for the fate of her dear husband.

Major Hawkins held up his hand to forestall her question. "I have no news on the fate of Luis."

The relief on Carmen's face quickly died as he continued.

"It appears that the Entente was laying a trap near Girona and the Republicans walked right into it. The Republican Air Force that was supporting the attack is being wiped out. Their ground troops are still slowly advancing but they're paying a very heavy price."

Carmen leaned on the back of one of the chairs to keep from falling down and bit her lip to keep from crying. It seemed like the French would once again put a puppet on the Spanish throne.

Major Hawkins gave her a moment to gather herself before continuing. "Our information says that Luis was part of an attack made through Besalú to attack the Entente troops from behind. They were supposed to attack over an hour ago. No one has heard anything from them."

Tears welled up as Carmen stared into the face of a British officer who'd had practice delivering bad news during his career. She closed her eyes and said a short prayer for her husband. Her spirits lifted a little when she opened her eyes and saw that Major Hawkins had his head bowed and eyes closed as his lips moved in a silent prayer. If both Catholic and Protestant were praying for her Luis, maybe there was hope.

She waited for the Major to finish and open his eyes before asking the question she wasn't sure she wanted answered. "So, while you have no direct news of Luis' fate, you do not think things look good for him."

"No, Mrs. Esperanza. We do not think things look good for him or the Republican government."

Carmen closed her eyes and nodded. When she opened them again, she waved Major Hawkins toward his normal chair. "Your lunch is getting cold. I'll get your tea."

The Major was seated when she returned from the kitchen. She poured his tea while he stared questioningly at her. When Carmen sat the pot on the table and he still hadn't moved she uttered a deep sigh.

"Major, my husband has been in the army since near the end of the Great War. I've always lived with the possibility that he wouldn't come home just like your wife did. His fate and soul are in God's hands and I believe God will protect him. Until the day he's taken from me, I'll always hope and pray that my Luis will come home to me. When he is taken from me, I'll do the best I can for my son Carlos and anyone else I can help until the day the Lord calls me home to my husband's side."

Major Hawkins was at best a vaguely religious man. The will and strength that Carmen drew from her faith both awed and scared him. People of such faith could do tremendous things. People of such faith were part of the Catholic Entente that hated his country and countrymen. Religions always brought out the best and the worst in people.

Carmen smiled. "Thank you for letting me know what's going on in our fight against the rebels and the information on my husband. But please eat your lunch. I've still got to go to Lieutenant Higgens' quarters to clean this afternoon and the sooner I'm finished, the sooner I can get back to my son. I'm sure there will be plenty of rumors if things have gone as badly as you say."

Major Hawkins smiled a little before murmuring, "Yes, ma'am."

The fish and chips were gone within minutes. He admired the way Carmen went about cleaning things up after he'd finished and wondered how she was taking the war news so calmly. It was while she was washing his dishes that he realized that what he thought had been mutterings to herself were actually prayers she was saying under her breath. He hoped they were answered.

October 11, 1936
Figueres, Spain

Capitano Guido Nobili looked at what was left of his squadron as it headed back towards the battle for the skies above Girona. There were only four of them left flying. When he'd talked to the rest of his men, they'd all wanted payback. There would be time for mourning tonight, today was a time for vengeance and there was no way the French fliers would have it all.

His usual wingman, Sottotenente Corrado Ricci, had shown up just before they took off. The road Ricci had used as an emergency airstrip was just as bumpy as most of the back roads around here and the resulting crash finished what the Spanish fliers had started. A passing French ambulance brought him back to the airbase. They'd even set his broken arm along the way. Sottotenente Ricci had added his hopes for retribution to those of the remaining pilots. He also wished them a safe return.

In some ways, Capitano Nobili wished the French fighters had already destroyed the Republican air force. While Ricci's return had lifted the spirits of the squadron and raised their hopes for the return of their other missing pilots, his wish for a safe return had reminded Guido of the terrible losses they'd suffered. But if the Republican air force was gone, there would be no one on whom to wreak his vengeance.

They saw a number of French planes headed north as they headed south. Some were headed over the Pyrenees towards their French bases. Some seemed to be headed towards the base at Figueres. He identified the plane of Capitaine Claude Lefebvre. The French squadron based at Figueres was returning just after Guido's group bounced down the runway and headed back to the action. They weren't missing any planes and bore few wounds from the air battles. Capitano Nobili decided he really wanted to fly one of the French M.S. 406s in combat. He tuned his radio and broke out his best French.

"Nobili here. Welcome back, Capitaine Lefebvre. Did you leave any of the Spanish for us?"

After a moment, broken Italian came back through the speaker. "Hey, Capitano Nobili, Capitaine Lefebvre here. There are still plenty of targets down there. Our friends from up north have too long of a trip to stay in the fight for long. Good hunting."

"Thanks. Safe landing and we'll see you soon."

Guido ordered the group to climb as they approached Girona. It made his planes more visible but it also let them see farther. Given the tactical advantage the altitude gave them, Capitano Nobili hoped the Spanish fliers would be too busy to notice his newcomers.

It was his executive officer and current wingman, Capitano Francesco Rossi, that spotted the Spanish first. There was maybe a dozen of them trying to defend themselves from a like number of French fighters. Another squadron of the French fighters was chasing Republican bombers while a number of French bombers unloaded on the Spanish troops that were trying to press the attack on the ground. Burning tanks were providing a bit of a smoke screen for the Spanish.

As they approached the air battle, Capitano Nobili noticed that the Spanish fliers made tight turns to keep their guns towards the French aircraft as the M.S. 406s made their high-speed passes.

He radioed his depleted squadron. "Pick a Frenchman and follow him on his pass. We may catch the Spanish napping." He didn't like splitting from his wingman but he thought it was the best way to make their limited numbers count the most.

Guido dove toward an M.S. 406 that had just started a turn back toward several Spanish planes. His timing was good and his guess on the Frenchman's attack path was only a little off. He was about three hundred meters behind when the planes exchanged fire in a head-on pass. The French flier banked right and roared on as the Spaniard slipped right and turned left to try to get his guns back on the fast-moving fighter. Nobili fired from less than a hundred meters away at the belly of the turning Spanish plane. He then had to yank hard on his stick as he pulled his CR.32 up and left from the now smoking Spanish plane. Guido turned the maneuver into a barrel-roll that let him bank his nimble plane back toward where the Spaniard should be.

A smiling snarl spread across Capitano Nobili's lips as his chosen target came back into view. Flames were spreading along the length of the Republican I-15 as it nosed over towards the ground. A passionate part of Guido's soul wanted to pursue the aircraft as it started to tumble from the sky. A colder part of his soul wanted more of his enemies in front of his guns. Flying with an open cockpit was always chilly work and the colder part of him won the argument. Guido pulled the nose of his fighter up as he climbed again and looked for another target.

Capitano Nobili was only peripherally aware of the radio as he chose another target. Italian voices were shouting cries of vengeance while indignant French ones were complaining of being robbed of their kills. His estimate of the French flier's attack path was better this time, although he did have to throttle back to give the Frenchman more of a lead. His cold smile turned to loud curses as the wing-man of his stalking horse came into line barely twenty meters in front of Guido.

Nobili snarled for a different reason as he nearly stalled his beloved CR.32 trying to put some distance between him and the faster French fighter. The snarl and yelled curses quickly turned to triumphant shouts as this Spanish flier had waited for the second plane before making his turn. The second French pilot had accidentally forced Guido into the right place for another close-range shot at an I-15's belly. Too close of a range as it turned out. Capitano Nobili avoided running into his fifth kill of the day but he couldn't avoid the flying debris when that Spanish plane exploded.

His beloved plane was wounded but still flying and the bloodlust that had overcome him subsided as he worked to get the damaged aircraft up and away from the fight. As he calmed, thoughts of his duties as squadron commander came back to him.

All of the French airplanes were still in the air while only three of the Republican fighters were still in the air. Capitano Nobili ordered his men back to base. He radioed the French squadron commander and apologized while explaining the Italians' thirst for vengeance.

They headed north with the tirade from the French commander still running as his voice broke up. They flew in silence for a few moments before Capitano Rossi's voice came over the radio.

"I got one of the bastards."

A "Me too" and a "Same for me" quickly followed.

Guido replied with "Two more for me" after a moment. While the remnants of his squadron would be mourning their friends tonight, they would at least be able to offer the departed some measure of vengeance. He was more than a little jittery as the remnants of his squadron headed north. Shooting down some of the enemies that had so wounded the squadron would help but now was the time to rest and regroup. Guido just hoped his airplane would be ready for another round tomorrow.

October 11, 1936
40 miles east of Barcelona, Spain
Vice Admiral Sir Geoffrey Blake leaned on the railing around the *Marlborough's* bridge. The late-afternoon view was one he loved but it didn't have its usual calming effect on him. He was more frustrated than he'd ever been. He'd reported the papal ship and been ordered to steer clear of it. That meant it was more difficult to keep an eye on the Italian fleet. At least they weren't pushing towards Barcelona. The lone scout he had keeping them under surveillance reported them still heading northwest at around ten knots. The question he kept coming back to was why the Pope was going into a war zone. He was sure that question was being discussed in Whitehall by now.

Sir Geoffrey also used his scouts to try to keep an eye on the battle north of Girona. While his fliers weren't allowed over Spain, they did have permission to operate in their territorial waters. There was no way he could explain violating that order so most of his information was based on what his men saw heading northeast from Barcelona and what they saw coming back.

That balance did not look good. There was a steady stream of troops headed to the fight but the vehicles appeared to be just as loaded on their return trips. Barcelona's hospitals were already full and the bodies of dead and maimed men were backing up into the streets. The Republican side of the air battle was easier to track but no better in its outlook. Around three quarters of the Republican fliers had returned from their first sortie. That number had dropped to barely half as the fight wore on. British spotters on the ground in Girona said that while the offensive was moving forward, it reminded them of some of the slaughters from the Great War.

Vice Admiral Blake tried to come up with some way to influence the battle of Girona. The Republicans were fighting for their grip on power and if they lost, Gibraltar would be put in a tenuous position. He hated being in a position where his command's future was in the hands of people he wouldn't trust to make his breakfast. He just hoped that the Spaniards would be able to break the French lines.

The air battle was what worried Sir Geoffrey the most. The ground agents in Girona couldn't see what was going on in the skies above the smoke-filled battlefield. The reports from the last week had put the Entente's air strength at just two dozen planes. The problem was that there was no way twenty-four planes could carry enough ammunition to shoot down the number of Spanish planes that weren't coming back from the battle. He had checked with Captain Cedric Holland of the *Ark Royal*. The opinion of him and his air wing commander was there had to be more airplanes on the Entente side, probably a lot more, to cause the kind of air losses they were seeing.

If their assessment was correct, then there were probably a lot more Entente ground troops in the area too. If that was the case, the Republicans had probably just walked into a trap. Things could get ugly for the British agents in Girona. He turned back to the bridge and tried to get Commodore John Moore's attention. Unfortunately, he was reading a report so Sir Geoffrey had to settle for the seaman next to him. That young man quickly got the attention of the *Marlborough's* captain. With a couple of quick hand signals, Commodore Moore conveyed that he would be out in just a moment. After he finished his reading, he came out to join the Vice Admiral with the report and a map in his hands.

"Sorry, Sir. There was a new report from our Girona agents. It seems that the Republicans tried a flank attack through Besalú this morning. It did not go well."

Sir Geoffrey looked at the map to see where Besalú was before responding. "Did they just screw it up or did they run into more Entente troops than they expected?"

Commodore Moore looked surprised at his boss's ability to figure out what had happened.

"Both, Sir. The Republicans blasted the Italian positions on a rise east of the town and then sent a battalion of Russian light tanks over the knoll into what was apparently a trap. There were French tanks on the other side of the knoll and the Russian tanks were wiped out. The rest is a bit confused. It seems the officer commanding the Republican regiment decided that the locals were playthings for the amusement of him and his officers. When the infantry was ordered to follow the armor, it mutinied and surrendered to the French."

Vice Admiral Blake removed his hat and closed his eyes. He ran his hand over his head a couple of times before sighing heavily. He opened his eyes and replaced his hat before finally responding to the report.

"Order our men in Girona to move to Sils and be prepared to pull all the way back to Barcelona. Pass their report and my orders on to Gibraltar along with my expectation that the Entente will be driving on Barcelona soon. I also believe the Pope will be on the ground in Spain soon, probably to try to quell unrest in Republican territory. And find out how the hell we know what's going on in Besalú."

Commodore Moore looked surprised but hurried back to the bridge while Sir Geoffrey returned to looking at the sea. He shook his head every few minutes as if he was disagreeing with something. He was still standing there ten minutes later when Moore returned.

"Sir?"

"Well?"

"Our men in Girona don't know why, but apparently an agent was tasked with keeping tabs on a particular Spanish Sergeant. The Spaniard was arrested last night but was freed today and apparently led the mutiny."

"Do you know if that's why we were shadowing him?"

"I don't think so, Sir. Girona said he had been a model soldier up until today."

Vice Admiral Blake went back to staring at the sea and it was a few moments before Commodore Moore cleared his throat. Blake turned back to him and held up an admonishing hand before he could say anything.

"Let's see... I originally called you out here to tell you to warn Gib and Girona that this looked like a trap and they should be prepared for that possibility. Captain Holland believes the likely reason for the Republican air losses we've observed is that there are a lot more Entente planes in the air over the battlefield. Our men in Girona haven't been able to get a good look at what's going on in the skies but they have reported that the Republican troops are getting mauled on the ground. We also know that the Entente has been clearing their supply route and everything east to the coast. Even with that, they had enough extra men and armor to set a trap on the only major route around their flank.

"That was the last nail in the coffin. The Entente seems to have a lot more available for this fight than we thought they did which means we shouldn't be thinking Jutland, we should be thinking Great Yarmouth. The Entente poked the Republicans and got them to chase them right into a trap. Only this time the other side has more ships they can commit to the fight.

"I expect that the Entente will counterattack with fresh troops tomorrow and the Spanish will break fairly quickly. The roads south from Girona will be clogged so if our scouts want to get out, they need to do it before the counterattack or they won't make it. Sils looks like a good way point. If I'm wrong, they can head back to Girona. If I'm right, I doubt the Spanish will offer any effective resistance before they hit Barcelona.

"Finally, there's only one reason that the Pope would be sailing around off the coast of Spain while the Entente clears that coast of Republican combatants. He plans on going ashore. And the only reason the Entente would want him to do that is to help get the locals to fall in line with the Nationalist agenda. The Pope already excommunicated Azaña. Now he needs to convince the Spanish people that the Nationalists are doing God's work. If he can do that, the Spanish won't be an occupied country, they'll be an ally.

"If that covers your questions, you should probably head back inside. I'm sure Gibraltar would like those answers, too."

October 12, 1936
Manstein Residence, Berlin, Germany
The breakfast of ham, eggs, and pancakes is delicious as always but I find I have little appetite. I try my best but there's still half of my normal breakfast staring at me from my plate when Beatrice comes in to remove the dishes. She starts to say something but stops and

looks at me for a moment with a concerned expression on her face. When she decides that I'm not sick, she nods her head and places her hand on my shoulder.

"I'll fix up something for you to take into work. It'll be next to your coat when you leave."

I murmur my thanks and watch as she closes the kitchen door behind her when she leaves, her signal that we can talk in private. At the other end of the table, Otto sits back. He had to answer the door twice in the middle of the night so he knows there was something going on. He didn't have to read the reports he passed to me so he got a lot more sleep than I did. He also knows that I've been running short on sleep since the Entente intervened in Spain. Brent, who can sleep through almost anything, has been patiently waiting with the hope it was news I could talk about. He leans on the table with his chin in his hands and looks at me expectantly. I sigh before I begin.

"Yes, I can talk about it. Most of it will be in the morning news broadcasts. No, it's not good. The Republican forces in Spain launched their counterattack yesterday. They claim that they are pressing forward and driving the invaders from Spain. Unfortunately, that's not how our agents in Girona see it. Their report says the Spanish have pushed the Entente forces back less than half a mile and paid a huge price for it. Based on the number of wounded heading south from the battlefield, they think the Spanish have already lost ten to fifteen thousand men, up to a quarter of their attacking troops. It's worse with their panzers and in the air where our men think the losses may be as high as seventy-five percent."

Both Brent and Otto can tell that I have more news so they simply nod in acknowledgment and let me gather my thoughts before continuing.

"I finally received responses from both Presidents Hoover and Schuschnigg. Neither the USA or the USGA will intervene in Spain. They've declared it a local affair and warned us to stay out of it. They will be discussing a possible censure of France and Italy by the League next week. If that's agreed to, they may start a trade embargo.

"The British have also rebuffed our overtures about any kind of intervention in Spain. They seem to be pinning their hopes on the Republican attack turning the Iberian Peninsula into the same type of quagmire it was for Napoleon. Based on the Republican losses so far, I just don't see that happening.

"And finally, the Russians appear to have taken this opportunity to attack the Turks. At least, that's what Prime Minister İnönü says. General Secretary Stalin says the Turks raided across the border and started the incident. I honestly don't care which of them started it as long as it doesn't blow up into a full-scale war.

"Strangely, I didn't get a lot of sleep last night and now it's time to go into work and make decisions that will affect the future of our country."

I look up from the table and find both Brent and Otto wearing expressions of deep concern.

"Sorry, that sounded a bit like whining to me."

"Dad, I think you should take the morning off. You've always told me to stop what I'm working on when my thinking starts getting fuzzy, I'd end up causing more problems than I fixed. I think you should do the same. We might not be able to fix a decision you make based on fuzzy thinking."

"I think my brain will just get fuzzier as the day wears on."

I know I must look bad when Otto joins the conversation on my son's side. "I'll send Weber to get a sleeping draught from the drug store. Four or five hours of unconsciousness should help."

As he leaves, Brent stands too.

"I'll tell Beatrice that you and Otto will be here for lunch and I'll take her snack to school. Now go upstairs, get undressed and crawl back into bed."

I push back from the table and stand up with a smile, Brent giving me the best stern look he can muster. It breaks when I come to attention and snap of my best parade ground salute to him.

"Yes, Sir!"

"Right, Dad. Just go get some rest, okay?"

My quiet "Love you, son" is greeted with an eye roll and an embarrassed grin.

"Love you too, Dad. Now go."

I head back upstairs and manage to get mostly undressed before I stop while sitting on the edge of my bed. My brain starts running through scenarios for dealing with each of the problems I'm currently juggling. Most of my solutions end up causing more problems for me to keep in the air.

I'm still sitting there when Otto arrives fifteen minutes later. He sets down the glass he's carrying and helps me get my pants off. He pulls back the bed covers before sitting me back down on the edge of the bed. He passes me the glass he came in with.

"Drink this."

I down it in one pull and wave the empty glass in his general direction. He takes it and sets it aside then pushes me back into the bed. He pulls the covers over me and takes the seat by my desk where he picks up a pen and notepad. Twice before I've worked myself to exhaustion and Otto knows that I'll fight the sleeping aid if I don't have him there to write down anything I may mutter. If he's there, I won't worry that I'll come up with some solution that I can't remember when I reawaken.

October 12, 1936

Besalú, Spain

The previous night had been interesting. Commandant Philippe de Hauteclocque had paced easily around Lieutenant-colonel Roger Noiret's command tent once he arrived with the rest of their two battalions. The Lieutenant-colonel had been seated in one of the two folding chairs by his small folding table and had told him about the events of the day. Philippe smiled bitterly as Lieutenant-colonel Noiret finished recounting the battle and its aftermath.

"And there I sat with nothing to do except direct traffic while you got to have all the fun over at Besalú."

Roger had rolled his eyes. "Yeah, fun. Burning, stinking dead bodies, crying wounded, body parts strewn about, that's not my idea of fun."

"At least it wasn't our men."

"True but there were a lot of Italian casualties. It reminded me too much of the Great War. Let's hope it meant something."

"At a minimum, it meant that the three infantry divisions and the two armored regiments that headed to the front north of Girona got there in plenty of time to smash the Republican forces. That appears to have been the plan all along."

"And here I thought that Gamelin was just dawdling. Things would have been dicey if the Spanish at Besalú had managed to get to Figueres. I'm still glad that they decided to give up. God showed them the error of their ways."

"God and some stupid officers." Philippe didn't share Roger's conviction when it came to God. Then again, as long as Roger didn't start depending on God's intercession, he did trust Roger's battlefield judgment. "Have they gotten anything useful from the prisoners you brought back?"

Roger shook his head. "We're pretty sure that the Russian tanks had Russian crews. The bodies were wearing Russian uniforms and what writing we could find was in Russian, too. The Republican officers aren't talking. Even the Sargento who led the little rebellion won't tell us anything. He just keeps saying it's up to his countrymen to make their own decisions.

"I do know that the Spanish enlisted troops he was with look at him as their leader. The Italians reported that all the prisoners are doing just what he told them to do. They haven't caused any problems at all. The way it's going seems to be healing the rift between us. I think he'd make a good Warrior for Christ."

de Hauteclocque had been so surprised by Noiret's pronouncement that he had to sit down. In the year Philippe had known the Lieutenant-colonel, he had recommended exactly one person for the Warriors. Then Captain Robert Olleris had been accepted into the order and was now the executive officer of Noiret's battalion. The implication was that Lieutenant-colonel Noiret would trust this Spaniard with his life even though they had just met and were enemies.

Roger's men had found the Republican plans for their attack when they had searched the offices used by the now deposed Spanish officers. The attack through Besalú had been the extreme left flank of their ongoing attack and it didn't appear that the Republicans had gotten word of the fiasco that had transpired. His suggestion of rolling up the Republican flank had been enthusiastically endorsed by headquarters as long as he coordinated his attack with the main attack tomorrow. Philippe leaned over the table as Roger spread the Spanish maps out.

"Anyway, Gamelin is planning a general counterattack tomorrow and he wants us to push south and flank the Republicans. The attack is kicking off at seven and we're supposed to move out at nine. He's promised us air support but he's left a lot of leeway in our orders. So if you're up for it, here's what I have in mind...."

This morning, Lieutenant-colonel Roger Noiret had a cold smile on his face. Whether through planning or sheer luck, Gamelin was going to get the battle test he wanted. An infantry battalion had taken over the security for Figueres and a sizable French force was concentrating near Bàscara before attacking today. The remains of the Italian infantry battalion would secure Besalú and keep an eye on the Spanish prisoners of war.

Lieutenant-colonel Noiret checked his watch, it was five minutes until nine. Father Louis Lobau had finished his blessing of Roger's troops while the French troops of the main force had been attacking the Republican positions southwest of Orriols for almost two hours. Reports said the Spanish were beginning to give ground. His attack would begin in five minutes.

"Let's mount up and start the final check," he ordered.

Commandant de Hauteclocque blew a whistle and men who had been taking a final chance to stretch their legs began loading into their vehicles. Moments later, the engines of ninety armored fighting vehicles and dozens of trucks growled to life. Roger looked at the skies southeast of the column as Caporal André Rinck received radio checks from the rest of the battalion. A hundred meters ahead of Roger, Lieutenant Richard Levesque ordered the infantry arm of A and C Companies to begin forming a ragged skirmish line centered on the road that ran southeast from Besalú. It joined the road from Figueres several kilometers north of Girona and all of it was behind the Republican line. The skies to the southeast were full of French airplanes so there was little chance his force would be detected from the air. The only worry there was having his men misidentified by those planes. That's why every vehicle in his convoy had a French flag draped on its top. The dismounted infantry would have to take its chances.

Roger closed his eyes and bowed his head. He prayed for both his men and his foes. He had known intellectually that the Republican troops were fellow Catholics who would hopefully end up as allies.

The time he'd spent with Sargento Esperanza had driven that point home on an emotional level, but until this war was over they were enemies to be defeated. Roger opened his eyes and he surveyed his combined command with pride. This is what he and they had trained for. His smile grew a bit predatory as he looked down and watched the last few seconds tick by.

"Move out."

Caporal Rinck relayed the order while Sergent Pierre Murat put their tank in gear. The column headed into battle.

Most of an hour had gone by and the column had passed through Fares and Serinyà with little fanfare. Most of the locals had fled when the Entente forces had taken Figueres. The few who remained had been working in their fields and simply stopped to stare at the force coming down the road from Besalú. Ahead lay Melianta and Banyoles, towns that were large enough for Lieutenant-colonel Noiret to expect some resistance. It wasn't long before the skirmishing infantrymen stopped and went into crouches. Moments later, Caporal Rinck passed on their report.

"Levesque reports about thirty guns ahead. They appear to be seventy-fives and are positioned along the road firing east for effect."

Roger consulted his map for a moment. Most of the Spanish forces were engaged with Entente forces east of the road. That didn't mean that there wouldn't be reserves west of the road.

"Send go for plan alpha."

Things were going as well as they had hoped when they were coming up with plans last night. The Spanish forces hadn't noticed them and they were right where air reconnaissance had said they'd be. Lieutenant Levesque moved all of his men east of the road. They would advance on Melianta and the area north of it to cover the main column as it drove past. They would be joined by C Company of the 4e

Cuirassiers. They were supposed to link up with a French infantry division led by the 505th armored regiment which was attacking southwest from Esponellà.

Commandant de Hauteclocque would take his A Company on a raid southeast of Melianta and hit the Republican line from the rear in an attempt to panic their forces. His B Company would screen Banyoles.

Commandant Robert Olleris would take the position the enemy artillery currently occupied. His B Company would then form the reserve while simultaneously guarding and coordinating the combined artillery resources and supply trucks of the two battalions.

Lieutenant-colonel Noiret would take the Char G1s of A and C down the road towards Girona on a raid intended to disrupt the rest of the Republican forces. They would be accompanied by an ammunition truck that would trail them by half a kilometer. Speed, surprise, confusion, and God would be their armor. That and the tough skin of their tanks whose all-around protection would be pushed to the limit. They had priority on artillery support from Olleris and the Entente air force was supposed to help. The frontal attack by the Entente forces pushing south and west from Orriols should have pulled any Republican reserves forward. If everything worked right, they would capture or destroy most of the Republican forces in the area. At least, that was the plan.

Commandant Olleris saluted Roger as B Company drove past on their attack of the enemy artillery position. Roger rolled A and C Companies thirty seconds later and the rest of the column fell in behind. By the time they passed Levesque's infantry, Roger's tank was up to forty kilometers per hour. B Company had opened a two-hundred-and-fifty-meter lead on them and was halfway to the enemy guns.

Even though the road was paved, the racing tanks were sucking dust into the air and Noiret couldn't see what was happening at the front of the column. There hadn't been any news over the radio so

Roger assumed all was going well. It was another twenty endless seconds before Caporal Rinck called "Contact!" through the tank headphones. The report was followed almost immediately by a large explosion from the area south of the Spanish guns. Hopefully it would be mistaken for a lucky hit from Entente artillery or a strafing plane.

"Send it up the chain," replied Lieutenant-colonel Noiret. Their only hope of coordinating with the air force was the long radio link through Figueres. The fliers and artillerymen had been warned to avoid this road until they got the contact notification and then to be mindful that French tanks would be driving down it. Roger's biggest worry wasn't the Spanish in his way, it was mistakes by his own countrymen, a point driven home by yesterday's incident with the Italians. The dust his tanks had been kicking up was beginning to obscure the flags they'd mounted on their back decks.

Roger was crouched behind his cupola machine gun as they closed on the enemy position. The Republican artillery had fallen silent but he could still hear the staccato retort of machine guns as they approached the fight. They were barely thirty meters from Olleris' tanks when Rinck came over the headphones again.

"Clear, Sir!"

Roger smiled as he stood and replied.

"Go on phase two and add that flags should be checked to make sure they're still visible from the air."

Caporal Rinck passed the order to the rest of the command while Roger scanned the road for enemies. Commandant Olleris saluted again as Roger and the rest of their tanks rolled by his position. Roger nodded in reply, refusing to take his hands off his machine gun. Just because it was supposed to be clear didn't mean that an errant Spaniard wasn't waiting to take a shot at the exposed drivers and commanders.

It would take time for the artillery to get into position to provide any support or for the air force to get the message and begin strafing the road. For now, it was just Noiret and his thirty tanks driving down the road behind enemy lines. Lieutenants Jacques Jeannin and Francois Martin were in the lead tanks cruising side by side down the road. Roger's tank was twenty meters behind them, second in line on the east side of the road. His tank and the column equally spaced behind him had their main guns pointed about thirty degrees east of the road. The tank commanders had their cupola guns pointed even further off the line of advance. Roger spared a glance to make sure the right column was mirroring their stances.

The two columns split to go around a burning crater barely a hundred meters down the road. A dark plume was rising over it and growing by the second. It looked like an ammunition truck had been hit by one of Olleris' tanks. The crater was over fifteen meters across and at least five deep. At least the ground was firm in the area so the tanks didn't have to slow down much. Roger thought for a moment.

"Rinck, radio command and pass that column of smoke up the chain as a reference for our fliers. Maybe we can keep from getting hit by our own bombers."

"Yes, Sir!" came the barely registered reply.

Roger turned his attention back to scanning the roadside with glances down their line of advance.

The rolled on for about a minute in relative quiet. Explosions and sounds of artillery fire were clearly audible but none were in their immediate vicinity. Lieutenant-colonel Noiret had just taken a glance forward when the tanks leading the column opened up with their hull mounted machine guns. A truck fifty meters ahead of them slewed sideways and drove off the road before bursting into flames. Luckily, it didn't explode. Since it appeared to be headed southeast, it was probably a supply truck returning after having dropped off its cargo. The column rolled on.

Another minute passed before they approached the next crossroad. There didn't appear to be any artillery here but there was a collection of vehicles. Even from his position in the second tank, Roger could see what looked like radio antennae sprouting from several spots. Caporal André Rinck's radio message confirmed it.

"Jeannin reports what looks like a headquarters unit up ahead."

"A Company off road and suppressive fire. C Company advance."

Roger clung to the handles of his machine gun as his tank and the rest of those in his company slowed and jolted their way across the open fields beside the road. Jeannin's tank was the first to fire though Martin's was only a split second behind from the other side of the road. Roger's tank ground to a halt ten meters from the road. Caporal Guy Morin selected a target and fired the main gun just as a loud clang came from Jeannin's tank.

"Anti-tank gun at the crossroad! Martin and Jeannin both targeting it."

Rinck's relay of the information would keep Morin from zeroing in on the gun and let him select another target for his attention. As his company's tanks fired their second shots, Roger noticed with satisfaction that his men had followed his orders and concentrated their first shots near the road while these were further afield. No one wanted to accidentally hit one of the C Company tanks that were now approaching the enemy forces.

"One more then follow C Company."

As Morin reloaded, Lieutenant-colonel Noiret took the time to look over at Jeannin's tank. A shiny scar now decorated the side of its turret, a testament to the accuracy of the Spanish gunner as well as the armor of the Char G1. As he watched, Lieutenant Jeannin reached out and ran a hand over the dimpled armor and shook his head. When he looked up and noticed Noiret watching him, Jeannin made an elaborate show of wiping sweat off his brow and patting the big tank. A meter to the right and Jeannin wouldn't have been there.

Their tanks each fired a third round before they rolled back to the road to advance and support C Company. Commandant Henri Dubois had his tanks almost to the crossroad by this time. Their machine guns were chewing up anything that moved while their commanders and gunners looked for targets that weren't already shattered pieces of men and equipment. A quick check confirmed that there had been no casualties among his men, though Jeannin's tank was a little slow on its traverse now. The whole engagement had taken less than a minute but that was long enough.

"Report to command that surprise is blown. Tell Dubois he has the lead to the next engagement. Have Olleris bring B Company here unless de Hauteclocque needs him. Also, have everyone load out with extra rounds when the ammo truck gets here. There's no telling when our next chance to reload will be."

Ten minutes later and his men had finished their reload. Everyone had taken turns stretching their legs and getting some water. Noiret and Olleris had even grabbed a quick bite of their rations. Their men had simply stared at them in disbelief. Morin broke their silence.

"How can you eat that stuff, Sirs? It hasn't been that long since breakfast and that stuff tastes like cardboard."

Noiret looked at his executive officer with a knowing grin before answering. "When in battle, eat, drink, and pee as often as you can. You never know when your next chance will be."

His men just stared for a moment. Noiret and Olleris finished their snack and turned their backs to the road as they unbuttoned their pants. After a few shrugs, their men started wolfing down ration bars and drinking their water. Five minutes later, the column of tanks rolled south.

October 12, 1936
Gibraltar

Carmen Esperanza stopped her cleaning of Major Thomas Hawkins' quarters long enough to say a quick Hail Mary. It was her third of the morning and it wasn't even eleven yet. It had been an unusual morning and she was developing a sense of dread. As she walked to work this morning, she felt like she was being followed. She had just decided it was just nervous fears left over from last week's attack when she arrived at the Gibraltar gate. There she was greeted by Sergeant Irvin Havens but once again his usual companion at the gate, Sergeant Terry Sanders, had been absent. When Carmen asked about Sergeant Sanders, Sergeant Havens had cheerfully told her not to worry. He had been sent on an errand by the brass but would be back shortly.

The oddities continued when Carmen got to Major Hawkins' quarters. He was already fully dressed and claimed to have eaten breakfast. He let her in and almost immediately headed out the door. When Carmen looked around, there were no dirty dishes so she doubted he had actually had anything. It was almost as if he didn't want to be in the same room as her. And the only reason Carmen could come up with that Major Hawkins wouldn't want to be around her was that something had happened to Luis. So she cleaned and tidied and worried and prayed.

It seemed like it had been hours but it was only half past ten when Carmen was surprised by the return of Major Hawkins. She had just run his sheets through the ringer and was going out to hang them up on the clothes line when he met her at the door.

Major Hawkins had a look on his face that convinced Carmen he had news of Luis and it wasn't good. He held the door open for her and said, "Please come and see me inside when you're done."

Carmen knew she wouldn't be able to keep a tremble out of her voice if she replied so she simply nodded and hurried out to the clothesline. She probably set a record for hanging up the sheets while also praying. She knew she didn't do a very good job of it and hoped they wouldn't blow off the line in the persistent Gibraltar breeze.

When Carmen opened the door to Major Hawkins' quarters, she found him standing in his living room with both hands behind his back. He waved her towards one of the chairs.

"Please take a seat, Mrs. Esperanza."

Carmen did and closed her eyes. She said one more silent prayer and inhaled deeply before opening them and looking up at the Major with a nod.

He nodded back before beginning.

"First and foremost, we don't know that anything has happened to your husband."

Carmen released the breath she hadn't realized she was holding and thanked God that there was still a chance that Luis would come home to her.

"If you remember, Sargento Esperanza's unit had been sent to Besalú."

Carmen inhaled sharply. Did he think she was likely to forget where her husband was? Calmly, she thought to herself and nodded once again.

"Our intelligence says they launched an attack to clear some Italians out of their way yesterday. We have a man about eight or nine miles north of Gerona in town called Banyoles. He saw your husband's unit along with about sixty tanks head to Besalú on Saturday. The problem is that he just reported seeing French tanks heading south on the Besalú – Gerona road. He knows they aren't friendly because they shot up a Republican position that was just east of Banyoles. Some of the tanks and infantry turned off the road and are advancing on the town."

Carmen was confused. Major Hawkins seemed awfully worried even though he said they didn't know anything had happened to Luis.

She had taken to wearing her rosary beads on her left wrist. Now she took them off and began to fidget with them.

"I don't understand, Sir. If you don't have any news about Luis, why are you so worried?"

Major Hawkins nodded his head as he realized that Carmen didn't understand what he was trying to tell her.

"I'm sorry, Mrs. Esperanza. We know your husband's unit marched to Besalú on Saturday. We know that his unit was supposed to be involved in an attack from Besalú yesterday. There are French tanks coming from Besalú today. We do not know what happened to his unit but we don't believe it is in or around Besalú any longer."

Carmen looked thoughtful for a moment before replying.

"So, if the French are coming from Besalú and that's where Luis' unit was, they would have fought. And if your man reported French tanks heading south from Besalú, then Luis' unit lost that fight."

"Exactly, ma'am."

Carmen closed her eyes for another quick prayer before continuing.

"Is it possible that his unit withdrew from the fight in a direction other than towards Gerona?"

"It's not likely, ma'am. All of their food and ammunition was coming to them through Gerona so they would have done their best to defend the road to it."

Carmen couldn't keep a slight tremble out of her voice.

"So... what you are saying is that you believe that Luis has either been killed or captured. Yes?"

"Yes, ma'am. And we won't be getting any updates for a while since our man had to abandon his location. We wanted to let you know as soon as possible. Is there anything I can do?"

Carmen was still fidgeting with her rosary and closed her eyes for another quick prayer. She then stood, put the rosary back around her wrist and straightened her dress.

"Thank you for telling me, Sir. Please let me know if you get any more information and if you get a chance, Mrs. Sanchez would dearly love some more of the candied apricots."

Carmen then headed back outside to check the sheets while Major Hawkins stared after her in hope and fear.

October 12, 1936

East of Figueres, Spain

Capitano Guido Nobili pulled the nose of his plane up and eased the stick to the right. The M.S. 406 lumbered through the barrel roll and Guido lost more altitude than he was used to losing in his CR.32. He felt like a falcon when he flew his CR.32, nimble and deadly. The French plane he was flying now felt more like a pig with wings. Okay, maybe it wasn't that bad but it would definitely take some time before the plane felt like an extension of himself. And time was something the Capitano didn't have.

Sergente Giovanni Battista had been very definite, Guido's airplane wouldn't be flight ready for days. The Sergente's plaintive tone as he listed off the damage done to the CR.32 had matched the pain Nobili felt for it. All of the squadron's surviving planes were full of holes. Capitano Nobili was grounded at just the time his soul cried for vengeance on those who'd killed his friends and so abused his plane.

Last night the remains of the squadron had imbibed more than a bit of anything alcoholic they could find. Their friends were dead and their planes were too. Only Guido had moderated his drinking. He'd stayed out as late as the rest of his men but when they staggered back to their bunks to pass out into alcoholic oblivion, Guido began writing the letters to his lost comrades' kin. Writing the letters had renewed his anger and his sleep had been elusive and fitful. That was when he'd come up with his plan.

The French squadron based here at Figueres had suffered far less damage. Eight of their planes hadn't been hit at all, though the French pilots were worn and needed a break. They'd only gotten back from the air battle over Girona about a half an hour earlier. Guido had talked with Colonel Jacob Sarbone, the Frenchman in charge of flight operations, and convinced the Colonel to let him fly one of the French planes. The one condition had been that Capitano Nobili stay out of combat. Sarbone had almost made Guido fly without any ammo but Guido convinced him that it might be nice to have some if any of the Spanish fliers appeared in the skies over Figueres.

That's how Capitano Guido Nobili found himself testing the capabilities of this unfamiliar plane as he "accidentally" drifted southwest towards the air battle over Girona. He'd had to fly east to convince Sarbone that he was going to stay out of the fight in the unfamiliar plane. Unfortunately, every maneuver he tested seemed to take him closer to what was left of the air battle. They also cost him more altitude than he was used to losing in his CR.32. That's why he found himself dropping like a stone towards the Spanish countryside. Well, that and trying to cross himself while flying the M.S. 406 upside down.

He was just north of a small fishing town named Sant Pere Pescador when he started another barrel roll. Like all fighter pilots, he had been trained to keep an eye on his surroundings so he was halfway through the maneuver when he spotted the column of vehicles on the road headed into the town. Fighter pilots are expected to have keen eyesight and Guido was no exception so he also noticed the strange flags flying from one of the vehicles. It took his brain a moment to realize it was the Papal flag. He was flying above the Pope and could clearly see his Holiness staring up at the French plane. Guido crossed himself and started to say a prayer before he noticed that the Pope was getting larger and larger. The devout catholic yanked the control stick with one hand while his other slammed the throttle forward. His right ankle ached as he tried to push the rudder pedal through the floor. Thoughts of an eternity in Hell for killing the Pope raced through his mind as he screamed a plea to God for help and the big French plane continued to lose altitude.

It wasn't really that close, at least that's what Guido kept telling himself. There had been at least fifteen meters of clearance. Everything was fine. Just because when he circled back, he saw men getting off a pile that had the much-rumpled Pope at its bottom didn't mean anything.

All thoughts of getting back into the fight had fled his mind as Guido headed northeast before he turned back to the west and Figueres. He didn't want anyone to know where he'd come from if there were reports of the incident. Guido decided he'd had enough flying for now. Colonel Sarbone might not be able to prove it was Guido if he got back to Figueres quickly enough and the incident was reported. Guido pushed the French plane for all it was worth and worried all the way back.

After he landed, Guido almost jogged to Sarbone's office. All seemed quiet when he got there so he breathed a sigh of relief. He was about to leave when Colonel Sarbone came out of his office.

"Ah, Capitano Nobili, how was your flight? I didn't expect you back for another half an hour or so."

"It was very nice, Sir. Your 406 has better speed and power than my 32 but I still prefer the agility of my plane."

"You didn't have any problems while you were out, did you?" Sarbone asked with a slight smirk on his face.

Guido kept his best poker face in place as he replied, "No, Sir. I just flew over to Roses and practiced a few dog fighting maneuvers to get a better feel for the plane."

Sarbone nodded his head and started to turn back towards his office. Guido had just started to relax when Sarbone's turn stopped and the base commander turned back to Guido.

"I'm glad to hear that. I was worried that you might try to get back into the air battle around Girona."

"No, Sir. That may have crossed my mind but your orders were pretty explicit against me doing so."

"Good. I wouldn't want you to get into any trouble." Sarbone turned back to his office and took a step in its direction as Guido relaxed in relief. Then the French Commandant stopped again and Guido tensed once more.

Without turning, Sarbone said, "I guess it's a good thing I didn't order you to NOT scare the heck out of the Pope."

Guido's wide-eyed look of horror was wasted on the back of his base commander as the chuckling Sarbone went back into his office and closed the door.

October 12, 1936
40 miles east of Barcelona, Spain

Vice Admiral Sir Geoffrey Blake was pacing back and forth in the flag bridge of the *Marlborough*. It looked like his assessment of the Entente plan had been right on the mark. The Republican troops were out in the open and getting hammered.

He was supposed to be on another arms run to the guerrillas based in Roses but that wasn't happening. The Italians were in the area in force both on the ground and at sea. Sir Geoffrey wasn't surprised by that considering that the Pope appeared to be in the area. Scouts from the *Ark Royal* had spotted the papal yacht berthed at Roses and not far off the coast was a good chunk of the Entente navy. Four Italian battle ships had been joined by the unmistakable *Richelieu* and *Jean Bart*. Two quadruple turrets up front made them stand out. Add in eight cruisers and a dozen destroyers and you had a nice little fleet.

Vice Admiral Blake was confident that his force could make a mess of the French and Italians but his battlecruisers didn't have the armor for a stand-up fight. It would be messy on both sides. That and he was under orders to avoid a fight. Eakes and the *Firedrake* were loaded up with another bunch of small arms and explosives that might cause some damage, but there wasn't anything that would help the Republicans in a real fight. Sir Geoffrey turned to Commodore John Moore who had been watching the Vice Admiral pace since news of the Entente counterattack had reached them twenty minutes ago.

"Moore, check to see if we could arrange a meeting with a Spanish fishing boat based out of one of the ports southeast of Girona."

"Lieutenant Caldwell, contact Gib intelligence to see if we have any smuggling contacts southeast of Girona and get some detailed maps of that coastline up here."

Lieutenant Travis Caldwell's "Aye, Sir" was lost to Sir Geoffrey as he stopped his pacing to stare northwest towards the Spanish coast.

Five minutes later, Lieutenant Caldwell was back with the detailed set of maps. He handed one end to Commodore Moore and unrolled the map for their perusal.

"Gib says we've got contacts at both Palamós and Calella. They'd like to know what you have in mind, Sir."

Sir Geoffrey looked over the map for a few seconds and seemed to weigh options before responding.

"I want to offload the *Firedrake's* cargo where it will do some good and there's no way we're getting to Roses to do what's scheduled. If I'm right and the Republicans have walked into an Entente trap, then I think the front line is going to be at Barcelona in no time. The stuff we're delivering is only really useful for ambushes and sabotage but I think the locals in either of those ports are going to want that kind of equipment all too soon. So why not go ahead and deliver it where it will do some good.

"I think Calella is a better bet. There's better access to both of the main roads that head southwest from Girona and they can get to the roads without going through one of the larger towns in the area."

Sir Geoffrey stopped and looked at Commodore Moore for his opinion. Commodore Moore looked at the map so he could follow the Vice Admiral's train of thought and assess the plans merits.

"Well, Sir, if the front does collapse that badly then I think you're right about dropping off the payload and where it should go. My question is whether either Gib or the Spanish will be willing to admit the possibility and allow us to make the delivery."

"True, but we aren't going to deliver it to Roses so we either drop it off here or cart it home. I doubt we'll be able to get anything arranged before tonight and we should know more about how things are developing by then. Let's sell it as a contingency plan even if it's what we expect to do."

Commodore Moore thought for a moment before giving a firm nod of agreement and turning to the young Lieutenant.

"Got it, Sir. I'll give 'em my best pitch and call you in if I need help." Lieutenant Caldwell scurried off to the radio room.

October 12, 1936
The Chancellery, Berlin, Germany
I used to look forward to Mondays. I was recharged from the weekend and looked forward to the possibilities of the new week. Today was different. So many events shaping the world are beyond my influence and I feel like I'm not having much of an impact on those that aren't. Well, at least not the way I hoped.

News of the Republican counterattack had been in the newspapers and on the radio. To both parliament and the League of Nations, this meant that things would take care of themselves in Spain and there was no need for Germany to do anything. I hope they're right. At least I should be able to make them pay attention if I'm right about the Entente's plans. The dozen seventy-five-millimeter artillery pieces and the ammunition of our first aid shipment should get to Barcelona by Thursday. I hope it gets there in time to do some good.

The Reichsmarine and Reichswehr are both confident they could deal with any threat from the French or Italians and they're probably right. At least for now. Things might be a bit dicey if the reports we're getting on the new French panzers and planes are right. I still can't tell whether Generalfeldmarschall Werner von Blomberg thinks the reports are credible. I know he's got men looking at ways to deal with the possibility but getting him to actually implement those ideas will be a tough sell. If the Republican counterattack succeeds, then the reports were overblown. If it fails, then they're probably just exaggerations by face-saving Spaniards.

Regardless, the French are pushing forward with new equipment and parliament, supported by von Blomberg, thinks the equipment we have will do the job. The Social Democrat Party is pushing for more reform issues and wants any money they can squeeze out of the budget spent on their pet projects. Sometimes I wish Wilhelm hadn't relinquished most of his power. At least then there would only be one person I had to convince. Sigh.... At least they were willing to buy the naval and army expansions as projects that benefited the workers by creating stable, good-paying jobs.

Britain and the Soviets seemed to be concerned with what's going on in Spain. Or at least they're willing to meddle to further their own agendas. Both are working for a Spain that follows their ideology. I'd be happy if it stayed a mess for a few years. That would keep it from joining either block and shifting the balance of power. Hopefully the fighting will drag on long enough for the League to get a response organized. Spain joining the League would probably help stabilize things in the area. If it doesn't, maybe a protracted fight will keep them from having any post-war impact on international events for a decade or two.

A knock on the door interrupts my musings. I do a quick job of straightening the mess of papers and charts on my desk before answering.

"Come in."

Oberst Ernst Weber opens the door. I can see the sheaf of papers clutched in his right hand and the almost triumphal grin on his face. It looks like things are happening in Spain. He closes the door behind him and obeys my wave to have a seat. After he's settled, he looks at me expectantly. I refuse to ask. I just give him my best "get on with it" look which earns me a sigh of resignation. He knows I'm tired so he just launches into his summation of the reports in his hands.

"The Entente counterattack has begun and the Republican forces are getting slaughtered. Our agents in Gerona say that barely a third of the Republican planes that left airbases in the area have returned. The Republicans had a division in reserve there yesterday but it moved to the front last night. The only thing that's come back since then has been a constant stream of ambulances that were overflowing. Then at about half past ten this morning, the ambulances stopped.

"Several empty ambulances returned about eleven and reported that there were French panzers blocking the road about four kilometers north of Girona. There was a battle raging on the north side of the French position but a couple of the panzers were facing Girona and the ambulances turned around and ran for it. Their lead driver said he got close enough to the French to be able to see one of them making shooing motions with his hand. The driver decided it was good advice.

"The Republicans are trying to scrape together a relief force but they've already committed their reserves. By eleven-thirty the Spanish had less than a hundred men, armed mostly with pistols assembled.

Our agents are using their discretion and pulling back to at least Sils and may end up all the way back at Barcelona." Oberst Weber winds down with a shrug.

"So much for the hope that it wasn't a French trap."

Weber shrugs with a sour look on his face. "I know, but the threat to their power base was bad enough that the Republicans had to react even if they knew it was a trap."

"We need to get a message to our aid shipments to make sure they don't deliver our guns and themselves into Entente hands."

Weber picks a pencil up off of my desk and jots a note on his papers before looking back up at me. "Anything else?"

"Yes. Check with Generalleutnant Liese over at Heeres-waffenamt to see how the special projects are coming along. I know Liese's reports are filtered by von Blomberg, so find out if Research has any possibilities that the commander of the Reichswehr isn't passing along."

Weber goes back to writing while I try to find the report that disappeared on my desk when I "straightened it up." I find it while he's still writing so I get to keep my mystique of organization for another day.

"I'll need a...," Weber begins as he finishes his note and looks up to see me holding out the copy of the research projects I received from von Blomberg. He smiles as he reaches for it. "Thanks, Sir. Anything else?"

I scratch my head and think for a moment before replying. "Set up a meeting with the party leaders of parliament for tomorrow afternoon if they can, or Wednesday morning at the latest. I don't think I'll be able to convince them to go for any major changes just yet, but at least I can point out the cliff we seem to be headed for.

"I also want a report of the resources we ran short of during the Great War and essential items that we currently import, price trends, and who we get them from. We'll need to compare that to what we're currently stockpiling and get projected war use rates for it all from the Reichswehr.

"I've got my copy of the budget so I'll try to find money I can get parliament to agree to re-appropriate. Won't that be fun. Maybe they'll pay attention if things go badly enough in Spain."

I finally stop babbling and look up at Weber, who's still furiously writing. It's another couple of seconds before he looks up at me with a silly grin on his face.

"Anything else? I'm sure you can squeeze in a few minutes to handle world hunger or bringing harmony to the world's religions."

I startle myself by actually laughing.

"I know. That's a bit of a pile of work and I don't expect to have all the answers tomorrow but I think we need to start really planning for the next war. Unlike the last one, there are at least five possible sides for the next one."

The startled look on Weber's face shows he hadn't thought about it in those terms. All he says is "I'll get right on it, Sir" before taking his leave to do my bidding.

I'll need to get Edna to set up meetings with the various ambassadors next week to see what can be worked out. If the world community stays as fractured as it currently is, factions may get picked off before they can offer effective opposition to the Entente's aggressive policies. I'll also need to get von Blomburg to tell me how the Reichswehr would fight each of the other alliances. If our army sees a weakness, there's a good chance the French see it too.

October 12, 1936
Four kilometers north of Girona, Spain

Lieutenant-colonel Roger Noiret wiped dirt and blood off his face before he went to sit back in his seat in his tank's cupola. He was exhausted. It was just after three in the afternoon. That meant he and his men had been here for less than five hours but it felt like they'd been here for days.

It had been ten twenty when they got to the juncture where the roads from Besalú and Figueres met. There had been an artillery battery firing like mad to the northeast but no one was watching the northwest from which the French tanks were approaching. It had been another slaughter. Roger had wondered why easy victories always left a bad taste in your mouth. The Republicans troops that hadn't fled were charred pieces of meat strewn about the crossroads.

Lieutenant-colonel Noiret had spread his tanks out fifteen meters apart across the road to Girona, ten to a side facing to the north. Two platoons from A Company were on the west side of the road while two from C Company took the east. The flank tanks were about five meters back and canted off to the sides. The tanks of third platoon from each company were fifty meters south of the main line and about thirty meters apart. Roger's tank and the tank of Commandant Henri Dubois were nearest the road. These faced south so the drivers and radiomen could keep an eye out for any relief force coming up the road. The Spanish could simply go around him if they wanted to, but retreating troops don't always do rational things, especially when it looks like their line of retreat is blocked.

While Roger's tank crews had done their best to improve their positions before anyone showed up, Sergent Claude Richard had his men distributing ammo from the supply truck and setting up the two machine guns they'd brought with them. Roger had them position the guns on either side of the road between the command tanks. It was the most protected position Roger could come up with since the truck crew refused to head back to the rest of the battalion. They left the now empty truck sitting in the middle of the formation on the road. Roger had to smile when one of the first things Sergent Richard and his men did was set up the portable radio and attach the flag to the antenna. The tricolors flapped lazily in the light breeze, announcing to one and all just who owned this particular piece of ground.

Barely five minutes had passed before several trucks came down the road headed south towards Girona. The tank crews scrambled to man their guns as the vehicles approached. They looked like ambulances so Roger's men had held their fire. The lead truck stopped about two hundred meters away and one of its men got out with binoculars. Lieutenant Jacques Jeannin had stood up in his cupola and made a beckoning gesture. He had seemed disappointed when the Spaniard had climbed back in his truck and they beat a hasty retreat. The bravado caused a bit of joking among the men as they found a way to release some of their nervous energy.

Fifteen minutes were spent coordinating their position with headquarters via Commandant Robert Olleris. Roger had Olleris fire several artillery shots to zero in the areas on both sides of their position. The ranging shots on the northern side broke up a group of Republican infantry that had been slowly gathering. Since his communications were dicey, Roger set up a "don't shoot" check in with Olleris. If Olleris didn't receive a call every ten minutes, he was to assume Noiret's force was under attack and fire for effect with three quarters of his fire directed north of their position and the remainder to the south.

Roger's radio man got his chance to show the officers how it was done while the ranging shots were landing on the north side of the position. This time the trucks were coming north from Girona and Caporal André Rinck had stood through his hatch and made shooing motions at the Spaniards. Once again, the trucks were ambulances that beat a hasty retreat. Lieutenant Jeaninn had saluted the Caporal while the rest of the group had laughed.

Things were quiet until almost eleven thirty. Roger was happy to see that his men were taking his advice on food, drink, and relief while they waited. Roger was facing south scanning for any signs of a relief force coming from Girona when he received Jeannin's report of infantry building to the north. He gave the order and Caporal Guy

Morin began spinning their turret to face north just as the bullets started to fly.

The Republicans had set up a couple of heavy machine guns that were laying down suppressive fire while their infantry advanced. They also seemed to have a few mortars with them but no actual artillery. The French tanks responded quickly and the attack lasted for less than two minutes. That it lasted that long was a testament to the courage of the Spaniards. Roger had seen some ugly sights in the Great War but the sight that greeted him surpassed them all. Thirty seventy-five-millimeter guns and fifty machine guns on a such a narrow front had been devastating. There were hundreds of bodies littering the ground between the Republican forces and his tanks. The cries of the wounded were plainly audible. A quick check found that his men hadn't even been scratched.

During the short engagement, Roger had discovered two things about the Char G1 that didn't make him happy. Twice during the quick, sharp action he had issued orders to the rest of his command. Both times he'd watched the machine guns of his tanks fall silent as the radio operators and commanders received and responded to the orders. The second time had allowed a squad of attacking infantry to get within a hundred meters of his line. He'd also watched as Morin, his normally quick-firing gunner, had quickly slowed the pace of his shots. It wasn't that he was tired, it was that after he loaded a shell, he had to reassess the battlefield to determine where to shoot. The previous set-piece engagements hadn't shown these weaknesses.

While musing about these problems, Lieutenant-colonel Noiret thought about Sargento Primero Luis Esperanza. The Spanish soldiers weren't the Entente's real enemy and they might end up being their allies. He climbed out of his cupola to grab the French flag attached to the back deck of his tank. He folded it as he returned to his seat.

"Rinck, tell Dubois that he's in charge until we get back. And have everyone restock on ammo while it's quiet."

"Are we going somewhere, Sir?"

"North."

Caporal Rinck had hesitated for only a moment before relaying the message and passing Dubois' acknowledgment back to Roger.

"Alright, Murat, take us north on the road, nice and easy. Let's see if we can't talk to these gentlemen."

Sergent Pierre Murat wasn't sure what his commander's plan was but he knew better than to question it. He eased the Char G1 out of its position and headed toward the Republican forces they'd been shooting at mere moments before as Caporal Morin spun the turret back around to line up with their direction of movement.

Roger had folded the French flag so that only the white stripe was visible. He then stood in his cupola holding the white flag of truce over his head as his tank approached the Spanish forces. He also prayed.

The tank was about fifty meters from the lead Republican infantry when Roger heard a whuff and the telltale whistling of in inbound mortar round. He waved the white flag as he crouched down and yelled at his own men not to return fire. The mortar round landed a few meters to the side of the tank. Most but not all of the blast was absorbed by the tanks armor. Something banged off his helmet and made Roger see stars so it was an extra second or two before he realized that something had also hit him in the left shoulder. The ringing in Roger's ears was quickly replaced by yelling from both inside and outside the tank.

As Roger's eyes refocused, he found Morin doing his best to help him from inside the turret while several Spaniards charged the tank. He tried to squeeze the trigger for his machine gun but found that his right hand was holding the now bloody flag against his left shoulder. Strangely, his left arm didn't seem to want to do his bidding either. It took him another moment to figure out that the reason Rinck wasn't defending the tank with his machine gun was that the charging Spaniards had red crosses on their helmets and medical kits in their hands.

Roger had his wits back under control by the time the Spanish corpsmen arrived and swarmed up the side of the tank. Their quick assessment was that the shoulder wound would need a few stitches and Roger's helmet had saved him from any serious head trauma. Roger found that there was a Republican officer standing beside his tank when the medics finally quit fussing over him.

When he had Roger's attention, he spoke. "My apologies for the violation of the flag of truce. I am Comandante Ibañez. What can I do for you?"

Roger closed his eyes for a moment and said a quick prayer before replying. "I offer a truce while you tend to your injured men in the field. Ambulances will be allowed to proceed to Girona if they stop and let us make sure they aren't carrying guns with them. There's no need for good men to die uselessly today."

The Spanish officer stood still for a moment as he digested the offer of compassion from his enemy. He then came to rigid attention and saluted, a gesture Roger did his best to return. "Thank you, Sir!" was all he said before he turned and jogged back towards his own men.

Roger sat heavily in his seat and called down to his crew, "Okay, Murat. Take us back to our side."

Murat spun the tank slowly around and headed south towards their fellow Frenchmen as Roger had Caporal Rinck relay the deal to the rest of his command. Sergent Claude Richard relayed the information up the chain of command with instructions to suspend any bombing or strafing runs until further notice. The check-ins every ten minutes would continue just in case things went bad.

It was almost noon when the first Spanish ambulances rolled south through the French line. Sergent Richard and his men did quick checks for weapons before the loads of wounded were allowed on their way. Minutes later, several ambulances approached from the south with requests to go pick up casualties. Roger watched all of this through a pounding headache as his men looked on with concern. He even dozed for a few minutes. That lasted until he was awakened to find a Spanish medic leaned over him with a concerned look on his face. Roger refused an ampule of morphine so a bottle of sangria was requisitioned from one of the ambulances and Roger was told to drink small amounts of it to help with the pain. Blood was soaking through his shoulder bandage and the young corpsman decided it needed to be stitched up then and there. Somehow almost half of the bottle of sangria disappeared in the process and Roger went back to sleep in his cupola.

He was awakened again at just after two. The Spanish officer he'd talked with earlier was approaching his position and waving a white flag. Roger did his best to look presentable although he found it hard to do so with his left sleeve torn from his uniform and a bandage rather than a helmet on his head. He had started to climb down from his perch atop his tank before realizing that Comandante Ibañez was talking to him.

"Please, Sir, stay where you are. We have done enough to dishonor ourselves when you were injured under a flag of truce."

His French was a bit muddled but that could have been the bandage on Roger's head. Roger sat back down before replying. "What can I do for you?"

The Republican officer bowed his head and replied, "More of my countrymen are streaming in. The front line is disintegrating and we are beaten. I ask for terms of surrender."

Despite his abused condition, Roger stood and came to attention, snapping off a parade ground salute.

"I'll be happy to accept your surrender, Sir. I'm not really sure what I can do with your men but I will report it to my headquarters so we can try to avoid any more killing. If you could wait just a moment."

Ibañez nodded and watched Roger carefully climb down from his tank and head over to the mobile radio that Sergent Richard and his crew had set up. It was a few minutes before Roger came back. As he approached his tank, he called for Caporal Morin to bring him his Bible from under his cupola seat. Then he turned to Ibañez with a hard look in his eyes.

"I have talked with General Gamelin and he is happy to accept your surrender. Unfortunately, we do not have the men or facilities to deal with the surrender of so many prisoners."

Ibañez' face went pale and he swallowed hard when Roger paused.

"I proposed a solution that General Gamelin is willing to agree to IF I believe it will be honored. Your men are to approach with their guns on their shoulders, muzzles down. One of my men will remove their weapons. Your men will then advance and swear on the Bible that they will no longer participate in this conflict and will accept the government that ends up in charge. They will then be allowed to proceed down the road to Girona."

It took Comandante Ibañez a moment to understand. "We are being released?"

"You are being paroled. Your men will swear on their souls and be allowed to go home. It will be up to you to honor these terms but you have to know that there are spies all over this country reporting what's going on to their governments. We will find out if it appears that your men are violating their paroles. The repercussions will be severe if they do. We do not want your countrymen dead or your country consumed in a guerrilla war. We are here to end the bloodshed."

The Republican officer stood very still for a moment before replying. "It is the duty of every soldier to fight and if captured, to try to escape to return to the fight. Your proposal removes that as an option."

Roger nodded. "The other options are worse. We could accept your surrender and hand your men over to the Nationalists where they will probably be at best, starved and beaten. Or, we could reject your surrender and your men's deaths would at least be quicker. Neither is what General Gamelin nor I want."

The Spanish officer thought for a moment before coming to attention and saluting. After Roger returned the salute, he dropped his hand.

"These terms are acceptable to me but because of the oath, I cannot speak for my men. I will tell them the terms, and those that agree will come forward and follow your directions. The rest will be on their own."

"That's the best we can hope for, Sir. Good luck."

Ibañez headed back towards his countrymen and a stream of Republican soldiers began heading towards the Frenchmen. Two more bibles were found among the detachment and Roger, Sergent Richard, and Lieutenant Jeannin stood by the side of the road as the Spaniards placed their hands on the bibles and gave their oaths. Sergent Richard's men were busily divesting the arriving soldiers of their guns and tossing them onto ever expanding piles. Within five minutes the Spaniards were simply going to the piles to drop off their weapons while Richard's men looked over those lined up to give their oaths. All the while, Commandant Henri Dubois and the rest of the Frenchmen kept station at their weapons in case of any trouble.

Comandante Ibañez had been the first to lay his hand on Roger's Bible and say, "I swear I will not take up arms again in this war, nor will I ever take up arms against the government of Spain." Ibañez had made four copies of the oath and he and three other Spanish officers coached their soldiers through their oaths. Several chaplains were among those surrendering. They took positions with the Frenchmen to accept the oaths of their countrymen. The third one took Roger's place and sent him to rest.

The rumbling noise of the steadily approaching battle that had been building through the afternoon abruptly ceased at three thirty and Roger drifted into oblivion once more. He slept through the minor panic caused by a squadron of French fighters flying low over the Spanish lined up to surrender. He managed to sleep through three different medics checking on his condition. He also slept through his men rigging a little shelter to keep the afternoon sun off him. It was almost five when he was shaken awake by Caporal Morin.

"Sorry, Sir, but I need to take a leak."

Roger simply nodded and climbed out of the cupola so his gunner could go relieve himself. There was a bit of confusion as the slightly groggy Lieutenant-colonel stood and found himself enveloped by the shade his men had built for him. There was a bit of laughter and even Roger joined in after a moment. He got down from the tank and walked around a bit to clear the cobwebs from his mind. His headache was down to just annoying and his left shoulder still throbbed but it wasn't too bad. He surveyed the area and found that Jeannin and Richard had also been relieved by Spanish priests. Commandant Henri Dubois ran over and snapped off a grinning salute.

"Feeling better, Sir?"

"Better? Yes. Good? No. What's the situation?"

"There's been a local ceasefire since three-thirty. We've been paroling the Spaniards as fast as we can with the help of their priests. We've gotten several reports from the ambulance drivers headed north that the brass in Girona is having a fit since their men are refusing to pick up weapons and get back into the fight. Comandante Ibañez and one of the priests headed south after that was first reported. General Gamelin sent a 'Well done' and is sending an infantry battalion to relieve us. They should be here in about half an hour. Olleris and de Hauteclocque say they've got about twenty dead and fifty wounded between them. One of the SOMUAs was taken out by an anti-tank gun. That's about it."

"Thanks for keeping an eye on things, Dubois. There hasn't been any trouble from the Spanish?"

"No, Sir. If anything, they seem to be in awe of you, Sir. I noticed a number of their soldiers talking and pointing at you as they passed through. I asked one of the priests and he said that the tale of the French commander who had been shot at and injured while under a flag of truce and still offered generous terms to his foes is spreading faster than gossip of where to find friendly women."

Roger rolled his eyes and started to shake his head before deciding that was a bad idea.

"Sorry, Sir. But I think the tale will do as much to get the Spanish to keep their oaths as swearing on the Bible will. With all of the mess that's going on in their country, your act of honor and kindness is something they will probably cling to."

Roger sighed. "Whatever the reason, I'll be happy as long as they do keep their word."

"Morin is back in the tank. I think you should get something to eat and drink and then go sit back down, Sir. You're still looking a bit pale."

Roger's sense of duty warred with his intellectual appraisal of his subordinate's suggestion. Common sense won out.

"Carry on then."

October 12, 1936

La Linea, Spain

Carmen Esperanza made her last turn for home in a fog. She was worried about Luis and the rumors that something bad had happened to the Republican forces near Girona. There hadn't been any news in Gibraltar, but she'd passed several groups of people on the way home who were talking about the French counterattack and heavy fighting. Most said that things were going badly for the government's forces and the jovial mood of the few Nationalist troops patrolling the streets seemed to confirm it.

Carmen stopped and worked to mentally pull herself together. If she got home like this, Carlos would catch her mood and things would spiral downward. She prayed for a good thirty seconds before straightening her shoulders and continuing her walk home. She waved at Mrs. Sanchez as she went by. Isabella Sanchez hadn't missed Carmen's pause on her walk home.

"Is everything okay, Carmen?" she called.

"It's fine, Mrs. Sanchez. Just a trying day at work."

Mrs. Sanchez just looked at Carmen for a moment, making sure the younger woman knew her story wasn't believed.

"If you're sure that's all it is, then okay. Let me know if there's anything I can do."

Carmen nodded her thanks and continued home.

Carmen was two doors down and headed towards her front door when Mrs. Sanchez quietly said, "Bring him here, Amber."

The lethargic-looking dog sprang down the stairs and galloped down the street to a man who had been a good hundred meters behind Carmen. She stopped in front of him and gave a single low throaty woof.

The man stopped and nothing happened for a few seconds. Amber gave a menacing growl and Mrs. Sanchez stood up from her rocker. She tilted her head to the left as she stared at the man and waved her hand as if commanding him to come forward.

The young man paused briefly then gave a shrug and began to make his way across the street. Amber followed close behind him as he approached the porch. He could have almost passed for one of the locals but his complexion was too light and his back too straight. Mrs. Sanchez sat back down as he approached the bottom of the stairs. His eyes seemed to be surveying the area though they did linger on the candied apricots next to her rocker.

"Ma'am." His accent was a little off, too.

"You wanta tell me why a Brit is in Spain and following Miss Esperanza around?"

The young man seemed chagrined but still smiled.

"Orders, ma'am. She's well liked at Gib and we know she's been having some issues with some of her neighbors."

"Ain't her neighbors that have been bothering her."

"Yes, ma'am. That's why we keep an eye on her until she gets here."

Mrs. Sanchez looked him over for a few moments as the young man stood rock still. She clucked her tongue and Amber bounded up the steps to resume her position at their top.

"That's fine then."

There was a hint of a twitch from him as she added, "And thank you for the apricots."

He bobbed his head before wishing her a good evening and turning to walk down the road.

Mrs. Sanchez sat back down in her rocker and picked up one of the treats with a self-satisfied smile.

October 12, 1936
Figueres, Spain

Capitano Guido Nobili was finally flying a mission in one of the French M.S. 406s. The French pilots were worn out from flying three missions earlier in the day so Colonel Jacob Sarbone, head of operations at the Figueres airbase, had allowed the Italians to take the French planes on a mission. The fact that the Republican air force had been driven from the skies and there was a ceasefire over most of the battlefield probably had something to do with his decision, too. It also probably meant that the Pope wouldn't be in the area of their patrol.

Commandant Juin's men weren't that keen about the Italians taking their planes into harm's way but Colonel Sarbone had overruled their objections. They were still a bit sulky but it helped that all of Guido's men had already flown a 406 when they'd been delayed at Toulon. It also helped that Guido was Italy's first ace since the Great War.

Guido was just happy to be in the air again. While his men were still feeling out the French planes, Guido was glad to be doing anything to take his mind off the last twenty-four hours. Four of his men, his friends, were dead. While his remaining men had passed out into alcoholic oblivion, Guido had written the letters to his lost comrades' kin. Writing the letters had renewed his anger and his sleep had been elusive and fitful. He'd tried to find more vengeance this morning while his men slept off last night's salutation to their fallen brothers, but almost crashing into the Pope had brought the world back into a sharp focus.

After he got back to Figueres, Guido rounded up his men and made sure they ate and were sober enough to do what they kept asking him to do for them. They wanted back in the air. They wanted to do almost anything other than sit around and dwell on their lost friends. Sottotenente Corrado Ricci had mostly wanted to puke his guts out. Ricci's broken arm would keep him from flying for weeks so he'd tried to do the drinking for himself and all four of their dead brothers. While his men ate, showered, and prepared themselves mentally, Guido had braced himself and plead their case to Colonel Sarbone. Colonel Sarbone had mostly smirked as he kept denying Guido's arguments. That stopped after Sarbone was given a message by his clerk. Then Sarbone had agreed with a smile. What damage could the Italian fliers do with a temporary ceasefire over most of the battlefield.

Capitano Nobili's men had been excited to get back into the fight until Guido told them about the ceasefire. The pilots had grumbled a bit before Guido pointed out that their orders allowed them to shoot at any Spanish planes they encountered and that their patrol area now extended fifteen kilometers south of Girona. That put them halfway to Barcelona with the chance of running into fresh Republican fliers.

That had been a forlorn hope. There was almost nothing else in the sky. The only thing they'd encountered was a squadron from the French bases north of the Pyrenees. They were only remarkable because they were flying the brand-new Dewoitine D.520. Guido had heard a little about them but this was the first time he'd actually gotten to see them. Guido knew the M.S. 406 he was flying was more than a hundred kilometers per hour faster than his beloved CR.32 but the new French planes passed them like they were standing still. In their brief encounter, Guido also noticed that the 520 appeared to carry even more guns than the 406, which also outgunned his 32. There were several gasps and whistles over the radio but it was Capitano Francesco Rossi who made the first real comment.

"Capitano Nobili, when can you get us up in one of those?"

"Trust me, I'll do my best," replied Guido.

His other men whistled and proclaimed their hopes while Guido thought about what the new planes meant. He got back on the radio.

"I do know that I wouldn't want to face one of those in my CR.32."

His comment caused quick silence on the airwaves. Once again, it was Rossi that broke it.

"So, Capitano, what does that mean for us? Hell, our CR.32s can't even catch our own Ba.65 bombers that came out last year. I know Fiat is working on the G.50 but that will just about match these M.S.406s, though I don't think it's supposed to have as much firepower. That doesn't sound good for us if we get into combat against one of the other alliances."

"I don't think any of the other alliances are as far along as the French are but I do think they'll be doing their damnedest to cut into the French lead. And I think we need to be doing the same thing or we're going to end up as nothing but targets.

"The same thing goes for tanks. We've all seen the tanks the French have stationed at Figueres. Does anyone think our army would fare any better against them than we would against these new French planes?"

The resounding silence that greeted Guido's question was the emphatic answer that all of the Italian pilots feared. A few minutes passed as the truncated squadron patrolled the skies south of Girona, each pilot wondering how they would last in the skies of a future battle until Guido interrupted their morose musings.

"The sun will be setting soon. It's time to head back to Figueres."

His men acknowledged and they began a lazy sweep east as they turned towards the north. Tenente Guillermo Bianchi broke the mood when he came over the radio.

"Capitano Nobili, it looks like there's some kind of warship off the coast."

"Okay. You and Rossi go take a look but don't get too close. The rest of us will fly a holding loop to wait for you."

The two pilots peeled east but were back in five minutes. It was definitely a lone British destroyer with what looked like two Spanish fishing boats. The new question of the day was why it was there. At least there was something to report from their mission.

October 12, 1936
40 miles east of Barcelona, Spain

Vice Admiral Sir Geoffrey Blake was in a foul mood. The speed of the collapse of the Republican forces north of Girona had surprised even him. That had been the beginning of his problem. His own cleverness had done the rest.

The stream of troops headed down the road towards Barcelona had clogged them thoroughly. A number of the retreating soldiers had decided to take the coastal road from Sils which meant they were headed straight to where the *Firedrake* was supposed to be making its delivery. Then the smugglers he was working with had moved up the timetable so they could be finished before there were too many prying eyes around.

Sir Geoffrey reported the change to Captain David Eakes and warned him the mission might be aborted so he should "do his best to make sure his radio was in good working order" in case there were any changes from Gibraltar. That was the fleet's standard code for his Captains to make sure their radios weren't working because Sir Geoffrey expected an order he didn't want to follow. Sir Geoffrey was damned if he was going to lose any chance he could to twist the Entente's tail. When Sir Geoffrey reported it to Gib, the Admiralty had reacted about how he had expected and decided to abort the delivery mission.

Sir Geoffrey had tried to contact the *Firedrake* but had gotten no response and he had congratulated himself on his ability to predict and get around his orders. He'd stayed smug right up to the point where the air patrol from the *Ark Royal* had reported a pair of French planes taking an interest in the actions of the *Firedrake*. Of course, the rendezvous had to be taking place at that exact moment.

Sir Geoffrey was sure that the encounter would be reported up the chain and Entente diplomats would cry foul over British violation of the Non-Intervention Agreement. London would point out the Entente violations and nothing would really happen other than the Admiralty being forced to notice that the incident had occurred. Maybe he could pass it off as an actual problem with the *Firedrake's* radio. He knew Captain Eakes would have made sure there was one, but he also knew their cover story would fall apart if an Admiralty board looked too closely at the issue. If that happened, Sir Geoffrey would make sure the Admiralty knew that he was responsible for circumventing the orders and he might end up in jail. Regardless, his career would be over. Hopefully the good intelligence and predictions he'd made would get the Admiralty to simply give him one of those silent reprimands that let him know that they knew what had happened but they weren't going to take official notice of it.

Commodore John Moore interrupted his musings.

"Sir, *Firedrake* is back on the air and Captain Eakes reports being sighted while transferring weapons to our contacts from Calella. He sends his regrets about the unfortunate timing of their radio issues and requests that the system be torn down and looked at when we get back to Gibraltar."

Sir Geoffrey thought for a moment before replying. If Captain Eakes wanted his radio checked when they got back to Gib, then he was sure that something would be found. That meant he had a contingency plan that should keep them both out of hot water. The big question would be how Eakes acted in the coming days. Eakes would know that Sir Geoffrey understood his subterfuge to cover their arses. If Eakes brought up his actions, it meant he expected Sir Geoffrey to do favors for him down the road. In that case, Sir Geoffrey would have to find a way to quietly shuffle him off to another command. If Eakes kept his mouth shut about his actions, it meant he was demonstrating initiative and planning without expecting a reward. That would mean the career of Captain Eakes was on the rise.

"Send my compliments to Captain Eakes and let him know that the unfortunate timing of his equipment failure will be reported but it won't adversely affect his record of exemplary service."

Commodore Moore smiled and bobbed his head. "Aye, Sir."

October 13, 1936
The Chancellery, Berlin, Germany
I settle down to the pile of reports left on my desk by Oberst Ernst Weber. He must have been here all night. There's a lot of the information

I requested, though it's marked as preliminary. He even managed to get a meeting with most of the party leaders of parliament scheduled for tomorrow morning. Maybe it's time to think about promoting him.

The first thing on the pile is a report on the status of the border incident between Turkey and Russia. Both sides are claiming the other started it and both sides are claiming to show restraint to reduce tensions. I jot down a note to send both of them congratulations on their efforts to maintain the peace. I also roll my eyes.

Next comes the report on critical materials. Most of them are things we now get from Lithuania-Poland or the Ukraine. The biggest issue will be oil. The supply from Romania should be secure as long as we don't get into a shooting war with the League but it's not enough for our peacetime needs. It won't be vaguely enough for wartime needs. The Soviet Union supplies enough for the rest of our peacetime needs. Can they expand production to meet our wartime needs and will they if they can? And what will that oil cost us? I jot down another note—expand oil reserves. I wonder how bad the war use estimates will be.

On to the special projects report. Generallieutnant Liese doesn't have much more to offer than von Blomberg reported though he does think the rocket program has more potential than von Blomberg. They both think it will produce something useful before Einstein's group does. Liese did add that he thinks the new explosive has the possibility of making a bigger impact on the balance of power. Time for another note—expand yellowcake reserves from, I shuffle through the materials papers, the USGA. My stomach growls at the thought of cake and I sigh and look at it despondently. Back to the report.

According to Liese, the synthetic oil project is having a few more issues than von Blomberg reported but it is progressing. Another note—keep an eye on synthetic oil production, may be exaggerated some, check von Blomberg for conflict of interest. There's probably some way that he's making money from the development process. Hopefully he's not skimming funds. That's the problem with every government there's ever been. They're run by men who are fallible and easily tempted out of the purest of motives.

I stop for a moment and think about the plans I've come up with to work around parliament if they don't see the looming danger from the Entente. Am I really thinking about subverting our process to save it? That's a sure path to tyranny. I dig back through my notes until I find the ones on diverting funds should it be necessary and write across it in big letters, NEVER DO, END OF GOVERNMENT. I put the reports and notes off to the side of my desk and just sit there wondering how I'd ever contemplated abusing my position.

I'm still sitting there when Edna opens the door and sticks her head in.

"Sir, Sir Eric Phipps is here to see you."

She mistakes my shudder as a reaction to the United Kingdom's ambassador.

"I know he doesn't have an appointment but he says it's urgent."

"Give me five minutes then send him in."

Edna nods with a smile and closes the door behind her as she heads off to stall the ambassador. I start cleaning up the reports and make sure everything is away from prying eyes. I thumb through Weber's reports until I find the one that deals with Spain. I can't think of any other reason that Phipps would be here. Everything else goes into cabinets and drawers.

Weber knows how to be succinct. The Entente trap worked to perfection. Less than ten percent of the Republican forces escaped and almost none of their heavy equipment. The only thing left to defend northeastern Spain is the anarchist group that's been running Barcelona since late July. There are about thirty thousand of them but they don't have much beyond rifles and homemade bombs. The Republican forces are losing ground on every front. Apparently, they stripped more than just their reserves to launch the counterattack north of Girona. There seems to be a sense of panic among the Republican forces. I scan the estimated losses and put the report away. I finish with time to spare. There are at least fifteen seconds before Edna knocks on the door again and ushers Phipps into my office. I stand to greet him.

"Good morning, Sir Phipps. Have a seat." Since both of us are named Eric, we decided long ago to not use our given names.

He shakes my hand and thanks me before we both take our seats. I let him get settled before asking, "What can I do for you today, Sir Phipps?"

"Thanks for seeing me, Chancellor Manstein. I'm here because of the situation in Spain."

He stops and looks at me expectantly. I simply smile and look at him expectantly.

"The Republican forces in northeast Spain have collapsed and the Entente is rolling southwest. The Republicans are also falling back on just about every other front. What we once thought would drag on for years, now rates to be over in a few months. Even before their civil war is over, Entente troops will be just outside of Gibraltar and the possibility of an accident that precipitates a war will skyrocket."

Sir Phipps pauses and looks at me expectantly. After a moment I relent.

"And exactly what would you like us to do to help you prevent this possibility?"

"We've come up with several options, Sir. We don't believe the League will act until after the American elections. And if Roosevelt wins, they probably won't do anything until after he takes office. Regardless of any other actions taken, we believe we should enact trade restrictions on both France and Italy. We believe a partial mobilization by you on the French border might force them to withdraw some of their strength. Another option is to blockade the Spanish coast, but we feel that if we enact it unilaterally it will raise rather than reduce tensions. Publicly supporting us would lend legitimacy and present a united front to the Entente that might get them to scale back or pause their operations. There's also the option of sending an international force to create a buffer around Gibraltar to keep our forces from accidentally clashing. Then there's always the possibility of active intervention."

The British diplomat stopped when I leaned forward in my chair.

"So one of your options to avoid an accident that might cause a war is to go to war? Really?"

"The active intervention would be against the Nationalist forces of Franco, not the Entente."

"And you think there would be a lower chance of accidents that way than if we just let the Republican government fall?"

Sir Phipps at least had the decency to look uncomfortable at my question. I shook my head in derision.

"You want us to engage in sanctions against several countries with whom we do little trade. You want us to crowd our border with France which will result in a high possibility of one of those accidents you're so worried about. Or you want us to publicly support a blockade, something which is an act of war. Or you want us to join you in actively shooting at Spaniards in their own country. And all of this is because you're worried about the possibility that there might be an incident between you and the Entente. Why would we ever be interested in doing any of those things?"

Uncomfortable or not, Sir Phipps soldiers on.

"Treaty and trade considerations are available that would make the arrangement beneficial to all concerned parties. We can guarantee deliveries of limited resources such as oil so your country wouldn't experience undo economic distress should there be open conflict."

It seems I'm not the only one who's decided to look at the supply side of an upcoming conflict. I start to tell him where to shove his offer before I remember my thoughts from earlier. This decision is not mine to make, it's the parliament's. I think my sudden change of expression gives Sir Phipps the wrong impression.

"I have a meeting with leaders of our parliament tomorrow. If you have written details of your proposals, I'll present them at the meeting. That's the most I can commit to at this time." I don't tell him what my recommendations will be when I talk to my countrymen.

"Thank you, Sir. That's all I can ask. I'll have everything written up and sent over to you via courier this afternoon."

Sir Phipps rises so I do too. I even manage to keep a smile on my face as he turns to leave.

My relief is short lived as I escort Sir Phipps to my outer office only to find the French Ambassador, André François-Poncet, waiting there. The two ambassadors put on their best plastic smiles as they exchange pleasantries and ask about each other's families. Edna gives me an exasperated look that almost makes me laugh. Otto is standing near the outside door and his expression never cracks. He does take a deep breath and slowly let it out. It's his version of an exasperated eye roll.

"Give me a couple of minutes," I tell Edna and head back into my office, closing the door behind me. I want to review all the details in the Spain report. I also want André to think I'm clearing away details from my meeting with Sir Phipps. I have learned a little about diplomacy over the years.

When Edna ushers André into my office, I greet him cordially and expect something similar to what transpired with Sir Phipps. I quickly find out how wrong I am. André gets down to business once he's settled in his seat.

"Chancellor Manstein," he begins and alarm bells start going off in my head. André has been at his post for over five years and we've been on a first name basis for the last two. "We are both signatories of the Non-Intervention Agreement. We have been criticized for sending troops into Spain in violation of the agreement by everyone else. We claimed it was in response to the actions of the other signatories and I'm here to offer proof."

He reached into his briefcase, removed several photos, and presented them to me.

"The first ones are Soviet tanks that attacked an Italian outpost near Besalú. Here are pictures of a British destroyer off-loading weapons to Spanish smugglers. They've been using them to shoot at our men since we first entered the country. We have examples of their equipment that were captured in the first days of October.

"We have NOT found any evidence that the Central Coalition has violated the Non-Intervention Agreement and we want to thank you for honoring your commitment. We also want to assure you that we are there only to end the conflict that other countries wish to prolong and profit from. We have no intention of keeping troops in Spain or threatening Gibraltar from Spain. We have appealed to the Pope and escorted him to Spain in an effort to end the bloodshed as speedily as possible. We sincerely hope that the Central Coalition will continue to remain neutral in the conflict since we hope that a representative from your country will act as the arbitrator when the peace negotiations begin."

André stops for a moment and then smiles before he continues. He places what appears to be a written copy of the speech he just gave onto my desk.

"Sorry, Eric. I was given explicit orders on that. de Gaulle wrote it himself. We finally got a picture of the Brits yesterday and heaven and hell were moved to get me a copy as soon as possible. We've been trying to get proof on them for a while. Any questions or comments?"

I think about the tone and information in the missive. I'm not surprised by it considering what I know of de Gaulle. He always came across as prickly and self-righteous. He also seemed to care deeply about the honor of both himself and his country. I also realized I needed to make sure that weapons shipment we sent got diverted or stopped.

"Tell him I said thank you for the compliment. We will do our best to see that we keep it. I have a meeting with leaders of our parliament tomorrow and will pass along the information. Everything you've said matches what our intelligence has come up with so it's likely to be believed." Though the part about them withdrawing their troops might be taken with a grain of salt.

André sat back for a moment and looked at me. "None of that was news to you? Not even the part about the Pope?"

His reaction and questions startle a laugh out of me. His candor inspires me.

"To tell the truth, we had noticed that the Pope had gone missing but we weren't sure what the significance was. Would you believe it was my son's art teacher that put it together?"

That left André with a stunned look on his face.

"What was an art teacher doing with access to your...." He wound down as he saw me shaking my head.

"He did it off of newspaper reports. He apparently gets them from all over and combs through them. He made his prediction last Thursday, right after he said your Girona offensive was a trap. He made a couple other predictions too. I'm thinking about offering him a job."

I could see the emotions warring on André's face between his personal enthusiastic support of my idea and the dread his professional persona had of us having someone that good at connecting the dots working for us. We both laughed a little nervously before going back to good natured banter that had nothing to do with our jobs. He left after another ten minutes. I began doing my best to make sure our aid shipment to the Republicans was either stopped or not traceable back to us. Weber's reports would have to wait. Appearances needed to be maintained.

October 13, 1936
Orriols, Spain

Lieutenant-colonel Roger Noiret was enjoying what he felt was an undeserved rest. His head was tender around the lump it now sported but at least it didn't throb anymore. His left shoulder was working on developing a spectacular bruise but the piece of shrapnel that hit it had apparently ricocheted off another part of his tank so it hadn't done major damage. They'd been pulled back to Orriols last night after they'd been relieved by advancing infantry from the main front. Those men had seen much harder fighting than he had and he felt guilty that he and his men were relaxing while they were still in harm's way.

Okay, his men were doing maintenance and Commandant Robert Olleris was doing paperwork so technically Roger was the only one in his battalion who was relaxing. Commandant Philippe de Hauteclocque had joined him after breakfast in their command tent and while his uniform was in its usual impeccable condition, the same could not be said for its wearer. Philippe had the tired, slightly haunted look of most commanders who had just seen their first combat. Father Louis Lobau had led a service for their fallen comrades last night but Philippe looked like he was still wracked by the responsibility of ordering men to their death. They'd been sipping on coffee for a minute or two before Roger decided to speak.

"Still trying to figure out what you could have done to keep fewer of your men from getting killed?"

Philippe looked startled as if he'd forgotten Roger was even there. He had just shrugged and nodded, guilty as charged.

"Good. That means you have the makings of a good field commander. Learn from it but don't let it consume you. Send a letter up the command chain if there were things we were trained to do that could have been done better. Maybe you'll save some lives down the road. And don't feel guilty about those you killed if they would have killed you given a chance."

"Thanks. They did a good job of preparing me for everything except sleeping afterwards. Wine helped a bit but I still woke up several times with images of the dead drifting through my mind."

"You learn how to deal with it. It'll get better. Just hope it never gets easier. It should never become easy to take another person's life."

Philippe contemplated Roger's advice while Roger went back to sipping his coffee. After a few minutes, Philippe sighed and seemed to decide it was time to return to the world. He looked more like his old self when he started up the conversation again.

"How are you doing this morning?"

"The shoulder and head hurt but not too bad overall. I am feeling a little guilty about taking it easy when my men are off working on our tanks and our countrymen are still in harm's way. Then again, that's another lesson I learned in the Great War. Rest when you can for your turn will come. How are you?"

"I'm fine, other than the lack of sleep. I think our men performed very well yesterday, and I think you're right that we'll soon be called on again."

Both men sat in thought for a few minutes before Sergent Murat announced his presence with a "Colonel, Sir?"

Roger looked up out of his light doze and told Murat to enter.

The Sergent came to attention. "They want to see you over at headquarters, Sir."

Roger stood and stretched. "Any idea what this is about, Murat?"

"No, Sir."

"Should I bring de Hauteclocque?"

"No, Sir. They said just you, Sir."

Roger thought that was curious. de Hauteclocque was second in command of their combined units. Roger couldn't think of anything that he should know that the armored cavalry commander shouldn't. He glanced over to the seated Philippe and found a reflection of his own puzzled look.

"Well, Philippe, I guess I should go find out what's going on. Stay here 'til I get back."

Noiret shrugged and left the tent with his driver.

For once, de Hauteclocque had been left with no idea of what was going on. He'd heard nothing from any of his informants and felt lost. He sat in the tent trying to envision possible scenarios that would cause this circumstance. Philippe came up with an official review of his actions (rarely a good thing), a special mission that his men wouldn't be a part of, or they could just want to talk with Roger about his actions to determine what kind of medal to recommend. Philippe decided it was time to sit on aristocratic derriere and wait.

Lieutenant-colonel Noiret returned about ten minutes later. de Hauteclocque rose but Roger had immediately waived him back to his seat. Roger then took his own seat and settled in without a word. The smile on his face made Philippe refrain from breaking the silence. It looked like more waiting.

Five minutes went by before the Commandant's curiosity got the best of him. When Philippe started to say something, Roger simply held up his hand. This was followed by a smirk when de Hauteclocque sighed heavily.

Another five minutes and de Hauteclocque heard someone approaching the tent. There had been a muttered exchange and the guard outside the tent was replaced by a newcomer. The "It's clear, Sir" had shown that the replacement was Sergent Murat. Another minute and two more men approached the tent. Philippe sat straighter in his folding chair and glanced once more at Roger before returning his attention to the tent flap. When the flap was thrown back, Commandant Robert Olleris and the Spanish Sargento from Besalú entered. Both came rigidly to attention. Philippe found little to distinguish the dark-haired Spaniard other than some swelling and bruising around his left eye. Philippe turned his gaze back to Roger and found the Lieutenant-colonel looking back with a smile on his face.

Roger turned back to the standing soldiers, one French, one Spanish, both as puzzled as Philippe. Since he knew that both Olleris and de Hauteclocque understood Spanish he switched to it for his conversation.

"At ease. Sargento Primero Esperanza, this is Commandant Philippe de Hauteclocque."

The Sargento did his best to snap to attention and saluted the Frenchman who returned it from his seat before Roger continued.

"Sargento, can I have your word that you won't repeat anything I'm about to say?"

The Spaniard thought for a moment before replying, "If it is not of military value to my countrymen, I will not repeat it."

Roger smiled. "It is of military value, but I don't think you'll repeat it."

Sargento Esperanza looked no more puzzled than did the two French officers.

"The Republican forces around Girona have been routed. The current government of Spain is doomed. Our high command wants to end the bloodshed as soon as possible and has been preparing for this situation.

"We have been given a very special mission. If you agree, we will escort you into Girona and forward through the Spanish countryside."

Roger paused for a moment and smiled as he watched Philippe and Robert try to guess how this Spanish Sargento was going to affect the war.

"Gentlemen, we are to meet Pope Pius XII east of here at Valveralla." Roger paused again while his audience took turns staring at him and each other. "We will escort him forward to Girona and beyond. We will provide security as he tries to end the fighting."

Sargento Esperanza was the first to find his voice. "And why am I here?"

"We hope that you will help the Pope. He has spoken against the sins of your current government but he has not witnessed them directly. You have and you were willing to put your life on the line to try to stop them."

Sargento Esperanza thought for a moment before giving his answer. "Barcelona will be the tricky one. It has been controlled by anarchists since July. I will be honored to assist His Holiness but I will want you, Lieutenant-colonel, with me."

Roger looked puzzled and started to ask why but Sargento Esperanza quickly held up his hands.

"You are the one who was shot at and still offered generous surrender terms, yes?"

Roger nodded that he was.

"My men know of what happened in Besalú. Others do not and may not understand why we surrendered. The men you paroled, the men whose lives you spared, are spreading out ahead of your forces. Tales like that spread quickly. My men surrendering might seem important to you, you showing mercy will be important to my countrymen. I will gladly go and tell my story if you wish, but it is your story that may end this conflict, not mine."

Roger sat in stunned silence at the Spaniard's simple view of how his actions would impact the fighting. When his eyes refocused, he looked back up to see a smile on the Sargento's face.

"And I will also tell my countrymen that I believe it was not a ploy but a genuine act of compassion. One from which we can all benefit."

October 13, 1936
Gibraltar

Carmen Esperanza was pensively waiting for Major Thomas Hawkins to arrive for lunch. The liver and onions she'd made for him were still sizzling in the pan and had been ready minutes ago. Major Thomas had arrived at his quarters for lunch with clockwork precision at five after noon for as long as Carmen had worked for him, until today. And that worried Carmen. She hoped it had something to do with their conversation this morning and nothing to do with Luis.

Mrs. Sanchez had visited her last night and told her about her British shadow. Carmen had been fairly certain that the man following her was Sergeant Terry Sanders and had become sure when he'd been missing from his normal gate post again this morning. She'd thanked Major Hawkins for his concern and that of his men. She'd pointed out how the actions of the Nationalist lieutenant had put both her and Carlos under the protective eye of the rebel soldiers. She'd assured him that she was far safer now than she had been since her husband went to war. She'd also pointed out that since they were keeping an eye on her, there was a chance they would notice what Mrs. Sanchez had noticed. If that happened, Sergeant Sanders might be put in a very bad position. Major Hawkins had smiled and told her he would see what he could do.

It was almost a quarter past when the front door finally opened and Major Hawkins made his appearance. Carmen hoped the liver wasn't too overdone and plated it while she whispered another prayer for Luis. She put it and a glass of water on the table and waited for a few heartbeats. The smile on the Major's face made her heart flutter with hope. He was gracious enough to put her nervousness over his stomach.

"Luis is alive and captive, or at least he was yesterday."

Carmen sank into one of the seats at the table as she exhaled the breath she hadn't known she was holding. She closed her eyes and bent her head in a prayer of thanks and hope. When she finished it, she realized she was sitting at the Major's table and almost bounced out of the seat.

"Excuse me, Sir."

Major Hawkins would have laughed at how flustered she was if he hadn't known how scared she'd been moments before.

"It's fine, Mrs. Esperanza. Please sit while I tell you what we know."

"But your lunch will get cold and I need to clean up the kitchen."

Major Hawkins heaved a sigh of forbearance before nodding his head in surrender. He sat and attacked his favorite food with gusto even if things were a bit overcooked. That was his fault, not Mrs. Esperanza's. He finished with a smile and sat waiting patiently as Carmen whisked away his plate and cleaned it along with the rest of the pans and dishes she'd used to make his lunch. It felt like hours had passed but when Major Hawkins looked at the clock, it had just reached twelve-thirty. He knew he would have indigestion this afternoon from eating too quickly.

The sounds from the kitchen dropped to a bare whisper, Carmen was down to drying things. Another minute and a few clatters as things were put away, and Carmen finally entered the dining area with a smile on her face. Her eyes looked a little puffier than they had. Major Hawkins decided she must have been crying and used cleaning up as a method of hiding it. He hoped his news wouldn't quench her joy.

"I'm ready, Sir."

Major Hawkins directed her back to the chair she'd occupied earlier and waited for her to get settled.

"Here's what we think happened. Your husband was part of the forces sent to Besalú. Another part of those forces was a Russian tank regiment. The officers, both Spanish and Russian, decided to take liberties with the local women, including several nuns at a church."

Major Hawkins waited until the wide-eyed Carmen finished crossing herself and seemed ready to hear more.

"They also took everything of value they could find from both the church and the people of Besalú. The priest and a soldier tried to stop them. Both were beaten and imprisoned. That soldier was your husband."

Tears welled up in Carmen's eyes but all she did was nod and say "That's my Luis. How is he?"

Major Hawkins held up his hands in a plea for patience.

"The Russians attacked on Sunday as their part of the general attack the Republicans launched. The Russian tank force was wiped out. Once the Russian tanks had left, the Spanish soldiers in Besalú mutinied, took their officers prisoner, and released the priest and your husband. After what the officers had done, the soldiers decided they wanted nothing else to do with defending the government that had put them in charge. The soldiers decided to surrender and Luis and the priest were put in charge of handling it. The French who ambushed the Russians accepted the surrender and then took Luis and the priest to a local doctor in Besalú. Several of the men who lived in Besalú slipped out Sunday night to let people know what had happened. Unfortunately, they didn't know who to talk to or where to find them so things had gone bad by the time their information made its way to the people in charge of the Republican attack."

"So as of Sunday, Luis was a captive and being treated by a doctor in Besalú, right?"

"Yes, ma'am. That's all the information we have on him. There are also some rumors that the French were treating those they captured well, but we haven't confirmed them yet."

"Thank you, Sir." Carmen stood up to get back to work and was startled when Major Hawkins rose, too.

"Why don't you take the rest of the day off? I understand there's a dog waiting at the gate for you and Sergeant Sanders has some treats for Mrs. Sanchez's dogs and some candied apricots for her."

Carmen smiled and thanked him before straightening a few more things and heading home. For the first time in months, she looked forward to the trip.

October 13, 1936
Figueres, Spain

Capitano Guido Nobili and his men were examining maps again. Girona had fallen this morning and Entente troops were expected to reach Barcelona this afternoon. The word was that there might be some resistance there. The combined Italian-French wing would be providing air cover for the advance today but not tomorrow. The current plan was that two of the French squadrons from Perpignan would move to an airbase just north of Mataró later today and provide air cover on the drive through Barcelona and beyond. That meant his men would get a new job.

A French armored regiment and an Italian mountain division would push toward Vic and Manlleu tomorrow. His men would be providing air cover and performing spotting duties. They would also be back in their CR.32s. Guido wasn't quite sure how he felt about that. He still loved how his biplane made him feel like a bird of prey but the French M.S.406 made him feel like a hunter. He knew he wouldn't have that same feeling of power he was used to when he flew his plane. And from what he'd seen of the D.520, that feeling of vulnerability was going to get a lot worse.

He looked around the table and saw looks of concern with an undertone of worry rather than the usual looks of anticipation and self-confidence. They would lose their edge if he didn't do something.

"We'll be running air cover this afternoon between Girona and Barcelona. There shouldn't be much in the way of opposition since the Republican forces have been virtually wiped out. It should be mostly spotting and making sure that there aren't any crazy Spaniards in the air who decide they need to take a shot at our men."

"Thank goodness for that," muttered Capitano Francesco Rossi.

Guido hadn't expected his executive officer to be one of those who were having doubts. Then again, Guido was having them too. Only Sottotenente Corrado Ricci seemed to be immune to the nervous attitude that pervaded his command. Then again, Ricci's broken arm had kept him from flying yesterday's mission in the French planes. He'd flown one when they were in Toulon but there seemed to be more of an impact for those who'd flown them on a combat mission. He also hadn't seen how badly the D.520 outclassed the M.S.406.

"C'mon, Rossi, you know we've done well against the Spanish when they didn't out number us ten to one."

That got grudging nods of acceptance from his men.

"Yes, Capitano, but what are we going to do in the next war? I know they're working on the CR.42 and the G.50 but neither of those would stand up to the new French plane. And if the French have it now, how long before the Germans and British have something similar?"

"That worries me too. That's why I talked with our airbase commander, Colonel Sarbone, last night. I told him that if he wants us to be effective partners in the Entente, we may need some French help in upgrading our equipment. He said he would send the request up the chain but it would be better if it came from someone in our development program. I told him I'd see what I could do about it. So, I wrote a letter with my observations to our wing commander, Maggiore Fagnani. Hopefully he can push things along. Let me know if you come up with any other suggestions.

"Until then, we do our duty and use our skill to show what Italian pilots are made of. We don't dwell on what might happen in the years to come, we deal with what comes our way with the sweat and courage that makes us feared by our foes."

Guido paused to see what effect his pep talk had on his men, but his attempt at seriousness was ruined by Ricci.

"And plaster."

Everyone looked at him in confusion.

"You said sweat and courage. You forgot plaster," and he waved the cast on his broken arm.

Everyone chuckled and groaned but it had the effect of breaking the gloomy mood that had pervaded the group.

October 13, 1936
40 miles east of Barcelona, Spain
Sometimes Vice Admiral Sir Geoffrey Blake hated it when he was proven right. The collapse of the Republican front north of Girona had been swift and total. Entente forces were pushing into Spain against virtually no opposition. He had hope that the Confederación Nacional del Trabajo, the anarchist group that ran Barcelona, would resist the Entente advance, but he wasn't sure if they would. Most of their equipment was small arms or home-made. They would at least have a couple of anti-tank guns if they got the equipment that Captain Eakes and the *Firedrake* dropped off yesterday. On the other hand, scout planes from the *Ark Royal* reported that the Papal yacht was at sea again. That meant the Pope was probably somewhere in Spain and Sir Geoffrey didn't like thinking about the possibility of one of the CNT anarchists taking a potshot at the Pope with British equipment.

He sat at his desk in his cabin with bowed head and rubbed his forehead worriedly. If something like that happened, he was sure the

Entente would publicize that they'd seen the *Firedrake* delivering something to local Spanish ships just yesterday. Not only would that put Britain in the crosshairs of the world's Catholics, it would make them a pariah that no one wanted to deal with. It would also end the career of one Vice Admiral Sir Geoffrey Blake. Sometimes his own cleverness was really annoying.

Time to quit dwelling on past mistakes and figure out what he could do about the future. Maybe the Entente would pull a Napoleon and the Spanish people would see their new Nationalist leader as a puppet. Sir Geoffrey had no doubt that there would be a new government running Spain, and probably soon. A lot would depend on how the Entente treated the new government and how it treated its people. A better armed CNT might be an asset then. Regardless, using Gibraltar as a base and shipping through the Mediterranean might become a tenuous prospect. Malta would have the same problems.

The First Battlecruiser Squadron would have to be stationed somewhere else. Speed doesn't work as armor if you're sitting at anchor and his ships would become more vulnerable the longer they sat. Virtually all of northwest Africa would be under Entente control. Ascension Island or Saint Helena might work as bases for protecting the south Atlantic but the fleet facilities would have to be built from scratch. The Canary Islands would have to be taken from Spain so they were out, barring a shooting war with the Entente. The mainland African colonies were surrounded by Entente colonies too. That left the eastern Med, somewhere in the Americas, or the Azores. And the Azores were Portuguese so controlling them was dubious.

Sir Geoffrey didn't like where his thoughts were headed. It looked like the First Battlecruiser Squadron would be relegated to guarding the sea lanes or sitting in the eastern Med with forays towards Malta and the east coast of Africa. If Britain was going to keep a naval presence at Gibraltar, it would have to be some of her battleships and even they would be vulnerable. Sir Geoffrey doubted they would come from Home Fleet. If they came from the Eastern Fleet, it might lead to Japanese or American expansion in the area. Odds were that the battleships would come from the Mediterranean Fleet based in Alexandria. The *King George V*-class battleships stationed there were a few knots slower than his battlecruisers but they had better armor protection. The problem would be the hideously vulnerable escorts.

Sir Geoffrey shook his head. Those were questions for the Admiralty and his boss, Sir Dudley Pound, the commander of the Mediterranean Fleet. He would just be expected to make some recommendations. Recommendations that would have an impact on his career as well as the defense of the Empire.

Those were things to let his hind brain mull over. What he needed to do was to come up with some way to slow down the Entente's advance without being seen in Spanish territorial waters or actually shooting at them. Spain claimed six nautical miles for its territorial waters while the United Kingdom only recognized it out to three. Maybe maneuvers in the disputed zone "to reestablish international standards" would work. If nothing else it would show the flag and limit the area the Entente ships could use for any bombardment or demonstration missions. It might give advancing ground troops a reason to pause or at least slow their advance. It would also put his ships in a more vulnerable position if shooting broke out, but it was the best plan that Sir Geoffrey could come up with. He got up and headed to the bridge of his flagship.

Commodore John Moore was in an earnest discussion with Lieutenant Travis Caldwell but both looked up when he arrived.

"Never mind, Caldwell. The Vice Admiral seems to have known we were talking about him."

"About what, Commodore?"

"Scouting report from the *Ark Royal*, Sir. The three other *Littorio*-class battleships have joined the fleet north of us. They have also been joined by all four of the French *Richelieu's*, the *Béarn*, and half a dozen French cruisers."

"Great. Pass it along to Gib and make sure Sir Dudley gets a copy. Are there any reports of transports with them?"

Commodore Moore looked confused for a moment before answering.

"The report is already on its way up the chain, Sir, and no reports of transports. What's up with the transports, Sir?"

"There's only a couple of reasons the Entente would mass eleven battleships off the coast of Spain. One is fire support for their troops. They seem a bit late to the party for that given the way the land action is going. Two is to test their rendezvous procedures, in which case we don't care. Three is to make a display of force to keep the Republicans or the CNT in Barcelona from fighting back. And four is to invade Gibraltar and start a shooting war here and now. Check with Gibraltar to see if they have any reports of transports being loaded that we don't know about and why we're asking. Also, find out if there are any reinforcements they can send our way."

Commodore Moore simply nodded at Lieutenant Caldwell who trotted off to send the query.

"Unless we get different information from Gib, I'm going to assume that the Entente is doing this as a test of their command and control with the intention of demonstrating off of Barcelona to keep the CNT from getting feisty. Place the squadron on alert. Be prepared to send destroyers and the *Marlborough* and *Benbow* to perform our own little demonstration off the Barcelona coast. You'll have command of the detachment and I'll transfer my flag to the *Lion* while you're gone.

"I want you to run the destroyers about four miles off their coast while you keep the battlecruisers about a mile further out. If anyone asks, we're refusing to acknowledge the Spanish claim of extended territorial waters and asserting the international standard of three miles. Be prepared to shoot but only return fire if someone fires something dangerous at your ships or you're about to be rammed. Otherwise, act like you've got the only ships in the area and don't yield an inch to anyone. I'll have the rest of the squadron with anything we can get from Gibraltar about two miles further out to sea.

"If something does happen, don't spend time checking with me for a response. Handle it. I trust your judgment and I'll back up any action you take. Seconds will be critical if anyone starts shooting."

"Very good, Sir."

Sir Geoffrey sized up his flag captain for a moment before giving a satisfied nod and heading back to his cabin.

October 14, 1936
The Chancellery, Berlin, Germany

I sit down and stare at my desk. I went by both Weber and my secretary Edna on the way in. Both simply got out of my way. I don't know if it was the look on my face or if Otto was shaking his head as he followed me but they knew things had not gone well in my morning meeting with parliament. The Bundesrat had been agreeable enough, but then it's always been for a stronger military because of the strong contingent representing Prussia. The Reichstag had been an entirely different beast.

Alfred Hugenberg, leader of the German National People's Party, had fully supported the idea of increasing military spending. The conservative leader could usually be counted on to keep an eye on foreign threats. Unfortunately, the other three major parties in the Reichstag were solidly against the idea. Ludwig Kaas, leader of the German Centre Party, was dead set against the idea of anything that might provoke the Catholic Entente. That wasn't really a surprise considering that they're sometimes known as the Catholic Centre Party. Nor was the opposition by Ernst Thälmann, leader of the Communist Party. The surprise had been the total opposition by Otto Wels, leader of Germany's Social Democratic Party.

Wels had talked with Generalfeldmarschall Werner von Blomberg, commander of the Reichswehr. Wels said that von Blomberg had assured him that the army could defend us from any attack but he had also expressed his belief that Germany should take her "rightful place" as a world leader and the best way to do that was a strong military with a totalitarian government. Strangely enough, Wels was now solidly against giving any more toys to someone who wants to radically change our government.

I can't say that I blame him.

I get my "things to do" notebook out of my desk and grab a pen. "Replace von Blomberg" is added to it, then underlined a few times. I stop and look at it for a moment before adding several exclamation points. When the leader of your military thinks there should be a different type of government, it's time for him to go. I would have to talk with Wilhelm III to replace him. Edna can set that up and he should be gone by the end of the week. Finding a replacement will take a bit longer but I need to get it done as soon as possible.

The only upside I can see of their refusal to increase funding for the military is that they were equally adamant in their opposition to the proposal from Sir Eric Phipps. They wanted no part of the British ambassador's informal alliance. They were also quite happy with André François-Poncet's comments. They weren't happy with me for withholding the French ambassador's comments until after the discussion on military spending.

I may have to see what kind of deal we can make with the Entente if the Reichstag keeps refusing to expand the military. That assumes we got the arms shipment to Spain stopped. I agree with von Blomberg that we can currently stop the French if they attack but I don't think we'd be able to push into their territory. That means all the fighting and damage would be in Germany. I also know that the French are continuing to upgrade their combat capability and I wonder how long it will be before we can't stop them.

The only bright spot was that the Reichstag leaders were willing to increase our reserves of strategic materials. They were very interested by the list that Weber prepared and agreed to work on building up at least a three-month supply of our critical imports.

Time for more notes. Institute national air and car races. Push air, panzer, and gun designs that are easy to mass produce.

Have Weber research strategic material issues experienced by France, Italy, and the United Kingdom during the Great War—best guess for Lithuania-Poland and the Ukraine.

October 14, 1936
Barcelona, Spain
Lieutenant-colonel Roger Noiret was both proud and more than a bit nervous. He and Philippe had met Pope Pius XII and been blessed by him personally, definitely something to include in his next letter to Catherine and the boys. The men of their battalions had been blessed in a mass ceremony. But while the Swiss Guard was still responsible for the safety of the Pope, his assignment was to provide security against any major threats.

This wasn't a role he or his men had trained for but he'd done his best. The Pope's first stop had been at the Cathedral of Girona this morning. Task Group Pius, as General Gamelin had begun calling the battalions of Lieutenant-colonel Noiret and Commandant Philippe de Hauteclocque, had established two rings around the cathedral. Roger's B and C Companies were a kilometer out blocking roads and making sure that no heavy weapons got near the Pope. Philippe's B and C Companies formed an inner ring a half a kilometer out. The A Companies of both battalions were in a ring barely a hundred meters from where the Pope delivered his message of peace. The Swiss Guard controlled everything inside that final ring.

He'd left Philippe in charge when the Holy Father had asked him to say a few words to the people. He and Sargento Primero Luis Esperanza had both spoken about their actions and the Pope had praised them as examples of what good men could and must do. The Pope had called for forgiveness and reconciliation among the people of Spain. That was the path for healing and returning Spain to her place as a spiritual leader in this world. His Holiness had also promised the people of Girona that the French and Italian troops would leave Spain once the fighting had ended. That was something that Roger hadn't known about. He'd had a few concerns about what would happen when the Nationalists were in control and hoped that de Gaulle had a plan.

The initial reception in Girona had been a bit subdued but hopeful. The crowds had been much more enthusiastic after the Pope's message. An older man in the crowd even started to pat Roger on the left shoulder as they left, but Sargento Esperanza stopped him. The man looked indignant until Luis had reminded him of Roger's wound. The congregant had been sheepishly apologizing by the time Roger even became aware of what was going on. Roger had turned and offered his right hand which the man quickly grabbed and shook vigorously while grinning from ear to ear.

Task Group Pius had stopped at Sils for lunch and Roger had spent most of the time going over security details for the afternoon sermon at the Cathedral of Barcelona. The CNT, anarchist forces that ran Barcelona after the Nationalist's failed uprising in the area, had initially stood their ground when the Entente forces had arrived there this morning. The leadership of the CNT seemed to draw courage from a squadron of British warships that had been visible a few kilometers off the coast. That bravado had lasted for about fifteen minutes before a much larger Entente naval contingent had sailed between the British ships and Barcelona. The CNT had quickly agreed to stop armed resistance for the duration of the civil war but there had been no oaths and no disarmament of their men. Then again, it had been hard to identify exactly who their men were. That Barcelona's cathedral was in the middle of a densely populated area hadn't helped Roger's peace of mind. He'd prayed for a safe and peaceful afternoon.

Things had not gone well once they entered Barcelona. The people of Girona had been swayed by the tale of Roger's mercy for the Republican soldiers. In Barcelona, that tale didn't seem to mean as much to the people and a somber crowd had begun to gather around the Pope and his entourage. Task Group Pius had kept the crowd well away from the Pope as they'd made their way to the cathedral but they had to let them in once they were there. After all, the whole point was for the Pope to bring his message of peace to the people.

Things had gone well and the crowd seemed to be relaxing after Pope Pius XII had delivered his initial message. Sargento Esperanza had finished his tale and Roger had just arrived at the pulpit when all hell broke loose. A man stood up yelling "Death to the fake Pope!" and threw a hand grenade at the Pope. Roger had no idea of how he'd gotten it past the Swiss Guard but he had. Everyone had been stunned for a moment before they reacted.

It was a moment that seemed to last for hours. The people next to the attacker had jumped on him even as members of the Swiss Guard were scrambling in his direction. Some guardsmen were diving for the hand grenade while others tried to interpose themselves between the grenade and the Pope. The grenade detonated just as one of the Swiss Guard landed on it. Pieces of his body and equipment were blown in all directions. The Archbishop of Barcelona died when a piece of shrapnel embedded itself in his forehead. Three other members of the clergy were injured but none seriously. There was only one other casualty. Sargento Primero Luis Esperanza had been the closest to the Pope when the attack began and had shielded the Pope with his body. The blast had driven parts of the wooden railing into his back. Several splinters were sticking out of his back, but it was the large one protruding from the base of his skull that sealed his fate.

Roger didn't remember moving but found himself holding the crumpling Sargento as they slid to the floor. His attention was distracted for a moment as he looked up to see how the Pope was. The Pope had risen from his seat and appeared unharmed as he bent over the two soldiers. Roger turned to look back at the man he'd come to think of as a friend and watched the light go out in his eyes as he heard the last rights being given by the Pope. The Pope had then kissed Luis' forehead before kissing Roger's.

Roger settled Luis' body on the ground and stood to find himself and the Pope surrounded by the Swiss Guard. After a deep breath, he helped His Holiness to his seat and tried to find out what had happened. Duty called and it wouldn't make any exceptions for him.

October 14, 1936
La Linea, Spain

Carmen Esperanza was headed home. It seemed like it had only been a few minutes since lunch. Major Thomas Hawkins had arrived at his house with such a big grin on his face. Carmen could see he was bursting with news but didn't want his lunch to get cold so she headed off his outburst.

"Luis is okay?" she asked.

"I'd say he's more than okay, Mrs. Esperanza."

"Thank you. Now eat your lunch while it's still hot. You can tell me of Luis afterwards."

Major Hawkins just stared at her for a moment before shaking his head with a grin. He bowed to her and took his place at his table while Carmen hurried into the kitchen to plate and present his lunch. He enjoyed his favorite liver and onions while he listened to Carmen humming a wordless tune as she cleaned up in the kitchen. That was something she hadn't done in months and it brought a smile to the Englishman's face. He'd been planning on just blurting out his news to Carmen but came up with a different plan while he ate. He finished his meal and waited patiently for her to clear away his plate. Another minute or two passed while he listened to Carmen washing, drying, and putting away his lunch dish and utensils. She finally returned to the dining area with a smile and an expectant look on her face. Major Hawkins waved her to a seat and waited as she settled into it before launching into his news.

"Sargento Esperanza doesn't appear to be a prisoner of war any longer."

"He has escaped?"

"No, ma'am. He seems to be traveling in the company of a French gentleman, though the report did say they had a large escort traveling with them."

Carmen looked puzzled as Major Hawkins grinned at her.

"I don't understand, Major. Why would my Luis be traveling anywhere with a Frenchman if he wasn't a prisoner?"

"That's a good question, Mrs. Esperanza. We wondered about it too. It seems the French gentleman simply asked your husband to accompany him and Sargento Esperanza agreed. There was even a suggestion that your husband had turned traitor."

Carmen looked alarmed and confused so Major Hawkins held up his hands placatingly while his grin grew even broader.

"I'm sorry, Mrs. Esperanza. Did I forget to mention that the French gentleman who asked for your husband's company was Pope Pius XII?"

Major Hawkins started chuckling at the dumbfounded look on Carmen's face. It was almost a minute later before she quit sputtering and actually got an intelligible question out. When she did, it was one long stream.

"The Pope? The Pope asked for my Luis to accompany him? Where are they going? What is the Pope doing in Spain? Why would the Pope want my Luis to go anywhere with him? Luis has met the Pope? The Pope knows who my Luis is?"

Carmen sputtered down as Major Hawkins continued to chuckle. Yes, this had been a lot more fun than simply telling her.

"Let me see if I can answer all of that. The Pope was at the Girona Cathedral this morning where he delivered a message of peace. He wants the Republican forces to quit fighting and neither side to seek retribution after the fighting ends. It seems that the tale of your husband's actions in Besalú were brought to the Pope's attention and he decided to take your husband with him on his tour. Sargento Esperanza was introduced by the Pope and spoke at Girona Cathedral this morning as an example of what good men must do."

Carmen looked bemused and smiled wonderingly. "The Pope knows my Luis and thinks he's a good man. I'll never win another argument."

Major Hawkins had just chuckled at Carmen's comment.

The rest of the day had sped by in a euphoric cloud. Luis was fine and traveling with the Pope. The people at church who had been shunning her because her Luis was fighting for the government would be fawning over her on Sunday. That would show them. Carmen prayed her thanks for Luis several times. She also prayed to ask forgiveness of her pride in her husband.

Sergeants Terry Sanders and Irvin Havens were both at the gate when she finally headed home. They noticed the bounce in her step and asked her what her good news was. She spent several minutes distracting them from their duties to tell them all about her husband's brush with fame before finally greeting Mrs. Sanchez' dog Amber and heading home.

She didn't notice that most of the people on her way home looked shaken and were discussing something in hushed tones. She also didn't notice that several people along her path stared at her and crossed themselves though Amber started getting skittish. She walked dreamily along until she made the last turn onto her street and saw Isabella Sanchez standing on her front porch.

Part of Carmen's brain noted that Mrs. Sanchez never stood on her porch, she was either going somewhere or she was in her rocker. It sent up warning alarms when it noted that Mrs. Sanchez had a bottle of wine in her hand and tears in her eyes. But the rest of Carmen's brain wouldn't let anything interfere with the joy and pride she carried for her husband as she bounced up the steps of the porch.

"Mrs. Sanchez, you'll never guess what's happened! My Luis is traveling with the Pope! The Pope asked for Luis by name and even had him give a speech at the cathedral in Girona this morning! I can't believe it! Luis is going to be famous! I'm so proud of him even if it means he'll be insufferable for months. He'll strut around...." Carmen wound down as she noticed a tear rolling down the old woman's cheek and she felt terrible for not noticing that something was wrong sooner.

"What's wrong? Is everything okay?"

"It was on the radio, Carmen. Someone in Barcelona tried to blow up the Pope this afternoon. They would have succeeded if it weren't for the heroics of one of the Swiss Guard and Sargento Primero Luis Esperanza, both of whom were killed."

October 14, 1936

Figueres, Spain

Capitano Guido Nobili walked into the field office of his base commander, Colonel Jacob Sarbone, and brought himself to attention. The order to report had been relayed by Sergente Giovanni Battista, his mechanic, when he landed from his last patrol of the day. Sergente Battista claimed he had no idea why the Colonel wanted to see him, though he did say that Guido was supposed to clean himself up a bit before he reported. Guido presumed the wing would be moving forward and maybe getting some replacements for his dead and injured men. He was right on two out of the three reasons for his orders.

"Capitano Guido Nobili, reporting as ordered, Sir."

"At ease, Capitano. Have a seat."

Colonel Sarbone looked Guido over for a moment before he emitted a small grunt as he shrugged his shoulders.

"I doubt you've heard what happened in Barcelona so here are the basics. One of those damned Confederación Nacional del Trabajo anarchists tried to blow up the Pope at the Barcelona cathedral a couple of hours ago. The rest of the Spanish started turning the CNT members into our ground troops in the area. Chaos reigns in Barcelona but we're getting a handle on things and it may actually work in our favor.

"A Spanish soldier was killed saving the Pope and the Pope is using his example and the actions of the CNT to help inspire cooperation with us and it seems to be working. Groups of CNT members are being turned in with many of them beaten black and blue.

"Because of this, our timetable has been moved up and we will be moving to the El Prat airport the day after tomorrow. We'll be joined by half a dozen more Italian pilots to bring the wing back up to strength. You will not be joining us."

Guido sat up straighter in his seat and looked at his commanding officer questioningly.

"Capitano Rossi will take over your squadron. You are being sent back to Italy. It seems Mussolini wants to pin the...," Colonel Sarbone consulted a piece of paper on his desk to get it right, "Medaglia d'oro al valor militare on Italy's first ace since the Great War. You're due in Rome this Saturday the seventeenth. You fly out tomorrow morning."

Guido sat in stunned silence for a moment while the French Colonel just stared at him with a wry smile on his face. Colonel Sarbone could see in his eyes when Capitano Nobili's brain started working again and he began digesting the news. There were a few more beats before the Italian ace asked questions.

"How long will I be in Rome?"

"I don't know. Your orders are open ended. I think the brass is still deciding what they want to do with you. A lot will probably depend on how things go on the trip back to Rome and how you do when you meet Mussolini. He'll pin your medal on you in some big ceremony they're planning. Considering how things are going here, I don't expect there to be much for you to do if they do send you back so you might want to pay close attention to any offers you get for other postings."

"Yes, Sir. I just wasn't expecting anything like this."

"I know. Just make the most of it. You'll probably have more influence during the next week than at any other time in your career. If there are things you want, don't be shy about pushing for them."

"Will do, Sir. Have my men been told?"

"Some of it. They know that you're getting a medal, that there's going to be a party tonight, and that they have tomorrow off. Giorgio Cenni and his photographer will be with you when you tell them the rest. He's a reporter who's here to get the story on Italy's new war hero. He wanted to catch the reactions of your men. That's why I wanted you to straighten up a bit before you reported."

"As long as my men don't start making things up just to mess with him and me."

That got a chuckle from Colonel Sarbone. Guido was dismissed and found Cenni and the photographer waiting for him outside Sarbone's office. After quick introductions and a couple of pictures, Guido led the way to the Italian barracks where they found his men cleaned up and ready for the anticipated party. Capitano Francesco Rossi called the room to attention as Guido entered and had the men salute to honor him. There was a little bit of confusion when the photographer's flash bulb went off. Guido brought himself to attention and returned their salute and then all formality went out the window as they just became friends who had fought and bled together. Guido was cheered, clapped on the back, and even carried around on his men's shoulders at one point although that was probably more for the photographer than anything else. Drinks were passed around and Guido was toasted. Capitano Rossi eventually called for a speech and the rest of his men quieted down as Guido stopped smiling and bowed his head. There were tears in his eyes when he looked up.

"Men, friends, thank you. First and foremost, to those of us who didn't make it back."

Guido and his men somberly raised their glasses and drank. The photographer was treated to angry looks and muttered comments when the flash bulb went off this time. Guido thought for a moment before continuing.

"Don't be mad at them. They're here to document our success and part of that success is the price we've paid to achieve it. Everyone back home should know the names of the men who gave their lives for us and for Italy."

Giorgio Cenni spoke up. "I'll make sure that everyone in the squadron is in the story with a special mention of those who didn't make it back. I'll want to talk to each of you tomorrow about your experiences and memories of your lost comrades."

There were a few more mutters but that seemed to soothe the pilots' pain and feelings of being violated by outsiders intruding on their grief. Guido gave his men a moment before continuing his little speech.

"To those of us who did make it back."

This time no one seemed to mind the flash as they drank and smiles returned as the mercurial mood of the pilots headed back to celebration.

"Tonight, we party. The cantina in Figueres has been reserved just for us so maybe Bianchi will finally have a chance to chat up that waitress he's been pining over."

Tenente Guillermo Bianchi blushed a bit as the other pilots teased him about his prospects for success. Guido continued after they settled down again.

"Tomorrow, I'll be on a plane to Rome while you bums get a day off. Rossi will be in charge of the squadron until I get back."

Rossi interrupted. "We knew you were getting a medal. They didn't tell us that you were going to Rome to get it."

"They're planning some big ceremony. Mussolini himself is supposed to pin the medal on my chest."

A couple of his men muttered "Holy crap!" while others asked incredulously, "You're really going to meet Mussolini?"

Capitano Rossi quieted them down before asking his commander the next question on his mind.

"How long will you be gone and what will we be doing while you are?"

"The squadron is moving forward to the El Prat airport southwest of Barcelona on Friday so you'll need to pack up while you're recovering tomorrow. Six new men will be joining you there to bring us back to full strength. As for me, I don't know how long I'll be gone. A lot depends on what the brass wants to do with me after the ceremony. Colonel Sarbone says I'll be talking with a lot of the upper brass so let me know if there's anything you want and I'll see what I can get."

Rossi's comment of "I want one of those new French planes" was quickly followed by a chorus of "Me too" from the rest of the men. Guido smiled and added his own.

"Me too. I'll see what I can do, but for now, it's time to get this party going. Let's head to the cantina and try our luck with the ladies here one more time before we leave."

The lively banter as they headed off masked their sadness at the probability that Guido would be leaving the squadron.

October 14, 1936
30 miles south of Barcelona, Spain
Vice Admiral Sir Geoffrey Blake sat at his desk and reread his orders. This was definitely not what he'd expected. The Second Battlecruiser Squadron and the Second Battle Division had sailed from Scapa Flow. They should arrive off of Gibraltar in a week. Sir Geoffrey's First Battle-cruiser Squadron would continue to harass the Entente forces until they were relieved, then they would sail for Scapa Flow. *Hood* and *Tiger* were still in drydock, so *Lion* and *Princess Royal* would be transferred to the Second Battlecruiser Squadron. The First Battlecruiser Squadron would be brought back up to strength when *Hood* and *Tiger* finished their refit.

The Second Battle Division, with its five older *Queen Elizabeth*-class battleships would continue on to Alexandria to relieve Admiral Sir Dudley Pound. He would also sail to join the Home Fleet at Scapa Flow with the Fourth Battle Division and its five *King George V*-class battleships. It looked like the Admiralty had given up on extending the conflict in Spain. Sir Geoffrey didn't know if that was because the *Firedrake* was seen on its delivery run or because of the attempt on the Pope. He decided it was probably the combination.

It also looked like the Admiralty was concentrating its newer and faster battleships in the Atlantic. That would make it easier to counter any moves the Entente fleet might make. Sir Geoffrey stopped his train of thought and wondered if he was reading too much into it. Maybe it was just a routine change of deployment.

Regardless, Sir Geoffrey was relieved to be leaving the Gibraltar post. He didn't like the cat-and-mouse games he'd been ordered to play. Dealing with smugglers and being ordered to harass the French and Italian fleets without the option to shoot were not his idea of what the British Fleet should be doing. He'd felt hamstrung ever since he'd arrived. In Sir Geoffrey's opinion, if you were going to threaten someone you better be ready to carry through. If you weren't, the other guy would eventually figure it out and quit responding to your threats. When that happened, you were down to two options, do nothing or start shooting. The constant and obvious bluffing meant there was no longer a middle ground.

Sir Geoffrey stood and paced around his cabin. Would the Entente see the redeployment as a British retreat? That was the real question. Sir Geoffrey rubbed his chin for a moment and gave a disgusted sigh. Maybe he should quit trying to read the minds of friend and foe alike. He still had harassing to do and needed to get the squadron in motion. He went to his cabin door and opened it, causing the excitable Lieutenant Travis Caldwell to nearly leap to his feet to demonstrate his readiness for Sir Geoffrey's orders.

"My compliments to Commodore Moore and have the squadron make course for Palamós, twenty knots."

"Aye, Sir. Palamós and twenty knots."

The young lieutenant headed off to pass on the orders while Sir Geoffrey closed the door and headed back to his desk. He'd only been in charge of the squadron for about three months but it felt like he was failing. He'd carried out his orders but it didn't feel like he'd made any difference in the Entente's timetable. Maybe it was the encounter with the Entente fleet this afternoon. He'd put his ships in danger to create a show of force for the Spanish. Then the damned French and Italian ships had sail between his ships and the Spanish coast. They'd kept every one of their guns turned towards the Spanish, too. It may have been their own display of force but it also showed incredible contempt for the British warships, HIS British warships, sitting just a few miles away. And now he was back to the empty threat problem.

Maybe he could jolt them out of their nonchalance by threatening their supply lines. The scout planes had reported a number of Entente merchant ships heading for Roses and Palamós. They would probably be using Barcelona to offload supplies soon. If Sir Geoffrey couldn't convince their battle fleet to pay attention to him, maybe he could scare their supply ships into yelling for help.

October 21, 1936
Manstein Residence, Berlin, Germany
I prepare myself for another day of dealing with people who refuse to believe my warnings. The collapse of the Republican forces in Spain wasn't due to the strength of the French army, it was because of Spain's weak and inept troops. Please pay no attention to the fact that we were praising the fortitude and esprit de corps of those same Republican troops less than a month ago. If we can blame it on Spanish ineptness then we don't have to spend more money on the military and we can fund our pet projects. Sometimes I wish I'd stayed in the military.

I finish shaving and dress for breakfast. I can hear Brent getting ready for school as I head down the stairs. The aroma of bacon and frying potatoes greet me when I get to the dining room. Otto is already there reading the morning paper. Another copy rests on my seat at the table. I greet them as I have on so many other days while I take my seat.

"Good morning, Otto. Good morning, Beatrice."

I tried greeting Beatrice first when she joined us but that only lasted for about a week. She informed me that Otto had been with me for a lot longer than she had and had earned the right to be greeted first. I had just been trying to make sure she felt welcome in my home. Otto had simply rolled his eyes and shrugged.

Otto peered at me over the top of his lowered paper. "Good morning, Erich."

As always, Beatrice waited for Otto's response before giving her own "Good morning, Sir." I still hadn't been able to get her to use my given name.

"Omelets and potatoes today, Sir. Rolls and blackberry jam, too."

"That sounds almost as wonderful as it smells, Beatrice." She'd gotten flustered the first time I complimented her. At least she had gotten used to that in the last eleven years.

"Thank you, Sir" had become her usual response.

I pick up my newspaper but hesitate before reading it. Some people might think our morning routine is boring and needs more variation to keep things interesting. I get more than enough excitement from my job. Boring and predictable at home are the moments that I cherish. I think the same applies to Otto. Tension and wariness are his constant companions once we leave the house. It's only here that he can relax some. I've talked with him about having a life away from us but he wasn't interested. Brent was like a son to him and I was his best friend. Decades of being wary and looking for hidden dangers had made it too difficult to deal with the general public. Those same decades of working with me also made him almost as big of a target as I am. I think that may be why Beatrice keeps things formal and avoids being around when we discuss things. The less she knows, the safer she feels. I wonder if this is how things work in other households where matters of state or business are discussed and I treasure her discretion.

I turn my attention to the paper to see what their view of the world is and how closely it resembles mine. Sometimes there are bits of information I haven't seen. Their speculations with fewer facts are just as important. The theories they come up with shape how the average person interprets world events. How the people see things determines the policies and agendas of the political groups that represent them. Those agendas are what I have to deal with to keep our country safe and working. On more than one occasion we've had to leak information to keep the people informed enough to make good decisions or prevent panics. The papers and radio have used their control of information to push their agendas for so long that I wonder who really runs the country.

The hall clock starts chiming six o'clock and Brent graces us with his presence. Otto and I fold our papers and put them away in expectation of Beatrice's presentation of today's enticing morsels. We all smile and nod through the presentation routine though Brent seems to be on the verge of drooling. He loves her omelets as much as I enjoy her strudel. Talking can begin once Beatrice has returned to the kitchen. As usual, it also has to wait for the initial assault on our repast to wane. Brent, who can wolf down food with that speed reserved for teenagers, opens the conversation.

"Have the Republicans managed to get any kind of defense organized?"

"The paper says they've stopped the Entente drive towards Lleida."

Brent just rolls his eyes at me before uttering, "But?"

"That's because the Entente isn't pushing towards Lleida. Most of the troops around Barcelona and the Pope headed south through Tarragona to Valencia."

Brent cocks his head to one side and looks a little confused for a moment before responding. I take the opportunity to get in a few more bites.

"Isn't Lleida somewhere about halfway between Barcelona and Zaragoza?"

I'm impressed he knows where it is and nod my agreement.

"And hasn't Zaragoza has been under the control of the Nationalists since they started shooting?"

I nod again and smile, wondering if he can figure it out.

"So why aren't they trying to link up with the Nationalists to consolidate their gains?"

Brent gives me a sour look as he drums his fingers on the table. I simply smile as I continue eating. Brent turns his gaze to Otto who swallows his latest forkful before responding.

"Why are there Entente troops in Spain?"

Brent starts to roll his eyes again but stops midway and gets a thoughtful look on his face.

"According to them, it's to stop the killing of the Spanish people and stabilize the government. Which means that their objective isn't to control Spanish territory, it's to control the people of Spain.

"Whoever wrote the article is thinking in terms of the trench warfare from the Great War as opposed to the initial war of maneuver. And with the disparity of forces, it's extremely unlikely the Entente will bog down. They would be more limited by their logistics than Republican resistance. So, going down the coast makes more sense because they can secure more of the Spanish population and they can be supplied by sea."

I continue to eat and smile when he finishes which garners another sour look from him. He scratches his head for a moment.

"And... it also cuts down on the amount of supplies that can be shipped in to support the Republican forces while stretching the line they have to defend around Madrid. Anything I missed?"

"Not much. Just the ability to pull the Pope to one of their ships for treatment if there's another attack and that by pushing into the rear areas now, the Republicans forces have less time to recover and organize any kind of defense."

Brent nods at my addition to the reasons for the Entente's direction of advance.

"And how many of the Reichstag members think the same way as the article in the paper?"

Now it's my turn for a sour look.

"Most of them. It 'proves' that the Republicans can stop the Nationalists and the Entente when they try. Which means that when the Republicans forces fall apart, it will be due to a Spanish collapse of morale, not Entente strength. Politicians see what they want and interpret things to fit their perceptions."

"Aren't you a politician, Dad?"

Otto laughed so suddenly he almost blew milk out of his nose.

October 21, 1936
30 kilometers north of Valencia, Spain
Lieutenant-colonel Roger Noiret was bone weary. It had been a week since the attempt on the Pope's life. His men were here to protect the Pope from large unit military action. The Swiss Guard were responsible for the immediate security around His Holiness.

Roger knew that was the arrangement but it didn't keep him from feeling like he had failed. The death of Luis Esperanza, a man he'd come to know and respect, hurt as much as the stitches he'd torn in his left shoulder during the attack. The Pope had prayed with Roger and Roger had at least been relieved of any feelings of guilt, but the shoulder was a constant reminder of his sense of loss and failure.

Task Group Pius had been covering about fifty kilometers a day. The Papal caravan stopped at least twice a day to spread its message of peace and healing. Roger usually spoke at one or two of the stops while Luis' place as a speaker had been taken over by Capitaine Gabriel Müller, the leader of the Swiss Guard. Part of Capitaine Müller's participation was to tell Luis' story and praise his actions, part of it was that the Capitaine wanted to be in a better position to see any threats to the Pope.

General Gamelin had rightly been pushing the advance from Barcelona. The Republican forces were in disarray and any pause would give them time to reorganize and mount some kind of resistance. But pause they would, at least for today. The rest of the 507th armored regiment were still sixty kilometers behind Roger's command. Their Char B1bis heavy tanks were being slowed down by mechanical problems. The rest of Commandant Philippe de Hauteclocque's cavalry regiment, the 4e Cuirassiers, were about twenty kilometers back with the hard-marching 2nd North African infantry division. Only the 1st Motorized infantry division had kept up with Task Group Pius, and a number of their trucks were running rough. Today, they would be working their way towards Valencia on foot while everyone else got some time to catch up on maintenance and rest.

All Roger knew was that he was grateful for today. He was glad that some other unit had the lead, that he didn't have to look over Commandant Robert Olleris' shoulder to check his deployment of Task Group Pius, or over Capitaine Müller's shoulder to coordinate with the Swiss Guard. Mostly he was grateful for not having to give a speech. Roger thought for a moment before deciding that wasn't true. He was even more grateful that Caporal Jean Martin was doing the paperwork so well that Roger only had to spend about fifteen minutes a day on summaries and signing his name. And that they hadn't lost any more men. And that the Pope was safe. Roger stopped and bowed his head for the shortest prayer he'd ever made. He simply prayed, "Thanks."

Roger felt as if a great weight had lifted from his shoulders when he finally opened his eyes. He was still physically tired but the mental fatigue of the last several days was gone.

He went to his field desk and wrote a letter to his wife, Catherine. He sent his love to her and their sons and told her of his adventures over the last week. He only touched briefly on how the Pope's actions and words had prevented a slaughter in Barcelona, though he did mention how the actions of the people in Barcelona helped prevent reprisals. He wrote of the boy in Reus who was about Junior's age. How the boy had walked up to Roger, come to attention, and saluted. Roger had returned the courtesy and asked why he'd done it. The boy's father had been one of the men they had furloughed north of Girona. He wrote of the little girl in Amposta who had given him a flower for similar reasons. He wrote of how much he missed her and how glad he was that she had agreed to be his wife.

He decided to wrap up the letter before he got too maudlin. Hopefully Caporal Martin could get the letter safely on its way. He could drop it off with his clerk when Martin came by later today for a more in-depth look at the paperwork Martin had been handling. Roger also needed to visit the doctor to get his shoulder checked out. And he needed to spend some time with his officers to see how things were going. He had more than a few things to do on his "day off."

October 21, 1936
La Linea, Spain

Carmen Esperanza had just gotten home. The last week had been a whirlwind of planning, thanking, eating, and crying, so much crying. She had been stunned last Wednesday when Isabella Sanchez told her of Luis' death and was sure there must be some mistake. But the radio reported it again as she sat on Mrs. Sanchez' porch sipping a glass of brandy. It was several minutes before Carmen moved. She bowed her head and prayed before looking up again and seeing the new world in which she lived. Tears had streaked her face but there had been things to do and her son to look after. She stood, wiping the tears from her cheeks.

"Where's Carlos?"

Mrs. Sanchez had looked at her intently before nodding her head. She knew Carmen was strong and taking care of Carlos would help her handle her husband's death. "He's in your garden with Reina. He doesn't know."

Carmen had passed the now empty glass to her friend.

"I'd best be getting home, then."

Mrs. Sanchez had taken the glass with a bitter smile.

"Maria will bring dinner around at six. Everyone else will take turns for the next week or two. Let me know what else we can do."

"Thanks" was all Carmen had said before she headed home. It was the first of many. The street had been decidedly empty as she walked to her house. Carlos hadn't really understood when she told him his Papa wouldn't be coming home from the war. He had been more confused than anything when Maria Avilar had arrived with food for dinner. Despite their differences, Carmen's thanks had been heartfelt.

Like most of her neighbors, Maria supported the Nationalists and had been distant with Carmen since the civil war began. But Maria had hugged Carmen fiercely before serving paella with shrimp and mussels followed by flan for dessert. Carmen and Maria had chatted about everything except Luis over dinner. When Carlos had brought out his medal to show Maria and said he couldn't wait to show it to his Papa, he didn't notice how both of the women shuddered with tears in their eyes.

Maria's boys, Jose and Pedro, had shown up after dinner to play with Carlos while Maria and Carmen slowly cleaned the dinner dishes in silence. They seemed to be reluctant to break the spell of companionship and actually finish but eventually there was nothing left to clean or put away.

"Thank you, Maria. That was delicious."

"It's the least we can do. Is Carlos going to go to school tomorrow?"

"Probably. I don't think he really understands that his father is dead and it would give him something to do."

"I'll have my boys keep an eye on him to make sure he's okay. What about you?"

"I don't know. If Carlos goes to school, I'll probably head down to Gibraltar for work. I think we'll need the money now more than ever. It'll keep me from dwelling on things and the British have been better informed than we have about most of the fighting, so maybe they'll know what will happen to Luis' body."

Maria had nodded. "That's probably best. I know Father Garcia will want to discuss arrangements with you. I'll let him know to stop by for dinner tomorrow. I'm not sure who's cooking tomorrow but I'll let Mrs. Sanchez know that they should expect an extra mouth to feed. Jose and Pedro will come over after dinner to keep Carlos occupied."

"Thanks" was all Carmen said as she closed her eyes and took a deep breath. She was startled by another crushing hug that started another bout of sobs from Carmen. It was a few minutes before Maria released her and stepped back to dry Carmen's face.

Maria's "Mustn't let Carlos see too much" earned another mumbled thanks from Carmen and the two women went back to chatting like they used to. The Avilars stayed late and it had been later still when Carmen finally got Carlos to bed. Carmen was exhausted when she turned in but sleep wouldn't come. She lay there, quietly crying for hours. She didn't know if she had actually gotten any sleep, but she was startled when the alarm went off.

That Thursday morning had been surreal. Her brain was foggy from lack of sleep but Carlos was his usual bouncy self. He'd been on his best behavior and helped with the dishes without even asking. Things had been better at school since he'd gotten his medal for helping her with her attackers and he'd been eager to go since then. Carmen wondered if the past two weeks had simply been too much for her son and started to say something to him when he stopped in his school preparations to take her hand.

"It'll be okay, Mom. I know Dad isn't coming home but I'll take care of you."

Carmen had nearly broken down at that point, but only one tear had escaped her eyes as she ruffled his hair.

"And I'll take care of you, my little man."

Carlos had hugged her before he finished getting ready for school. He hadn't even protested when she kissed him on the cheek before he left.

The walk to Gibraltar had been quiet. Amber had crossed the street and nuzzled her when she got to Mrs. Sanchez' house. The dog seemed to sense her loss and simply ambled along beside Carmen. Twice people had stepped out of her way. Both times they had bent their head in prayer and crossed themselves as she passed. Both times, the pain and grief had welled up and nearly overwhelmed her.

Carmen found that the British knew of her husband's death when she approached the gate. Both Sergeants Terry Sanders and Irvin Havens were in full dress uniform and came to attention as she approached. They both snapped off parade ground salutes as she bid them good morning. As usual, Sanders took the lead on their side of the conversation.

"Morning, Mrs. Esperanza. Terrible business, ma'am. Major Hawkins has some information for you at his quarters. Let us know if there's anything we can do. We are so sorry for your loss."

"Thank you. At least he's sharing God's grace."

"If there's anyone with that right, it'd be your husband, ma'am."

Carmen had bobbed her head and continued on towards her morning work. She hadn't been sure she could carry on a conversation without breaking down and both of the British soldiers seem to understand her pain. Carmen wondered how many friends they had lost over the years and said a prayer for them as she crossed the quiet ground.

Major Hawkins had been in full dress uniform too when he greeted her at the door to his quarters. She didn't even get the chance to knock.

"Morning, Mrs. Esperanza. Please come in. Don't worry about your usual routine, just have a seat at the table if you would."

Carmen headed toward the Major's dining table and found Lieutenant James Higgens holding a seat for her. The young lieutenant looked dashing in his dress uniform. She took the proffered seat and waited as the British officers settled in their chairs. Major Hawkins looked deeply into Carmen's eyes with evident affection and concern before speaking.

"We were going to go by your house to pay our respects but I thought you might come to work so we waited." He paused for a moment before continuing. "I know it's not adequate, but we're sorry for your loss. I lost my wife and son eleven years ago in childbirth. Nothing anyone said could dull the pain, but I found refuge in my work." He paused again, bowing his head, and Carmen realized the single tear rolling down his cheek was mirrored on her own. He took several deep breaths before he raised his head and continued. "Your job will be here for you whenever you feel the desire or need to work. Higgens and I will pay you regardless of when you make it. Sergeant Sanders will come by at least once a week to check on you and Carlos. Let him know if there's anything you need. Okay?"

Carmen simply nodded and Major Hawkins continued.

"We do have news that you may not have heard. Last night, the Pope arranged for your husband's body to be flown to Málaga tomorrow. The casket will be driven to La Linea on Saturday. You should be able to have his funeral on Sunday or later. We would be proud to attend if that's okay with you."

Carmen felt remarkably composed when she responded. "That will be good. It will help to have Luis close where I can talk with him. Thank you for letting me know and sharing your grief. Now if there's no other news, I'd like to get started on your breakfast."

Major Hawkins had simply nodded and then both he and Lieutenant Higgens stood as Carmen rose and headed into the kitchen. Carmen had thrown herself into her cooking and cleaning routines and was grateful for the time where she could turn her brain off. She headed home with a prayer and a little more peace of mind.

When she had finally turned onto her street, she found Mrs. Sanchez on her porch with Father Garcia. He rose and crossed the street to her, pausing to give the faithful Amber a pat and scratch as she headed home. They walked to Carmen's house in silence that was broken only when Carlos opened the front door and greeted his mother with a hug and the priest with a wary look.

"I finished my schoolwork, Mama, and cleaned my room. I was thinking about doing some weeding in the garden."

"That would be good, my young man. Thank you."

Carlos gave her another tight hug before heading out the back door. Carmen watched him go with pride in her heart before finally breaking the silence with Father Garcia.

"Would you like something to drink?"

"Water, please."

She went into the kitchen and returned moments later with two glasses of water. She invited the priest to a seat at the dining room table and joined him, taking a deep breath.

"The British say that Luis is being flown down and should arrive on Saturday. Can we have his funeral on Sunday?"

"We can, but the Vatican has asked that we delay it until Monday. They're sending a Cardinal from Rome and he won't get here until Sunday evening."

Carmen's eyes had widened but after a sigh, she'd simply nodded. "I still want you to do the service. You knew my Luis."

"I'll be honored to. I'll send someone over on Saturday when Luis arrives. I know Mrs. Sanchez has everything organized around here and I've told her to come to me if you need anything. Is there anything I can do?"

"I think Carlos and I are okay but a few minutes of prayer wouldn't hurt."

Father Garcia and Carmen prayed and then he excused himself and promised to see her on Saturday. Food and the Avilar boys arrived a little later with Sofia Martinez disappointed that Father Garcia had already left. That night, Carmen almost believed that nothing had changed until she heard Carlos sobbing quietly in bed. She invited him to her bed and curled around him protectively as they both drifted off to sleep.

Friday had been much the same. Saturday had seen Carlos and the Avilar boys running around the neighborhood. Carlos was trying to stay distracted while Jose and Pedro were enjoying their lack of supervision. Carmen had cleaned and cleaned. It was her way of keeping herself from dwelling on Luis' death.

It was almost four when cars had arrived outside. She had just finished sweeping the kitchen for the third time when there was a knock at her door. She found a gentleman in an outfit straight out of the sixteenth century when she opened it. The Swiss Guardsman asked her to accompany him to the church. Carmen started to object because of Carlos but then saw another guardsman walking up the street with him in tow. The trip was somber and both Carmen and Carlos broke down when six guardsmen removed Luis' casket and placed it in the church. They then draped a Papal flag over his coffin and two guardsmen took positions beside it. Their detachment commander explained that Luis had been posthumously made a member of the Swiss Guard and he would receive the same send off as the other guardsman who had given his life to save the Pope. More would be explained when the Cardinal arrived from Rome.

Mass on Sunday had featured a sermon on service to the Lord. Old friends who had distanced themselves when the civil war broke out hugged, blessed, and extended their sympathies. Twice, Mrs. Sanchez and father Garcia had to spirit Carmen and Carlos away to quiet areas of the church so they could compose themselves. After several requests, Carmen agreed to allow other parishioners to view Luis' casket. It seemed like forever but the crowd eventually headed home while Carmen and Carlos stayed and rested at Father Garcia's house.

The Cardinal had arrived at half past four. He presented them with tokens blessed by Pope Pius XII and said the Holy Father would come by to personally thank them once the war was over. He also told Carmen that she would receive the equivalent of fifty ounces of gold and the monthly pay of a Capitaine of the Swiss Guard for her life and that of Carlos. He knew it couldn't replace her husband but the Church hoped it might ease her other burdens.

Despite being on a Monday, virtually everyone attended the funeral. Even school had been canceled. The four British soldiers in their dress uniforms had stood out almost as much as the six men of the Swiss Guard who acted as pallbearers. Eating, drinking, and celebrating Luis' life continued for most of the day as people who had laughed contemptuously at Luis mere weeks ago, now sung his praises and mourned his loss. Most of it went over Carlos' head but Mrs. Sanchez called out more than a few members of town for their hypocrisy. Carmen appreciated her efforts more than she could say.

Exhaustion had let her sleep that night but Tuesday had brought reality back into focus. She and Carlos both slept late but after a brunch of leftovers, they both found they wanted to return to their normal routines. Carlos had headed off to school while Carmen headed to Gibraltar to catch up on her work.

Sergeants Sanders and Havens had greeted her at the gate and tried to keep to their normal morning routines even if Carmen was several hours late. She could see and hear their guarded concern but was surprised when she saw their pride too. She knocked at Major Hawkins' quarters but he was off at work. He had told her where he kept his spare key for just such occasions but it still felt weird when she let herself into his home. Carmen had lunch waiting for him when he'd arrived. It was strange but Carmen decided that making lunch for the Major had long been a substitute for preparing meals for Luis. It was probably why this routine helped settle her.

Major Hawkins had smiled when he found Carmen working. After finishing his meal he'd asked Carmen to join him at the table.

"We know things are going to be tough with the loss of Luis so Lieutenant Higgens and I are going to increase what we pay you. I doubt it will cover your shortfall but it's our honor to help."

Major Hawkins misinterpreted her initial shallow smile and quickly became perplexed as a giggle followed by a full laugh escaped Carmen. His consternation grew as tears joined the laugh and he wondered if she was having a breakdown. She finally stopped and looked down at the table as a few remaining tears pelted its surface. She looked back up with tear-pooled eyes.

"Thank you, Major. I needed that laugh. I appreciate your offer but have to refuse. The Vatican will be paying me a stipend and the Church will assist me with any needs I might have. Money will never be a problem for me or Carlos again. What you and Lieutenant Higgens can do is just let me work. Normalcy is what I need right now. I'll have to decide what I want to do down the road but right now, all I want to do is what I'd be doing if Luis was still alive."

Major Hawkins had nodded his acquiescence. There had been extra goodies from the Sergeants on her way home yesterday, but today had been nearly normal. And she cherished it more than she could say.

October 21, 1936
Rome, Italy

Capitano Guido Nobili sat in his hotel room enjoying a drink of chilled amaretto. The plane rides to Rome had seemed to take forever, probably because he hadn't had anything to do. He'd arrived in Rome last Friday morning and been greeted by a Sergente who had driven him to the Hotel Hassler atop the Spanish Steps. Guido's thoughts that he might be in heaven were confirmed when he met his liaison for his stay in Rome. Aurora Esposito was ten centimeters shorter than Guido with long black hair, an athletic figure and a face that belonged on an angel.

Aurora was there to help him get settled in and guide him through the schedule for his medal ceremony. She had also been assigned to show him the sights of Rome. She had been a bit cold and professional when Guido first met her and his inherent shyness had made that Friday afternoon and evening more than a little awkward. She loosened up slowly during the day as they toured the sights that he seemed to know as well or better than she did. After dinner, she had leaned back and looked at him questioningly.

"You're not at all what I expected. Most fighter pilots are cocky and pushy but you seem to be quiet and watchful. My info says you've never been to Rome and I've lived here all my life yet you know more about it than I do. You're here to receive a medal as Italy's first ace since the Great War and yet you haven't said a thing about your combat experience. Just who the heck are you?"

Guido smiled and even blushed a little bit before answering.

"Yes, I'm a fighter pilot, but I'm also a squadron commander who lost a third of his command. Men who died while I couldn't help them. Friends who died needlessly. Our planes were better than the Spanish, but I think we would have all made it back if they had been as good as the French. So I've had a little of that cocky attitude knocked out of me. It's not exactly something to brag about.

"As for Rome? I've always wanted to visit but I'd never made it before now. That hasn't kept me from reading everything that I could about it in preparation for today. And now that I'm finally here, I'm staying in one of the best hotels in Rome and being shown those dreamed of sights by the most beautiful woman I've ever met. That she's charming, funny, and paying attention to me just convince me this is all a dream. Sorry if I've managed to disappoint you."

They had stared at each other for several silent minutes before Aurora had looked at her watch.

"You need to get to sleep and so do I. A car will be by to get you at nine sharp."

Their goodnight wishes were awkward but Guido hoped he would get to spend some more time with her. As he prepared for the award ceremony on Saturday morning, Guido found it very strange that he was more nervous about possibly seeing Aurora again than he was about meeting Mussolini. Maybe this was why he'd never had a serious relationship. It distracted you at odd times, and distracted in a dog fight meant death. Guido shook his head then checked his appearance before heading downstairs.

Another Sergente picked him up and drove him to Quirinal Palace. Guido was amazed at its size and beauty as they drove up. Then he'd seen Aurora waiting at the entrance and the palace seemed to fade into the background. She guided him on a private tour of the grounds. Despite Guido's fascination with history, he could only remember the Courtyard of Honour, the mirrors room, and vaguely the gardens when Aurora finally led him up the Staircase of Honour to the Throne Room. Part of his distraction was simply being overwhelmed by the sights, part of it was that Aurora had taken hold of his arm after the first few minutes.

Guido had been last in a line with three other people who were receiving honors. Aurora told him what he was supposed to do but it seemed to have vanished from his head so he paid more attention to what the other recipients were doing than who they were. He approached the throne when they called his name and began reading out what honor he was receiving and why. He bowed to King Victor Emmanuel III and then turned to face Benito Mussolini. Guido was surprised to find that Mussolini was only slightly taller than he was even though he was standing on the first step of the dais. Mussolini pinned the Medaglia d'oro al valor militare on Guido's chest and then saluted him, an honor Guido quickly returned. Photographers punctuated the exchange with flashes from their cameras. Then as they shook hands, the fascist leader had spoken and handed him a small box while more flashbulbs popped.

"Well done, Maggiore Nobili. Let me know if there's anything Italy can do for our dashing pilots."

"Get us planes like the French have, Sir" was out of his mouth before Guido could think to stop it.

They stopped in mid-handshake for a moment as Mussolini glared at Guido before he recovered. The handshake continued and Mussolini smiled for the cameras before kissing Guido on both cheeks and releasing him to return to the audience. Aurora had given him an alarmed and questioning look when he returned to her side but Guido wasn't about to do anything else to draw attention to himself.

When the ceremony wrapped up a few minutes later, Guido found an army Capitano had appeared by his side.

"If you would come with me, Maggiore" was all he said.

It took Guido a moment to realize the Capitano was talking to him. His mind played back the medal ceremony and Guido looked down to his left hand where the box containing his new insignia waited. He'd been promoted not one, but two grades. Aurora released his arm as he turned to the other officer.

"Certainly, Capitano."

The army Capitano guided him through the crowd to a much smaller office where Mussolini sat behind a large oak desk. Guido drew himself to attention to start the ritual for reporting when summoned by a superior but Mussolini stopped him.

"That's not necessary, Maggiore Nobili. Have a seat and tell me what you meant by your comment."

Guido sat in the indicated chair and collected his thoughts for a moment. He decided that brutal honesty was his best choice if he wanted things to change.

"Sir, my squadron was stationed in Figueres along with a French squadron. They had M.S.406 fighters that were a bit less maneuverable than our CR.32s but they are also a hundred kilometers per hour faster. My men were all happy with our planes and made fun of the lumbering French planes right up until the Republican counterattack."

"Didn't our planes perform well against the Soviet planes?"

"Yes, Sir, they did. But we were heavily outnumbered and as we ran out of ammunition we couldn't break away. Five of my men were shot down, four of them died. I expected to join them and would have if French reinforcements hadn't shown up. The extra speed would have saved my men's lives."

There was a short silence as Mussolini got a faraway look in his eyes while he absorbed the information. Guido continued when he appeared to refocus.

"We got to fly some of the French planes on patrol after most of the air battle was over. Between that experience and watching them in combat, all of my men wanted the 406 over the CR.32 even if it meant we had to learn new tactics. That was when we got another rude shock as a squadron of the new French D.520s flew by us like we were standing still. We all agreed that we might be able to defend against a 406 but there was no way we could compete with the D.520. And all of my men admitted they would be afraid to even try.

"I know that Fiat is working on the G.50 but that would only put us on a parity with the 406. By the time it gets to our fighter squadrons, the French will still be flying circles around us. And if the French have shown the D.520, then other countries, ones that we my face in combat, will be working to match or better it. We need to radically improve our air force if we want our pilots to have a chance."

Mussolini had looked thoughtful as he appraised Guido. "Thank you for your candor. Please go and enjoy Rome. I'll send word when I've decided what to do with your information."

The army Capitano had been summoned and Guido was escorted back to the waiting Aurora. She waited until they were outside of the palace before rounding on him for details on what had happened. They walked around Rome as Guido ran through the meeting. Guido developed a sense of dread when Aurora pointed out that Mussolini didn't like bad news and asked if Guido had forgotten that Mussolini was the Minister of the Air Force among other things.

The rest of Saturday had been a bit muted as Aurora showed Guido around town while he did his best to get out from under the cloud of doom he felt following him around. She'd even given him a goodnight kiss when he headed to his sumptuous room that now had the feeling of a gilded prison. Sleep had not come quickly that night.

Aurora had taken Guido to mass at the Vatican on Sunday and followed it up with sightseeing there. There was a message waiting for Guido when they returned to his hotel for dinner. It was a summons for the following morning. Dinner and drinks lasted for hours as they learned about each other. Aurora invited herself up to Guido's room when the evening waxed late. Guido objected since he might be a condemned man but Aurora would have none of it. The night had been magical. Even though he'd had little sleep, Guido's only regret in the morning was that he might not get to repeat it.

He gave Aurora a long kiss when he left for his appointment with Mussolini. He hoped it wouldn't be his last. The ride to the Quirinal Palace seemed to be over far too quickly while the wait for the actual meeting seemed to drag on endlessly. He was eventually summoned to the same office he'd been in on Saturday and Mussolini had again interrupted the formalities and directed Guido to a seat.

"Why do you seem to be nervous, Maggiore Nobili?"

"I told you things that you may not have wanted to hear last Saturday. Some people in positions of power don't react well when that happens."

"Huh. Not a bad answer considering I'm one of those people who has a reputation of not reacting well." Mussolini sat back in his chair and contemplated the decorated pilot for a moment. "I was not happy to hear your analysis of our fighters considering we have a major program working on an upgraded version of the CR.32. That doesn't mean it wasn't true.

"You've caused me a lot of extra work. Our intelligence and the French themselves agree with your assessment of the French fighters' capabilities. Rather than ask your men if they agreed, we asked them if they would like to have their planes replaced with either of the French fighters. While they would prefer the D.520, every single one of them was willing to trade in their CR.32 for even an M.S.406."

Mussolini raised his voice. "Send her in."

Aurora entered the room with a smile as Guido's jaw dropped at her appearance in uniform. She was a full Colonnello in intelligence. He'd started to rise automatically but both Aurora and Mussolini told him to stay seated. Aurora took the other seat in front of Mussolini's desk.

"Any problems with him, Colonnello Esposito?"

"He snores a bit, Sir, but no he doesn't talk in his sleep and he didn't spook when I tried to scare him about you."

That earned a small snort of amusement from Mussolini.

"Very good." Mussolini turned back to face Guido before continuing. "I'm going to need someone to work with the French if we're going to fix the issues with our fighters. Would you like the job?"

A number of questions ran through Guido's mind, most of them concerning Aurora but he focused on the question. "I think I'd like that very much, Sir. And if I may, you might want to do something similar with our tanks. Their new ones also seemed to be a lot more effective than anything else in the field."

Mussolini had simply nodded tiredly before dismissing him. The details were still being worked on but Guido would assist in upgrading the Regia Aeronautica and it turned out that Aurora really did like him and would accompany him. Guido would be in Rome for at least another week before being sent to Paris. Aurora was looking forward to the trip almost as much as he was.

October 21, 1936

Gibraltar

Vice Admiral Sir Geoffrey Blake was clearing out his quarters on land. The Second Battlecruiser Squadron and the Second Battle Division had arrived this afternoon. The *Lion* and *Princess Royal* had been transferred and all that was left had been to tidy up and take the rest of his truncated command back to Scapa Flow. Vice Admiral Sir Andrew Cunningham, commander of the Second Battlecruiser Squadron, told Sir Geoffrey that the Admiralty was not censoring him. The Admiralty wanted to do in depth interviews with Sir Geoffrey and his men to see what they could learn about the latest French and Italian battleships. They also wanted the faster *King George V*-class battleships available in the Atlantic rather than stuck in the eastern Mediterranean.

That meant a lot of time sitting in port while the interviewers worked their way through the crews and shore leave when they didn't want you. Sir Geoffrey smiled at the thought of seeing Jean and their daughters. It had only been three months instead of the expected year so he hoped Jean wouldn't be too put out by his return. It also meant combing through all the reports and seeing what he could glean from them.

Most of the information would probably come from the last week when they'd led the Italian battleships on a jaunt around the western Med. The *Littorio*-class ships had not been slow to follow Sir Geoffrey's command when they had headed northeast from Barcelona. Since they'd begun their journey after dark, there were probably Entente submarines stationed as lookouts around the area of operations. That was an area where Britain was woefully behind.

They had sighted a number of Entente cargo ships carrying supplies to the troops in Spain but only about half of them were military. There was a high probability that any extended operation that required sea supply would have a long-term impact on the Entente's economy since those cargo ships wouldn't be available to carry the food and resources they imported. They had also been sighted by a number of patrol planes so surface operations might be untenable but stationing a number of the newer S-class submarines in the western Med might be very profitable.

Sir Geoffrey's squadron made a couple of high-speed dashes as they cruised off the French and Italian coasts. The five Italian battleships had slowly lost ground on each dash. They appeared to have a top speed of thirty knots which meant they were faster than any of the Royal Navy's battleships and were probably more heavily armored than his battlecruisers. Not a good combination for the Royal Navy.

The Entente squadron had been traveling with fewer escorts than the Royal Navy used so they might be more vulnerable to submarine or air attack. Sir Geoffrey decided he needed to do a closer examination of the photos from the *Ark Royal's* scouts.

Sir Geoffrey sighed and realized he'd been dithering. He had finished packing and needed to head for the launches to return to his ship. Regardless of what Sir Andrew said, he felt his mission had been a failure. They had gathered some intelligence on the Entente fleets but hadn't actually stopped them from doing anything. Now he was back at Gibraltar preparing to go home while the Italians had rejoined the French off of Valencia in an effort to threaten one of the few remaining Republican cities. It wouldn't be long before they collapsed and Spain was wholly under Nationalist control.

Assuming they joined the Entente, the western Med would be ringed by Entente territory. Commerce through the Med would be problematic at best and Gibraltar might become untenable. Shipping and ship movements would have to go around Africa, greatly increasing their cost and slowing their speed. Throw in that a lot of that African coast was Entente colonies and things would get even dicier. Things were definitely not looking up for the British Empire.

October 28, 1936
The Chancellery, Berlin, Germany
I sit at my desk waiting for my nine o'clock appointment. The French ambassador, André François-Poncet, will want to discuss the Spanish situation. Sir Eric Phipps, ambassador from the United Kingdom, is scheduled for eleven. It might prove to be an interesting morning. At least the Reichstag is paying more attention after Valencia.

It's nine on the dot when Edna opens the door to my office and announces the French Ambassador. I rise to greet him.

"André, good to see you."

"Good morning, Erich."

We shake hands and sit down. André seems relaxed so maybe there won't be any surprises and he has some answers for me.

"Thanks for seeing me on such short notice. I know you're busy so I'll try to keep this brief. The Swiss Guard have finished their investigation and they believe that the grenade used in the attempt on the Pope came from the British. The Pope intends to announce this during this Sunday's sermon."

"You know they'll simply deny it or claim it wasn't intended for that purpose and was stolen by the assassin."

"Maybe, but the Swiss Guard have records from the CNT that show the grenade was from that destroyer we photographed and that the attack was planned by the CNT. Whether or not it was what the British intended, they knowingly gave weapons to anarchists while we were heading their way. It hasn't gone over well in Paris or Rome."

"The Swiss also found something else. There was a cargo ship in the Barcelona harbor that had a dozen artillery pieces and several hundred rounds of ammunition for them. They appear to have come from the Ukraine."

I do my best to only look concerned before responding. "I'll see what I can find out about how they ended up there. Hopefully it was just an overzealous army officer and doesn't extend to anyone in their government violating the Non-Intervention Agreement."

André just looks at me for a moment. "Hopefully that's all it was. We too hope no government in the Central Coalition was involved."

I think I've had enough of the veiled threats. "Even if they were involved, what's a dozen guns compared to the ten infantry divisions, five tank regiments, and hundreds of airplanes the Entente sent into Spain. And let's not forget your battleships that blew the crap out of Valencia last week."

André at least has the courtesy to look abashed. "I told you, Erich. We're only there to end the bloodshed as quickly as we can. Our troops will pull out soon. Madrid should fall within days and we'll pull most of troops out once that happens."

"But you'll leave enough there to make sure your puppet is in charge and secure, right? And Valencia?"

"The Republicans sent a division to defend it and refused our calls to surrender. I guess they thought we wouldn't attack since we didn't at Girona. They were wrong. We had no intention of letting them recover and build up their defenses to drag this out. We got Franco's okay and hit them hard by land, sea, and air. We think there were around twenty thousand casualties between their soldiers and civilians when they broke. It's still probably a lot cheaper than if we had drawn it out."

"That's pretty callous when we're talking about women and children."

"Erich, we weren't going to wait around to see what other goodies the Brits, Russians, or Ukrainians could slip into the city. A call was made, the fighting should be over soon, and our men will get to come home."

André's facade has slipped a little and he looks more than a bit pissed off. Maybe the French have rightly decided we were behind the Ukrainian shipment but they can't prove it yet. It might be best to ratchet this down a notch or two.

"I understand that we're sometimes faced with difficult choices and I appreciate the warning about the attempt on the Pope. Was there anything else you wanted to discuss?"

André visibly calms himself before continuing. "We think the British will again try to get the Central Coalition to work with them and the Japanese. We urge you not to and hope we can at least be peaceful neighbors and trading partners."

"Peace is all we wish, but I know there are many members of your country who still long to retake Alsace-Lorraine and treat my country to the taste of defeat. The price for such attitudes can be very high indeed."

"And that is why we too desire peace. Those elements are being kept in check. Hopefully the elements in your country who also thirst for war are also being reigned in."

"I do my best, André. I do my best."

"That's all we can ask, Erich." André pauses for a moment before standing and extending his hand. "And now I should take my leave. Thank you for your time and good luck with Phipps."

I stand to shake his hand and he heads off to report to his superiors. I sit back down as Edna pops her head in.

"Anything I can get you, Sir? Water? Schnapps? Something to eat?"

I laugh at our old running joke. "Nothing to eat. He didn't leave that bad of a taste behind. Water would be good. Maybe some Schnapps with lunch."

She smiles and heads off to get me a drink. She always seems to take the edge off of my anxieties. I stare at where she had been and wonder if maybe Otto was right about me needing a woman in my life.

Edna ushers Sir Eric Phipps into my office right at eleven. If nothing else, these ambassadors seem to be punctual.

We greet each other and settle in our chairs before he dives into the reason for his visit.

"Good morning, Chancellor Manstein."

"Good morning, Sir Phipps."

"I hear that the French Ambassador was here earlier today. Would I be right in presuming that he made his slanderous claim about us be responsible for the attack on the Pope?"

I simply shrug and nod.

Sir Phipps shakes his head and rolls his eyes.

"What a shock. We supply arms to the rightful government of Spain but when something goes wrong, those idiots in the CNT just happen to write everything down so the Entente can point an accusing finger our way. You know it's a setup, right? The CNT can't even tell you how many members they have within a thousand but somehow they have written records for hand grenades."

"The thought of it being a setup has crossed my mind."

Sir Phipps gives an obvious sigh of relief. "The home office said you'd buy it hook, line, and sinker. I'm glad I was right."

"Please, Sir Phipps, I'm sure that neither you or André would ever skew evidence to influence Germany."

That draws a disdainful frown from Sir Phipps before he shrugs with a smile. "Score one for you."

"If all you're here for is to make sure I don't think the attack on the Pope was an English conspiracy, rest assured that I don't think it was. And if that theory comes out in our press, I'll point out just how unlikely their 'evidence' is."

"Thank you, Sir. There is another point. We know that the Soviet Union has been probing the eastern defense of your Central Coalition and wonder if you might be interested in creating an anti-communism agreement with us and Japan to prevent its spread."

I sit back in my chair. That was one I hadn't seen coming.

"I'll take any proposal you have to parliament and share it with our allies. What do you have in mind?"

Sir Phipps opens his attaché case and removes a folder which he passes to me. "Basically, it's a defense pact where we would come to each other's aid if any of us were attacked."

"Are there specific commitments or is it just generic aid that's promised?"

"The details are up for negotiation but the intent is that both military and economic aid would be guaranteed based on the severity of the Soviet Union's attack."

"So, something along the lines of the agreement we have with Lithuania-Poland?"

"Along those lines, though we would prefer a more definitive level of commitments. From what I've seen of Lithuania-Poland's agreement, they get to decide when and what they'll commit."

"True, but they're also on the front line with the Soviets and know that any attack on Turkey or the Ukraine will probably spill over to them given time."

"A similar thing could be said about Japan. This agreement would keep the Soviet Union from concentrating its forces on either front and guarantee a multi-front war if they get aggressive against any of us."

We discuss it for about a half an hour more before Sir Phipps rises to return to his masters. I'll read through it and present it to parliament but it looks like another attempt to drag us into a wider alliance with Britain and Japan. I'll have to pass it along to our allies, too. I'm sure the Brits will if they haven't done so already. And if we don't pass it along, our allies may wonder why.

Maybe this whole proposal is just an attempt to drive a wedge between our countries. I wouldn't bet against the Brits presenting it as a safety net in case we're involved in a fight against the Entente and can't send many troops to aid our allies against invasion. The question is whether or not our "friends" will actually consider it or just use the possibility to try to wring more commitments and concessions out of us.

One group blithely explains away shelling innocent civilians while the other tries to bribe us to forget the injuries they've inflicted on us in the past. Sometimes I wish I'd stayed in the military. The fact that I'm really looking forward to Schnapps with lunch makes me wonder if my job will turn me into an alcoholic before I give up on it entirely.

Reference: Part II

The Spanish Civil War

HISTORICAL FIGURES

FRANCE

Roger Noiret –   Officer who fought with the Free
                             French.

Philippe de Hauteclocque –   Officer who fought with the Free
                             French.
                             He used the name Leclerc to protect his
                             wife and children in occupied France.

Maurice Gamelin –   Commander in Chief of the French Army
                             1933–1940.

Charles de Gaulle –   Army officer and statesman who led
                             Free French forces. He rewrote the

French constitution and was President of France for ten years.

André François-Poncet – Ambassador to Germany 1931–1938.

ITALY

Guido Nobili – Fighter pilot with nine claimed victories during the Spanish Civil War.

Benito Mussolini – Politician and journalist who founded the National Fascist Party. Led Italy from 1922 to 1943.

TURKEY

İsmet İnönü – Prime Minister of Turkey 1925–1937.

UNION OF SOVIET SOCIALIST REPUBLICS

Joseph Stalin – General Secretary of the Communist Party of the Soviet Union 1922–1952.

GERMANY

Erich von Manstein – One of the best strategists and field commanders during WWII.

Werner von Blomberg – Chief of the Troop Office during the Weimar Republic.

	Minister of Defence 1933–1935. Reichsminister of War 1935–1938.
Kurt Liese –	Chief of the Waffenamt (German Army Weapons Agency) 1933–1938.
Alfred Hugenberg –	Chairman of the German National People's Party 1928–1933.
Otto Wels –	Chairman of the Social Democratic Party 1919–1939.
Ludwig Kaas –	Chairman of the German Centre Party 1928–1934.
Ernst Thälmann –	Chairman of the German Communist Party 1928–1933.

UNITED KINGDOM

Sir Geoffrey Blake –	Commander of the Battlecruiser Squadron and second in command of the Mediterranean Fleet from July 1936 to July 1937.
Sir Dudley Pound –	Commander-in-Chief of the Mediterranean Fleet from March 1936 to June 1939, when he became First Sea Lord.
Sir Eric Phipps –	Ambassador to Germany 1933–1937.

Sir Andrew Cunningham –   Succeeded Sir Dudley Pound as Commander-in-Chief of the Mediterranean
Fleet. A post he held until 1943 when
he became First Sea Lord.

TIMELINE:

Nov. 1936   Spanish Civil War ends with Nationalist victory.
Pope Pius XII helps heal Spain.
FDR wins US election.

Jan. 1937   Spain and Portugal join The Catholic Entente.
France helps Italy begin modernizing forces.
Older equipment is used to pay for resources.
Roosevelt takes office, tries to restore the prestige and
influence of the League of Nations.

Mar. 1937   Pius XII begins South and Central American tour.
French and Iberian agents seek agreements.
Third Serbian insurrection ends.
USGA Senate formed.

June 1937   Brazil, Uruguay, Paraguay, and Bolivia leave The League
of Nations to create The Organization of American
States (OAS). Trade agreements are signed with the
Catholic Entente.
Brazil receives the Italian battleships *Conte di Cavour*,
and *Giulio Cesare*.
All receive older Entente tanks and airplanes.

July 1937 Japan invades China.

The League of Nations imposes sanctions on exports to Japan.

The United Kingdom increases exports to Japan.

Sept. 1937 Chile joins the OAS and receives two French heavy cruisers as payment for resources.

The United States begins expansion of military.

US Congress approves military aid for Argentina to keep them in the League. The US sends 50 M2 light tanks and 50 P-36 Hawk fighters.

Nov. 1937 USSR attacks Turkey in Caucasus.

Finnish troops lead the way.

Large French maneuvers on German front.

Belgium joins The Catholic Entente.

Ukraine and Lithuania-Poland mobilize.

In an attempt to deescalate the situation, Germany does not.

Dec. 1937 Rape of Nanjing begins.

Jan. 1938 Venezuela joins the OAS and receives the older French battleships *Dunkerque, Strasbourg.*

Peru and Ecuador also switch alliances.

All receive older Entente tanks and airplanes.

The League of Nations votes down intervention in Turkey.

Feb. 1938 France renounces claim to Alsace and Lorraine.

Central Coalition and Catholic Entente sign five-year non-aggression pact.

Benelux split into spheres of influence.

All major French naval units are moved to ports on the Bay of Biscay.

Britain reinforces their Home Fleet.

German troops head east.

US Congress approves military aid for Colombia to keep them in the League. The US sends 50 M2 light tanks and 50 P-36 Hawk fighters.

Mar. 1938   Bulgaria begins genocide in Macedonia.

Soviet advance in the Caucasus stalls as troop are moved to the Ukraine-Poland border.

Apr. 1938   USGA intervenes in Macedonia with approval from The League of Nations.

Bulgaria invokes Coalition defense clause.

Germany defuses situation.

Tensions between the Central Coalition and the USGA remain high.

May 1938   South America erupts in war.

Venezuela, Peru, and Ecuador invade Colombia.

Much of the Colombia is overrun by the end of the month.

Brazil, Chile, Paraguay, Uruguay, and Bolivia invade Argentina. Buenos Aires falls in the first week. Argentina establishes a temporary capital at Bahía Blanca.

The League of Nations imposes sanctions despite protests in the United States.

Neville Chamberlain looks for diplomatic solution and fails. Naval units are sent to Argentina to protect British economic interests.

The League of Nations protests intervention by the United Kingdom and imposes sanctions.

Charles de Gaulle smiles.

Erich von Manstein knows he will soon be sending his son to WAR.

BIBLIOGRAPHY